I0847003

To Julia. You found my earring that one time.

For more information, or to book an event, contact :
olivedwilson19@gmail.com
Book design by Olive Wilson
Cover design by Olive Wilson
ISBN - Paperback: 9798991029308
First Edition: July 2024

A Path of
Vanquish &
Victors

Prologue

Richalle skidded around the hall as the explosion shook the walls. She leaped to the side as the ceiling crumbled above her. As soon as the rubble hit the ground, Richalle broke into another sprint.

She couldn't slow.

She couldn't afford it.

If she didn't retrieve the explosives before the base perished to dust, she would suffer a fate worse than death.

After all, the Empress had a reputation for a reason.

Bronze battalions rushed from the broken building. Their weapons hung loosely at their sides; vulnerable to a potential attack. But it didn't matter. Their opponents were not in the corridors, but in the wall.

Richalle didn't know who they were, only their name. The name that had been terrorizing the Empire and League of Red Doves alike. Three women, each more threatening than the last.

Black Cyanide.

Richalle weaved between soldiers running the opposite direction. One grabbed her wrist, stopping her sprint.

"Commander," the soldier huffed, his voice fast with panic. "We need to go! This place is coming down!"

Richalle didn't turn. "I can't! If those explosives get into the wrong hands–"

She was interrupted by the crumbling roof. Richalle scrambled back as rubble came between her and the man. The debris made a wall; there was no way she could get through.

Richalle drew a shaky breath. She needed to keep going. Duty came before all grievances.

She sprinted through the halls, her heels pounding against the ground. Dust drifted around her, clouding her strained lungs. Concrete clattered to the disintegrating floor as ear shattering booms shook the building.

Dangerous, of course.

But so was the Empress's hard rasp.

Richalle leapt around the corner to find her office. She pushed the silver doors open, revealing a dimly lit room. Carpets padded the floor, and pictures of Emperor's drifted along the walls.

She rushed in, tearing the room apart to find the bombs.

"Dammit!" she screeched as she tore out a drawer. "Where is it?"

"Where's *what*?"

Richalle's gaze turned towards her chair. There, legs swung over the side, was a woman. Braids scattered her coffee curls, and her black eyes gleamed with chaos.

Beside her were two other women. The first had tan skin and glittering green eyes. The red strand in her hair matched the red arrows strapped to her back.

The third was smaller. Her black hair was strung into hundreds of braids that ran down her back. Instead of the thrum of chaos that lit up the other two's gaze, this one's blue eyes were filled with timidity.

Coffee Curls placed a bag on Richalle's desk. Her eyes widened as she recognized the explosives.

"How *dare* you!" Richalle stepped forward, teeth grit. "Give–"

Her foot caught on a string. A hiss rang through the air as the room became a faded blue.

The women placed gas masks over their faces, malicious smiles spreading across their lips.

Richalle stumbled towards the desk, her head throbbing. Her stomach bubbled as nausea rose in her throat. She couldn't think. She was in danger, yet her head could only form one thought.

Cyanide.

Richalle extended a hand to Coffee Curls. The woman's grin only widened as she waved back, eyes glittering with blood lust.

Richalle couldn't breathe. Her head was swamped, her lungs were blocked, and her brain couldn't think of a way out.

Wait–

Cyanide.

Black Cyanide.

The last thing Richalle saw was Coffee Curl's chaotic gleam, and she fell on the desk.

Chapter One
Alohi

What the fuck? What the fuck? What the fuck?

The heist may have been over, but Alohi couldn't shake the feeling of impending danger. Of course, the feeling wasn't uncommon when one lives among the two most dangerous criminals in Thine.

She supposed Quilla didn't get enough excitement out of simply blowing up a bank vault. So when they journeyed back to the Pirate Colonies of Salenian, the bastard made them climb in through the highest window.

"Are you sure this is necessary?" asked Alohi, desperately clinging to Lilith's makeshift grappling hook.

"Yes," Quilla drawled, not caring to elaborate.

Alohi shivered as a gust of ocean wind made the rope twist and flip. They hung over a massive cliff, the turquoise ocean rumbling beneath them. Sprays of salty water occasionally reached to touch Alohi's boot, causing her to jump.

"I would appreciate a reason." Lilith responded, brushing a stray vine from her face. "If it wouldn't be too much trouble, Quill."

Quilla groaned. "Florian doesn't want us to get seen. He prefers our entrance to be inconspicuous."

"Oh, yes because three teenagers grappling into a window isn't suspicious at all."

"The point, love," Quilla said, continuing her climb. "Is not to be seen. That's quite a hard task if we were to enter the front door."

Alohi rolled her eyes. She knew damn well Florian had said nothing about the subject. She was even more certain the pirate was not one for discretion.

She didn't dare voice her concerns, given that Quilla's boot was dangerously close to her face.

Fortunately, she didn't need to.

"What the *fuck*?" just ahead of them, a head peaked out the window. Braided hair ran past their shoulders and gold teeth glittered from their jaw. Loosely tied around their hairy chest, was a robe.

"Florian!" Quilla exclaimed, climbing through the window. "I would have met you downstairs–"

"If you weren't so busy scaling the cliff?"

Alohi and Lilith pulled themselves over the sill, excitedly awaiting the sibling dispute.

"It's more discrete," Quilla shrugged. "I didn't want to draw attention."

Florian rolled their eyes. "Come now, Kiwi, you have no problem with 'attention.'"

Quilla scowled at the nickname. "As much as I do enjoy giving a show, I'm not in a mood to draw the eyes of the Empire every time I happen to come here."

"It's not the Empire you should be worried about." Florian said. "It's the League."

"What about them?"

Florian pulled a letter from their back pocket and handed it to Quilla. "I believe it's from your *friend*."

Alohi perked. No matter the situation, the pirate seemed to enjoy using the word 'friend' to describe Nikolai.

Alohi and Lilith rushed to Quilla's side, peering over her shoulder. Alohi read the letter so fast she didn't retrieve the information, and had to try it a second time.

Quilla, Lilith and Alohi,

Good afternoon, hope all is well. I know the pirate will give you this, so consider this your official demand to surrender. Come to the beach with your hands up and weapons on the floor, and we will not harm you or the Pirate Colonies.

Be warned, failure to act will result in the extermination of this little base, along with everyone who resides within.

Best regards,
Nikolai Lone.

"His writing sounds like a drugged ferret with a blade to his throat." Alohi commented.

Quilla ignored her, pulling a pen from her pocket. Lilith and Alohi leaned over her shoulder, their eyes widening with every new word.

Nikolai,

Hope this letter finds you well. Unfortunately, we have to decline your kind offer to spare our lives for a few short hours so you end it at Camp Fifty. So, this is your official demand to shove your surrender up your hairy ass.

Go fuck yourself,
Quilla Cercel Thorne.

PS: Be ready,

Quilla swiftly folded the letter. handing it to Florian while dropping her bag at his feet. "Send this to him. The bag's yours."

Florian raised an eyebrow. "And the one strung around your shoulder?"

Quilla grinned, showing fanged teeth. "That one's mine. It helps with certain... *business.*"

"Explosives," Lilith clarified. "It helps her explode things."

"Thank you," Florian growled. "I know how bombs work."

Quilla strode to the window, bombs slung over her shoulder. Out on the sea was a platoon of ships, each bearing the red dove of the rebellion.

"Florian, get out of your robe and put some decent clothes on." Quilla grinned, turning to her crew. "And once you're done, be ready to fight." She drew her knives, positioning them between her fingers. "We have a dove to catch."

Chapter Two
Nikolai

On the first day of the invasion, Nikolai sent a letter formally requesting Black Cyanide's surrender.

On the second day, Quilla wrote back, formally requesting he shove his surrender up his 'hairy ass.'

Nikolai stood at his desk, looking at the signature with curiosity. Funny how someone so rooted in chaos could have such neat handwriting.

"Well," Killen said, looming over his shoulder. "At least we know it's not forged."

Nikolai looked at him, unamused. "Signatures exist for a reason."

"Anyone can fake a signature," Killen scoffed. "But to forge that level of profanity against you? That talent is Quilla's alone."

Nikolai glared. "Who's side are you on?"

"I don't take sides, I am simply here to watch the spectacle."

"You seem to be standing on my ship, hence my side."

Killen raised his eyebrows. "Oh no. I simply enjoy watching a couple angsty teens with *way* too many explosives go head to head. I get a better view from here."

Nikolai tilted his head. "You're awful."

"Correction: I'm bored."

"Aren't you always?"

"Not when I'm with you!" Killen grinned. "Speaking of which, don't you have a meeting?"

Nikolai pulled a pocket watch from coat. When he saw the time, he nearly threw the thing across the room.

"Well," Nikolai said, tucking the trinket in his pocket. "We have a plan to explain, don't we?"

Nikolai strode across the deck and towards the cabin, Killen on his heel. The wind ruffled his combed hair, brushing against his long, black coat. Nikolai clasped his hands behind his back, letting out a breath. The warmth of the air turned white in the frigid atmosphere.

He flung the cabin door open to find his men crowded around a table. Five of his most trusted generals. Well— his father's most trusted. The privilege to choose who he associated with was removed long ago. Each man looked at him with expecting, judgmental eyes.

Nikolai cleared his throat, placing Quilla's letter in front of them. "Unfortunately, there will be a fight."

There was barely any emotion around the table. Of course, no one was expecting a surrender, much less wanting one, but Quilla's words were unusually unprofessional. The League didn't appreciate the stark disrespect.

"Little whore." One murmured.

"Here's the plan," Nikolai said, laying his palms on the map. "The majority of our fleet will bomb the entrance. The Pirate Colonies will fight them, while we sneak in through the back and kidnap Black Cyanide."

A scrawny soldier raised his hand. "Yes, um, how are we going to find them?"

"With your eyes." Killen growled.

Nikolai ignored him. "Knowing them, they'll most likely be leading the battle. Miss Thorne can't resist a fight, Miss Cole refuses to let her die, and Miss Windlem is lost without the two. If we're discrete enough, we can sneak in as a pirate and kidnap them from behind."

"And when we do find them?" asked the soldier. "It's not like they'll go willingly."

"We're going to knock them out," Nikolai said. "Raven, I have tranquilizer arrows for you. As soon as I get Black Cyanide out of the crowd and away from the pirates, you shoot them. We then carry their bodies back to Camp Fifty."

"What happens when we get back?" Raven asked, her bright red curls bobbing with every movement. "What then?"

Nikolai drew a shaky sigh. "Then Black Cyanide will face due punishment for their crimes."

As if on cue, there was a crash. Nikolai's head flew up to hear footsteps on the roof.

"Change of plans," he drew his swords. "We're taking Black Cyanide here and now. Raven, get to the crows nest, the rest of you are with me. Let's go."

As it turns out, Raven had no time to get to her perch. In fact, none of them got the chance to walk out the door. They were stopped by Quilla, knives drawn and a sick smile spread across her lips. Her messy, tangled curls wavered with her tattered coat. She ran her tongue along her teeth.

"Nikolai!" she exclaimed. "How– oh *shit*!"

Nikolai jabbed a sword at her stomach. She leaped in the air, bounding off Nikolai's blade and landing opposite him.

"Miss Thorne," Nikolai growled, reeling around. "Ready to die?"

"Titles are so last generation," Quilla's blade came whirring at his head "Come now, Nikolai, I thought your pleasantries went with your sobriety."

"Brave of you to say," Nikolai's foot came at her shin. "I suppose you're hungover now?"

Quilla shrugged, leaping over his boot. "The headache makes me more homicidal."

"Does it now?" Nikolai dove to the side as an arrow flew at him. His vision shot upward, catching a red blur hiding amongst the sails. "Oh, hello Miss Cole."

"It seems you are the only one eager to exchange pleasantries." The voice was familiar— soft and gentle. But there was nothing kind in the woman's tone. "Why not do us all a favor and cram it."

Nikolai found Alohi's eyes. He barely had time to open his mouth before the politician's needles came at him. He dove to the side, only to find himself face to face with Quilla.

"Little help?" Nikolai called to his clearly absent crew.

As soon as the words left his mouth, an arrow came at Quilla's head. She dove to the side as the weapon stuck into the wood.

"Ugh," she groaned, brushing Nikolai's swords away from her as if they were simply sticks. "You never let me have my fun."

Nikolai dodged a fistful of knives. "Most likely because you're supposed 'fun' gets people killed."

Quilla shrugged, pulling something that looked suspiciously like an avocado from her pocket. She threw it before Nikolai could comprehend the object wasn't a squishy fruit.

The stern exploded. Splinters of wood flew from the wreckage. Screams mixed with the chaos as more 'definitely not avocados' exploded from Quilla's grasp.

Nikolai face planted onto the boards as the boat tipped. Crystal water crept along the sides of the ship, consuming the wood.

With all his strength, Nikolai leapt from the boat. He grasped a hanging rope, swinging onto the horizontal mast. As soon as his feet found a stable grip, he wished he let the water engulf him.

"Nikolai," Alohi drawled, needles already in hand.

"Alohi," Nikolai said, an equal tone of exasperation in his voice. "I wish I chose a different mast."

"I don't!" Nikolai turned to see Killen perched behind him. The swordsman looked like an eager child awaiting the circus. "This is going to be the most thrilling thing I've ever watched!"

"As much as I agree with you," the low crackle of a voice joined Killen's excited giggles. Florian took a look at Nikolai, then at Killen. "The two of us are on opposite sides, and unfortunately have to duel."

Nikolai let out a groan. "Yes. It seems you do."

Killen lazily grasped his swords, while Florian pulled his cutlass from his waist. They looked like they were stalling to fight each other.

Alohi, however, was quite eager. Her style was flawed, of course, but her attacks were so quick Nikolai barely noticed the holes. Alohi's needles came at his joints like blades, piercing bits of cloth and exposed flesh. Nikolai bounded back as Alohi swung at him. He pushed his swords under Alohi's legs, causing her to lose her balance.

Alohi dug her needles into the wood to stop her fall. Her pirate clothes wavered in the light wind and her blue eyes matched the ocean. For a moment, Nikolai wanted to help her up. Because those were the same eyes that supported him through everything. The same eyes that cried into his arms when her father hit her. Those eyes were the closest thing he had to a family.

Then, a second ship crashed into the mast.

Nikolai toppled from the wood, plummeting towards the crystal water. Killen grabbed his wrist, struggling to hold his own balance. When he turned, he saw Quilla and Lilith driving a pirate ship directly into the wreckage. Nikolai had no idea where they got the thing.

"Alohi!" Quilla called. "Florian! Stop messing around and get on the god damned ship!"

Alohi grinned, hauling herself onto the mast. She raced along the wood, and leaped towards the criminals.

Florian, however, resembled a disappointed child. He moped towards the ship, failing to hide his distaste for the newfound peace.

As the ship finished propelling itself through the wreckage, Killen lost his grip. He and Nikolai plummeted into the water where the rest of his crew waited.

Nikolai clenched his fists, watching as Quilla waved him goodbye from the boat's stern.

Chapter Three
Lilith

"What the fuck are you doing?" a pirate snapped, his chair scraping the floor as he stood. "From my perspective, you three are freeloaders leaching from our riches."

Quilla tilted her head, placing a hand on her temple. "Did you simply forget about the array of explosives we brought to you just a few hours ago? You and your filthy gang of seagulls couldn't manage a heist half that."

"See?" a blonde man banged his ringed fist against the table. "Cocky, Florian. Just stuck up teenagers with no idea what they're doing."

"Not cocky," Lilith retorted. "Smart. We know our worth. We also know the worth of those explosives."

Alohi rested her cheek in her hand. "And their firepower."

She only mumbled. Barely loud enough to touch the conversation. But when all voices vanished and the argument came to a halt, Alohi eyes widened in the terrifying revelation that everyone had in fact heard her comment.

"Alohi." Quilla hissed. "*No.*"

Every being in the meeting room glared daggers at Alohi. Both Quilla and Lilith passed threats around like candy. She probably didn't see why it was such a problem when she engaged. "What?"

"Disagreements and conflicts may arise, Windlem." Florian stood, brushing their long braids behind their back. "But threats are never dealt. We are one organization. Infighting, no matter the severity, is not allowed."

Alohi tucked her knees to her chest, her cheeks becoming a rosy pink. "You guys threatened the League all the time."

Lilith rolled her tongue around her mouth. "Well, yes. But us and the League were never quite..."

"Sociable." Quilla finished. "The difference is, Alohi, we were more than happy to dig a dagger into Grandez's pretty little nose. No one here would ever hold a blade to one another."

"Got it," Alohi blew a stray strand from her eyes. "Sorry."

No one seemed to acknowledge her apology. They simply carried on like nothing had ever happened. Retorts were tossed, arguments were thrown. The only one who didn't talk was Florian. The pirate sat at the head of the table, their hair draped over their shoulders. They watched with a blank expression, lips occasionally twisting into a smile. It was like they were watching a play, anxiously awaiting the inevitable conclusion.

"We have brung you a steady stream of income since we arrived here!" Quilla said. "I don't see any of you going on heists every other day."

"I don't see any of us leading an army to our doorstep." The pirate to her left retorted.

"It's either the League or the Empire." Lilith drawled. "I don't know about you, but I would prefer the incompetent one."

"If you three don't get out of our hair—" the pirate rasped. "We'll experience the wrath of both competent and the opposite of such."

Quilla seemed to have a retort on the tip of her tongue, but it vanished as Florian stood. The pirate placed their jeweled hands on the table, digging their nails into the wood.

"You have a point." Florian pressed a manicured finger to their lip. "The Empire and the League will be naturally drawn here. I can't risk my people's lives for you, Kiwi, as much fun as I have with you."

This time, Quilla didn't retort. Instead, she gave her friend a respectful nod.

"But then again," Florian tilted their head. "You are a good asset. Even your destruction gives us more advantages than money ever could. I'd like to keep that, if possible."

"Your support is valuable, Florian." Quilla said. "I'd like to aim to keep it."

Florian sat back in their chair, resting their chin on their wrist. "I do enjoy my time with you. Tell me, do you miss Hanslack?"

"Not in the slightest."

"What a shame," Florian hummed. "The city loves you two."

"The city respects us." Lilith retorted. "They do *not* like us."

"Oh?" Florian tilted their head. "Perhaps it's time to remind the gangs who owns them? Who is *really* in control."

Quilla raised a finger to her lip, a smile gleaming on her features. "I suppose I need to remind Gillen of the significance of a rose."

"Personally," Lilith added. "I'm excited to see how he got on without us."

"I'd assume the Serpents territory has gone down by at least half." Florian commented. "They probably lost every dime within the first week you left."

"I'd give them two weeks before going broke." Quilla commented. "Just on pure momentum."

"What momentum?" Lilith retorted. "Gillen can barely find the balance to get out of bed. He couldn't get a squadron together if an arrow was at his throat."

"Ahem," a pirate cleared his throat. "Can we please get back to the conversation at hand?"

Florian rolled their eyes. They crossed their legs and clasped their jeweled fingers through each other. "So serious," they shrugged. "Come now, can't we have a bit of fun?"

"It seems, Florian," the pirate commented. "That you may be going on a vacation to Hanslack. You'll have weeks of 'fun' with your darling misfits."

Florian raised their chin. "It seems I will." They grinned. "So we're in agreement? I'll go to Hanslack with my comrades and—" Florian stood, wandering around the table. Their manicured hands hovered over the heads of each pirate. They raised their fingers, pinched their lips, and withdrew their hand, moving to the next person.

"Sir," a pirate who was currently under Florian's grasp murmured. "What are you doing?"

Florian pinched their lips. "Choosing."

They continued for another few minutes. Florian would hover their hand over one man, consider him, and quickly move to the next. When they circled the table for a second time, Quilla got fed up.

"Florian," she drawled. "Could you ever so possibly speed— whatever this is— up?"

Florian shot her a glare and stepped back from the table. They pointed a ringed finger at the table, scanning the people who stared blankly at them.

"You." A small man perked when Florian's finger landed on him. "You lead the colonies while I'm gone."

The pirate's eyes widened. He glanced behind him, as if Florian was pointing to someone else.

"No, not the window," Florian said. "You're babysitting."

"I don't—" the man stammered. "I don't know—"

"You'll figure it out. If you have any questions, ask someone else. If I need anything, I'll send a bird." Florian turned towards the door, gesturing for Quilla, Lilith and Alohi to follow. "Don't break anything while I'm gone. I'll be back..." they paused, pressing their finger to their lips. "When I'm back. Good luck!"

With that, Florian closed the door, the wood clanging with a bang.

Chapter Four
Alohi

Alohi usually liked boats.

But this one was lonely, as if all the life she previously felt had evaporated.

She leaned against the taffrail, gazing at the orange sunset. The light glittered on the water in a pink reflection. Quilla and Lilith were in their cabin, and Florian... she didn't want to guess where the pirate had scurried off too. It was just her and her thoughts. As of now, she hated her thoughts. They weren't being kind.

It's your fault. A voice rang. *You killed your parents, you were an awful friend to Nikolai, and you couldn't hold your political power.*

Alohi grit her teeth, pressing her elbows into the wood.

None of this would have happened if you just kept your poise. You are pathetic, Windlem. You always have been and always will be. There's no changing this. No matter how hard you try, you will always be weak.

Alohi shoved her fingers in her ears, attempting to block the voice that resonated within her head.

"Shut up." *You think you can fix this, Windlem?* "Shut up!" *You are coming to Quilla Thorne's heel like a hound. No mind of your own, no opinions that aren't influenced. You are a pawn, Windlem.* "Shut *up!*"

Alohi punched the taffrail. Her hand recoiled as soon as it made impact. She shook her fist, wincing at the pain.

The voices continued, criticizing her every move. They critiqued the way she walked, the swing of her arms, the tone of her voice.

And Alohi was sick of it.

She turned from the ocean, nearly sprinting towards the several boxes Florian loaded onto the ship. She hadn't guessed what was in them, she didn't have too. Quilla and the pirate were becoming a bit predictable.

She flung a crate open, peering inside the box. There, were bottles of alcohol. The liquid was a golden brown, sloshing around the murky glass with the rise and fall of the ship. She didn't know what kind they were; she didn't need to. All she knew was if she drank enough, it would get her drunk.

"Is this what you want?" she asked. The voices seemed to nod excitedly.

Alohi flicked off the cork and chugged the liquid.

~~~

The door flew open. Quilla and Lilith turned to see a tipsy Alohi leaning on the doorframe. Her blue eyes wavered in a drunken glitter. Her weight tipped from side to side, sloshing the bottle in her hand.

"Dear god," Quilla murmured.

"Alohi," Lilith started, moving to stable the politician. "Sit down."

Alohi giggled: the liquor sloshed in its bottle.

"Do you–" Alohi let out a disfigured snort. "If I... if I were to piss on Nikolai's leg next time he–" she hiccuped. "He does something stupid, do you– do you think he would stop being a bitch?"

Lilith made a pleading glance at Quilla.

"Yes, Alohi, wonderful plan." Quilla said, making her way to Alohi. "Why don't we sit down so we can discuss it further."

Alohi leaned on Quilla, her rose scent overwhelming. The alcohol had seduced her thoughts and now her brain couldn't form a sane idea.

"He's such a bitch." Alohi murmured, sitting on the bed. "Such a fucking... hmm..."
~~~

Alohi collapsed on the pillows, grinning as she took another sip of alcohol. The bitter taste made her cough. Liquid came out her nose.

"That's enough of that," Lilith snatched the bottle.

Alohi groaned. She reached for the liquor, tipped too far off the bed, and fell on her face. She made a sound that resembled a dying moose, and giggled.

"Okay, Alohi," Quilla said, helping her to her feet. "Why don't you tell me more about Nikolai? 'He's such a fucking... hm?'"

"Fucking bitch." Alohi giggled. "He– he– he has a stupid nose."

"Really?" Quilla asked, resting her chin on her palm. "Tell me more."

Alohi collapsed on the pillows, drooling on the sheets. "His nose– he looks punchable. Like– like– I just wanna–" Alohi swung her fist in the air, blowing a dramatic breath. "He looks like he needs to be punched."

"Couldn't have said it better myself." Quilla grinned. "Everyone needs a bit of punching or they grow up disfigured."

Lilith nudged her. "Stop encouraging it!"

"What? It's better she gets it out when she's not near Nikolai. Besides, drunken blackmail is the best kind of blackmail."

"Nikolai is disfigured. He has a stupid nose, stupid lips..." Alohi trailed off, her eyes glazing in a daze. "Soft eyes, soft lips, good jawline..."

Quilla was grinning ear to ear. "Alohi, don't say anything more. I need to get Florian–"

"No, you will do nothing of the sort." Lilith grabbed Quilla's wrist and pulled her to the bed. "Quill, what do we do?"

Quilla giggled. "You mean besides enjoy the show?"

"Yes, besides that," Lilith groaned. "I mean how do we get her... you know, back to normal?"

"We can't," Quilla shrugged. "We just have to wait. It's better to sleep it off."

"So...." Alohi didn't hear the rest of what they said. She was too busy attending to the stupid idea she crafted. She slipped past Lilith and out the door. Once she was there, she tripped to the stern and stood on the taffrail, letting the wind ruffle through her clothes.

But they were too restricting, too... trapping. They needed to come off.

Alohi unbuttoned her blouse, letting the thing fly behind her. She undid her fly, nearly slipped into the ocean, and threw her pants behind her. Next, Alohi stripped from her bra and underwear, letting the wind take her clothes.

She extended her arms, letting the wind fly through her hair. She smiled as a gust of air hit her cheek. The spray from the ocean flew from the waves and onto her tongue. She loved it. She loved all of it.

"Quilla!" Alohi turned to see Florian. The pirate was crumpled on the ground, hiding their eyes with their hands. "Help!"

Quilla and Lilith barged on to the deck to find Alohi naked on the taffrail. Lilith's face disfigured into one of horror, while Quilla burst into laughter.

"Alohi get down!" Lilith called, rushing towards her. In a moment of mischief, Alohi turned and freefell towards the water. Lilith caught her by the wrist and pulled her onto the dock.

"Quill," Lilith said, seething. "Can we tie her up?"

"*Way* ahead of you," Quilla grinned, already holding rope. "If she wants to jump off the ship, she's going to have to drag the bed with her."

Alohi let out a strangled giggle, leaning against Lilith.

"That's enough," Lilith grabbed Alohi's ear, pulling her towards the cabin. Alohi squealed like a piglet. "You are going to sleep this off. Oh, and the next time you get drunk I'm going to toss you in the ocean myself."

Chapter Five
Cercel

The crowd erupted below Cercel, their applause like thunderous validation. She stood with her hands clasped behind her back, golden robes flowing in the gentle breeze.

"We will end this reign of tyranny! We will stop the tax increases, and we will make sure everyone has a say in this democracy!" the crowd thundered with cheers as the words left Cercel's lips. Politics, when you thought about it, was quite easy. Tell the people what they want, and they won't bat an eye when you do the exact opposite.

Simple, really.

Cercel was surrounded by idiots. And she wouldn't have it any other way.

Next to her, on the balcony, were the most abscond fools of them all. Tricked by morals to follow her like ducklings. And all she had to do was deploy a bit of sympathy.

Her naive siblings.

In their defense, they weren't blood related.

"A new light will shine on Thine!" Cercel declared, her phrase echoed by announcers below. "No more will you go hungry because of my father's greed. No more will this country be divided unevenly. Poverty will vanish, normalities will shift to their rightful, true nature. Peace will scatter the air, and the demands of unrighteous rebellion will be stomped *out!*"

Screams of delight echoed around the mountains. Cercel smiled, savoring the validation. It may have been brought by lies, but the pleasure was real, and it was directed at *her*.

"Empress Ghan! Empress Ghan! Empress Ghan!" the crowd chanted. Cercel waved a final time, and her and the Golden Class slipped inside the palace.

"Empress Ghan! Empress Ghan!" Lamia chanted, putting a hand on her shoulder. "That was amazing, Cercel!"

Cercel shrugged, brushing her grasp off. "It's politics. Just tell the people what they want to hear and they'll cheer for you. Simple."

"Still," Casimir joined. "Your political brilliance is admirable. Your truth, resilience and leadership is something to be desired."

Cercel should have felt something. She should have felt victory with the praise. For once, Rosalie wasn't the one with the recognition.

And yet? There were no flutters. A smile was the last thing her lips wanted to morph into. She felt *nothing*.

"I'm tired." She said, already striding up the stairs. "I'm going to my room."

Before they had time to answer, Cercel left the corridor. As soon as she was sure they couldn't see her, she sprinted. She needed to run. She needed to get away. There was something chasing her, and it would *never* go away.

The worst part was, she would never truly escape the monster.

Because it was a creation of her mind.

Of her past.

Cercel slammed the doors to the Empress's chambers. She crumpled to the ground, hiding her face in her hands. She couldn't do this. She couldn't face the demon that wrapped its icy hands around her shoulders. Yet the demon didn't give her a choice.

She was never fucking in control.

Cerce, Rosalie cooed. *How pathetic, your rooms a mess.*

The hallucination was right. Shattered glass smothered Cercel's floor. The covers were thrown off her bed and the walls bore holes— mostly due to Cercel's episodes. It seemed everything around her was cracking. The walls, the glass, and her own sanity.

"Stop it." Cercel whimpered, pressing her head deeper into her knees. "Go away,"

Honestly, Cerce, Rosalie chirped. *Have you really spiraled this far from grace? Rosalie held this weight as a child and didn't go insane. As did Father; yet, you crumble.* Cercel gasped as Rosalie's icy hands wrapped around her shoulder. Her fingers trailed up her neck, brushing her throat. They were strangling her, yet there was no pressure applied. *My question is, why?*

"You're not real." Cercel chanted, not daring to look up. "You're not real. You're not real."

Aren't I, Cerce? Rosalie said. *Your jealousy's real. Your failure's real. Your broken little mind–* Rosalie tapped her forehead. *Is all too real. I'm a product. So doesn't that make me real?*

Cercel looked up. Tears coated her black, angry eyes. Her mind was trapped. Every thought, every memory– it was all too painful to run through her mind.

Except one. One cold, horrible goal.

The goal that was the only reason she was still alive.

Revenge.

"I am going to kill Rosalie Ghan." Cercel chanted. "I am going to kill Rosalie Ghan. I am going to kill Rosalie Ghan–"

Louder.

"I am going to kill Rosalie Ghan!" Cercel hollered. "I will cut off all her fingers and string them on a necklace. I will torture her friends. All the friends she *left* me for. I'll make her beg, and kill them in front of her. Then, I'll cut her arms, her legs, her stomach. She'll bleed from so many places she won't be recognizable. Then I'll chain her to the palace roof and let the birds finish her off!"

Yes, Rosalie edged, her breath icy on Cercel's cheek. *Kill her. Drag her name through the mud. Just as you were dragged.*

Cercel stood, Rosalie rising next to her.

"Yes, I will banish my grudge against Rosalie," she said. "Then I will lead as Empress. I won't follow in Father's footsteps. I'll be good."

Rosalie hissed, her sharp nails digging into Cercel's jaw. *Those two goals are mutually exclusive. Don't be a fool, Cerce. You are cruel, through and through. You are broken; shattered beyond repair.* Rosalie let out a chortle. The laugh drifted into the air, as if it was simply a breeze. *Your past defines you. Your pain shapes your actions. Don't pretend you have control, you and I both know the past has a collar around your neck.*

"Stop it!" Cercel shouted, crumpling to the floor. "Stop *tormenting* me!"

What's wrong? Rosalie cooed. *Too afraid to accept constructive criticism? That's the difference between you and me, Cerce. I learn; you fail with the same overdone, useless tactics because you refuse to be better. You refuse to give the energy needed. So you're here. A broken failure who hallucinates her sister because the real one left.*

"No, no, no, no." Cercel chanted, pressing her knees into her temples. "Please, stop..."

Rosalie grabbed her jaw, jolting her face from her lap. Her fingernails dug into Cercel's skin. Not real. Not real. But somehow the pain felt so *physical.*

"Rosalie..." Cercel pleaded, tears sliding down her cheek. "I'm *begging* you. Leave me alone!"

Rosalie grinned, her mint breath hot on Cercel's cheek. Her curls hung over her glittering eyes in messy strands. She ran a tongue across her fanged teeth, relishing Cercel's tears.

Never.

Chapter Six
Nikolai

There was never peace in the League of Red Doves.

Not for Nikolai, at least.

Of course, as he strode into the base, he was immediately flocked by messengers. Some asked if he succeeded, some already knew about his failure. But most were simply telling him he was late to a meeting.

Nikolai nearly stabbed them.

Instead, he showed incredible restraint and brushed past the messengers without saying a word. Though every inch of him was screaming 'don't go,' the more logical part knew his father was a blood hound when it came to finding him.

The assembly hall, like most places where the League resonated, was paper white. He pushed open the doors and strode into the room. Seats lined the circular auditorium, velvet stairs circled the chairs, leading to the esteemed balcony. There, staring him dead in the eye, where to most vile, asinine, critical people Nikolai had the displeasure of knowing.

"Nikolai!" his father's wall shaking *boom* was the first to scold him. "Get the hell up here!"

Nikolai blinked, and headed to the balcony. There, he found the four members of the council. Tanor Unighast had replaced Alohi, and Nikolai had a particularly strong distaste for him.

"Nikolai," Grandez huffed. "I'm assuming you have not retrieved Black Cyanide?"

Nikolai had to lock eyes with Unighast to keep them from rolling into his head. "No, Father, I did not."

Grandez groaned, rubbing the bridge of his nose. "Nikolai–" he breathed. "I asked one thing of you. For heaven's sake, they are *teenagers*."

"Yet somehow they are sabotaging the organization made by you, Father."

Grandez shot him a look. Nikolai's tongue had become increasingly free. He had adopted tenfold the safe amount of sarcasm and used it with ease. For some reason, fear didn't register anymore.

"Black Cyanide may be coming at the League of Red Doves, but they aren't succeeding. Name one way they've hindered us."

Nikolai didn't hesitate. "The Archives is now a pile of dust."

Grandez grunted, flaring his nostrils. "That was Thorne's doing."

"And Thorne–" Nikolai grinned. "Is a part of Black Cyanide."

"She wasn't a part of the damn cult yet."

"She made the thing, she was a part of it before it existed."

Grandez looked ready to punch him and Nikolai returned the urge. They glared at each other, baring their teeth.

"Now then, men," Nikolai recognized the voice as Unigast's, mostly because his blood pressure rose to an ungodly level. "There is no need for baseless violence."

Nikolai was about to baseless violence his genitals.

"Let's take a breath," Unighast inhaled. On his exhale, there was a distinct smell of smoke.

Nikolai obnoxiously hacked.

"Fine," Grandez growled. "Nikolai, there will always be other chances. For now, we need to discuss military strategy."

"I'm afraid you'll actually need a military for that, Father."

Grandez seethed. "We have a god damned military–"

"Not a good one." Nikolai smirked.

"Are you making a point of being uselessly critical?"

"Yes, I am. Glad you noticed."

"Now, now," Unighast stepped between them. As did the smell of drugs. "We are wasting valuable time discussing fruitless matters. Let us begin."

Nikolai and his father groaned, then turned to the map on the table. Nikolai immediately recognized the rough mountains of Brighan and the massive structure that was the Golden Palace.

He let out a snort. "You can't be serious."

Grandez, perhaps tired of the constant interruption, ignored him. Though it took a considerable amount of effort on his part.

"First, we gather all our forces on ships and sail across the sea to Thine. When we dock, we will make a two day trip to Brighan."

Nikolai kept three fingers in his hand. He was counting the plan's flaws.

"After that, we attack." Grandez continued. Nikolai covered a snicker with a cough. "All our force, centered at the front of the Empire. Our opponent only knows snippets of our power, never the entire thing."

Nikolai's mistake count had grown to five.

"While the Empire's soldiers are fighting our main battalion, we will send you, Nikolai, to kill the Empress." Grandez pointed a manicured finger at his chest. "Don't fuck up."

Nikolai chuckled. "Oh, don't worry father, I believe you will fail *long* before I have the chance."

Grandez snarled. "I can tell you have more to say on the matter, so spit it out. *What?*"

Nikolai laughed. It wasn't hard, just a simple chuckle. As if he was chuckling at a tasteless joke.

Because all of this was utterly, profoundly *stupid*.

And it was fucking *hysterical*.

"I'm sorry," he hummed. "But honestly, Father, that was the worst plan I've heard since the one I constructed when I was seven. Really? Have you ever seen a successful battle plan, because you have somehow achieved the opposite."

Unighast heaved a heavily smoked breath.

Nikolai held up seven fingers, lips split in a grin "This is how many fatal flaws I found in your plan. I am about to break down all of them. *Every single one.*"

The room went silent, waiting for him to continue.

"First, your approach is *awful*. I mean, honestly, do you know how many resources just a boat ride across the sea needs? Let alone forty carrying all our troops. Next, you expect our battalions to *walk* through the woods for two days, which, may I remind you, are more Empire train tracks than trees." Nikolai scoffed, rolling his eyes. "What? Did you think they would just let us *stride* to the Golden Palace?"

Grandez groaned. Dacnoff, Spin and Bolian looked embarrassed, and he was half sure Unighast was dying for another shot of narcotic.

"And, on the off chance you do make it to the palace, you'll be met with another round of problems. The largest of which being our troops are going to be *exhausted*. I know none of you have ever walked more than a couple feet, but try and imagine a life beyond your spoiled indulgences, will you? Our troops will barely be able to stand, let alone fight. Not to mention they'll be carrying supplies for the trip. The Empire soldiers will simply be able to push us over and be done with it." Nikolai blew a sigh. "We wouldn't stand a fucking chance."

"Language." Unighast breathed.

"So, Mister Lone, what would you propose?" Spin asked, her tone drenched in passive aggression.

"The point of a good strategy is to attack our enemy's weak point." Nikolai explained. "For the Empire, it's their sea travel. They have ten max, poorly scouted sea routes. It's one of the few things the League is better at. A bloody fucking miracle in my opinion."

Unighast snarled. "Language."

"So you suggest we have a sea fight." Grandez groaned. "That's messy."

"We're talking war," Nikolai retorted. "I don't think it matters the terrain, it won't be clean."

"Would you stop with the sarcasm?" Grandez growled. "It's not helping matters, and you're getting on my last nerve, Nikolai."

"Am I?" Nikolai grinned. "Personally, I wouldn't worry if I was in your shoes. Once we go through with you elementary suicide strategy, I won't have nerves to get on."

"You dare?" Grandez advanced on him, his hot breath on Nikolai's cheek."

Nikolai didn't flinch; instead, his grin widened. "I do."

The constant hostility must've worsened Unighast's hangover, because he stepped between the two.

"Please, councilors." Nikolai and his father looked ready to string his intestines on the wall. "It's getting a bit hot in here, why don't we get some air."

Nikolai fantasied bashing Unighast's head against a banister while Grandez romantically looked at the decorative blades strung to the wall. Reluctantly, the two stepped away from each other, letting the tension fizzle out.

The council members dispersed, leaving Nikolai and Unighast alone on the balcony.

"I must say, Nikolai," Unighast drawled. "You never fail to make things entertaining."

"Well, someone has to make sure we aren't obliterated."

Unighast pierced his heavily buttered lips. "Hm, perhaps you do." He gazed longingly at the bathroom. "Mind if I powder my nose?"

"Be my guest, talking to you is draining."

Unighast barely reacted, instead practically sprinting to the bathroom.

Nikolai sighed, collapsing into a chair and pressing his fingers against his temples.

Finally, peace.

Well that's what he thought, until the distinct smell of heroin drifted into his nostrils.

He groaned, tilting back his head to see the gray air drifting from the bathroom. He sprang from his chair, the familiar bubble of nausea rising up his throat. *That fucker.*

"Seriously?" Nikolai groaned as he leaned against the bathroom door. "Are you so dependent that you can't survive a minute without your drug?"

Unighast looked up, smoke leaking from his lips and curling to the ceiling. "It's only when I'm around you, Lone." He took another puff of cigar. "Why do you care anyway? It helps me. Isn't that what you want? For council members to be at their best?"

"'Best' and 'high' are not synonyms." Nikolai said, polishing his swords against his coat. "In fact, they're antonyms. If anyone were to see you smoking, the League's reputation would crumble. The drug doesn't enhance your performance, it makes life the tiniest bit bearable. A selfish reason, really. There is no place for addicts in my organization, so put the drug down and suffer the withdrawals."

"And if I don't?" Unighast growled, licking his yellow teeth.

"Then you will be withdrawn from your position."

Unighast huffed a cracked laugh. "You can't fire me. Who the hell else would you hire from Woodran?"

Nikolai chuckled, whacking the cigar out of his hand. The thing clattered to the floor, spilling a piss yellow liquid. "I am not above fudging the rules, Unighast. You are expendable. Drug or job? Narcotic or reputation? The choice is yours." Nikolai turned towards the door. "Choose wisely."

Unighast laughed, the sound and awful chortle. "Bold words for someone who also has a crutch."

Nikolai stopped, Unighast's phrase lingering on the walls. He lowered his swords to the floor, a crisp clang echoing through the room as the blade touched the ground. A low chuckle crept up his throat, breaching his lips. "Beg your pardon?"

"I–" Unighast stammered. "Nothing."

"If I ever hear of this again–" Nikolai turned, advancing on him. "I will cut off your fingers and string them to the noose I will hang you with. Before that, I will scorch your toes and burn you with your own cigar. After that I will cut off your balls and shove them in your mouth before hanging you on the ceiling butt naked in this very council room." He grabbed Unighast's collar, throwing him to the floor. Nikolai's blade lifted his chin. He met Unighast's tear filled eyes; his sword twitched with the addict's trembling body. "Do you want that?"

"No, sir." Unighast whimpered.

"So we have an agreement?"

"Yes, sir."

"Lovely!" Nikolai smirked, lifting his sword from Unighast's throat.

"Good chat, dear friend." Nikolai licked his teeth, grinning at Unighast's pathetic body on the floor. "Always *wonderful* to reconnect."

Chapter Seven
Alohi

Alohi felt like her head had been bashed against a fence.

Not only that, but the embarrassment was killing her.

Of course, she didn't remember the previous evening. But that didn't stop Quilla from recounting the entire thing in detail. The entire telling took more than an hour, and Alohi spent an additional period of time relentlessly apologizing to Lilith and ignoring Florian at all costs.

Now, she was striding down the wet streets of Hanslack. Though she had never been to the city, she heard stories. Stories that concerningly matched up to Quilla and Lilith's personality.

She did not, however, expect to be the center of attention. As they walked down the street, heads turned to look. Merchants, business men, and thugs couldn't take their eyes off them.

But it wasn't 'them.' It was one person. Someone who held herself together better than Alohi ever could. Someone who righted her sweep and brushed her hair behind her back. Someone who had played this game before.

"Chin up, eyes ahead." Florian murmured in Quilla's ear. "One wrong move, one faulty step, and these people will tear you apart."

Quilla straightened her posture and widened her stride.

"Don't give them a reason to doubt you. You are their queen. The best of them. They will believe you as long as you don't show *cracks*." Florian strode next to her, tattered cloak falling behind them.

Lilith walked next to her, matching her partner's pace. "Quilla, where are we going?"

Quilla didn't smile. If she showed any emotion whatsoever, Alohi didn't catch it. "Home."

~~~

Alohi's head throbbed as Quilla kicked open the door to a gambling den. It was small, its ceilings uncomfortably low; but as soon as they entered, all heads turned to them. Numerous dark, lifeless eyes centered their gaze on the four. Alohi shrivelled backward. Quilla strode into the crowd.

Lilith and Florian headed in after her, keeping their chins high. It seemed that only Alohi was trying to slip in unnoticed.

Quilla stopped on the stairs, turning to the agape crowd. "Where's Gillen?"

Silence was her only answer.

Quilla rolled her eyes, trying again. "Well? Where the hell is Gillen?"

No one moved.

"Look," Quilla groaned. "I know you've all heard of me. You've either heard rumors about my morals, or you've witnessed my lack of such. Either way, all of you know I don't take kindly to insolence–" she drew a blade from her coat, toying with it. "So let me ask a final time. Where the *hell* is Spencer Gillen?"

This time, she got a response.

The room erupted in pointing and shouting. Through the chaos, Alohi made out a set of directions. Quilla did too, because she headed up the stairs and into the heavenly quiet hall.

"Why did you do that?" Lilith asked. "You know where Gillen's office is."

Quilla didn't have to respond, Florian did it for her.

"A show, my dear." They exclaimed. "She's been gone for a while. People need to be reminded that she is not one to be walked over."

"So–" Alohi stammered. "Why didn't you... uh, give them more of a performance."
~~~

Quilla shrugged. "They're not my enemies. They aren't friends, but tolerable acquaintances. There's no need to kill them."

"What about Gillen?" Alohi asked. "Is he a tolerable or intolerable acquaintance?"

Quilla opened her mouth to respond when a door flew open. Out strode an old, frail man with the worst posture Alohi had ever seen. It may have been her hangover, but the elder gave a suspicious resemblance to the pigeons that gawked along Hanslack's streets. He took one look at Quilla, and his gaze shrank into a glare.

Ah, intolerable acquaintance.

"Gillen," Quilla drawled, her face a neutral line.

Gillen wrinkled his nose. "Quilla Thorne." He strode around her, as if assessing a specimen. "Long time."

"I suppose it has been." Quilla kept her eyes on the wall, not daring to move.

"Well, I see your archer is still alive." Gillen pinched Lilith's cheek, only for his hand to be slapped away. "That's a surprise."

Gillen moved to Florian. The pirate towered over him, their beaded locks falling onto Gillen's hunched shoulders. "Florian," Gillen examined the pirate with curiosity. "I haven't seen you in years."

"Trust me, Gillen," Florian snorted. "I'm grateful for the fact."

Gillen chuckled, and moved on. "A politician, Quilla. How *intriguing*."

Alohi would have fought back from Gillen's touch. Instead, she was too busy holding back vomit.

Gillen strode back to Quilla, his tired eyes narrowing on her face. "What do you want, Quilla?"

She pulled a sack of money from her coat and shoved it in Gillen's chest. "It may not look like much, but that is a million kangue. The money from the job. It's not split, I took no piece of it. It's all yours." Quilla met his eyes, though it seemed to take a considerable amount of effort. "In return, I ask that you give us a place to stay. I will continue to pay you and pay my own affairs. No legal trouble. No strings attached. Way too much money for a couple beds; that is all I ask."

Gillen paused, looking at the bag. For a moment, he seemed to be considering the offer. Then, an earsplitting cackle rang through the air. His laugh was chipped, age wearing down his high notes. But nevertheless, it was a laugh.

"Oh, Quilla," Gillen chuckled. "You naive little girl. You think you can fool me? Honestly, the posters are everywhere. Everyone in the city knows who you are; hell, I would guess everyone in the country has some clue. You can't promise no trouble when trouble defines you. Money is worth nothing if I'm hanged in the gallows for harboring a traitor. Really, Quilla, I thought Emperor Ghan taught you better."

Quilla's breath stopped.

As soon as Gillen saw this, he snorted. "Oh, so you didn't know. Your face is everywhere, Quilla. Or should I call you Rosalie? That is your name, isn't it? Your *real* name? Who you *really* are?"

Quilla took a step back.

"You've failed, haven't you, Rosalie. Your entire life has been a sequence of defeat and anguish." Gillen lifted her chin, breathing down Quilla's neck. "You dug your grave, now lay in it."

Quilla was pushed into Florian's arms. The pirate steadied her, murmuring in her ear– "No cracks."

As if on cue, Quilla's vulnerability shattered. She straightened her posture, ran a hand through her hair, and grinned.

"Bold," Quilla said. "Really, Spencer. Hypocritical, actually. That's a better word for it. Tell me, when was the last time you stood on your own two feet? You said it yourself, all those years ago in this very room. I am a talent. I work hard. There's no denying that. You however, don't. I may be Ghan's daughter, but I worked for my reputation here. Heads turn when I walk by. Fear ripples through hearts when they smell my roses. I have a reputation, while you've leached off of mine."

Gillen growled. "Bold words for someone who's asking a favor of me."

Quilla chuckled, snatching the money back. "Well, you've made it pretty clear your hospitality would be more a hindrance than leverage. I withdraw my proposal. To you, I wish good luck. It will be a fun show watching you struggle without your lieutenant."

Gillen snarled. "We've done great so far."

Quilla grinned, gazing at the cracked, dim lights and peeling paint. "Have you?"

The group turned, heading after Quilla. Just as they were about to ascend down the stairs, Quilla stopped.

"On second thought, keep the money." Quilla flung the bag behind her. "Consider it charity."

Chapter Eight
Quilla

"Why'd you do that?" Florian asked. "We could have used the money, not to mention that much of it. He's an asshole, why should he get it?"

"True, true," Quilla grinned.

"So why did you do it?" Lilith pressed. "I mean you proved a point, that's for sure, but it wasn't at all necessary."

"I did prove a point," Quilla confirmed, smiling like a toddler. "And no, it wasn't necessary."

"You aren't answering our questions." Florian said. "Why did you do it?"

Quilla giggled. "I like to imagine what happens when he opens the bag."

Lilith raised an eyebrow. "What happens?"

"Well, I believe I put just enough cyanide in it to make him vomit uncontrollably, but not die."

Lilith blinked. Florian let out an amazed cackle. "Oh, you fabulous fuck."

They had just left the Link and were strutting along the wet streets of Hanslack. The concrete was damp, as always, and the buildings dripped remnants of the previous rain. Quilla didn't like it, but this city was home.

"So why go back to the Link?" Lillith asked. "Other than to make Gillen hurl?"

"I want to see where our reputation stands." Quilla said. "The best way to do that was to ask Gillen. The need for a place to stay was simply my excuse to be there."

"So," Florian started. "Where is the money?"

"Most likely in Grandez Lone's slimy fingers."

Florian groaned. "Why would you make me imagine such an awful sight? I was having a good day."

"You didn't take the money with you?" Lilith asked.

"No. When I was facing death row my thoughts were more focused on surviving than grabbing kangue."

Lilith sighed. "Fine, but how are we going to get food and supplies?"

Quilla blinked. "You've known me for two years and yet you still can't predict my methods?"

Florian grinned. "I love doing jobs with you! You always add a bit of *zest*!"

"A bit?" Lilith raised an eyebrow. "She has a crippling addiction to explosives."

"That's a recent thing." Quilla conceded. "It was only about a month ago when I discovered how *wonderful* they are."

Lilith put an arm around her. "And since then they've been your one and only true love."

"Second only to you–"

"Hey guys?" Alohi's cautious tone cut through their conversation. "You might want to see this..."

They turned to see Alohi gazing at a wall. Posters were plastered to the bricks, their own faces staring back at them.

Quilla stepped closer, staring into her own black eyes. "Quilla Thorne or Rosalie Ghan. Wanted alive. Prize of one million kangue." She tilted her head, examining the name at the top of the page. "Ordered by Empress Cercel Ghan."

"Woah," Lilith ran a finger down her poster. "Since when is Cercel Empress?"

Quilla's gaze shifted to the floor. She couldn't think. The same haunting voice tainted her thoughts. It asked how. It asked why. And it told her over and over again that it was *her fault.*

"What happened to Ghan?" Florian asked. "You know, the male one?"

"I don't know." Quilla whispered. "But this is bad. Really fucking *bad.* Ghan didn't put up wanted posters. Ghan never told anyone about the absence of his heir. It's a trick for advertising. To say his favorite daughter ran away— well, that brings up questions." She took a shaky breath, tearing the poster from the wall. "Cercel doesn't care. She isn't interested in the good of the country; only herself. She's been consumed by so much vengeance it's blinded her." She turned to them, crumpling the poster in her hand. "She wants to end me, and in the process, she'll burn this country to the ground."

~~~

Quilla swung her foot into the wood. Whatever was holding it close snapped, and the door creaked open.

"Well," Lilith began. "It, uh– it has a roof."

They found an abandoned farm house on the outskirts of Hanslack. The thing had cracked windows, creaky boards, and more spiders than nails. But nevertheless, it was somewhere to stay. Quilla's favorite part about the place was its proximity from the beach. That was why she vouched for the farm house instead of the underground sewers. She liked her water to be salty rather than... *that.*

"Better get comfortable," Quilla said. "This is where we're staying until the war ends."

Lilith opened her mouth to reply but closed it when she heard a belch. They turned to see Alohi collapsed on the lawn, vomiting into the grass.
~~~

Lilith rushed to hold back her hair, Quilla on her heel. Florian looked like they were about to copy Alohi's action.

"How long have you been holding that in, Alohi?" Quilla asked as another round of throw up spewed from Alohi's mouth. "Tell me, is this worth the drunken happiness?"

"Oh, do shut up," Lilith told her, still holding Alohi's hair. "You've been so much worse."

Quilla shrugged. "Actually, no. When I'm hungover, it just makes me want to kill more. Of course, I worked up my tolerance."

Alohi wiped her face, shakily getting to her feet. "I'm never drinking again," she rasped. "Never again."

Quilla laughed, "You keep telling yourself that." She kicked a piece of vomit from her shoe. "But we didn't come here to seek sobriety."

"Right," Lilith smirked. "We came here to fulfill our one and only purpose in life."

"*Your* only purpose." Alohi wiped a gob of throw up from her lip. "My life has plenty of purpose."

Quilla ruffled her hair, beaming at the sulking politician. "Pish posh, Windlem. You're with us now, and you conform to our moral compass."

~~~

The group assembled on the tattered couch, watching Quilla with anticipation. Quilla looked back at them, waiting for someone to say something.

"So," she threw up her hands. "Anyone have any ideas?"

They stared blankly at her.

"I thought you had a plan!" Lilith exclaimed.

"I have a vague idea."

"Uh huh," Florian grumbled. "What 'vague idea?'"

"Well," Quilla said. "I know it's going to involve the Empire, the League, and a *fuck* ton of explosives. That's about it."
~~~

"Okay, so essentially you're looking for advice on what to explode?" Florian asked, crossing their arms.

"That about sums it up."

"Okay," Lilith started. "And you need it to harm the League and the Empire?"

"That would be preferable."

"That should be pretty simple." Florian said. "I mean, the League relies on the Empire more than they would ever let on. Destroy the Empire's resources, and you'll destroy the Leagues."

Lilith bit her lip. "But we have to keep in mind that harming the Empire helps the League. We want to hinder each more than help."

Quilla nodded. "You're right. We need to do something so detrimental, so *enormous*, that neither side can look at it as a victory. The question is, what?"

There was silence, each of them running through every strength and weakness.

"What about the trains?" Alohi mumbled.

Quilla raised an eyebrow. "What about them?"

"Well," Alohi pressed a finger to her chin. "The best thing the Empire has going for them is their train system. At the same time, it's the League's only source of food. Transportation, supplies, military; those are all things both sides heavily rely on. To destroy those would be too much of a loss for both sides. Neither could count it as a win."

Quilla raised her knuckle to her lips. "Well, Windlem," she grinned. "You should get drunk more often."

"Trust me, alcohol is nothing more than a hindrance."

Quilla's smile widened. "In that case, I should stop taking your knowledge for granted. Well done. We're going to blow up the largest train port in Thine."

"Which is?" Lilith pressed.

"Great question!" Quilla exclaimed. "Alohi?"

"I haven't the slightest clue."

Florian threw up their hands. "You're a political prodigy and you don't know your enemies greatest strength?"

"*Political* prodigy. Not geographical, not strategic. *Political.*"

"What Alohi's trying to say is she's really good at insulting people." Quilla amended. "Nothing else."

Alohi scowled. "You're twisting my words."

"Aren't I always?"

"Okay," Lilith said. "So as you were saying, Quilla, we have a plan but we have no idea where to execute it. I think before we go deeper into the details, we need to locate the place we plan to blow up."

"True," Quilla said. "I'll find the train port. Lilith, find water. Alohi, help Lilith and then drink as many glasses of said water as possible. It'll help with your hangover. And Florian–" Quilla grinned, turning to the pirate. "I'm putting you on grocery duty."

Chapter Nine
Lilith

The door creaked open and Lilith crept in. She padded to the desk and wrapped her arms around Quilla, resting her face on her shoulder. "Hey, Quill."

Quilla giggled. "Hey, Lili."

"I brought you something," Lilith placed a cup of tea on the desk. By some miracle, Florian had gotten the stove to work. As soon as they did, Lilith decided that all of them would do well with some hydration.

Quilla smiled, taking a sip of the tea. "No coffee?"

"I'm not feeding your addiction."

Quilla hummed a groan. "How unfortunate."

"So," Lilith started, moving her hands to Quilla's waist. "How's it going? Have you found the port?"

Quilla's tone shifted. She drew a sigh, leaning heavily on her desk. "Yes, I did."

"And?" Lilith pressed. "Where is it?"

"It doesn't matter. We're scrapping the plan. It's not happening."

Lilith perked. She flipped Quilla's shoulders, locking with her gaze. "Why? It's such a good opportunity. I mean, the amount of harm that it would cause to the League and the Empire—"

"It doesn't matter." Quilla said, averting her gaze to the ground. "We're not going *there*. I'll find something else."

"*There*?" Lilith asked. "Quilla where's *there*?"

Quilla sighed. She kept her gaze on the floor, eyes taking on a worried color. "The Grave Desert."

Lilith tensed at the name. She bit her lip, unsure of what to say. "Oh."

"Yeah," Quilla breathed. "It– I'm not making you go back there."

Lilith sighed. She didn't want to talk about it. She hated remembering her days in that place. She hated the tears that welled in her eyes. She hated when she was thrust back into the sand.

"I–" Lilith stammered. "I can't step in sand without feeling scared. I think– well, there's nothing that could hurt me in the sand, but I'm– I'm terrified."

Quilla gazed at her. Her black eyes were kind and compassionate. "Hey, sit down," Quilla led her to the bed. "Let's talk."

Lilith sat down, her hands trembling in her lap. "Trains are hard for me. I– I can deal with it and hide it, but– I, um, it makes me nervous. Really nervous. Really *scared*." She bit her lip, looking at her shaking fingers. "Sorry, this probably sounds pathetic."

Quilla laid a hand on her leg. "No, no, don't be sorry." She gave her a small smile. "Stop calling yourself that. It's not true." Quilla sighed. "I have the same thing. Dark alleyways. Gillen's office. Hell, I'll see an extravagant door and my mind thinks it's Ghan's. It's so weird. The smallest things send me into flashbacks."

Lilith leaned on Quilla's shoulder, closing her eyes. "I don't get flashbacks as much. Sometimes there are little bursts of the memory; flashes, almost. But mostly–" she took a breath. "Mostly it's just sudden, uncalled for rushes of panic. I'll get nightmares, but– but they don't feel like nightmares. They feel–"

"Normal?" Quilla asked. "Yeah, I get those too. For me it's like an unpleasant reality. For most people, it's a dream. But for me, it was what life was like. I dealt with it, and survived."

Lilith blinked tears from her eyes. "God, why did we survive?" she buried her head in her hands. "Out of all the people, why are we still alive?"

Quilla hugged her, resting her face on Lilith's shoulder. "Chance. That's what I amount it too. Just pure fucking luck."

Lilith looked up, tears pricking her eyes. "No, it wasn't chance. You were a brilliant swimmer, that's why Ghan chose you. My dad protected me with his life, that's why I'm alive. No chance. Just luck."

"Lili," Quilla squeezed her. "You never told me about your dad."

Lilith flinched, tears leaking from her gaze.

"Only if you feel comfortable," Quilla reassured. "No pressure."

"No, it– it's okay," Lilith took a shaky breath, placing her hand on Quilla's knee. "I want to talk about it. He was really– um, kind. He supported me, let me help with the farm work, and taught me how to shoot a bow. Before– you know, you."

Quila smiled. "He sounds wonderful."

Quilla let the words resonate. She didn't speak— she didn't need to. The past demanded time to creep into the present.

"He was," Lilith choked, tears bordering her waterline. "It– it was my fault we were taken. The Empire locks you up for minor crimes. It's unfair. I–" she paused, hands shaking. "I tried smoking with my friends. Little did I know it wasn't something simple. We were doing crack. We got caught, and–" she rubbed her temples. "The next day, a group of Empire soldiers came to our house and dragged us to the Grave Desert."

"Oh," Quilla placed hand on her shoulder. "That wasn't your fault. Trust me, Lilith, you didn't do anything."

"Yes–" Lilith stammered. "Yes I did, Quilla. How can you say that? It is *all* my fault."

"No." Quilla said. "It's not. Look, the Empire's criminal justice system is... messed up, to say the least. I never really had friends, but I'm pretty sure it's normal to try drugs as a teen. You were a farmer, right? Well, the system is designed to discriminate against people of lower social class. To the Empire, you're better as slaves than citizens."

Lilith looked at her hands, unsure of how to respond. Quilla was right; some part of her knew that. But somewhere deep inside her was dwelling on the fact that *all of this* was her fault.

"I– I'm not done." Lilith continued. "When we got to the Grave Desert, it– it was really hard. We worked all day. Little to no food. Just– awful. I– I did something, and they were about to whip me. Dad stopped them, and–"

Her voice cracked. Tears poured down her cheeks. She buried her head in Quilla's chest, gripping the back of her blouse. Quilla stroked her hair, resting her lips on Lilith's head.

Quilla took a breath. "You don't have too–"

"They killed him." Lilith blurted. "They slammed his head against the tracks until his skull caved in. I held his bloodied corpse while they ran away laughing. The blood stayed between my fingernails for *weeks*! They didn't let me say goodbye; they didn't let me say *sorry*. They didn't even fucking let me *talk* to him!"

Lilith stood. She grabbed her bow from the nightstand and flung it against the wall. The thing clattered to the floor, not a crack from the impact.

Lilith crumpled to the floor. She slammed her hands over her ears and put her head between her knees. It needed to shut up. All the voices, the laughter– it needed to *shut the hell up.*

It was all too much. They were all laughing. Laughing at her. It was Cercel, it was Zinglor, and it was those awful guards who killed her father. They were cackling. Telling her she was weak, incapable: pathetic.

"Hey, hey, Lili," Quilla drew her hands away from her head, weaving her fingers through her partners. "Focus on me. Breathe, breathe."

Lilith didn't realized she stopped. She squeezed Quilla's hand, and tried. But the breaths were uneven, coming in strangled, panicked gasps. *In, out. Repeat. In, out. Repeat.*

Lilith leaned into her partner's chest. Quilla held her, keeping her breathing steady and predictable. That's what she needed. She matched her breath with Quilla's, prohibiting the intake to be any quicker than the release.

There was no speech. Quilla didn't talk; she didn't need to. Just having her presence was everything to Lilith. She needed Quilla by her side. They were each other's teathers. When one's own head flung them into madness, the other was the rope that brought them back to earth.

Quilla was Lilith's rope. And Lilith was Quilla's.

But best of all, they inspired each other. Quilla's craving for revenge caught Lilith's fall. Lilith's urge to forgive kept Quilla from going insane.

Vengeance was a useful tool, in low doses.

"I'll do it." Lilith said.

Quilla raised her eyebrows, concern glittering in her gaze. "Lili, are you sure–"

"Yes." Lilith sat up, looking Quilla in the eye. "You understand, right?"

"I–" Quilla stammered. "Understand what?"

"The need to kill," Lilith said. The phrase was so plain, so blatant. But it was the only string of words that could put together what she was feeling. "I want to go back there, and I want to laugh at them. I want to *destroy* everything they've ever worked for. I want to free the captives, and make the slavers die hard, *miserable* deaths. I want them to *suffer*, just as I did."

Quilla stared at her, an unreadable emotion on her features. Then, a smile twisted her features into a malicious, vengeful grin.

"Well then," she said. "In that case, let's go play with explosives."

Chapter Ten
Cercel

Oh, Cerce, Rosalie chatted. *How naive can you be?*

Cercel grit her teeth, focusing on the stride of her walk.

I mean, honestly. She continued. *Do you expect this to work out? He doesn't love you. He never has!*

Cercel took a breath. She couldn't respond. She couldn't show cracks. She couldn't let anyone see that slowly, she was being driven insane.

Rosalie scoffed, placing her icy hands on Cercel's shoulder. *Are you really not going to answer me?* She taunted. *Oh please, Cercel. All you have is your jealousy and hate. That's the only thing that will never leave you. The only thing you will ever be. You are nothing more than your vengeance.*

Cercel's lip curled. She rammed her heel into her shin, exhaling as the pain slithered through her limbs.

Rosalie flickered. Her shape shifted, becoming distorted. Her voice wavered, syllables dancing in different octaves. A moment after she glitched, she regained her poise, grinning at Cercel with white, perfect teeth.

Not quite, Rosalie snickered. *You're going to have to cause more pain than that.*

Cercel punched her arm.

More.

Cercel punched the wall.

Again.

Cercel bit down on her sore knuckles.

Harder.

But this time, she didn't follow Rosalie's orders. Instead, she ran. She sprinted through the hall: she didn't know if she was running away from Rosalie or towards the man she hated more.

She stopped just before Father's cell. Her heart pounded, her mind raced. But as she peaked behind the barred doors, her anxiety vanished.

Father was pathetic. His pants were tattered and his shirt had vanished. His skin gave a yellow glow and his stomach retreated into his ribs.

Hm... Rosalie scoffed. But that was all she said. Just a thought.

"Where are you going?" Cercel muttered, only loud enough for the figure in her mind to hear.

Rosalie cackled, the noise fading away with her distorted body. *You don't need me anymore. The real torment is about to begin.*

Cercel straightened her posture, ran a hand through her hair, and unlocked Father's cell.

As soon as Father saw her, the pathetic aura vanished. Instead, it was replaced with a sick grin.

"Cercel," he cooed. "What are you doing here?"

Cercel growled, tossing him a ration bar. "Food, eat it."

Father grinned, licking his teeth. "So, tell me," he began, tearing into the bar like a wild animal. "How are your first few weeks as Empress?"

"Why do you care?" Cercel drawled, leaning against the wall. "You've never really shown much interest in my success."

Father grinned, flashing his yellow fangs. "Can it really be success when you spend all your time hanging around a dirty prisoner? Honestly, you could send any one of your servants to come and feed me, yet, you come yourself." Father stood, his chains clattering against the floor. "My question is, why?"

Cercel dug her nails into her palm, concealing the panic resting beneath her smirk. "Maybe I just like to watch you *suffer*."

"Or perhaps," Father waltzed towards her, his hot breath hitting her cheek. "You need my help."

Cercel let out a stout cackle.

"You are slipping, Cercel. Slowly. Just slow enough you think anyone will notice. But people *do* notice. They notice the fire in your eyes, the downwards curl of your lips. Tell me, do you really think Rosalie is next to you, whispering orders in your ear–"

With those words, Cercel lunged. She grabbed his collar and pinned him to the wall, his frail body barely a weight in her hand.

"Don't talk to me!" she growled. "I am your Empress, not your fucking pet! *Treat me like one!*"

Father smirked, his features displaying an infuriating tranquility. He tilted his head, examining Cercel. From her royal robes to her combed hair. He wasn't judging, simply looking.

"You've grown." He commented.

Cercel blinked. "Beg your pardon?"

Father grinned. "You've gotten taller."

"Yes, I know what 'grown' means." Cercel rolled her eyes. "It's just an unusual comment, given you and I's relationship."

"What?" Father tilted his head. "Can't I compliment my *daughter*?"

Cercel let out a strangled gasp. She released Father, watching as he crumpled to the ground.

"What did you just call me?" she growled.

It looked like Father tried to answer. He opened his mouth, the familiar twist of a phrase forming on his tongue. But instead of the carefully crafted words, he let out a string of coughs. Blood flew from his throat, scattering the floor with a mix of spit and phlegm.

"Look," he drawled, his voice choked. "I'm sick, Cercel. I took pills as Emperor to soothe it, but–" another string of hacks rose from his throat. "Without them, I don't expect to live another year."

For a moment, Cercel felt the foriegn sting of pity. Father always seemed so powerful— so *untouchable*. To see him crumpled on the ground, blood spewing from his tongue, it was surreal. Cercel had imagined him on his knees many times, but unlike in her fantasies, she never imagined feeling an ounce of sympathy.

Nevertheless, masking was always a wonderful option.

"Why do you think I care?" Cercel demanded. "You abused me for years! I don't care if you're dying! Fuck, I should be *glad*!"

Father simply looked at her, his black eyes glittering with curiosity. "But are you?"

"Am I what?"

"Glad?" Father grinned. "That I am to be dead?"

Cercel opened her mouth to respond, but couldn't. She didn't have the words. Because unfortunately, he was right. Father was her lifeline. As much as she hated to admit it, she had no idea what she was doing. She knew how to order, she knew how to please people. But to fulfill any of her promises? She was shooting in the dark. Father hit his target.

"You're lost." Father said. "You put on a ruse of understanding and knowledge, but the truth is, Cercel, you don't have a clue how to rule."

Cercel sat on the floor, tucking her knees to her chest. "How did you do it?" her gaze wandered around the cell, refusing to meet Father's eyes. "Run this fucking shithole."

Father grinned. "It was different back then. I had to win an election. I won't bore you on how that happened, but once I was Emperor, I was lost."

Cercel groaned. "That doesn't help me."

"I'm not done." Father retorted. "Once I was in power, I recognized that I needed to stay in power. There was a Rebellion, Lunan Renel, so I nuked them. I made sure the raging river that was once the League of Red Doves dwindled to the trickle. The point is, Cercel, you have to define your goals. Make sure that no matter what, they can't take you out of office. Then, you can do whatever you want. So tell me, child, what do you want?"

Cercel hesitated. Her one true desire was to kill Rosalie Ghan. However, it may not be best to tell that to a person who worshiped the ground she walked on.

"I want to extinguish the League of Red Doves. I want to kill any spark of rebellion. I want to be legendary. I want my name plastered on palace walls and *worshiped*."

Seemed pretty plausible.

"Well then," Father's lips twisted into a smirk. "Let's start with the League. Do you know where they are?"

"Obviously not," Cercel retorted. "If I did, I wouldn't be asking you for advice."

"I suppose," Father cooed. "What if I told you *I* knew where they were?"

"I would strengthen your prison security."

Father paid no mind, brushing off her comment. "I know where they're hiding, Cercel. I know their status, and I know they are vulnerable to an attack. Abush now, and you could end the League of Red Doves."

Cercel pinched her lips, considering this. She could do it. She could demolish the Empire's largest nuisance and be a legend in history.

But that wasn't what she really wanted. No, she didn't much care what happened to those incompetent peasants who called themselves a rebellion. She wanted one person. One woman to fall to her knees before her.

She was going to kill Rosalie Ghan.

Cercel tightened her glare. "Where are they?"

"Ah-ah," Father waved a shriveled finger in her face. "Cercel, look, I–" he let out another string of blood filled hacks. "I don't have much time, but I want to help you." He reached to touch her face; Cercel let him. "But I need my pills. They'll keep me alive for at least another three years. I can guide you, Cercel."

"Why?" Cercel murmured, Father's hand still on her cheek. "You never cared for me before. Why now?"

"Cercel," Father tilted his head. "I was hard on you because I was scared. Scared of your power, your potential. But I was wrong. I should have taught you, not Rosalie. You were always the most competent of your siblings. I was scared of your power, I thought you would overthrow me. But Cercel–" Ghan cupped her cheek. "You have grown into such an amazing young woman, and I am so, *so* proud of you."

Cercel cracked. Tears pricked her eyes, trickling down her cheeks and pouring to the ground. Father brushed them away with his thumb. It was so surreal— the care, the *love*— so foreign Cercel entertained the possibility that it was a hallucination.

"Why are you saying this now?" she snapped. "What advantage does this give you?"

"Oh Cercel," Father's eyes melted. "I am so sorry. I never realized the extent of my-" he opened his arms. "Come here."

Before, danger would have howled in her ear to run. Before, she would have stabbed Father. Any other time than the present, she wouldn't have believed he was offering a hug.

But now, Cercel only wanted to hug him back.

She flung herself into Father's arms, pressing her face into his shoulder.

"My amazing daughter." Father said, stroking her back. "My beautiful, amazing daughter. You are going to be an amazing Empress."

"And you're going to help me?" Cercel asked, her voice a begging child's. "Right?"

"Yes," Father whispered. "But please, Cercel-" he choked, blood coming from his mouth. "Get my pills."

Cercel nodded. She picked herself up from Father's arms and nearly skipped to the door. "I'll be right back." She said, "Then you can teach me?"

Ghan grinned; not one of ambition, but one of true good nature. "Yes, I will train you to be the greatest Empress this country has ever seen."

Chapter Eleven
Nikolai

Nikolai's swords hit Killen's with a clash. His master bounded back, legs bent in the defensive. Nikolai didn't hesitate; he raced towards Killen, blades raised above his head.

Killen dove to the side, rolling to his feet and twirling around Nikolai. He was like a dancer: soft, delicate, precise. Nikolai was a lion: strong, wild, unrelenting.

"Sit still!" Nikolai hollered as Killen spun around his blades.

"Is that what you're going to tell your opponents?" Killen growled. "'If you would be so kind, sit still while I decapitate you.'"

Nikolai growled, not pleased with the high squeal Killen used to imitate his voice. He tightened his grip on his blades, lowering them at his sides.

"I thought you were supposed to be training me on defense." Nikolai said. "It's a little hard to do that when you're constantly avoiding the attack."

Killen dropped his blade to his side. "Well, it's a bit hard to stay on offense when you keep charging at my head."

"Is that what you're going to tell your opponent?"

"Fuck off." Killen growled. "I'm your master, I get to criticize you, not the other way around."

"Fine," Nikolai shrugged. "I'll try to be a bit less *aggressive*. Would that help?"

"Actually," Killen rubbed the back of his head. "I think we're done with sparring today."

Nikolai raised an eyebrow. "We have two hours left in our session."

"I know," Killen sighed, a new vulnerability in his tone. "Sit down, let's talk. Then you can have the rest of the time off."

Nikolai tilted his head, but didn't protest.

They sat outside of the ring. Their legs were close— not quite touching —but close enough to feel Killen's warmth. Awkward silence warped the room. Nikolai took a breath, eager to be rid of quiet.

"So?" he started. "What did you want to talk about?"

Killen sighed, pressing his fingers to his temple. "Look, Nikolai, there's no easy way to say this." He bit his lip. "But— well, there are signs. Signs that I've been noticing with you. I just–" he sighed. "I need to know. Are you–" Killen swallowed. "Hurting yourself?"

Nikolai's breath caught. He hid his addiction. Hid it *damn well*. At least he thought he did. He was always calm, composed. *Normal.* He took every precaution to make sure his habit remained unseen.

"Actually, on second thought, don't answer that." Killen took a breath. "I'm going to lecture, so be the brilliant student I know you are and listen."

Nikolai bit his tongue.

"Life hasn't exactly been fair to you, Nikolai. Not fair at all. Your dad puts an ungodly amount of pressure on you. You've been fighting a hopeless war since you were fourteen. Competition has been the only thing you can fall back on. I guess, what I'm saying is, no one would blame you if–" Killen weaved his coat between his manicured fingers. "If you fell into something."

Something.

Nikolai stared at his gloves.

"I guess–" Killen stammered, "I guess the only thing I can do in this situation is try to counter whatever asshole voice is repeating the words of your father. So, Nikolai, know that in my eyes, you are a brilliant, smart, resilient young man. If anyone else—*anyone* else— was in the same situation, Nikolai, they would fall. Falter. *You* haven't.

"In the three years I have known you, you've never faltered. It sends my mind spiraling every time I try to rationalize it. You betray the impossible, Nikolai. You do things thought to be undoable and make the world gape. I mean, you're a seventeen —eighteen, sorry— year old competing with grown adults. They might not realize how lucky they are to have you, but I do, Nikolai. I realize it. I know how *special* you are."

Nikolai's lips opened. He stared at his hands, not sure how to respond. Could he admit it? No, dear god no. The last time someone found out about his... *cutting* they left him. He couldn't have that. Not again.

"Killen, what are you talking about?" Nikolai laughed, the noise a poised fake. "Who in their right mind would *cut* themselves! I mean honestly, you have to be clinically *insane* to do anything like that."

Silence stung the air. It was only when Killen spoke that Nikolai realized he fucked up.

"Nikolai," Killen's face fell. "I said hurt yourself. Never cut."

Nikolai's eyes widened. Horror rapped her icy hands around his neck. He slipped. *Faltered.* One sentence— one fucking *word*— gave him away.

No! There was a way out. There *had* to be a way to right his words.

Just then, the door to the sparring ring flew open. Nikolai whipped around to find a League soldier.

"What is it?" Nikolai asked, standing.

"Mister Lone." The soldier bowed. "Your father wants to see you."

Nikolai didn't turn back to Killen. He simply strode towards the door, a practiced confidence in his step. He wanted to be out. He needed his secret to be hidden. Even if his reason to leave was to be ridiculed by his father.

It didn't matter how hard Grandez hit him. He would rather take a million beatings than share that secret.

~~~

Nikolai flung the door open and strode in. Though it was his house, it felt strange, unreal. He tended to avoid its white walls and gold lacing.

"Nikolai," Grandez was leaning against the living room door frame. "Will you ever stop wearing black? I just *adored* your white."

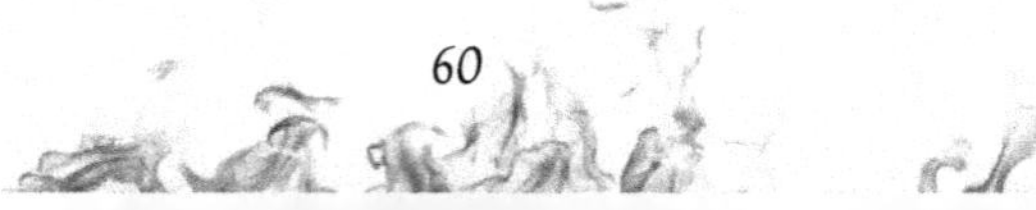
~~~

Nikolai gazed at his clothes. The white and blue had been replaced by dark cloth and lace. It was supposed to hide him, yet he could never avoid being the center of Grandez Lone's anger.

"I believe it's more efficient." Nikolai said. "Hides the blood. White stains so easily."

"Yes, I suppose it does." Grandez said. "However, your spilling of blood has been lacking. Especially in the necessary areas."

Nikolai swallowed.

"Why isn't Black Cyanide dead?" Grandez asked. "They haven't done anything *extravagant* for quite some time. Something is cooking. Thorne has something up her sleeve."

"Doesn't she always?" Nikolai rolled his eyes.

"Don't take that tone." Grandez huffed. "Listen! You are going to train harder than you've ever trained before! When Thorne makes her move, we can track her. You are going to find Black Cyanide, and kill them on *sight*."

"Dad–" Nikolai started. "Shouldn't we kill them in public? Set an example?"

Instead of a response, a low cackle came from Grandez's throat. As the laugh rose, Nikolai retreated back. His heeled boots clicked against the wood floor, carrying him as far as possible from his father.

"I see what you're doing." Grandez advanced on him. "You don't want to kill them. You cannot bear to plunge a blade into people thought to be your friends."

Nikolai took a breath. "Dad, no–"

"You are pathetic, Nikolai." Grandez slammed his fist against the wall. The fist narrowly missed his head, and Nikolai was left staring at his father's knuckles in the shattered plaster. "Incredibly *pathetic*. They betrayed you! I am all you have left. Your friends, they come and go. I am here *forever*."

Nikolai's eyes watered. He was trembling. He was about to show weakness. Weakness that he couldn't afford.

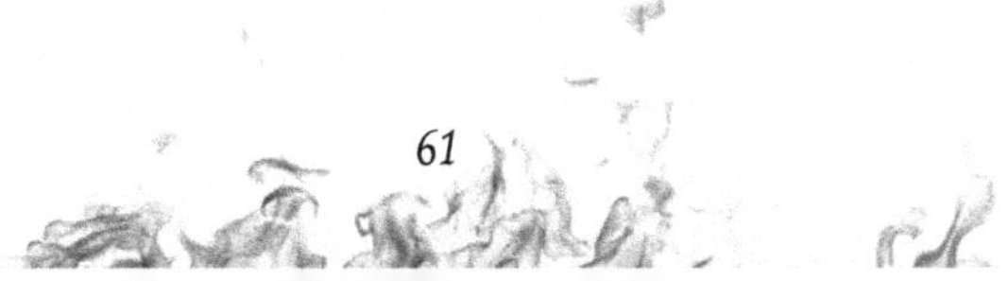

"Apologies, Father," Nikolai said. "It was a mistake to refuse your orders. I will kill Cyanide as soon as I get close enough."

Grandez grunted. He drew his fist from the wall and turned away. "Fine," he growled. "But be warned, Nikolai, my patience is running thin. You need to eliminate this enemy. You have yet to become the greatest. Kill the Empress. Take her place. This is your duty. This is all your life is worth. What use are you alive if you cannot complete this?"

Nikolai exhaled. Poise re-entered his tone. It was there, it was loyal. He knew the calm wouldn't leave him. He promised himself something after. A sick reward.

"Of course, Father." Nikolai said, clasping his hands behind his back. "This war will be over by the end of the year. I will kill Black Cyanide. I will kill Empress Ghan and I will eliminate anyone who gets in my way."

Grandez smiled. "Make it half a year."

Nikolai nodded. As soon as a satisfied expression touched his father's face, he strode towards the exit. If it wasn't for the promise of the euphoria, he would have run.

The door clicked behind him. He fell back onto the wall, sliding to the floor. His eyes shut, his breath steadied. The calm lingered in his bones, slithering through his body in swift, relieving shivers.

But it wouldn't stay for long.

He pulled a knife from his coat.

The metal made his heart perk. The gleam gave his wrist a tingle. His skin was numb. Preparing itself.

Nikolai grinned. He was going to cut.

Deep.

Chapter Twelve
Lilith

The click of the train clattered through the countryside as it sped towards the Grave Desert. Lilith stood, watching the ground morph into rocky doons. She leaned against the train door, the light of the sunrise reflecting off her braid. She was excited, sure. Well, at least she thought she was. This was revenge. Those people who enslaved her, beat her, killed her father, they would all pay. She would shoot an arrow into their throat. She would laugh as they choked on their own blood.

She should have been bristling with joy.

But instead, she felt a weird feeling of grief.

Sadness, vulnerability, *pain*.

As the trees slowly vanished and the dirt turned to sand, the flame of panic slowly engulfed her. Her lungs shrunk as her ribs closed around them. Her knees buckled, her balance shattered.

There were a million thoughts racing in her head, and yet?

Only one consumed her.

I can't breathe.

She needed to run. She needed to get far, *far* away. Because someone was about to come at her from behind. There was a whip raised to her back, a foot was going to be dug into her side. *Something* was about to happen.

"Quilla!" Lilith hollered, scrambling to her feet. "*Quilla!*"

"Lilith?" Quilla barged into the train car. Her black eyes were alert with panic. "Is everything okay?"

"Quilla–" Lilith stammered, "Quilla I can't–"

Quilla ran to her, engulfing her in a hug. Lilith crumpled to the ground, sobbing into Quilla's chest. Her teeth clattered, her breath came in short, panicked gasps. She couldn't do this anymore.

"Quilla–" she heaved. "I can't do this. I can't go back–"

"I know," Quilla said. "I know,"

"How will I ever face it?" Lilith sobbed. "How will I ever go back there? Just seeing sand makes me– makes me like *this*!"

Quilla didn't say anything. She simply held her tighter.

"Quilla?" Lilith asked, lifting her face from Quilla's blouse, "How did you do it?" she took a breath. "You know, face– *everything*."

Quilla sighed, her eyes drifting towards the ceiling. "I don't know." She said, "I just knew that if I didn't go back to the Golden Palace– to *them*, then I would never truly be free. I'm still not free. The memories still seize me at night. But I think I find comfort in the fact that I'm shaping my past into something bearable. I'm covering the wounds with bandages, and under those, new skin will grow."

"But–" Lilith stammered. "I mean, you went in there and you achieved everything you needed. The panic stays away when you need. How do you keep it at bay?"

Quilla sighed. "I don't. Look, Lilith, I know I look strong in the Golden Palace, but–" her voice cracked. "I– it's not always like that." She swallowed. "When I faced Ghan, I couldn't kill him. I had the opportunity too, but I couldn't. I just– I kept morphing between Quilla Thorne and Rosalie Ghan. Like I was two different people."

"But you're always so *strong*." Lilith whispered. "*How?*"

Quilla pierced her lips as her eyes drifted to the countryside. She didn't say anything, instead pressing her finger against her chin.

"Quilla?" Lilith asked. "Did I– did I say something wrong?"

"No, no, not at all." Quilla said. "Sorry, I'm just thinking."

"Oh," Lilith shifted her gaze back to Quilla's blouse. She couldn't look at the sand. Couldn't bear it. "Okay,"

"The way I combat panic is anger." Quilla said. "When the panic overwhelms me, I look at the source. I look at what— *who* caused it. And I make a vow. I vow not to stop until they suffer the same way I do. Until I have the final laugh."

Lilith gazed at her. "I thought you said vengeance was your cage."

"It is," Quilla admitted. "But it's also my wings."

Lilith bit her tongue. With a cautious breath, she shifted her gaze to the outside. The terrain was sandy, doons curving in the distance. The place was unmistakable.

The Grave Desert.

There was still fear. Still a lung-crushing panic. But in her pain, she found someone to blame. It wasn't her who gave her this fear. It was *them*. The people who caged her. Now she was free, and had an emotion to bandage her wounds.

Pure, filthy rage.

Lilith stood, ugly ambition pushing her to her feet. "Let's fucking do this."

~~~

"God dammit, Alohi!" Quilla howled. "Just jump!"

"Oh, excuse me." Alohi rolled her eyes. "My sincerest apologies for not being eager to jump out of a train car moving faster than any animal!"

The three of them stood in the doorframe of the engine. Alohi was gripping the walls so tight her knuckles turned paper white. Quilla loomed behind her, her hand dangerously close to the politician's back. Lilith lingered behind them, barely noticing their squabble. Her gaze was on the horizon.

"If your tone wasn't dripping with sarcasm, Windlem, I would have taken your apology." Quilla snarled. "Now stop wasting our time and *jump!*"
~~~

"You go first!" Alohi retorted. "If you're so eager!"

"Oh trust me, I would. But if I got off the train, your cowardice would keep you from leaping. You would be carried far into the distance and be used as a slave."

"Well would you look at that?" Alohi grinned. "The notorious criminal prodigy and wrath of Hanslack is looking out for her friend! What a surprise! Some would even say–" Alohi made a dramatic gasp. "She *cares* for her."

Quilla kicked her off the train.

As soon as Alohi tumbled onto the desert, Quilla followed. Lilith jumped after her, her gaze still resting on the horizon.

"Congratulations," Quilla prodded Alohi with her foot. "You've earned my 'care.' Is it everything you hoped and more?"

Alohi groaned. "I miss Florian."

"Why? So you can drunkenly flash him again? Hate to break it to you, but that wasn't exactly enjoyable for both parties."

Alohi glared at her. "Are you ever going to drop that?"

"Nope."

The two scowled at each other, both searching for another creative insult to throw.

"Guys," Lilith said. "There's a town over there. We can steal horses. That will give us a quick escape if needed."

"Speaking of which," Quilla said. "What's the plan?"

"I should be asking you," Lilith responded. "You know the train port's location and weak points."

Quilla shrugged, pulling out a map. "The thing is, the train port is also the largest slave hub. Over three thousand captured people work there. There are weak spots here–" she pointed to a doorway. "And here," she pointed to a skylight. "But our main course of action really depends on our goal."

"What is our goal?" asked Alohi.

"I think the only person that can answer that is you," Quilla gestured to Lilith. "So, Lilith, what do you want to do?"

Lilith's gaze shifted towards the sky. The sun beat down on her face, illuminating her green eyes. "I want to rescue everyone in that base." She said, locking eyes with Quilla. "I want them shipped on a train to Ueria, it's on the far side of Thine, very undermanaged by the Empire. No one will be able to catch them again. After that, I want to blow that place to pieces."

Quilla smiled, nodding. "Wonderful." She turned to Alohi. "Well, politician, are you in?"

Alohi grinned. "Of course. There's no way in hell I'm staying behind."

"Good," Lilith looked at the town, licking her teeth. "Let's blow these assholes into the sky."

~~~

Lilith plunged her arrow into a soldier's hand. He wailed, clutching his wound.

"Alohi," Lilith ordered, "Paralyze him."

Alohi obeyed, striking his limbs. They fell by his side, unmoving. Alohi pulled a knife from her coat, ready to plunge it into the man's face.

"Don't." Lilith said, "I want them alive. I want them to burn in the explosion. I want it to be *painful.*"

Alohi nodded. "I'll make sure they can't move a muscle, but feel every lick of the flame."

Lilith grinned, an ambitious glitter in her green eyes.

"Did you hear that?" she knelt down to the soldier. "You are going to die. Your body is going to be torn apart, limb from limb and eaten by the flame. By the end of the hour, nothing will remain of you but burnt pieces of *flesh.*"

The guard whimpered.

Lilith dug her foot into his chest.

"What next?" Alohi asked.

"Next?" Lilith stuck her tongue to the roof of her mouth, thinking. "We need to get to the barns. That's where they keep the slaves. Quilla's mid-hijack. She'll get a train here, we'll get them on it and send them straight to Ueria."
~~~

"I still don't understand why you sent her to do something *alone*." Alohi said. "She's going to ruthlessly murder anyone in sight."

Lilith grinned. "Exactly."

They sprinted through the gray corridors. Unlike the outside, the station was surprisingly neat. Train routes and maps littered the walls while the floor was a shiny concrete. Lilith hated it. She hated every inch of this place. Mostly because she experienced the conditions beyond these halls.

Just as they rounded a corner, she saw a group of Bronze soldiers. They were eating in what appeared to be a mess hall. They didn't see her; they were too focused on their conversations. Spouts of mindless laughter erupted from their throats. They were happy. *Joyous*, even.

Lilith saw red.

She loaded her bow, pointing it at the soldiers.

"Lilith–" Alohi started. "They aren't doing anything. We can leave them. If you shoot–" she took a breath. "We'll be caught."

Lilith's lips spread into a sick smile. "You're right, Alohi." She tucked the arrow back into her quiver, retrieving a second weapon. "This one will be much more efficient."

Her bowstring snapped. The arrow soared through the crowd, striking the wall. For a moment, there was silence. The soldiers gazed at the arrow, then back at her. Lilith grinned, waving.

Then the room exploded.

Lilith pounced on Alohi, shielding her from the fire. The eruption shook the halls, rumbling through the floor. As soon as the shaking stopped, Lilith got to her feet.

"Let's go!" she pulled Alohi up, "We need to run."

The two sprinted down halls, their feet pounding against the floor. Once in a while, a soldier would catch them. Before they could reach for their weapon, Lilith shot his hand to the wall. Each and every one of them would die by explosion.

As they ran, Lilith slammed explosives to the wall. They were little metal things. Almost cute, if you didn't know what they were.

"Do you even know where you're going?" Alohi asked, panting.

Lilith scowled. "Do you ever do anything other than complain? I'll find my way out eventually."

Alohi growled, but kept her mouth shut.

Just as she said, Lilith did find her way out of the building. The entrance they used, however, was heavily guarded. Alohi had to paralyze a lot of guards.

"There," Lilith said, pointing to a barn. "That's where they are."

The building was old, holes and chips burdening the wood. It hadn't changed. Lilith remembered her and her father weeping under its leaky ceiling. He held her tight, shielding her from the sand storm.

Now, she would send a course of fire through its fragile walls.

Lilith barged into the building, bow in hand. The air smelled of animals and piss. Men and women were shackled to the walls, their heads hung low. The lucky ones had rags. Most were completely naked.

As soon as they saw her, they scrambled back. They clutched their loved ones to their chest, looking at her with fearful eyes.

Lilith unstrapped her bow, throwing it to the ground. She gazed at them, looking at their scared, tired faces. It was as if she was looking in a mirror that reflected her past self.

"I'm not here to hurt you," she said. "I'm here to help. I promise."

They shied away, mistrust glimmering in their eyes.

Lilith gazed at the broken ceiling. She had been in their position. She had been in this very barn. These people were going through the exact same thing she had. So why couldn't she form words of comfort?

As if a brick hit her, she realized why.

Because there was none.

There was nothing she could say to make them trust her. They were too broken, too hurt. They had nothing left.

Meaning they had nothing left to lose.

"Listen," Lilith spoke. "There are no words I can say that will make you trust me. There is nothing I can do to erase what has already been done. But know, I was in the same place. I have been shackled under the same bonds. And yet? I stand here free. I stand unchained, my only limits being my mind. I got out. And I offer the same for you."

Their gaze changed. While fear remained, a new hope glittered in their eyes.

"My friend is coming with a train set course for Ueria. If you get on it, you will be nothing more than fugitives. I won't lie, your life will not be easy. Chances are, you'll end up mixed with criminals, each crueler than the last. But criminals have their own mind. They have their limbs with no chains bearing them to the ground. Work hard enough–" Lilith straightened her posture, exhaling. "And you just might live."

The crowd was silent. Their eyes, still scared, glimmered with new hope.

"How do we know you speak truthfully?" a man asked, standing up. Blood crusted around his ankles where shackles were bound far too tight. Scars riddled his limbs, carving white marks in his sunburnt skin. "How do we know you won't just ship us on another train to work as your slaves?"

"You don't." Lilith said. "And you have nothing but my word to convince you otherwise. But tell me, would you rather stay in this hell, or risk a worse one for freedom?"

Silence took control. No one spoke. No one dared utter a word. That was until the same man stood up.

"I'll go." He proclaimed.

A woman to his right stepped forward. "So will I."

And so the chorus started. Yells of compliance and hope echoed around the wooden walls. More and more people stood. The stench of weary fear was replaced by cautious optimism.

Lilith grinned, straightening her posture. "In that case, let's get you out of here."

Chapter Thirteen
Quilla

Quilla grinned as four bronze guards charged at her. She leaped, fired four knives, and landed. Her opponents collapsed in a pile, blood pooling at her feet.

She ran a hand through her hair and continued her sprint through the train. Lilith sent her to hijack the machine, already set on the route to Ueria. Admittedly, the job was the best she could hope for.

Quilla kicked the door open to the next car. Inside was an impressive array of silver soldiers. Without hesitation, they charged at her. Her knives were drawn within a second, fired within two. She danced through the crowd, her blades slashing their flesh like bread.

The silvers fell to the floor. The unfortunate ones that were still alive stared at her with fear. Their hands trembled by their sides as Quilla stepped over their collegue's corpses.

"I don't want to kill you," Quilla proclaimed. "I simply want to get to the..." she trailed off, searching for the right word. "What is it you call the engine? Hm, doesn't matter." The soldiers flinched back as Quilla grinned. "You, however, have a choice to make. Are you going to let me through—" Quilla gazed at the corpses on the floor. "Or are you going to end up like your friends?"

The silvers looked at each other. Then, they moved to the side, letting Quilla stride through.

She kicked open the door to the engine. The conductor flinched back, a sword clasped between his white knuckles.

Quilla rolled her eyes. She pointed to the corpses with her bloodied fingers. "Out."

The man obeyed, scrambling past her.

Quilla gazed at the controls. Now that she looked at them, a shocking revelation came to mind.

She had no idea how to work this thing.

To her, the train was a bunch of buttons and levers.

And unfortunately, this was the one thing she couldn't blow up.

Even worse, the train port was just ahead of her. A group of half naked men and women were waiting at the train tracks. She supposed Lilith had done her job.

Quilla gazed at the control board. There was no way she could make sense of it in time. There were too many buttons that did too many things.

She supposed the most reasonable solution was to press as many of them as she could until the train came to a halt.

Quilla punched the board, causing the train to make a sound resembling a dying chicken. She pulled a switch, which made the machine whistle. Yanked a lever, and recieved the desired screech of the wheels.

With all her strength, she held the brake. The train's wailing escalated to a new high as it screamed into the port.

Quilla thought her arms would fall off by the time the train came to a stop. She dragged herself out the engine and gazed into the sandy, beige landscape of the desert.

Lilith strode to her, crossing her arms. "Little risky on the breaks?"

"A little risk is a little fun." Quilla hopped from the train, landing next to her partner. She turned to the people standing behind Lilith. They were sunburnt, most teary-eyed and weary. "Are these them?"

Lilith nodded. "Yes."

"Woah," Quilla gazed at the captives, sympathy making her eyes water. "There's more than I expected."

"Really?" Lilith asked. "You've witnessed the full extent of the Empire's cruelty. I thought you would have expected as much."

"I've witnessed the full extent of *Ghan's* cruelty. I always had a tinge that the Empire was... well, moral."

Lilith let out a cracked laugh.

"So," Quilla said. "Where are all the guards? I mean, obviously you killed some, but I figured there would still be some alive."

Lilith giggled. "Most of them are alive. They're in there. With Alohi." She pointed to the train port building, a massive structure that was at least three stories tall.

Quilla tilted her head. "Why is Alohi in there?"

Lilith grinned. With the cruelty that glittered in her eyes, there might have been blood between her teeth. "I want it to be painful."

As if on cue, the door to the station flew open. Alohi strode out, kicking it shut. The politician looked lethal. She had her needles between her knuckles and sweat beaded on her forehead. She had a few cuts, but nothing serious.

"All of them?" Lilith asked.

"I ran around the entire building." Alohi proclaimed. "Three times. If they were in there, I found them."

Quilla looked at her, realizing. "You're leaving them alive. Unmoving, but alive. You want them to die in the explosion."

Lilith nodded. "They killed my dad in cruelty. It's an eye for an eye. I'm killing all of them. Not just for dad, not just for me. But for everyone that has ever been in this awful place."

Quilla nodded, a similar smile gleaming on her lips. "Then let's end it. For them."

<center>~~~</center>

After they got the people on the train and found someone who actually knew how to work the thing, Black Cyanide got on their horses.

"Are you sure this will work?" Quilla asked.

"Oh, I'm sure!" Alohi said. "I watched her plant those goddamn bombs. What I'm worried about is the explosion taking our skin with it!"

Lilith didn't answer. Her horse steadily raced into the distance.

"As much as I hate to admit it," Quilla sighed, pulling up to her partner's side. "Alohi does have a point. If you're too close, we'll be blown up with the station. If we're too far, the detonator won't work."

Lilith kept her eyes on the setting sun. "I'm not planning on using a detonator."

"Then how are you–"

"Don't worry," Lilith smiled. "That place is going up in flames. For now, let's make sure Alohi's prophecy doesn't come true."

Quilla nodded, and urged her horse forward. The three galloped through the desert, the hot sun beating on their shoulders. Eventually, they got so far from the station that Quilla could barely see it.

"Lilith," Quilla said, "Whatever you're planning, you should probably do it now."

Lilith grinned, pulling out her bow. "You're right, Quill."

The archer pulled an arrow from her quiver. At first glance, it looked like a regular weapon, but as Quilla looked closer, she saw the tip wasn't sharp, but circular. Even more odd, the stick seemed to have... wings.

Lilith placed the arrow between her drawstring. She pulled her bow back, centering her gaze.

"Brace yourself." Lilith warned, the sun glittering off her grin. She gave a small chuckle, and released the string.

The weapon sailed through the air, out of sight within seconds. For a moment, the desert was silent.

"So," Alohi raised an eyebrow. "Was that–"

She was cut off by an explosion. In place of the barely visible station, was a very visible mushroom of fire. Flames curled around each other, doubling as they catapulted into the air. Smoke rose from the massacre, pouring into the sky.

Before they could say anything, the air shock came rushing towards them. Quilla was thrust off her horse, plummeting into the sand. Alohi and Lilith landed next to her, eyes trained on the massive explosion.

Lilith sat up, grinning at the flaming port. Quilla and Alohi gazed at her, more in awe of her cruelty than the effects of it.

"You just–" Alohi stammered. "You just exploded that thing."

"Holy shit," Quilla cackled. "Holy fucking *shit*."

Lilith didn't say anything. Instead she turned around, gazing at the two with vibrant, green eyes.

Without warning, she flung her arms around them. Quilla hesitantly wrapped her in a hug while Alohi sat stunned.

"Thank you," Lilith said, holding them tighter, "Thank you so, so much."

Quilla smirked. "You did most of the work."

"Yes," Lilith said. "But you didn't give up on me. I couldn't have done any of that without you. Thank you for helping me." She gazed at them, her eyes sparkling with love. "Thank you for being there for me."

Quilla and Alohi smiled. "Of course," Quilla said. "Always."

"We love you, Lilith," Alohi said. "Of course, I'm a bit concerned about where your morals are going, but I still love you."

Quilla raised an eyebrow. "You aren't concerned about my morals?"

"No. That ship has long sailed."

Lilith laughed, squeezing them tighter. "Can we go?" she asked. "I want to go home."

Chapter Fourteen
Alohi

Alohi couldn't sleep.

She threw her sheets, tossing the pillows around her bed. The thoughts inside her head sung loud, howling insults. Her father's deep rasp, calling her *defectum*, her mother's soft plea, begging her to do something about the abuse. And worse?

Nikolai's tone, laughing inside her head. Though he wasn't mean. She wished he was mean. At least if he was cruel, she would have something to grasp. She would have an idea.

But no, he was kind.

He whispered praise, he laughed at inside jokes, he wrapped his warm arms around her. He held her when she cried.

And now he caused the tears.

She didn't want to miss the League. The League was awful. The pressure put on her was something she never wanted to recall. But there were good moments, mostly with Nikolai. Though she didn't want to admit it, she grieved her old home.

Alohi didn't like grief.

She threw her sheets off and slumped out of bed. The boards of the house creaked as she made her way downstairs. She barely heard the noise. She needed a supplement, a narcotic. She needed her head to shut the hell up.

"Dammit Florian," Alohi growled as she rummaged through the cupboards. "I know you have alcohol somewhere."

Her entire body melted as she pulled a bottle from the mess. Inside sloshed an amber liquid. She pulled the cork with her teeth and pressed the bottle to her mouth. She savored the liquid. The taste, though awful, was a reminder of the numbness about to come.

She pushed the liquid back, the hot sensation drifting to her throat. Before she could swallow it, something hit her from behind. The liquid flew from her mouth, coming out her nose.

Alohi leaned on the counter, her nose aflame as remnants of whiskey dripped from her face.

"Absolutely not!" Lilith snapped, leaning on the wood. "You are *not* about to jump into the ocean naked!"

Alohi stood agape. "That's not what I–"

"Cause and effect, Windlem," Quilla grinned, leaning next to Lilith. "As fun as it would be to see you flash Florian, I don't believe they would enjoy it." Lilith shot her a glare. "Oh yes, and we are–" Quilla cleared her throat, as if rehearsing a script. "'Concerned for your wellbeing and safety and believe that you are following an addictive path that will run your life into the gutter.'"

Lilith shot her a glare. Quilla shrugged.

"Anyway," Lilith said. "Look, Alohi, we're worried about you. We want to make sure you're okay,"

"I'm fine," Alohi said, wiping the whiskey off her face. "You don't have to worry."

"We know we don't," Quilla said. "But we are. Alohi, I've been there. We both have. We know what the thoughts are like, and we understand the urge to drown them out. Especially with alcohol."

Alohi's gaze shifted to the ground. "So why do you get to drink it?" she snarled. "And why can't I?"

Quilla sighed. "I– I'm trying not to. It's a bad habit that I unfortunately acquired at a young age. I know it feels good in the moment, and I know it's easier than healing. But it's not worth it. Healing is. You may not see it now, but there is a comedown."

"*Healing*?" Alohi hissed. "What do I have to heal from?"

Quilla and Lilith looked at each other, then back to Alohi.

"Alohi, sit down." Lilith said, gesturing to the couch.

Alohi obliged, though reluctant. The two criminals sat on either side of her, sending nervous glances to each other.

"There is no easy way to start this conversation." Quilla began. "But we're worried you're going down the wrong path. I mean, Alohi, you've had sort of a rough life. Your parents were, for lack of better words– well, let's just say there was room for improvement. You had a *tremendous* amount of pressure on you. The only person you really trusted betrayed you and was killed–"

"What Quilla's trying to say is," Lilith interrupted. "Your mind has a lot of memories that need to be processed. In mine, and especially Quilla's case, we tend to process our memories with narcotics. But all that does is make them swell until they consume your entire being."

Alohi bit her lip. "So," she began, not sure where she was going. "What do you suggest I do instead?"

Quilla and Lilith gave each other a pleading look.

"I would–" Quilla gazed nervously at the ceiling. "Talk about it?"

Alohi sighed. "Fine, I'll talk." She breathed a hard sigh. "My dads motto was be good or be disowned. Ranine was good, I played the line. When I was lucky, my dad would insult me, when I wasn't, he would beat me. I still have the goddamn scars."

She gazed at Lilith and Quilla. She expected a look of boredom, as if her problems didn't matter. But what she found was stable, steady kindness.

Alohi took a breath. "But–" she swallowed. "Sometimes Dad was kind. Sometimes we would work on my craft for hours. He would fantasize about my future, telling me great foretellings of my accomplishments. When I succeeded, it was better than sex! Not that I've ever had it. When I didn't, it felt like my entire being was ripped from me and shattered in front of my eyes. Of course, Dad's beatings didn't help."

Lilith looked at her, sorrow glittering in her gaze. "Oh Alohi," she said, her voice steady. "That's awful."

"Yeah, well, it happened. And now it's over."

"But it left scars." Lilith said. "Scars that have an effect. Scars that still *hurt*. We all have them, Alohi. It's not something to be ashamed of. Not at *all*." Lilith tilted her head. "Did you ever tell someone what was happening?"

"Yeah," Alohi breathed. "Nikolai. He was always kind. He never pushed me, never told me that I was pathetic. Why would he do that? Why would anyone..."

Lilith offered a sympathetic smile. "Maybe because he cares?"

"*Why*?" Alohi broke. Tears pricked her eyes, trickling down her cheeks. "He must have had some motive, some ambition! No one does anything for anyone else! Not from pure *fucking* kindness! He saw value in me! *Somewhere* he saw value!"

"And yet, do you see value in yourself?" Lilith asked.

Alohi opened her mouth to respond, but realized she didn't have the words. Instead, a sob rose from her throat. It wasn't a gentle cry, but a scream. A scream of pain. A scream of her past.

Lilith wrapped in a hug, letting her cry into her shirt. Quilla wrapped her arm around her, resting her head on Alohi's shoulder.

She must have cried for minutes. She hated everything. Her dad, her mom, Ranine, Nikolai, every fucking one of them. There were so many wrongs, so many times she was treated awfully. And yet? Somehow, she still felt a burning sensation of love.

"Alohi?" Quilla asked. "How are you feeling?"

Alohi sat up, wiping her eyes. "Angry." She said, "But free. It's weird."

"The mind rarely makes sense." Lilith said, laying a hand on Alohi's shoulder. "It's like trying to navigate through a hay bale."

Alohi giggled. "Yeah, I suppose you could look at it like that."

"Hey, if you're feeling better Alohi—" Quilla bit her lip. "I have a really burning question. Can I ask?"

Lilith snorted. "Fire away, Quill."

Quilla moved uncomfortably in her seat, like a child who had to piss. "Alohi, you mentioned something earlier. 'Sex?' What's that?"

Alohi's mouth fell. Lilith palmed her face.

"You can't be serious." Lilith groaned.

Alohi slumped onto the backrest. "Ghan never taught you, did he?"

"We were an elite group of assassins. I don't think telling us about 'cake' was high on his to-do list."

"Quilla," Lilith grasped her partner's shoulders. "Sex is *not* cake."

Quilla shrugged. "Everyone talks about it like it's a phenominal cake. What? Is it stacked with drugs?"

"No," Lilith said plainly. "Alohi, you brought it up. Explain."

Alohi shot up. "No! You're her girlfriend!"

"And?"

"Well the chances are you'll be having sex with her."

Quilla raised an eyebrow. "What's so wrong about having cake with me?"

"Quilla, not cake." Lilith snapped, turning back to Alohi. "And absolutely not. There is no way in *hell–*"

"You think I'm going to do any better?" Alohi asked, her voice shrill. "My mom's talk was essentially don't do it or you'll get pregnant!"

Quilla choked.

"I was told by my dad!" Lilith said. "His first time was in a bathroom stall!"

Quilla gazed at Lilith. "I've never been more confused."

"What if we just don't tell her?" Alohi suggested. "I mean, do you at least have some clue? Someone must've mentioned it in Hanslack."

"Oh, yes," Quilla made a face. "All the time. I was just too embarrassed to ask. It seemed like everyone knew what it was. Just common sense."

Lilith leaned back, placing her fingers on her temple. "I cannot *fathom–*"

"What the fuck is happening down here?" Florian called from the stairs. "I am trying to sleep, but you three are yelling–"

"Quilla doesn't know what sex means." Lilith and Alohi said simultaneously.

Florian snorted. "Oh." The pirate strode to the sink, grabbing a small cup. They filled it with water and waved it in Quilla's face. "Okay, so imagine this is Alohi's–" Florian gazed at the politician with a quizzical look. "Hole, and this–" they plucked a pencil from the coffee table. "Is Nikolai's stick."

Lilith sunk into the cushions. "Oh dear lord."

Florian sat on the coffee table. Alohi couldn't have looked more horrified when they stuck the pencil into the cup. Nausea rose to her throat as they jabbed the pencil up and down, splashing liquid on Quilla's leg.

Quilla raised an eyebrow. "Ew," she wrinkled her nose. "How would two women do it?"

Without saying a word, Florian grabbed another cup. They pressed the glasses together and shook, causing the liquid to splash.

Quilla pinched her lips. "And two men?"

This time, Florian didn't need props. "Sword fight."

"Got it."

"Did you have to use me as an example?" Alohi growled.

Florian shrugged. "I thought examples might help. You know, with the visual."

Quilla recoiled. "I didn't need a visual."

"Yes well," Florian grinned. "I enjoyed it."

"Oh," Lilith glared at them. "We all know. So Quilla, does that answer your question?"

Quilla pressed her fingers to her temple. "Why would anyone do that? It just seems so gross–"

"It feels good." Florian said plainly.

"*How*?" Quilla hid her face in her hands. "Actually, nevermind. I don't want to know. I'm going to bed to try and forget this."

"Ditto." Lilith said, following her.

Alohi sunk into the pillows, glaring at Florian. "Do you really think me and Nikolai have a thing?"

The pirate chuckled, taking a sip of water from 'Alohi's hole.' "Oh most definitely."

Chapter Fifteen
Nikolai

Nikolai swung his foot into the bag. As soon as it hit, he withdrew his attack, coming at the thing with quick punches. He drove his knuckles into the center, pretending the fluff was a stomach.

"Faster." Grandez growled from the sidelines. "Harder, Nikolai."

Nikolai's lip curled. His lungs filled with familiar frustration. The anger made his fist stronger, his moves quicker, and his body thrum with distaste for every move he made.

He swung his heel into the bag. Next, he pounded his fists into its top. He twirled around the thing as it swung back to hit him. Once he was on the other side, he swung his foot into the bottom.

Maybe a bit too hard.

The bag collapsed. Rice poured from the hole, making a pool on the floor.

"Fuck this," Grandez stood. "We're sparring."

Nikolai's eyes widened. His father barely ever took interest in his training. He usually hired a trainer to help him. A fact Nikolai was grateful for.

Whenever they did spar, Nikolai was never allowed to hit Grandez. He learned how to take his many punches; to stay light on his feet.

His father, however, had no bounds. He would swing his fist at him, elbow him in the gut, draw blood with his fingernails. Everything that would prepare him. Prepare him for a fight Nikolai didn't want.

Grandez stood, taking off his coat. His father wasn't exactly in shape, but given Nikolai's limited power and Grandez's indefinite will in the match, his poor stamina did little to hinder him.

Nikolai took a breath, wishing he had his swords. Grandez stood on the opposite side of the ring. He rolled up his sleeves, a sick smile spreading across his lips.

Nikolai swallowed.

Grandez lunged at him. Nikolai spun around his father's attack, only to be met with a fist to his face. He held up a hand to block it, but another blow flew at his stomach.

He stumbled back, grasping his chest and heaving for air. Grandez looked malicious. The gleam in his eyes told Nikolai he was about to get kicked.

When his father came at him, Nikolai scrambled backward.

"Oh come on, Nikolai," Grandez smiled. "Get yourself together and defend yourself!"

Nikolai ducked as Grandez's fist came at him. More blows fired at his head, and this time, he wasn't able to stop them.

Nikolai fell back, clutching his cheek. His father took advantage of his weakened state, and kicked his stomach. Nikolai collapsed to the ground, groaning.

"Get the hell up," Grandez said, leaning down. "I can't help but roll my eyes at this, Nikolai. I trained you to be *better*!"

Nikolai gasped for air, covering his face with his hands. He couldn't let his father see the tears rolling down his face.

Unfortunately, Grandez had other plans.

He took his hands, yanking them from his watering eyes. When he saw the tears, he kicked him.

"Get the *fuck* up, Nikolai." He growled. "*Now.*"

"Dad please–" Nikolai sobbed. "Please, I don't want to do this anymore!"

Grandez ignored him, grabbing his wrist and pulling him to his feet. As soon as the hand grasped his skin, the gloves slipped.

"Dad, no please–"

But his cover fell off, coming into Grandez's waiting grip. Nikolai folded his arms into his chest, hoping against hope that his dad would leave him *alone.*

"Hold out your palms, Nikolai." Grandez growled. "*Now,*"

"No," he gasped, the air in his throat tightening. "Please– Dad, don't make me do this!"

But his father had no remorse. He snatched his hand, looking at the scars with a mild curiosity. When he was done gazing, he snorted.

"God, you're sick, Nikolai." He spit on his cheek and turned away. "Fix it or don't, I don't care. As long as you don't bleed out, I have no problem with your mental insanity."

With those words, he left. Nikolai watched him go. He should have done something. He should have felt *something.* But he was so used to this he expected it. It didn't phase him.

Like clockwork, he pulled the blade from his coat. The metal glimmered in the bright light. Nikolai gazed at it, admiring the reflection. There was no rush to pull his glove off. There was no speed in any part of it. Instead, Nikolai relished the urge. He craved the way his body pulled himself towards the blade. There was pain, but there was solace in the promise of relief.

Nikolai pulled his remaining glove from his fingers. There were so many scars. They covered his arms completely, some inching up his bicep. Most had remnants of blood keeping them closed, the others had healed into deep holes.

Nikolai traced the blade down his arms. He ran the metal down his scabs, across the skin that was still rough, and the healed dents. He listened to the voices howl, he observed as the accents chanted. He told them to be patient, which only made them yell louder.

So he dug the knife into his skin.

Right next to the cut he made before the session.

Which was next to the one he dug this morning.

Nikolai smiled as the blood trickled down his arm. He gave a steady exhale as the warm red ran over the scabs.

The words telling him he was worthless had vanished.

The accents screaming disappeared.

The voices were gone.

"Nikolai?" he shot up as he heard the voice. Killen was standing in the doorway, sorrow coating his eyes. "Oh, Nikolai,"

"Killen!" Nikolai got to his feet, tucking his arm behind his back. "What brings you here?"

"Nikolai," Killen breathed, barely above a whisper. "Please, *please* don't pretend you're okay."

Nikolai swallowed. He had seen everything.

"It's okay," Killen said, making his way towards him. "I won't hurt you, okay?"

Nikolai recoiled as Killen touched his shoulder. The grasp made him want to vomit.

"No," Nikolai drawled. "*No*, you don't care. Stop *pretending* like you do!"

"Nikolai," Killen murmured. "Please, I do care, I want you to be okay."

"Stop *lying*!" Nikolai snapped. "You're using me! Just like everyone else in this goddamn place! I'm a paycheck to you, aren't I? Just another *job*? For the council, I'm a tool. For my dad, I'm a reputation. Why is it any different with you–"

"Because I love you, Nikolai!" Killen hollered. "You are like my son. I love you like a *son*, Nikolai. I care about you so, *so* much, and all I want is for you to be *okay*!"

Nikolai stared at him, his face emotionless. It had been so long since someone had loved him like *that*. There was Rex, who *died*. There was his mother, who *died*. And there was his father, who didn't mean it.

"No," Nikolai shook his head, clutching his wound. "You don't. No one has ever meant that. If they did, they died. So don't say that. Loving me will only hurt. So do yourself a favor and use me as a pawn. Judge me, Killen.

Take every misconjecture and savor it. I am a failure until I break the impossible bonds. Hit me, criticize me, and wait for me to crumble." Nikolai held up his wrist, watching the blood trickle down his skin.

"Just like the rest of them do."

Chapter Sixteen
Cercel

Cercel strode along the halls of the Palace. Her robes wavered behind her, brushing against her ankles. Surprisingly, a grin spread across her face. There were no more voices, no whispers of doubt. For once, she had it all. The power, the potential, and best, Father's love.

He was going to guide her. He was going to tell her how to succeed. There was a path for her, a way out. She was going to be a *legendary* Empress.

"Hey Father," Cercel called as she approached his cell. "I brought you some dumplings. I know you like–"

The tray clattered to the ground as she saw what dwelled inside. Or rather, what was missing. Instead of the man that was supposed to guide her, there was a spilled pill bottle. Just beyond the medication was a paperclip. He must have used the metal to pick the lock.

Cercel fell to her knees as her gaze wavered to the wall. Her breath caught, her teeth clattered, and ugly sobs rose to her throat. Her breath came quickly, rattling her chest and shaking her limbs. She couldn't breathe. There wasn't enough air in the world for her. The voices flooded her head like a storm, their insults clattering around her skull like a hurricane.

Pathetic.

Awful.

Failure.

But one word wasn't just in her head. It was simple. Just a few fucking letters. But when Cercel saw it, her entire body collapsed. It was the word she wished she would never see again.

But there, written in a dripping crimson, was the jagged, dreadful spelling.

Defectum.

Cercel's hands slid to her scalp, yanking her hair. A sob ripped from her throat, echoing around the walls. She flung her fist into her head: again, again and again. But the pain didn't suffice. Nothing made it go away. Nothing made it better. Nothing could. Father was gone. He abandoned her. Just like everyone else.

She had nothing. She was *nothing*. Father betrayed her. He earned her trust and shattered it. Left her for some life as a *criminal*. That was what she was worth. She truly had *nothing*.

Nothing except hate.

Nothing except *vengeance*.

"I am going to kill Rosalie Ghan." Cercel chanted. "I am going to kill Rosalie Ghan. I am going to kill Rosalie Ghan. I am going to kill... I am going to kill..."

You are going to kill Rosalie Ghan. Rosalie finished, wrapping her icy hands around her. *Rosalie Ghan will beg. Rosalie Ghan will shatter at your feet. Rosalie Ghan is going to feel the pain you have felt.*

Cercel sat up, welcoming Rosalie's cold embrace. She may have been hateful, she may have no other purpose than vengeance. But when all else was gone, the burning flame of hatred kept her warm. Vengeance held her when no one else would. Pure, unfiltered rage was her shield.

And her sword.

~~~

"What is this, Cercel?" Lamia asked. "Why are we here?"

Cercel gathered the Golden Class in the Emperor's chambers. She took her place on Ghan's throne, legs crossed. She should have felt victorious, she dreamed of this throne for so long. But now, all she felt was rage.
~~~

"I know where Camp Fifty is." Cercel drawled. "I know where Rosalie, Lone, and all the other incompetent fleas are."

"What are you planning?" Casimir asked. "What do you want us to do?"

Cercel grinned. She hopped from her throne, grabbing a map as she strode down the stairs. She rolled it onto the ground, beckoning the Golden Class to kneel with her.

"Camp Fifty is here," she said, pointing a finger at her jagged handwriting. "On an island, just off the coast of Woodran. The only way we can get in is through a giant hole in the ground, but that gives our troops a disadvantage."

"How the fuck do you know where–" Ezekiel snapped. "No. Nevermind. I don't want to know."

"And I don't want to talk about it." Cercel drawled. "You three are going to go in there and plant smoke bombs. I want there to be so much vapor it will kill a fucking elephant. Once the doves have flocked from their nest, we'll be waiting to cage them."

"What about us?" Lamia asked. "Won't we die from the smoke?"

"You'll have masks." Cercel said, "And once the smoke is released, you'll get out as fast as possible."

"Speaking of which," Casimir started. "How are we going to get in?"

Cercel ran her hand along the map. She traced the burrow with a smile, picturing its walls going up in flame.

"There's a ventilation system that comes out here, here, and here." Cercel pointed to each location. "You three will enter through them. Each leads to a separate section of the base. Casimir, you'll take the lower area, Ezekiel, you'll take the middle, Lamia, you'll take the top."

"Oh come on!" Ezekiel grumbled. "Why does Casimir get the fun stuff? The middle is just bedrooms. It'll be easy."

"I know," Cercel stared blankly at him. "Even you can't fuck this up."

Ezekiel groaned. His lips pinched to form the face of a pouty child.

"Cercel," Lamia asked, her voice sheepish. "What will you do when you round everyone up?"

Cercel grinned, her fangs glittering in the candlelight. "I want to give them hope. I want them to believe that everything will be okay. I want them to think I will show *mercy*." Cercel gave a cracked laugh. "Then, I want to make it *very* clear that their situation is very, *very* hopeless."

There was silence, no one dared speak. The Golden Class simply sat there, jaws ajar.

"And–" Casimir stammered. "And Rosalie?"

Cercel cackled, a low bubble rising from her throat. "I am going to make her watch all of it. All the deaths, all the *screams*. And when it's over, I'm going to make sure she knows it's *her fault* before I torture her and leave her to bleed out with her dead friends."

Chapter Seventeen
Alohi

Alohi had never been so scared of Lilith than when she was assigning household chores.

The woman was like a military commander, ordering them around like sheep. Alohi was sweeping so vigorously she thought the broom might snap. Then again, she didn't want to drop and give Lilith ten.

She was on dusting and sweeping duty, Florian had the fun task of tidying and organization, Lilith had given herself the duty of cook, and Quilla was out stealing groceries.

That would have been fun, if it wasn't pouring rain. Lilith practically had to drag her girlfriend out the door kicking and screaming. The more Alohi hung around Quilla, the more she compared her to a child. A very murderous, bloodthirsty child.

"Alohi!" Lilith sang, glaring at her from behind the counter. "Your broom has stopped moving!"

Alohi swallowed and continued her work. Despite her harsh words, the archer seemed to have a knack and an appreciation for spring cleaning. Though Quilla always seemed to be the neat one.

"Since when are you a clean freak?" Alohi asked, careful to continue cleaning. "I always thought Quilla was the tidy one."

Lilith shrugged, continuing to scrub the decaying kitchen counters. "Quilla knows how to organize. I know how to make people work together. If this space gets messy, we're all going to get grumpy."

"Quilla's always grumpy," Florian commented.

"No, actually," Lilith grinned, "You've been witnessing her calm side."

Alohi gulped. "I hope it stays like that."

"I do too," Lilith said, "And to make sure you three don't come at each other with pitchforks and pig heads, we have to keep this place manageable. That means some cleaning once and a while."

"Why you three?" Florian frowned. "Why wouldn't you fight? You're just as bloodthirsty."

"Yes, but I'm twice as bored and would love to watch that dispute unfurl." Lilith shrugged. "Besides, I love seeing Quilla fight."

Alohi smirked. "Don't you?"

She could tell by Lilith's face she had a string of curses on her tongue. Before she could use them, a knock tattered the door.

No, not a knock.

A disfigured clunk.

The three looked at each other, unsure of what to do. Alohi, who was closest to the door, padded to the handle. With a cautious hand, she nudged it open.

But no amount of weary fear could prepare her for what waited on the other side.

Alohi screamed.

Lilith and Florian rushed to her side, saw the crumpled mess of human flesh and let out their own terrified screech.

It was Emperor Ghan.

Emperor *fucking* Ghan.

"What the fuck?" Lilith grabbed her bow and arrows, shooting the Emperor's tattered clothes to the ground. "What the fuck? What the fuck? What the *fuck*?"

"Um," Florian touched Ghan with their foot, as if they were touching a rotting deer. "What do we do with it?"

Lilith placed her hands on her head. "I don't know. Is it conscious?"

"Yes," Ghan drawled. He looked awful. He was covered in bruises. Bags loomed under his eyes. He was soaked head to toe in mud, which added to his tired persona. "I want to see Rosalie."

"It's conscious." Florian said.

"Well fix that!"

Florian grinned like a child who was just given candy. They plucked a knife from their coat and held it above Ghan's head.

"Don't kill it!" Lilith screeched. "Quilla will know what to do. Just- knock it out."

Florian pouted and rammed their boot heel into Ghan's skull. The Emperor collapsed on the ground.

"Now what?" Alohi asked.

Lilith pressed her fingers to her temple. "I don't know! Tie him to a chair or something!"

Florian grabbed Ghan by the armpits and hauled him to his feet. Alohi swiftly grabbed a chair and placed it in front of Florian. Once they had his limp body in the thing, Lilith tied his hands behind the back rest.

The three stared at him, unsure of what to do.

"Well?" Alohi began, heaving a worried breath. "What now?"

Lilith breathed a sigh. "I suppose we wait."

<div align="center">~~~</div>

As soon as Ghan's eyes fluttered open, Lilith had an arrow held to his throat.

"Why are you here?" she asked, eyes slits of rage.

"Oh look," Ghan smirked. "You've finally done away with the 'it' pronouns. Maybe the pirate would like to add them to his collection."

Lilith punched him.

"I was trained by your apprentice, and Quilla is not afraid to torture," she picked him up by the collar, her face close enough to bite his nose. "So I'm not either."

Ghan simply shrugged. "Go ahead. I'm not going to talk to anyone but Rosalie."

"You've put that girl through enough."

Ghan cackled. "I made her a weapon any military could only dream of. She should be grateful."

Lilith's eyes ignited with rage. "She should kill you slowly, letting you bleed out alone in the rain."

"She would have, if she wasn't so *weak*."

Lilith swung her foot into Ghan's face. There was a sickening *crack*, and blood flooded from his nose. Lilith kicked him in the chest, causing the chair to topple over. As soon as the Emperor hit the ground, Lilith pressed an arrow to his throat.

"The next words that come out of your mouth better be my *goddamn* answer." Lilith drawled, tracing the weapon along Ghan's features. "Or I will cut you so many times it will be written in your *blood*."

Ghan snorted.

Lilith pulled his chair up. Still holding the back, she swung her fist into Ghan. Blood dripped from his lip, curling down his chin. More came with each swing, along with bruises and cracks that definitely weren't normal.

"I told you," Ghan grinned, blood seeping between his teeth. "I will only talk to Rosalie."

"That was not my fucking answer!" Lilith snapped.

Just as she was about to pound Ghan's face in, Alohi grabbed her fist.

"Lilith?" she began sheepishly. "May I have a word?"

Lilith sneered and followed Alohi to the door.

"You're leaving me alone with him?" Florian hollered. "*Why?*"

"You're grown, Florian," Lilith retorted. "You can handle a pathetic man bleeding out in a chair."

Florian whimpered, still looking horrified. "He's committed multiple massacres!"

"And is currently tied to a chair bleeding out!" Lilith shot back, "Suck it up!"

Lilith followed Alohi outside. They huddled under the roof, sheltered from the pouring rain.

"Don't you think you should go easy on Ghan?" Alohi asked. "You know, until Quilla comes back."

Lilith sighed, pressing her fingers to her temples. "Look, it might look cruel, but–" she stammered, hugging her shoulders. "I guess– I just want him to hurt like how he hurt me. How he hurt Quilla–"

"Who hurt me?" Alohi jumped to find Quilla standing behind her. The crime prodigy had two bags filled to the brim with groceries. A giant smile spread across her lips, just as it always did when she stole something.

"Quilla," Lilith clutched her partner's shoulders. "I don't quite know how to explain this. But– well..." she trailed off, unsure of how to continue. "We have a bit of a *predicament*."

Quilla raised an eyebrow. "What kind of predicament?"

Lilith and Alohi stumbled over their sentences, barely getting anything that mildly resembled a phrase out.

Quilla scoffed, her quizzical expression mixing with laughter. "Can it be any worse than what we've already dealt with?"

Lilith bit her lip. "A bit, yeah."

Quilla hummed a chuckle. She strode past Lilith, groceries in hand.

"Quilla wait–" Lilith pleaded. "I just want you to be prepared, it's–"

But it was too late. Quilla turned the handle and immediately dropped her bags. Florian stood in front of a very beat up Ghan, cutlass to his throat.

"What the *fuck*?" Quilla exclaimed, throwing up her hands. "I mean– I don't–" she turned to Lilith, "*How*?"

Lilith had bitten so much of her lip Alohi thought she might swallow it. "He sorta showed up at our door."

"And your immediate response was to tie him to a *chair*?"

Lilith shrugged. "Well, yes."

"Lili, look." Quilla placed her hands on Lilith's shoulders. "That is the most dangerous man in Thine. If you think your amateur knot tying skills will hold him, you are sorely mistaken."

"It's worked so far..." Lilith trailed off as she saw Ghan holding up too free hands.

"Has it?" the Emperor smirked. "Honestly, Rosalie. Given your immense skill, I thought your apprentice would be better."

Lilith already had an arrow at Ghan's face. The Emperor's grin widened. "There's no need to shoot me, little archer. I have nowhere else to go."

"Alohi." Quilla ordered. Alohi perked. "Paralyze him."

Alohi drew her needles, a spark of joy fluttering in her chest. "Permanently?"

"No," Quilla said. Alohi sank. "Just so we can move him."

"Move him where?" Florian asked, cowering as far away from Ghan as possible.

"The basement." Quilla said plainly.

"We have a *basement*?"

Quilla rolled her eyes. "Are you blind? It is behind the stairs. Or did you not know where that was?"

Alohi snorted. She tightened her grip on her needles and swung them at Ghan's pressure points. The Emperor collapsed limply in the chair, his lips still spread in an evil smirk.

Quilla yanked his collar. She dragged him down the stairs and to the basement, Lilith and Alohi at her heel. Florian stayed behind, his grip on his cutlass turning his knuckles white. Quilla swung open the door and threw Ghan inside.

"Are you going to tie him up?" Alohi asked sheepishly.

Quilla rolled her eyes. "Obviously," she held out her hand to Lilith. "Rope."

Lilith planted a snake of string in her hand.

Quilla strode forward, binding Ghan's hands and wrists. After she was done, she kicked him in the jaw.

"Rosalie, wait–" Ghan started. "I have information for you–"

"That I have no need for," Quilla finished. "Be good and I might feed you."

"Really?" Ghan asked, smiling with bloody teeth. "You don't want to know about Cercel?"

Quilla stopped. Her hands crumpled into fists as she clenched her jaw.

"Take that name–" she drawled. "Out of your *fucking* mouth."

With those words, she strode up the stairs, gesturing for Alohi and Lilith to follow.

Chapter Eighteen
Lilith

"Quill?" Lilith called as the door crept open. "Are you okay?"

Quilla was leaning over her desk, head towards the floor. Her white blouse was wrinkled and wet, given the rain. Her messy curls hung over her shoulder in a curtain. She looked torn– broken. Like her past had reclaimed her life.

"How?" Quilla drawled, "*How* did he find me?"

"Quilla–" Lilith started.

"No!" Quilla whirled around. Her eyes were tired, stress lines sinking beneath them. She looked old, tired, *hurt*. "He could have gone anywhere. *Anywhere*! But he chose to go to me. To torment *me*! Why won't he leave me the fuck *alone*!"

"Quilla, please," Lilith said, "Sit down."

Though she looked angry, she obliged.

Lilith sat on the bed beside her. Quilla kept her gaze on the wall.

"Look," Lilith began. "There's nothing I can say that will make this better. There are no words that will fix this. All I can say is that I will stand by you whatever decision you make."

Quilla sighed, placing her head in her hands. "I don't know what to do."

Lilith touched her shoulder. "Okay, then let's figure this out. You can ignore Ghan, you can see what he has to say, or we can cast him out in the rain."

"We can't cast him out." Quilla said. "As pathetic as the bastard looks, he could still cause quite a bit of damage."

"Okay," Lilith offered a small smile. "That gives us two options. Ignore him, or see what he has to say."

"He mentioned Cercel," Quilla said. "If she's planning something, I want to know what it is. We could try to talk to her again, or if worse comes to worse, overthrow her."

"Are you sure it's a good idea to talk to him?" Lilith asked. "I mean, I'm not saying you're subject to this, but he is pretty manipulative."

Quilla smirked, a true smile. "Oh trust me, I have methods for avoiding that."

~~~

Quilla body slammed Ghan against the wall, holding him by his tattered cloak. Lilith expected some sort of violent tactic, sure. But the pure force Quilla used felt a bit extreme.

"Listen here you little shit," she hissed, holding Ghan by his collar. "You mentioned Cercel, so spit it out. What is she planning?"

Ghan smirked, tilting his head. It was as if he was examining Quilla like a product for sale. "Rosalie, you've grown."

"Yeah, no shit." Quilla swung her knee into his balls. "That's how time works. What is Cercel planning?"

Ghan pinched his lips, unhurt by the sudden blow to his penis. "Now, Rosalie, did I teach you no manners? Put me down, then I'll talk."

Quilla threw him on the floor.

"It's Quilla," she snarled. "And I put you down, now talk."

Ghan's lips quirked into an evil smile. "A conversation like this wouldn't be very civil."

"I've tried civil, didn't like it. I prefer hostile."

"Oh Rosalie," Ghan's grin softened, showing a gleam of grief in his eyes. "You've changed so much."
~~~

Quilla kicked him. "Yes, if I could slaughter the bitch that used to be your daughter, I would. Her naivety got me into this mess."

"You were the one who decided to leave," Ghan said. "Not Rosalie."

"Yes and thank god for that one sane moment." Quilla retorted, "I'm only going to ask one more time. Spit whatever you have to say *out*."

"And if I don't?" Ghan growled.

"I'm not above using blades on family."

"Fine," Ghan relented, sitting up. "Cercel's angry. And with the state I left her in, I bet her fury has nearly consumed her. She knows where Camp Fifty is–"

"Wait–" Quilla interrupted. "How does she know that?"

Ghan scoffed. "Because I told her."

"And how did you find out?"

"It was pretty obvious," Ghan shrugged. "I mean, unregistered ships come out of a small island off Woodran pretty much weekly. All it took was a small squadron to tell me all the little details about your base."

Quilla clutched the bridge of her nose. "Of course. Grandez Lone is such a *goddamn* idiot!"

"Anyway," Ghan continued. "Cercel, the imbecile, says that she's going there to 'become legendary' or something like that. I wasn't really paying attention. However, I was able to see through her haze of deceit. She's not there to achieve power, she's not there to extinguish the rebellion." Ghan smiled, taking a breath. "No, she's there to accomplish a goal she's had since she was twelve. She's going to burn a fire that's been ready to rage for years. All her hatred, all her pain; she wants it gone; *out*." Ghan licked his bloodied teeth. "Into your chest, Rosalie."

Quilla's breath caught. "What do you mean? What is she planning?"

Ghan hummed a cackle. "Oh Rosalie. How naive can you be? Isn't it obvious?"

Quilla grabbed his collar. "*Dammit!*" she screeched, pinning Ghan to the wall. "Tell *me!*"

Tears pricked Quilla's eyes, threatening to slide down her cheek. Under Ghan's tattered cloak, there was the slightest tremble of her hands. Quilla was breaking: *snapping* under the weight of Ghan's presence.

"Quilla—" Lilith warned.

"No, stop." Quilla drawled. She turned back to Ghan, the smoke of extinguished rage floating her gaze. "*Fuck*! Why are you silent? *Talk* to me!"

"Rosalie," Ghan gleamed. "Compose yourself."

To her great credit, Quilla was able to regain her posture. She ran her fingers through her hair, let Ghan fall to the ground, and placed her hand on her hips.

"I'm only going to ask once." Quilla drawled. "What is Cercel planning?"

Ghan shrugged. "To go to Camp Fifty, of course. She thinks you're there." He got to his feet, leaning on the wall for support. "And if you believe nothing I say every again, Rosalie, believe this. Cercel is going to slaughter everyone there in search of you. And when she doesn't find you?" Ghan stepped closer, barely an inch away from Quilla's face. "She'll murder the entire dynasty until *you* step forward."

Chapter Nineteen
Quilla

"Quilla no–" Lilith begged. "Please, Quill, don't do it."

"I have too," Quilla said, stuffing her knives into a bag. "People are going to *die*. The rebellion is going to *die* if I don't meet Cercel. She wants me, only *me*. If I'm there, I can minimize the damage done to Camp Fifty."

"Quilla she'll kill you!" Lilith pleaded. "That's all she wants. We've tried to change her mind before, it doesn't work. It won't work this time. When she sees you, she won't hesitate."

"No," Quilla drawled. "She won't kill me, I know it. She's still my sister–"

"Quilla *please*!" Lilith was crying now. "She's tried! You can't say she hasn't! You saw her at the palace–"

"She was under Ghan's influence–"

"*No!*" Lilith hollered, pounding her fist on the desk. "Ghan's influence is the only reason you're not *dead*. Ghan wanted you alive. He wanted you back. Cercel wants to *kill* you."

Quilla lowered her head, a deep grief overcoming her. She gazed at Lilith, her eyes glossed with tears. "Please, Lili, she's still my sister."

"Quilla," Lilith put a hand on her shoulder. "I know, but she's too deep into the hole of vengeance. Your sister has been covered in a world of pain and anger."

Tears trickled down her face. Quilla raised a hand, wiping them from her cheek. "Lilith, they're the only family I have left."

Lilith's eyes welled with sorrow. "Oh, Quill," she wrapped her in a hug. "I'm so, so sorry."

Quilla clung tight, afraid to let go. She pressed her tearstained face into Lilith's blouse, sobbing into her chest.

"I'm so sorry, Quill," Lilith said, her voice soft. "This is all fucked up."

"It's my fault." Quilla cried. "She hates me because I left. Everything would've been fine if I sucked it up and *stayed*!"

"No," Lilith pulled away, cupping Quilla's cheek. "It wouldn't be. I would still be in that desert, Cercel would still be neglected by Ghan and you would still be in that *awful* place. You made the right choice when you left."

Quilla shook her head. "There was no right choice. Just two wrong ones."

"And you chose the one with the least fall." Lilith took a breath, stroking her partner's cheek. "Quill, look, you didn't cause any of this. If this war is anyone's fault, it's Ghan's. You're a casualty, you have no obligation to fix this."

Quilla drew a shaky breath. "Lilith, I may not have asked to be in this war, but I'm in it. The simple fact that Ghan dragged me into this doesn't change the fact that people are going to die. The flicker of rebellion will be stomped out, Camp Fifty will be demolished and so will any resistance. After that Cercel will find me and *slaughter* you, Alohi and Florian in front of me. She'll make me watch *everything*, before slitting my throat and leaving my body to be eaten by the seagulls!"

"Quilla no–" Lilith began.

"Lilith," Quilla grasped her shoulders. "I can stop it. If I can just convince my sister there is a better way of life, that she doesn't have to fill the gap that Father left in her, then it'll all be okay. The war will be over. No more blood spilled because of *my* actions."

Lilith bit her lip. "And what if you can't convince her? What if Cercel kills you?"

Quilla turned to her, tears glittering in her black eyes. "Then you'll live."

Quilla lifted her bag from the bed. Just as she was about to stride out the door, something grabbed her wrist.

"Quilla, I am *begging* you," Lilith pleaded. "Please, who cares if Grandez Lone dies? Who cares if the League is extinguished? We can go, we can run! Cercel won't find us! We'll hide in the woods!" tears poured down Lilith's cheeks. She was gripping Quilla's wrist so hard she thought it might lose circulation. "I am *begging* you, Quilla. Please, *stay!*"

Quilla's gaze rested on her. Tears trickled down Lilith's face, looping around her chin. Sobs shook her shoulders and a predetermined grief sunk her posture. Quilla bit the inside of her mouth. How could she leave her like this?

"Okay," Quilla dropped the bag. "I'll stay."

Lilith threw herself into Quilla's arms, pressing her face into her blouse. "Oh thank you," she breathed. "Thank you, Quill."

Quilla sunk into the embrace. "Of course," she drew a shaky sigh. "I love you, Lili."

~~~

The cold sunk into Quilla's toes as she stepped out of bed. Her bag was ready; she never bothered to unpack it. All she needed to do was get dressed and say goodbye.

She pulled on her clothes, careful not to make a sound. The cold air of the house stung her nose; a gentle reminder of the terror she was about to face.

Her gaze wandered to Lilith. Her partner was sleeping peacefully, her hand outstretched to where Quilla once lay. She was so calm, so beautiful.

"Goodbye," Quilla brushed a strand of hair from Lilith's face. The archer squirmed, she reached to grasp Quilla's hand, giving it a gentle squeeze.

"Quilla..." Lilith called, her eyes remaining closed. "Where are you going?"
~~~

Quilla swallowed. She knew she had to lie, but this was the one person she didn't want to lie to.

"I'm getting water," she croaked, the words hurting as they came out. "I'll be back in a second, go back to sleep."

Lilith turned, taking most of the covers with her. Quilla watched her drift back to unconsciousness, tears welling in her eyes. This might have been the last time she saw her. She let herself watch Lilith sleep a final time.

When the archer's breathing became rhythmic and her chest rose and fell in a stable rhythm, Quilla kissed her cheek. This time, Lilith didn't rustle.

"Bye, Lilith," she whispered, tears choking her voice. "Don't get yourself killed."

<center>~~~</center>

Quilla gripped the mast of the ship, rain blowing in her face as the vessel raced across the ocean. The boat was small, barely fitting a small bed below its deck. As tiny as it was, the thing raced across the waves faster than any of Nikolai's large vessels. She would be in Woodran by morning.

Tears streamed from Quilla's cheeks, blowing in the gust. Her heart weighed heavy, a feeling of longing overtaking her. She wanted someone hugging her, she wanted support, she wanted *love*.

Yet she couldn't have it. Because she was doing this for love. She needed to save her sister. To try one last time. Because she loved Cercel.

And if that love wasn't returned, if her sister drove a blade deep into her heart, at least Lilith would be safe. She would cry, most likely hate her for leaving. But she would no longer be on the same path as Quilla.

The path of inevitable tragedy.

Chapter Twenty
Nikolai

When Nikolai stepped into Quilla and Lilith's room, he half expected someone to be there. He would've grinned as he saw them. He braced himself for the overly critical remark about his dress by Quilla, and the playful nudge from Lilith. His arms moved to embrace Alohi, who would've flung herself into his arms.

But there was none of that. No smiles, no laughs, just the sound of his feet padding into the empty room.

The silence was sickening.

He walked around, running his gloved finger over the dusty sheets. He was supposed to clear the room out a while ago, but every time he tried, nostalgia overcame him. He could barely stand the quiet.

He slumped onto the floor, resting his head on the base of the bed. He exhaled, the breath turning white in the frigid air.

Quilla always liked the cold.

"This is funny," he mumbled. "All of this."

Silence was his only audience.

"I'm supposed to be happy now," Nikolai said, "I'm supposed to be glad for the quiet. My father is supposed to be the only family I ever need." He let out a harsh laugh. "And yet, I feel more alone than ever. I feel more pressure to perform, and I feel the heavy eyes judging my every movement."

Nikolai exhaled, a low cackle dripping from his mouth.

"The only good part about my life is my addiction." Nikolai paused, rolling the phrase on his tongue. "No, scratch that. It's not good, it's bad. Not just because others think so, but because I do. I hate the nausea, I hate the panic, I *hate* everything about this stupid drug!"

Nikolai withdrew his glove from his hand. Wounds scattered his wrist, trailing down his arm to his elbow.

"I hate you," he whispered. "God, I hate you."

He paused, taking a breath. "The worst part is, there's no way I can be rid of you. I'm stuck. If I quit, I'll become like Unighast and have smoke leaking from my mouth. I've felt the urge; just to ask him for a hit. Not like he would give it to me." Nikolai scoffed. "But the hard truth is, simply stopping won't fix anything. I need to get away from this hell. I need to get *away* from the League."

He let out a rough snort. "Like that's ever going to happen.

"But the weird part is, I thought it would all be better now," Nikolai sighed. "I thought my dad would love me, I thought I would finally have all that I wanted. But now–" he put his face in his hands, rubbing his temples. "Now I feel more alone than ever."

He looked at the ceiling, tears leaking from his eyes. He was trapped. Not just in his addiction, but in this role. A role he never fucking sighed up for.

"God what the fuck am I doing?" Nikolai growled, getting off the floor. "I'm talking to dusty sheets about problems that will never go away, I–"

He stopped as a metal trinket fell from the vent. The object clattered to the ground, clanging on the concrete before settling.

Nikolai cautiously strode towards it. He lifted the metal, rolling it between his fingers. He pressed the point into his palm, and was met by a sharp prick.

A golden needle.

Nikolai's head flung upwards as a rustling came from the vent. A lock of curly hair flew by, along with a flash of gold.

Then, smoke poured from the opening.

The revelation hit like a brick.

The Golden Class.

~~~

Nikolai raced along the halls, his shoes squeaking on the concrete. As he rounded the corner, he saw the Lone quarters. He flung the doors open and scrambled in.

"Dad–" he panted, out of breath. "We need to evacuate!"

Grandez Lone strode down the stairs. He was still in his robe, coffee in hand. "Why?" he yawned. "Nikolai, it's too early for your–"

"Listen to me for once in your life, Dad!" Nikolai hollered. "They're smoking us out, through the vents! I saw Lamia. Her needle dropped on the ground." He tossed the golden trinket to his father. "If we don't evacuate, everyone in here will die of smoke poisoning!"

Grandez nearly leapt down the stairs, alert sparking in his gaze. "There's a bunker at the bottom of the base. We need to get into that!"

"No!" Nikolai screeched. "That bunker's small! We need to get everyone out."

"Nikolai," Grandez growled, grasping his shoulders. "Why do you think they're smoking us out? Empress Ghan is waiting on the outside with enough troops to extinguish us. We need to get the executives into the bunker–"

"But the rest will die!" Nikolai screamed. "Either by smoke or blade! They will die–"

"And the rebellion will live on!" Grandez hollered. "Look, Nikolai, if the people running this place live, so will the spark of hope. We are surviving. This is *surviving*."

Nikolai bit his lip, anger rising in his throat. "Fine," he drawled. "Then let someone else take my place."

Grandez's jaw fell. "What, Nikolai no–"

"If our troops are meeting their end, I'm meeting it with them." Nikolai said.
~~~

Grandez rolled his eyes. "Nikolai, don't be ridiculous. You are the future of the League. You can't just give it up for some filthy peasant–"

"Yes I can," Nikolai retorted. "And I will. I'm giving it to a child. That child gets to survive–"

Before he could finish, Grandez grasped Nikolai by the collar. He threw him to the floor, his head slamming against the concrete. His vision blurred, his focus blackened. The only sense still prominent was the ringing in his ears.

His vision cleared to reveal a blade to his throat. The knife rested on his skin, its cold touch sending waves of terror through his body.

"Listen very closely, Nikolai." Grandez drew. "You are going to go down to that bunker, you are going to stay there, and you aren't going to say a word of this to *anybody*."

Nikolai snarled, his hateful eyes resting on his father. "What? Are you going to hold a blade to my back while we walk through the League?"

Grandez simply chuckled. "No, you will walk freely. Because you know that if you step one toe out of line, if there is one slip up, one thing for me to displease, the punishment will be much worse than any work I could do with a dagger." He got to his feet, tucking the blade in his robe. "Remember, there is one influence more lethal than a weapon," A sick smile spread across his face, the bright light gleaming off his teeth. "A parent's love."

Chapter Twenty One
Cercel

Dawn just broke when the flood of League citizens poured from their base.

Cercel stood at the exit, royal robes flowing behind her. The Golden Class lingered at her side, grins plastered on their faces. There was no one else. No army, no witnesses. No one other than her siblings could witness the full extent of Cercel's cruelty.

It took a long while for the first person to come out of that little hatch. So long that Cercel started to wonder whether her siblings had actually released the smoke. Despite Ezekiel's constant, desperate chattering, Cercel still had her doubts. *No one* was above lying to her.

Then, the hatch flew open. A child scrambled out, clutching his heaving chest. After him, came a mother, father, and brother. They didn't seem to notice Cercel. They were too busy heaving for air, their stomach's widening for the substance.

And suddenly, the boy looked up.

His hair covered his eyes, dark residue staining his frightened face. When the kid saw the Golden Class, he scrambled back in fear, recognition molding his features.

"Mommy!" he cried. "Daddy–" the family looked up, horror painting their faces. "It's the Empress."

Cercel raised her hands, her lips curling into a grin. "In the fucking flesh."

Cercel snapped and the Golden Class rushed to detain them. They bound the family's limbs and threw them to the soggy ground. The children screamed, of course. The parents hollered for their kids. A few sorry looks were passed around her siblings. When she saw this, Cercel rolled her eyes. Remorse was nothing more than a hindrance.

"Cercel–" Lamia stammered. "What are we going to do with them?"

Cercel snorted. "You'll see."

As the hatch flew open, more League citizens came pouring out. With an order, Cercel had them detained. Screams rattled the morning air, accompanied by begging and pleading. Once, she saw Lamia gazing at the prisoners with a sympathetic look. Cercel met this behavior with an elbow to her stomach.

No more remorse after that.

More hands were bound, more screeches rang and more pleas were forced. Each one became more aggravating, more *boring*.

Because one key part was missing.

Where the *fuck* was Rosalie?

The bastard had to come out by now. Nearly all the League was restrained on the field. Cercel recognized Tnil and Killen, who were flinging curses in her direction. And yet? Rosalie and her main three were nowhere to be seen.

"Where is she?" Cercel growled. She hadn't realized she voiced her displeasure until someone responded.

"Who?" Ezekiel blinked.

"The litter of kittens I want for breakfast." Given the look Ezekiel gave her, he might have taken the phrase seriously. "No, imbecile, *Rosalie*."

"Why do you care about her?" Casimir asked. "I know you have a sick vengeance for her, but in the grand scheme of things, her presence shouldn't matter."

"It doesn't." Cercel lied. "But having her on the loose would be catastrophic. I want her in custody."

"How do you know she's even here?" Lamia asked. "She could be somewhere else."

Cercel rolled her eyes. "Well, she obviously hates the Empire. This is where people who hate the Empire go."

"Actually," a crisp accent called. "It is possible to hate the League just as much as you despise the Empire."

Cercel's breath caught. Her heart pounded into a to race and her hands crumpled into fists. She knew that voice. She memorized the way its syllables danced along each other. That was the voice who matched her stride, the voice who criticized her to no end. The voice who took *everything* from her.

Rosalie.

The air tensed, its breeze coming to an icy halt.

Cercel simply held up a hand, stopping the Golden Class from advancing further. A smile curled on her lips as she ran her tongue along her teeth.

"No," Cercel drawled. "This is my fight."

Cercel strode to her sister, her robes flying behind her. Rosalie wore her usual attire, a black trench coat with white blouse. Her hair was unbrushed and wet. Light drops of rain pattered on her face, sliding down her cheek. Spreading across her face was a confident grin.

"Cercel," Rosalie chimed. "Don't you look extravagant?"

Cercel met her grin, letting her robes drop from her shoulders. "As do you, sister. A shame that wonderful white blouse will be stained with your blood."

"Actually," Rosalie tilted her head. "I was hoping we could skip that step. I'll drop my blades if you drop the League's ropes. After that, you can do whatever you like with me."

Cercel's smile widened. This was too easy.

"Fine," Cercel chuckled. "Drop your weapons."

Rosalie started by taking off her coat. Next, she pulled knives out of her shoes, then her belt, and surprisingly, her hair. When Cercel got the chance, she would figure out how she managed to do that.

"Wonderful," Cercel said. "If you would be so kind as to come here."

Rosalie stayed where she was. "Not until you release your captives."

Cercel gave a small cackle. She strode to Rosalie and hammered her fist into her face.

Rosalie collapsed to the ground, hands flying to her bloodied nose. Just as she sat up, Cercel swung her boot into her neck. Rosalie fell, clutching her throat.

But Cercel wasn't done. She pressed her knee to Rosalie's chest. Her sister gasped under her, muffled pleas escaping her mouth. Cercel swung her fist into her face, sending blood down Rosalie's lip.

Her sister's red dripped down Cercel's fingers, curling around her palm. She didn't want to stop. There was so much hate, so much *resentment* built inside her. It needed to come out.

"Cercel!" she barely heard the cry. She was too busy relishing the blood staining her hand. Too busy memorizing the tears springing to Rosalie's eyes as she *begged*. Begged for mercy, pleaded for forgiveness. Pleaded for her life.

And Cercel was having too much fun ignoring her.

"*Cercel*!" this time, someone pulled her back. "You are the motherfucking Empress! Can you please try to act less insane?"

Cercel turned to see Casimir holding her by the collar. She snarled, glaring at him, then Rosalie.

"You remember when we were kids in Renel and they told us to 'just be ourselves?'" Cercel smiled innocently. She was betrayed by the blood between her teeth. "I'm just being myself!"

"Unfortunately," Casimir said, rolling his eyes. "Most things they tell children are simply to protect their fragile sanity. Hence, most are lies. In this situation, it is a very bad idea to 'be yourself.' So please, Cercel, save the crazy for the safety of your own room."

Cercel groaned, brushing Casimir from her collar. She leaned down, grasping Rosalie by her collar. Once she dragged her to the group of League citizens, she threw her to the ground.

"Rope," Cercel commanded. "Now."

Lamia obliged, handing her the twine. She bound Rosalie's ankles, then her trembling wrists.

"Wait!" Rosalie hollered, blood seeping from her mouth. "You said you would release them."

Cercel gazed at her, pinching her lips. "'*You said you would release them.*'" She cackled, the sound ripping through the night air. "Oh come now, sister. Did you really expect me to be *honest*?" Cercel leaned down, grasping Rosalie's chin. "I know why you're here, sister. I know you think you can 'save' me. But listen here and listen now, I don't need saving. There is no aspect of me that is not cruel. This is me, through and through, no amount of pleading is going to change that."

"Cercel!" Lamia called. "Don't hurt her, she's our sister."

Cercel whipped around, her black eyes tightening into a sharp glare. "And? Why does that matter?"

"You– you said you cared for her," Lamia stumbled. "When Ghan locked you up."

For a moment, Cercel simply gazed at her. Her eyes softened with confusion– then malicious revelation. She laughed. Hard, rough cackles coming straight from her stomach.

"Oh, Lamia," she snorted. "You really thought that was true? You really thought I had your best interest at heart?" another string of cackles erupted from her throat. "I was *manipulating* you! Ghan never banished Rosalie, he fucking *loved* her! She was treated like a fucking princess while the rest of us had to work for every ration of validation! This is a game of survival, Lamia. How many times do I have to tell you, we are *not* family. We are *not* sisters. I *don't* love you!"

Lamia took a step back, tears glittering in her eyes.

"Lamia–" Rosalie tried, sorrow glittering in her black gaze. Before she could say anything, Cercel kicked her.

"Well," Cercel smiled. "Now that's done, I suppose we can get on with the real show." she held up her bloodied hands, her tongue running along her reddened teeth. "Let the festivities begin!"

Chapter Twenty Two
Nikolai

Nikolai clenched his jaw. His breath came short, rage catching his exhales.

He was in the bunker, a room large enough for around a hundred people. And yet? The only humans that dwelled inside were the four council members, a few military generals, Nikolai, and his father.

This was fucked up. All of it.

These people were supposed to be the best of the rebellion. Instead, Nikolai saw a couple lazy, fat, selfish bastards who didn't care for anyone but themselves. The League wasn't a resistance, it was a group of cowards who would sacrifice *anything* for their own needs.

And Nikolai was done enabling them.

His gaze shifted to his father. The man was sitting upon a throne, grinning. He was fucking *grinning*. It was as if this was what he wanted, as if this fate was *desired*.

Nikolai made a decision then. An opinion that had been submerged for years. He clenched his fists, grit his teeth, and centered his hate squarely on his father.

And at that second, he stepped from his place in line.

"Father," Nikolai growled, stepping in front of the councilmember's thrones.

"Nikolai," Grandez humored, tilting his head.

"We need to talk," Nikolai snarled. "*Alone.*"

Grandez snorted a laugh. "Whatever you have to say, you can surely say it infront of the council members."

Nikolai hesitated. He was about to protest when he realized he didn't have too. He was standing in front of an array of cowards. Each thought their power was tenfold what it was.

"Fine," Nikolai said. "I'm done. I'm leaving. There it is, flat out. This organization is nothing more than a bunch of drugged up cowards sitting upon a throne you haven't earned. I'm done doing your bidding. I'm done coming to your call like a dog. I'm *done* throwing myself away for a small piece of validation."

Grandez cackled. "Are you?" he mused. "Isn't that sweet?"

Nikolai tensed. His entire body thrummed with rage. But something was *different*. The voice in his head yearning his father's approval had vanished. No pleading accents commanded him to do as Grandez said. Rage was his new master, and for once, it was his own.

Instead of the obedience Grandez wanted, Nikolai let out a harsh string of cackles. The laughs kept coming, unable to cease. Tears welled in his eyes, pouring down his cheeks. But he kept laughing. It felt too good to stop. The cackles gave him power. Hot, thick, *wonderful* power.

"Oh, you're fucking *hysterical*, father." Nikolai heaved, overcome by giggles. "Are you really so far up your own ass that you can't take anyone seriously? Let alone your own *son*?" he let out another hard belt. "But I see now, I see something I was blinded to my entire life. Blinded by *your* illusions. The only way you will ever take me seriously–" Nikolai strode to him, confidence fueling his steps. "Is if violence fits the equation."

Before he got a reaction, Nikolai swung his fist into Grandez's face. The war generals stood, ready to sink a blade into his throat. As soon as Nikolai withdrew his knuckles, he reached for his swords, pressing the blade to his father's throat.

"Ah-ah," Nikolai grinned. "One step, one wrong movement and I will slit his throat."

"Nikolai," Grandez pleaded. "You wouldn't–"

Nikolai licked his teeth. "I don't see a reason not to. You hurt me all the time. Pin me to walls, throw me to the ground, pound your fist into my face. Just before this, you pressed a blade to my throat. What's wrong with this one act of hostility?" Nikolai leaned forward, breathing on Grandez's quivering cheek. "After all, like father, like *son*."

His father took a shaky breath. "What do you want, Nikolai?"

Nikolai's smile widened. "I want to speak my mind, and you're going to listen." He said, "First, you were wrong about Quilla. You were wrong about Alohi and Lilith. They are not heartless lunatics, they're *people*. People who have been through hell and back. People who hold more skill in their fingers than your entire fat body. They are the true rebellion. The people that are truly fighting for freedom, for what is *right*. All you are fighting for is your comfort."

Grandez cackled. "Like you are any better." He snorted. "You fight for your comfort just as much as we do. You hunt your friends like a pack of dogs! You don't fight for the common good, Nikolai. You fight for your own ass."

Nikolai straightened his posture. "You're right. I'm only looking out for myself. But now, that's going to change. I'm going to fight the Golden Class and free the League citizens. If I get out of that fight alive, I'm going to find Quilla, Alohi and Lilith and beg for their forgiveness."

For a moment, Grandez simply gazed at him. Then, he cackled, the sound rough and jagged. "Isn't that cute?" he grinned. "The cursed son finally finding–"

He was cut off by his own scream as Nikolai dug his blade into Grandez's arm. The war general's rushed to his side, only to be stopped by Nikolai's blade at his father's throat.

"No." Nikolai rasped. "You forget. *I* am in charge. *I* have been in charge from the moment I was born."

Instead of the expected demeaning remark, Grandez simply swallowed. Sweat beaded his brow as he nodded, fear coating his glossed eyes.

As soon as Nikolai withdrew his swords, the generals charged. First, an arrow came to his stomach. Nikolai met the weapon with his left blade. Next, a sword swung at his shoulder. Nikolai ducked and swung his blade into the flesh of his attacker.

More swords clashed with his own. They came from different directions, each aiming to take his flesh. But there was one constant. The swings were never deadly. They weren't trying to kill him.

Because he was still the White King.

And there was a much more efficient way to do this.

With one, swift movement Nikolai crossed his swords over his own throat.

There was a gasp, and it seemed the entire room jumped back.

"Nikolai," Grandez breathed. "What–"

Nikolai tightened his grip on his swords, pressing the blade into his own skin. "I'm warning you," he growled. "I'll do it."

The generals dropped their weapons, raising their hands in surrender. Grandez stood, slowly making his way to Nikolai.

"Why–" he stuttered. "Nikolai, you're bluffing."

Nikolai simply let his sleeves fall to his elbows. There, in the bright light, were his scars. The scabs shone while the scars indented deep into his flesh.

"Bluffing?" Nikolai let out a fierce laugh, pressing the blades closer to his neck. "Not my style."

For a moment, Grandez's eyes stayed emotionless. Then, he laughed. The noise was hard, Nikolai had heard it before. It was the sound that hurt most.

He had heard it often.

But this time was different.

Because he didn't care.

"You're sick, Nikolai." Grandez growled. "So sick you're useless. Who would ever want a broken king?"

Instead of the hurt he might've felt before, a smile spread across his lips. He licked his teeth, the hurtful words running on his tongue, ready to come out like an arrow. "The father who broke him."

With the phrase, Nikolai sprinted out the door. He ran through the smoky halls, cloak covering his nose.

Chapter Twenty Three
Quilla

"No, Cercel, *please!*"

Quilla was tied on the ground, squirming under her ropes. The rain had turned to a thunderstorm. The drops soaked her, running down her spine and sending shivers through her body.

Cercel was standing in front of her. A sick smile spread across her lips as she held her knife to the throat of a small child. The kid quivered, tears running down his red cheeks.

"Cercel, he's just a child!" Quilla pleaded. "You want *me*. Kill *me*. Let him go!" she let out a shaky breath, tears gliding around her chin. "I am *begging* you!"

Cercel tilted her head. She gazed at Quilla with curious, wide eyes. They were the eyes she grew up with. The eyes she learned to love.

"You've been begging a lot, Rosalie." Cercel observed. "Interesting, it doesn't suit you."

"Enough with the games, Cercel!" Quilla hollered. "People's lives are at stake! Take my life! I am *offering* it to you! Let them *go!*"

Instead of the blank expression, Cercel's features shifted into one of danger. An evil smirk curled around her lips, her voice cracking like a thousand shards of glass.

"I'm not playing a game!" Cercel drawled. "I am fulfilling a duty, Rosalie. For once, I have everything. I'm in power, I command a nation, a *dynasty*! I am *keeping* that privilege."

"Then switch!" Quilla screeched. "You can come with me! With us! We don't have to conform to the Empire's standards anymore! We can be free! Cercel, *please*!"

A horrifying cackle ripped from Cercel's throat. Without a thought, she slid the knife across the child's throat. Blood poured from the wound as life slowly drained from the boy's eyes. Quilla watched as Cercel threw him to the side, letting his blood soak the grass.

And deep inside, she knew his death was her fault.

All this blood; it was on *her* hands.

"Do you know why I can't switch sides?" Cercel grabbed her collar, her icy breath cold on Quilla's cheek. "Because I don't care about the war. I don't *care* about the lives that are lost or the blood that's spilled. All I care about is whatever side I'm on, it's the opposite of *yours*."

Tears glittered in Quilla's eyes. They poured down her cheeks, curving around her chin. "Cercel–"

She was cut off by a blade to her shoulder. Cercel's star traced her collarbone, carving the flesh into a neat line. Blood oozed from the wound, dripping down her shoulder. Quilla screamed, the sound slicing the air.

"Cercel!" Casimir hollered. "She is our sister! Don't do this!"

Cercel tilted her head, looking innocent. "Oh course," a malicious grin painted her features. "We should move on, shouldn't we?" Cercel straightened her posture. "Ezekiel, set the prisoners on fire."

"*No!*" Quilla shrieked. "Cercel *please!*"

"There are children!" Casimir retorted.

"They're innocent!" Lamia screamed.

"I don't *care!*" Cercel growled. "You want mercy, Rosalie? This world never gave me mercy. Never fucking gave me a *dime*. Why should I return the favor?"

"Because then you break the cycle!" Quilla screamed. "How many innocents have to die before someone decides they don't need violence! That vengeance isn't all there is to life? Or is the only point of life to continue killing?"

Cercel tilted her head. "But you're not any better, are you, Rosalie?"

Quilla sighed. "No, but I'm trying to be."

For a moment, Cercel stood still. Then, anger recovered her expression. "Ezekiel!" she called. "Light them on *fire!*"

With trembling hands Ezekiel ignited his blade. The fire danced along the sword in orange streaks. There were no more pleas, no more commands of violence. They all seemed to accept that fire was going to burn the lives of hundreds.

Quilla closed her eyes, tears dripping down her cheeks.

But there was no woosh of fire, no screams of agony. There was no bright light to shine through her eyelids. Instead, there was an eerie silence.

"This–" Ezekiel stammered. "This isn't right."

"*What?*" Cercel asked, stunned. "Ezekiel, what are you doing? Set them on fire!"

"*No!*" Casimir shouted. "I'm done following your baseless orders, Cercel. I'm done bowing to an Empress whose only goal is the death of her own sister."

Before Cercel could respond, Ezekiel charged at her. She ducked as the flaming sword flew over her head. Cercel threw her stars, each clashing with Ezekiel's blade.

Quilla gasped as someone hoisted her to her feet. She turned to see Lamia undoing her rope.

"Lamia–" she stammered, tears pouring down her cheeks. "I am so sorry–"

"What for?" Casimir materialized beside her. "We should be thanking you, Ros– Quilla. You saved us. Now we get to save you."

Quilla couldn't respond. Instead, she flung herself into Casmir's arms, pressing her tearstained cheek into his chest. Lamia joined, engulfing her in an embrace. She didn't want to let go. She couldn't lose them *again*.

She whipped her head around as Ezekiel shrieked. Cercel stood over him, blades in hand. His sword was cast into the weeds. Quilla ran forward, knives already in hand. Before she could throw them, two swords crossed between Cercel and Ezekiel.

Nikolai wore all black. His hair hung over his eyes in messy strands. When he saw her, he smiled. "Nice to see you, Quilla."

Before she could respond, Cercel swung at Nikolai. She threw her stars and he blocked them. Their movements were quick, each ready and willing to kill.

"Hey, Quilla," Ezekiel was by her side, hand on her shoulder. "Long time?"

"Yeah," Quilla choked. "It has been."

"Quilla, you and Nikolai need to free the hostages and get them on a ship." Lamia said. "We'll fend off Cercel."

"No!" Quilla begged. "You can't. You'll die! Please, I can't lose you *again*!"

Lamia stroked her cheek, tears trailing down her face. "It's okay. Really, it's okay."

"No, no, it's *not*." Quilla sobbed. "You don't deserve to die. *Please*, don't do this!"

"Quilla," Casimir laid a hand on her shoulder. "You left a long time ago. You've made your place. We don't have one."

"But you can!" Quilla pleaded, "*Please*, don't do this."

Ezekiel gave her a sympathetic smile. "Don't do anything stupid, rose bud."

"Ez, *please*! I need you! Don't *leave* me!" Quilla's begging was silenced by the woosh of Ezekiel's sword. The Golden Class charged at Cercel, quickly immersed in the fight.

Just as they entered, Nikolai was pushed out. He rushed to Quilla, his features wild with adrenaline.

"Quilla," he panted. "We need to untie them."

Quilla gave a swift nod and rushed to the hostages. First, she went to Tnil. As soon as the rope slipped off her wrists, she engulfed Quilla in a hug.

"I'm so sorry, Quilla," Tnil said. "You didn't deserve that."

Quilla simply nodded and brushed her off. "We need to untie the others."

She moved through the motions dully, one eye always on the fight. The battle had moved to the outskirts of the plain. Cercel seemed to have the upper hand, usually remaining on offense. But through the blurs of movement, flickers of a flaming sword, a gold arrow, and a shining needle crept into Quilla's vision. They were still alive. The Golden Class were alive and fighting.

"Quilla!" Nikolai called. "Everyone is free! We need to get to the ship."

Like clockwork, Quilla helped everyone to her feet. She rushed them to the docks, following up the back. Whenever someone slipped behind, she would urge them forward. She couldn't think. Barely a thought crossed her mind. She was drowning in so many emotions she was blind.

They picked a rather massive ship. When everyone was aboard, Nikolai released the sails and the boat rushed into the sea.

Quilla stood at the stern, watching the mess of the fight. As the ship lurched for the open sea, three people retreated from the fight. They sprinted towards the deck, their gold uniforms glittering in the rain.

"Nikolai *stop*!" Quilla called. "They're coming."

Nikolai, who was manning the steering wheel, turned to see the Golden Class sprinting. He twisted the wheel, causing the ship to veer around.

Her siblings raced through the field. Cercel was nowhere to be seen; she was either dead or hiding. It didn't matter. Quilla didn't care what happened to her, all she knew was that her siblings were alive. Alive and running towards *her*.

Just as Casimir stepped his foot on the dock, a star twirled into his back. His smile faded, and a choke of blood sprang from his lips. He toppled to his knees before falling onto his side, red rapidly pooling around him.

Next, Cercel went after Lamia. It was as if the Empress materialized. She flung her blade into Lamia's stomach before she had the chance to grasp her needles. Lamia collapsed, curling into the fetal position.

Ezekiel was the final target. To his credit, he was able to block two of Cercel's stars before the third spiraled into his chest. The flaming sword slipped from his grasp, the bright flame retreating into the hilt. Ezekiel fell onto his back, yanking the blade from his crimson chest.

"*No!*" Quilla hollered, falling to her knees. Tears consumed her gaze, yet her eyes couldn't turn away from the scene in front of her. Her siblings were on the ground, bleeding into the weeds. Cercel had grasped Ezekiel's sword, setting fire to the plants that would become her sibling's graves. They had almost made it. They had *almost* been a family.

Quilla felt everything at once. Every emotion swirled in her brain like a storm. And yet? Only one thought formed in her head. Only one truth mattered now. All the *rage,* all the *grief. Every single* misconception and mistake had led her to believe one thing.

Cercel was *not* her sister.

Chapter Twenty Four
Lamia

Lamia never felt pain like this.

But as the light of the sun became larger and reality started to shift, she realized one thing.

She wasn't going to die alone.

There was a woosh, and flames lit the grass around them. In the distance, there was Cercel's mad laughter. Not joyous. Almost in mourning.

Lamia didn't care.

She looked at Ezekiel. He was groaning on the ground, wincing in pain.

"Ez," Lamia croaked, blood coming from her throat. "*Please.*"

Ezekiel gazed at her. Instead of the terror she expected, a tranquility washed over him. He reached for her extended hand and they intertwined fingers, squeezing each other tight.

"Casimir–" Lamia choked, extending her hand.

She didn't have to continue, Casimir's hand landed in hers. They squeezed each other's fingers, not daring to remove their eyes from the clouds. The flame inched closer, thundering through the tall grass.

"Goodbye," Lamia turned to see flames licking Ezekiel's body. Tears formed in his eyes as his skin blistered with the fire. "It's been fun."

Before she could respond, Ezekiel let out a screech, and the flames curled around his hair. Blistered bubbled and popped on his reddened skin. For a moment, his wretched, terrified scream pierced the air. The sound only lasted a second, and Ezekiel's body lay still in the fire.

"See you on the other side." Casimir squeezed her hand. Lamia turned to see his dreads dancing with flames. His arrows caught and soon his body was engulfed in hot, orange light. A screech similar to Ezekiel's rang from his blistering lips, but like their brother's, it only lasted a moment. Then an eternity of tranquillity.

Lamia swallowed. She kept her eyes on the sky, focusing on nothing but the pound of the rain against her cheek. First, the flame reached her palm, burning her fingertips. Next, it danced around her feet, winding up her legs in hot pain.

Lamia grit her teeth, keeping her gaze on the clouds. She didn't draw her limbs back. She didn't try to put out the flame. This was the last few seconds of her life, she wanted to feel *all* of it.

Eyes on the sky.

The fire gripped her clothes, turning her gold uniform to ash. Her skin bubbled and blistered as the flame raged on.

Eyes on the sky.

The raindrops evaporated before they touched her skin. Tears replaced them, sliding only beyond her waterline before the fire swallowed them. Lamia braced herself, letting the fire crawl onto her lips, eating away at her chin.

Eyes on the sky.

Her hair caught. Her breath became overwhelmed with smoke. The fire consumed her nose, her head, her temples–

And her eyes were no longer on the sky.

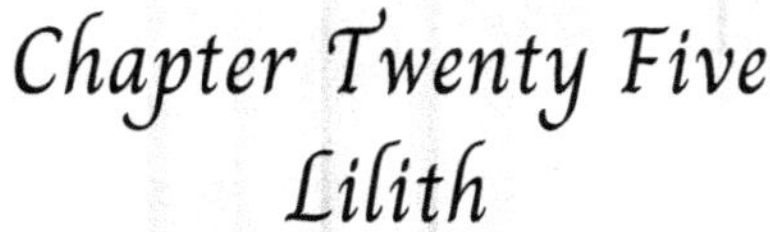

Chapter Twenty Five
Lilith

The rain pattered hard on the roof. Lilith paced around the broken house, her bare feet splashing in puddles from the leaks. Her head swam, her heart pounded. Worry overcame her. Not just worry, but grief.

Because deep down, she knew she ran out of luck.

Or more accurately, Quilla had.

She wasn't coming back. She made the sacrifice no one asked for. Lilith should have been mad, she should have been *furious*. But instead, she was just sick with fear.

But as she continued to pace the house, the slow revelation began to creep into her bones. She was alone. Quilla was gone. Earlier in the day, Alohi tried to convince her otherwise, but they both knew. Quilla was dead. Her heart punctured by Cercel's blade. Lilith just clung to the sliver of a chance that somehow, by some miracle, Quilla managed to escape.

Just then, there was a knock on the door. Lilith nearly flung herself at the handle. When she opened it, she let out a sob.

Quilla was being supported by Nikolai, arm over his shoulder. Her eyes were red and puffy. Blood dripped from every inch of her body. A large wound oozed on her shoulder. She looked broken, shattered. No light was left in her black eyes. Some part of her must've died— but at the very least, a fraction had *lived*.

Nikolai wasn't much better. Several gashes bloomed on his arms. His clothes were soaked and his expression solemn. But they lived. Both of them must have some generous deity on their side because they stood. Bloody, defeated, broken. But by god's name, they *stood*.

"Quilla–" Lilith flung herself around her, tears running down her cheeks.

"Lili–" Quilla choked, her voice a low, shattered rasp. "I am so, *so* sorry, Lili. I should have listened–"

"No," Lilith put a hand on her head. "Not now, it's okay."

"Lilith?" Nikolai asked, his voice a similar scratch. "Where's–"

"Second floor on your left." Lilith said, not taking her gaze off Quilla. "That's where she's sleeping."

Nikolai nodded and headed for the stairs. Quilla hugged her tighter, pressing her face into Lilith's blouse. Lilith placed her hand on her neck, holding her tight.

"Lilith?" Quilla asked sheepishly.

They pulled apart, Lilith's hand on Quilla's shoulder. "Yeah?"

"You–" Quilla choked. "You can hit me."

Lilith's eyes widened. "What? Why would I ever–"

"Because I was awful. I promised I wouldn't leave and I did. I deserve to get hit–"

"Absolutely not!" Lilith cupped her face. "Whoever taught you that is absolutely wrong. You don't deserve more violence than you've already endured."

"But–" Quilla stammered. "But aren't you mad?"

Lilith shrugged. "I'm frustrated and worried. But I understand why you did it. More than anything, though, I'm just glad you're okay."

For a moment, Quilla stayed still. Then, she flung her arms around Lilith, pressing her face into her chest. "I'm sorry. Lilith, *please* don't leave me."

"I'm not going too," Lilith said, kissing her hair. "Never, okay?"

"Thank you," Quilla murmured. "I'm sorry."

"Stop saying sorry." Lilith said. "Come on, you must be exhausted."

Quilla put her arm around Lilith, leaning against her shoulder. Lilith placed her hand on Quilla's waist, keeping her close. They walked side by side, both afraid to let go.

When they got to the room, Quilla collapsed on the bed. Lilith unbuttoned her blouse, revealing a gash on Quilla's shoulder.

"Quill?" Lilith took a rag and dabbed the wound. "When you're ready, can you tell me what happened?"

Quilla winced as the cloth touched her skin. "She did that."

"Your sister?" Lilith asked.

Quilla sat up, causing blood to leak from her shoulder. "She is *not* my sister anymore."

"Quill–" Lilith sat next to her, nudging her back onto the bed. "What did Cercel do?"

"The Golden Class," Quilla drawled, putting her head down. "They freed me. They told me they loved me, and they distracted Cercel while me and Nikolai freed the hostages. They were about to make it to the ship until–" Quilla swallowed, pain shimmering on her features. "Until Cercel–"

"Quilla," Lilith said. "You don't have to tell me–"

"Until Cercel stabbed them." Quilla blurted, tears breaking her waterline. "She stabbed them in front of me. Then, she lit them on fire. I watched it all. I watched them *burn*, I heard their screams and I saw–" Quilla took a sharp breath. "I saw Cercel's smile. Her *laugh*." She grit her teeth, tears pouring from her fiery gaze. "I want to gouge that laugh from her *throat*. I want to *carve* her organs. That woman is *not* my sister."

There was silence. Neither of them knew what to say. They simply sat, Quilla's words echoing around the quiet room. For a moment, Quilla's gaze remained consumed with rage. Then, it broke. The fire melted into smoke, and a sob escaped her lips. Lilith pulled her partner into her chest, resting her hand in Quilla's soaked curls.

"Quilla," Lilith breathed. "I am so, *so* sorry."

Quilla didn't respond. Instead, she simply nuzzled her face deeper into Lilith's chest.

"Hey," Lilith murmured. "I need to finish your wounds. Then we can sleep, okay?"

Quilla nodded, sitting up. "Okay,"

Lilith unbuttoned her pants, pulling the wet cloth off her. She undid her undergarments and wrapped a blanket around her bare body. Lilith dabbed her wound with a wet cloth, gently wiping the blood away.

When she was done, Lilith wrapped her shoulder in a bandage. Quilla flinched as it was tightened.

"Sorry," Lilith said. "You okay?"

"Yeah," Quilla croaked, "Can I– can I get some water?"

Lilith smiled, tucking her hair behind her ear. "Of course."

She headed out the door and padded down the stairs. The house was quiet, the only sound was the constant drip from the ceiling. Lilith filled a glass with water and walked back to her room.

"Hey," Lilith turned to realize the voice came from Nikolai. He was leaning against Alohi's door, legs crossed. He had gotten older since she last saw him, or at least that's what she saw. Bags loomed under his eyes and his white clothes had turned black. The once finely combed hair was now messy and tangled.

"Hey," Lilith replied, offering a small smile. "You look–"

"Awful?" Nikolai gave a small laugh. "I know."

"That's not what I–" Lilith sighed. "Nevermind. Are you doing okay?"

"I'm not the one to be concerned about." He glanced at Quilla's door. "How is she?"

Lilith sighed, slumping next to him. "I'm– well, worried." She lowered her voice to a whisper. "She asked me to hit her, Nik."

"Oh," Nikolai shifted his gaze to his hands. "That's–"

"Why would I ever do that? I'm frustrated and worried of course, but I would never hurt her. She thought she *deserved* it! How could *anyone*–"

"Lilith," Nikolai said, cutting her off. "She thinks she deserves it because people have hit her before. People who told her they loved her. When that happens you think it's normal. And because you've been deprived of that love, you do anything for it. So it makes sense that when she finally finds someone who truly loves her, she's willing to let herself be abused to keep you."

Lilith looked at her hands. "What does it feel like? To— you know— not ever have a parent's love?"

Nikolai looked at her. "Your dad died, didn't he?"

"Yes, when I was fourteen." Lilith said. "But that's different. He loved me. Actually *loved* me. I feel grief, yes, but it's grief for something I once had. What's it like to never have it?"

Nikolai sighed. "There's only one way to describe it. A hole. The insults they shoot will dull and the cuts they dig into your skin will scar. But there is always a hole. You need someone to love you like a father would for that hole to be filled."

"Did you have someone?" Lilith asked. "To fill that hole?"

"Many." Nikolai looked at the ceiling, blinking tears from his eyes. "Rex; he died. Killen; well, I fucked that one up. And in a way, my dad. But the truth is, Rex was my first mate, not my father. Killen was my master, not my dad. Those two relationships cannot be intertwined. As much as I wish they could, Killen will always care more about my skills than my health."

"Really?" Lilith gazed at him. "Or is that your dad?"

Nikolai bit his lip, looking ahead. "Fair point. Either way, when you find someone you love, you'll let them hit and beat you in order not to lose that. Or– at least in my case. But given Quilla's past, I think it might be similar for her."

"But I don't *want* to hit her!" Lilith exclaimed. "I don't understand how anyone could *ever*–"

"That's why she's so lucky to have you." Nikolai said. "If she wound up with the wrong person, things could be a lot worse."

"Yeah," Lilith took a breath. "I guess so."

"Speaking of which," Nikolai began. "You should get back to her. She went through a lot today, I want to make sure she's okay."

Lilith smiled, standing from the floor. "Thanks, Nikolai," she patted his shoulder. "I'm glad to have you back."

Nikolai saluted her. "Glad to be back."

Lilith returned his gesture and headed into the room. She gently closed the door, careful not to make a loud sound. "Hey, Quill–" she stopped as she saw Quilla's curled up figure on the bed. She was wrapped in blankets, sleeping in the fetal position.

Lilith gave a small smile. She placed the water on the desk and padded to the bed. With a gentle hand, she brushed Quilla's hair behind her ear.

"Hey Quill," Lilith said softly.

Quilla opened her eyes. "Hey, Lili."

Lilith climbed into bed, laying up next to her. Quilla nuzzled her head into Lilith's chest. Slowly, her breath became rhythmic and her chest rose and fell in even patterns. Lilith kept a hand on her head, gently stroking her coffee hair.

Chapter Twenty Six
Nikolai

Nikolai leaned against the wall, breathing a sigh. For a moment, he wished there was smoke seeping from his mouth like a stream of fog.

As much as he hated to admit it, he was alone. His father, though awful, was still his father. He was Nikolai's blood, the person who was supposed to love him unconditionally. And yet?

They hated each other. Maybe there was a time when Grandez really loved him, but that was long gone. Their relationship had morphed into one of pure *hatred*.

But that wasn't what he was sad about. Infact, his commune with his dad had become nothing but forced chivalry. When he looked back, all he could feel was the strong pull of validation and need to please.

Never once love.

But one thing hurt. The loss of a partnership that could've been brilliant. It could have been brilliant– could've filled the hole buried deep in Nikolai' chest.

And the worst part?

The betrayal was his own.

When Killen expressed concern about his mental wellbeing, Nikolai brushed it off. He laughed in his face, calling the habit crazy as if he didn't do it himself.

When Killen approached him on the ship, he was too afraid to talk to him. The only conversation they had was Nikolai telling him and Tnil to look after the citizens, nothing else.

Killen offered him love. *Unconditional* love. The type he craved. But he had been too afraid to take it.

Nikolai glanced at Alohi's door. He did the same thing to her. He was too afraid to confront his issues; to admit he wasn't always perfect. That fear destroyed one of the most valuable relationships in his life.

He groaned. He needed his head to shut up.

And there was another way to fill the hole.

Nikolai drew the blade from his cloak. The knife shone in the dull light, its edges glittered with excitement, as if awaiting its plunge into Nikolai's skin.

But this time, he didn't tease himself. He didn't let himself feel the cold of the blade press lazily on his skin. He didn't allow the touch to aggravate the voices

Instead, he simply dug the knife into his wrist. He cut diagonal, the dagger slicing through his scars. The scabs peeled away, blood seeping from the old cuts. More liquid trickled from his wound, dripping wearily down his arm. The red pattered on the carpet, one drop after another.

Then the drips turned to a pour.

Then a steady stream.

And a fucking *flood*.

Nikolai withdrew his knife, panic gripping his chest. He flung his coat over his wound; the blood simply soaked right through. He kept dabbing the cloth against his skin, only to make it red within seconds.

His head was light. His vision wavered. The pour of blood continued, pooling onto the carpet. He wanted to scream, he wanted to screech for help. But most, he wanted the blood to stop.

But it wouldn't. It never did. The red kept pouring from his wrist. The warm sensation turned cold as the liquid leaked from his insides to his skin.

Nikolai gasped. Black wavered along his vision. His eyesight blurred; and he collapsed.

Chapter Twenty Seven
Quilla

Quilla gripped her hair, pulling on her scalp as the voices got louder. There were flashes; sparks of Lamia's kind face, Cercel's evil one. The fire burned her memories like it burned her siblings. Ghan's drawl pounded in her head, telling her she was nothing, telling her she had no purpose on this earth. Telling her to *die*.

Come now, Rosalie. He chanted. *Do you really think you deserve to survive this? Do you really think your little archer cares about you? I mean, why would she? Face it, you are forever pathetic.*

Quilla turned in her sheets, placing her hands over her ears.

You have nothing to live for. This time, the voice was her own. The Empress's accent danced along syllables as her long fingers traced Quilla's cheek. *You really think that girl cares about you? She's lying! Obviously. Are you so naive that you can't see that? The only people who ever cared for you are your siblings. And guess what? They're dead.*

Quilla clenched her eyes shut.

I killed them. The accent was tainted by a rough rasp, tone scratched by years of bloody history. *I killed your family. You had the chance to kill me, and you couldn't. What use are you if not for your vengeance. It's not Ghan anymore, it's me. Cerce. Your sister.*

Cercel cackled, the sound drifted lazily into the night air, echoing around the walls.

But you can't kill me. You've tried, and you can't. So what use are you? Why not die, Rosalie?

"No," Quilla murmured. "No, please, stop."

Kill yourself. Ghan chanted.

Kill yourself. The Empress prodded.

Kill yourself. Cercel rasped.

Kill yourself. End your life. Commit suicide. Die, Rosalie. You have nothing to live for. Why not? What's stopping you? What is holding you back? Fucking kill yourself. You're worthless. Why live? Who the hell wants you here? Certainly not you.

Quilla jolted awake. The voices faded to the back of her mind. Her breath came short; whenever she tried to breathe, the air got stuck in her throat. Sweat beaded on her forehead, the droplets drifting down her temples.

She stepped onto the floor, the cold creeping up her ankles. Quilla pulled on her coat, then her boots. Just as she was about to stride out the door, her gaze caught.

Lilith was in a deep sleep. Her hand hung over the bed with an open palm. Her head lay on her bare shoulder; so peaceful. So *happy*.

Quilla couldn't leave without an explanation.

With shaky hands, she pulled a quill from its ink. She pressed the feather to the paper, tears pattering on the desk.

Hey Lili,

I'm done hurting people. I'm done being the cause of so many deaths. So I'm ending it. I'm sorry you had to find out this way, but at least you won't have to deal with me anymore. I'm a burden this world will be glad to be rid of.

I hope you have the life you deserve—

—Quilla

Quilla dropped the pen, the ink splashing on her foot. Tears poured from her face as she read over the letter. She left the paper on the nightstand. Lilith would find it in the morning. Quilla didn't want to imagine the events after that.

She strode out the door, her coat drifting behind her. As soon as she stepped into the cold outside, the rain soaked her. The drops slid down her cheek, washing away her tears.

The voices howled in her head. Each one had a different accent. A different piece of shattered glass that was her mind. They screamed, hollered, screeched, but Quilla didn't mind.

Because this time she was doing what they wanted.

Kill yourself, Thorne. End your life, Rosalie. Jump off the fucking cliff, Rose.

Her legs moved without her permission, gently drifting through the grass and towards the ocean. Her knives clinked in her coat, rattling against their own metal.

She could do it now, silence the voices once and for all.

But she wouldn't die that way. She didn't crave the touch of the blade.

She craved the lap of waves against her lifeless skin.

Quilla sped up her pace, striding towards the cliff. The dark of the night reflected off the black ocean, except for the occasional white when the moon shone through the clouds.

She smiled as she imagined her lifeless body. The salty water lapping against her blue fingers. The sand would slowly cover her body, then the crabs would pick apart her flesh, leaving nothing but her bones to be mistaken as rocks.

The grass brushed her ankle for a final time as she made it to the cliff. It was a steep drop; at least twenty feet of falling until she splashed into the turbulent waves. The water clashed violently against the pointed rocks. The stones were sharp enough to impale a human; the waves were strong enough to push a corpse deeper into the water.

Quilla smiled. *Perfect.*

Her heel drifted over the edge, the splash of the ocean dewing her sole. Quilla hovered her palm over the cliff, letting the sea water splash her fingers. She closed her eyes, breathing the salty water a final time.

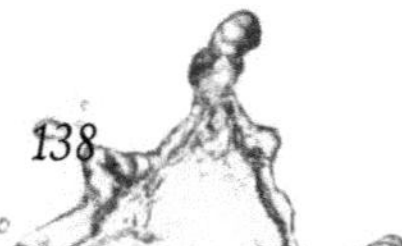

Before she would inhale it.

She lifted her foot above the water and released her balance. She drifted over the edge, eyes closed, tears sliding down her cheek.

Just as her toes slipped, something grabbed her wrist. Her eyes flung open, tears pouring down her face as she saw who was holding her.

"Lilith–" Quilla stammered. "You weren't–"

"Stop it," Lilith growled, pulling her into a hug. "Just shut up."

"Lili–" Quilla choked. "I'm so sorry. I don't know what got into me. You can leave me. I know you won't physically hurt me but you don't have to stay with me–"

"No," Lilith pulled apart. Tears drifted down her cheeks, along with the patter of rain. "No, I'm not leaving you. I get it, Quilla, I do. With all that's happened to you, I'd be surprised if–" she swallowed. "*This* didn't happen. But please, I am *begging* you. You have a future with me. We can build a life together. Grow up, have a family, be *happy*. I know it's hard, but Quill–" Lilith choked, cupping her face. "You're only seventeen. You've had a hard life. But trust me, Quilla, it will get *better*!"

Quilla's trembling hands reached for Lilith's. "Promise?"

Lilith gave a small smile. "I promise."

Quilla was about to fling herself around her. To apologize and thank her endlessly. To admit she wanted to live, she *wanted* to get better. She was going to do all those things– she was going to make life worth it.

Until the ground beneath her broke.

Quilla gasped as gravity took her. Her stomach was left behind as she dropped. Shock made her heart beat at tenfold speed.

Her fall stopped as something grabbed her wrist. She gazed up to see Lilith clutching her arm, eyes filled with panic.

"Lilith–" Quilla called. "Please don't let me go."

"I won't." Lilith choked. "I promise Quill, I won't."

Quilla peaked downward. The waves clashed angrily against the rocks, sending spray to touch her legs.

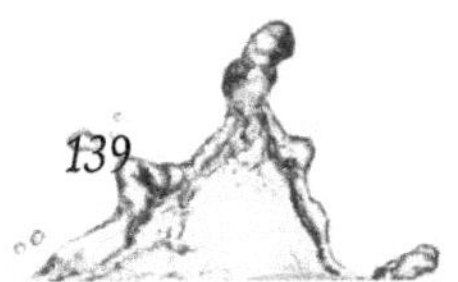

"Quilla!" Lilith screeched, panic scraping her syllables. "I'm slipping!"

She was right. Their hands slid from each other's grasp, Quilla slowly sinking towards the violent waves.

Just then, a wave crashed against the cliff. Quilla's grip slipped, and she fell. As she plummeted, time slowed. She saw Lilith's terrified green eyes. She felt the spray of the ocean on her back. And she smelled the thick scent of death enclosing around her.

Quilla splashed into the waves. The water dragged her under. The current smashed her against the rocks, sending her body flying into another stone.

Her arms pushed her to the surface, only for the waves to send her deeper into the ocean. The bottom was rocky, coral spiking along the pebbles.

Quilla's head whacked against another rock. She gasped, her mouth filling with water. Instinctively, she breathed in, only to have more liquid flood her lungs.

Why not let it take you? The all too familiar voice echoed. *Let the water drag you through its stones. You're so close! Why not let it kill you?*

For a moment, Quilla's body went limp. She stayed unmoving, letting the water toss and turn her. But something urged her forward— towards the surface. Maybe it was her enclosing lungs, desperate for a gasp of air. Or maybe it was the life waiting for her above the waves. The promise of a new beginning.

Quilla dug her feet into the pebbles. With one, fluid motion, she propelled herself to the surface. Just as she broke the water, a wave crashed on her.

The water wanted her to drown.

The world wanted her to die.

And since when had she ever listened to what the world wanted?

Quilla flung herself to the surface. She tried to breathe, only to have water erupt from her throat. The liquid spewed from her mouth, barely allowing her to gasp. Then, another wave crashed onto her.

She couldn't breathe. Whenever she tried, a wave pushed her under the water. Her chest tightened, her throat burned, and every inch of her yearned for the cold touch of air.

A current grabbed her, flinging her into a rock. Instead of paddling away, Quilla clutched the stone. Her nails dug into the layer of seaweed that clung to the rock.

She crawled to the surface, the water pulsing beneath her. But she wouldn't let go. She wouldn't let the waves push her under. She clung to the rock, she clung to the air, she clung to her *life*.

"Quilla!" Lilith called. The archer was racing along the beach, her messy braid flying in the wind. "Swim to me!"

Quilla took a shaky breath and bounded off the safety of her rock. As soon as she let go, the water took her. She was thrust under, the waves whacking her against the coral. She tried to breathe, only to have salty liquid flood her nostrils.

As soon as she was under, the waves pulled her back to the top. Quilla gasped for air, coughing up the vile liquid splashing down her throat. She gazed at the shore. Waves crashed over her, drenching her head in its violent grasp. But there was one common factor. No matter what, the waves would always carry her to the beach.

Quilla took a final breath and stopped swimming. Her arms rested, her legs stopped kicking. She sunk into the water, letting the current sway her body back and forth. It wasn't rough, it wasn't violent. It was peaceful.

When the waves pulled her above, she gasped for air. When they hauled her beneath and into the coral, she didn't fight it. She was a piece of the ocean. Another molecule among thousands. She didn't control where she was going, she didn't need to. She had faith the ocean would carry her where she was needed.

Just then, something grabbed her wrist. She was pulled to the surface to see Lilith's green eyes. Quilla tried to stand, only to fall into her partner. Lilith hugged her, her warmth a stark contrast to the water lapping at her knees.

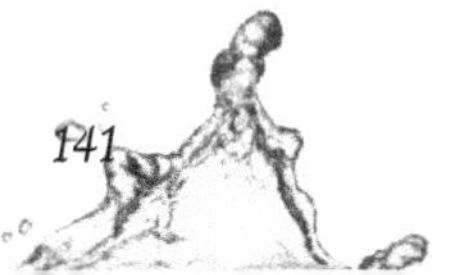

"Lilith?" Quilla murmured.

"Hm?" Lilith answered, not daring to pull apart.

"I–" Quilla stammered. "I want to live. I want a future. I don't want to be like this anymore. I don't want to be consumed by this– this anger anymore. There has to be more to life than vengeance!"

Lilith wrapped her in a tighter hug. "Good," she whispered. "And there is. You are a brilliant, amazing girl, Quilla. You have a bright future. Even if life hasn't been kind to you, it will be. You *will* have a good life."

Quilla pulled apart, gazing at her. "Promise?"

Lilith gave a small smile, tears trickling down her face. "Promise."

Chapter Twenty Eight
Alohi

Alohi's eyes fluttered open to the patter of rain on her ceiling. The rags and towels she used as blankets weighed heavy on her body. She didn't want to get up, it was warm in her bed.

After a minute of contemplation, Alohi stretched. She sat up and her rags slumping off her. She padded along the creaky boards, brushing a strand of tangled hair out of her eyes. She clasped the door handle, pushing it open to start her morning.

But it wouldn't budge.

Alohi tried again, this time harder.

The door halted just a crack open.

Alohi kicked it.

The wood thing swung back at her.

This time, Alohi opened the door slowly. She peaked through the crack, and screamed.

"Lilith!" she hollered. "Quilla! Florian!"

There were pounding footsteps, a gasp, and hands dragging Nikolai's unconscious body from the doorway. Alohi stepped outside, tears gleaming in her eyes as she saw her best friend soaked in his own blood.

"Quilla!" Lilith called. "Get my stitching materials. Florian, get a washcloth."

Alohi barely heard them. She was too busy looking at Nikolai's pale face. The blood that oozed from the gash on his wrist. That *huge* gash. The gash that was cut diagonally, the gash that could *kill* him.

But then she noticed the gentle rise and fall of his chest. The air that entered and left his lungs. He was breathing, his heart was beating, the same blood that covered the carpet was circulating through his veins.

He was still alive.

That was the thought Alohi clung too. She hugged it, clutching the fact with all her strength. She couldn't take her eyes off the rise and fall of his chest, the gentle part of his lips that inhaled and exhaled.

Before she knew it, Quilla and Lilith were carrying Nikolai into her bedroom. They set him on the sheets, his blood immediately soaking the towels. Alohi didn't care. Alohi couldn't care about anything but her best friend's life.

Lilith started the stitching as soon as Nikolai was on the bed. Her needle went through his pale flesh with speed. More blood soaked Lilith's hands, but she was unfazed. Her vision tunneled, all she was focused on was keeping Nikolai alive.

"Alohi..."

But there was more blood. It soaked through the towels, seeping onto the mattress. His lips were turning blue, his skin was purple under his fingernails, his breathing was getting shallow. It was slowing, his chest was beginning to–

"Hey, Alohi." Quilla placed a hand on her shoulder. "Let's take a break outside."

"*What?*" Alohi sounded like Quilla just asked her to defenestrate. "I'm not leaving him–"

"Look at me, Alohi." Quilla said. "You being here isn't going to do anything to help Nikolai. If anything, it will give you a stress heart attack. Lilith is skilled, I've seen her do this before. Nikolai has the best chance with her."

Alohi took a shaky breath and got to her feet. Her and Quilla padded out of the room, Alohi always keeping one eye on Nikolai.

"Hey," Quilla said, shutting the door behind her. Alohi eyed her best friend through the crack like a hungry dog. "Let's not think about that right now."

"How can we— what the hell happened to you?" it was the first time Alohi had laid steady eyes upon Quilla. Her hair was moist and scrapes littered her skin. Her eyes were tired, bags sagging under them. Beneath her coat, bandages wrapped what must've been an ugly wound on her shoulder.

"Great! That's another conversation." Quilla drew a shaky sigh. "I made a bunch of stupid decisions in a row and by some miracle I'm still alive."

"Not the first time." Alohi shrugged. "So... I guess Lilith's had her hands full?"

Quilla snorted. "It's a bloody wonder she hasn't broken up with me yet. I'm going to make her take a nap after she's done. She deserves it."

Alohi gave a stout cackle. "You think she's going to let you out of her sight?"

Quilla shrugged. "I'll lay next to her, how's that?"

Alohi scoffed. "Oh, well now you're just rubbing it in my face that I'm single."

Quilla grinned. "Well, you know, Alohi." She ran her tongue along her teeth, gesturing to the door. "You could shoot your shot."

"Quilla, there is a time and place—" Alohi snarled.

"What do you mean?" Quilla giggled. "He is on his deathbed, you're a mess. When he wakes up, you give each other a tearful apology and sex it out." Quilla placed her forearm on her head, falling back in a dramatic swoon. "So *romantic.*"

Alohi backhanded her. "First, it's fuck it out. 'Sex it out' is either grammatically incorrect or it hasn't been used in two hundred years."

"Alohi," Quilla clutched her chest, her face wrinkling with suppressed laughter. "Are you mansplaining slang to me?"

"You learned what sex was a couple days ago. I have every right to mansplain to you."

"Touche," Quilla amended. "But I have a serious question."

Alohi shot her a blank stare. "Last time you had a serious question Florian started playing with my 'hole' and Nikolai's 'stick.'"

"Don't remind me," Quilla growned. "But I have a different question. Do you have feelings for Nikolai?"

Alohi drew a sigh, her gaze drifting to the ceiling. "I don't– I don't think so. I mean, I feel safe around him. The *safest*. He's done so many things for me and yet– he betrayed me when I needed him most. How could I ever like him after that?"

Quilla was about to open her mouth when Alohi started talking.

"But then again, his father manipulated him. He was under a lot of pressure and found some unhealthy coping mechanisms. But who wouldn't? I escaped my home! If I stayed any longer, I would've developed something like he has. Even now, I have this— this *longing* for alcohol. I have my escape, he has his. But he's a lot better at hiding it. And– I don't think I helped. I was too busy telling him how bad it was to recognize the root of the problem. The problem is that he's *suffering*, not that he cuts himself. If he stopped suffering, or if it was lessened, maybe— maybe he would have stopped. *Maybe* he wouldn't have bled out."

There was silence. No one dared to speak. Quilla intertwined her fingers through Alohi's; a silent gesture of comfort.

"Nikolai–" Quilla stammered. "Nikolai cuts himself?"

Alohi couldn't bring herself to respond.

"Okay," Quilla took a breath. "I've seen this before, Alohi. The people in Hanslack– a lot of them do it. When you hurt yourself, it releases a small amount of the same hormone drugs like opiates release. That's why it's so addicting. That feeling– it's powerful. Pain feeds into addiction, so the addiction can't stop until the pain does."

"Oh," Alohi swallowed. "What was his pain?"

"I can't say for sure." Quilla said. "If I had to guess, I would say his father and the pressure that was put on him."

Alohi took a breath. "So, now that he's here, do you think he could have a chance at stopping?"

Quilla gave a small smile. "Yes, I think so. But you have to be patient. Recovery can go many different ways. Some quit cold turkey, and that's the only way they can do it. Others endure a painstaking process of relapsing and intense urges. If you want to help, I would recommend being patient with him. Don't expect his recovery to be linear. There are going to be ups and downs. The important thing is that you support him no matter what. I think that's going to be the best thing for him."

Alohi stared at the wall, tears forming in her eyes. "I did none of those things for him. *None.*"

Quilla placed a hand on her shoulder. "It's okay, everyone makes mistakes. What's important is that you are able to learn from them and correct yourself. That way, you can be a better... *friend* in future." Quilla turned to her, grinning. "Now, back to my original question. Do you have feelings for him?"

Alohi took a breath. "Sometimes I get knots in my stomach, like I just can't stop looking at him. When I go to sleep, I hug a pillow wishing he was next to me. I want to bury myself in his chest. I want to embrace him and I want him to hug me back."

"Got it," Quilla smiled. "So, for all the marbles. If he kissed you, would you kiss him back?"

Alohi looked at the door. The last time she thought about kissing him was on the boat. It was a powerful feeling, but it didn't feel right. This time, it felt comfortable, safe, *correct.*

"Yeah," Alohi breathed. "I think I would."

Just then, the door creaked open. Lilith padded out, holding her sewing supplies and a blood soaked cloth.

Alohi stood up so fast she banged her shoulder on the wall. "How is he?"

"He's breathing," Lilith laid a gentle hand on Alohi's shoulder. "And he'll make it."

Alohi practically threw herself into Lilith. "Thank you," she mumbled, pressing her face into the archer's blouse. "Thank you, thank you, *thank you*!"

"Don't mention it," Lilith said. "Do you want to see him?"

Alohi swallowed. She gave Lilith a sly nod and headed into the room. Nikolai lay on the bed, his chest rising and falling in an easy rhythm. His lips, once a chapped blue, were flushed with red. His skin had returned to the correct pale.

Her eyes cautiously drifted to his wound. The blood was cleaned; only remnants of crimson remained. The skin was neatly bandaged, covering the torn flesh. He looked better; *alive*.

"Hey Nik," Alohi clutched his limp hand. "Been a while, hasn't it?"

Only silence answered her.

"I tried alcohol," Alohi smiled. "I can see why you like it. Although, I think I might have had too much. Quilla won't stop teasing me about what I did."

Alohi chuckled, holding his hand tighter. "I don't think you would have let me forget it any sooner. When you wake up, I'm sure she'll tell you all about it. And then you'll both tease me." Alohi huffed a laugh. "You'll never let me forget it."

Her gaze shifted to the ceiling. "If you ever want to talk to me again, that is." Tears welled in her eyes, creating a gentle sting. "I talked to Quilla. She helped me understand what you went through. I'm sorry I didn't understand it at first. I should have realized, Nik–" Alohi choked. "I should have realized that what I did only hurt you. I shouldn't have blamed you, I shouldn't have gotten mad. You were there for me when I needed you. You kept my secrets when no one else would. And when you needed me–" she let out a sob, tears pouring down her cheeks. "I got mad. I betrayed you. And now–"

She ran a gentle finger down Nikolai's arm. She was always afraid of his scars. Afraid of what he did to himself. Now she was beginning to see them in a different light. They were marks of endurance. Marks of battle. When someone lost a battle, when someone was injured, you didn't hate and shame their scars. They were marks of sacrifice, marks of hardship, of *strength*.

"Now I see," Alohi murmured. "You fought every single time. Every scar is the mark of a loss. Those cuts were never on purpose. They were never careless. They were never out of spite, thoughtlessness or anger. They came from pain. Pain you needed to escape from. Who would blame you for wanting an escape?"

Alohi lowered her forehead to Nikolai's palm. "I'm so sorry, Nik. I'm so, *so* sorry. I was wrong, I was awful. I may have thought *this* was helping, but there's no excuse for my yelling. There's no excuse for the words I said. I did something wrong, and even though you can't hear my words, I hope you know that I *will* do better. I'll be there for you, every step of the way." Alohi took a breath, looking at Nikolai's closed eyes. "If you'll have me."

Chapter Twenty Nine
Lilith

"Hey," Quilla murmured as they entered their room. "Are you doing okay?"

Lilith perked, molding her expression into one of confusion. "Fine, why? Are you okay?"

Quilla sighed, sitting on the bed. "Come on," she patted the spot next to her. "Sit."

Lilith cautiously sat beside her. "Quilla, what is this? I need to make sure–"

"No," Quilla whispered, her tone soft. "You've done so much today. You barely slept last night. I want to make sure you rest."

Lilith scoffed. "Look who's talking."

Quilla's eyes softened, "Lili–"

"Quilla seriously, I'm fine." Lilith said, "If anyone needs sleep, it's you."

"Okay," Quilla took a breath. "Let's compromise. You take a nap and I'll go downstairs–"

"*No!*" Lilith grasped Quilla's wrist, tears forming in her eyes. "Don't– don't leave. Please."

Quilla stared at her, black eyes blank. "Look, Lilith," she moved her hands to Lilith's, intertwining their fingers. "I broke your trust–"

"That's not–" Lilith interrupted.

"No, it's okay." Quilla offered a small smile. "I know I did. It wasn't to hurt you, but I did. So let's talk this out. What would help regain that trust?"

Lilith bit her lip. "I guess–" she sighed, "I guess I want to know why. Why wasn't I enough for you?"

"Oh," Quilla drew a sigh. "In that moment, in my mind, I believed that I was a burden. That you would be better without me. I knew as long as I lived, Cercel would keep going after me— and hence you— until I was dead. In my mind, killing myself was the only way to keep you safe."

"So–" Lilith stammered. "You did it because of me?"

"*No!*" Quilla grasped her shoulders. "That was *not* your fault, in any way! You saved me, okay? You are the only reason that I am still alive! I did it because I felt like I was too much trouble than I was worth. I was tired of the flashbacks, I was tired of the panic, and I was tired of burdening you with it."

"It was never a burden," Lilith choked. "*You* were never a burden."

"I can see that now," Quilla said. "But at that moment, I thought I was. I thought it would be easier for everyone, and myself, if I just ended it. It– it was sort of like I lost control of my mind."

"Will you–" Lilith bit her lip. "Will you ever try again?"

Quilla drew a sigh. "I don't want to. As of now, I want to live. But–" she took a shaky breath. "I don't know if that will change. I hope it won't, but truthfully, I don't know."

"Okay," Lilith laid a hand on her knee. "Will you promise me you'll talk to me, then?"

Quilla offered a small smile. "I can promise that."

They gazed into each other's eyes. Quilla's were a glittering black, life gleaming in her iris. Before she knew it, tears welled above Lilith's waterline. The droplets poured down her cheek, curling around her chin.

Quilla pulled her closer, nuzzling her face against her chest. She stroked her hair, running her long fingers down Lilith's braid.

"Don't leave me," Lilith pleaded. "Please, Quill."

"I won't." Quilla pressed her lips into Lilith's hair. "I promise." She placed her hand behind Lilith's head. "Now please go to sleep, you've had a rough couple of days."

Lilith chuckled, gazing at her. "As have you. You need sleep just as much as I do."

"Right, well I care about your rest and wellbeing more than I care about mine."

Lilith snorted. "Then I suppose we're at a crossroads." Her lips curled into a grin as she wiped dried tears from her eyes. "Because I care about your health more than mine."

"So in conclusion," a brilliant smile gleamed on Quilla's lips. "We're both mentally fucked."

"Did you just realize that, Quill?"

"I had a haunch."

Lilith snorted a laugh, a bright gleam replacing her grief. "You know," she giggled. "With how smart you are, I'm surprised that thought never occurred to you."

Quilla shrugged. "There is only enough room in my head for the important facts. I tend to block out the things that are useless."

"Like sleep."

Quilla's smile widened. "Precisely."

Lilith tackled her, pushing her head onto the pillow. "Close your eyes!"

Quilla cackled, grabbing Lilith's shoulders and turning her onto the mattress. "When I'm the queen of hell."

"So now," Lilith squirmed under her. "You realize that was my first impression of you?"

"Really?" Quilla hummed as Lilith pushed her to the other end of the bed. "Is it wrong that I'm flattered?"

"Are you?" Lilith grinned, planting her hands on Quilla's wrists. "I give you more praise after you *sleep!*"

"Over my dead body," Quilla freed her hands, about to push Lilith onto the mattress. In a moment of pure genius, Lilith collapsed on Quilla, burying her head in her partner's chest.

"What the–" Quilla stammered. "Lili, what are you doing?"

"I can't hear you, I'm asleep." Lilith murmured, nuzzling closer to Quilla. "You must be *heartless* to disturb your girlfriend while she's sleeping."

"Oh, so this is our compromise?" Quilla giggled, the sound even more soothing when it came from her chest. "You smart bastard."

"Why thank you."

Quilla wrapped her arms around Lilith, placing her long fingers in her loosely woven hair. "Have a good sleep."

Lilith smiled, focusing on the gentle bump of Quilla's heartbeat. "Have a better one."

Chapter Thirty
Cercel

Cercel gripped her chest, tears dripping from her face as her legs collapsed beneath her. She scurried to a corner, sinking to the ground and onto the glass she shattered days before.

She placed her hands over her ears, plugging her fingers deep into the cartilage. Cercel scraped her fingers against the skin, blood seeping from the wound. It trickled from her ear, running down her neck and seeping into her shirt.

"Go *away*!" she screeched. "Stop it! Leave me *alone*!"

But they didn't stop. The hands grasped at her, their icy touch trickling down her shoulder, seeping into her skin and infecting her veins. There were a million of them, a million whispers, a million fingers scraping her cheek, pulling at her hair, scratching her flesh.

Cercel shut her eyes, not daring to look beyond her hands. Something was there. She didn't know what, but *something* had taken her vision hostage. Her senses were no longer portraying what truly existed. She was trapped. Trapped in the cage that was her mind.

The worst cage, in her opinion.

Because there was no key.

Cercel...

"Stop it..."

Cercel...

"Go *away*!"

Cercel... Cercel... Cercel... Cercel...

"Leave me *alone!*" Cercel stood, ramming her fist into the wall. Blood seeped from her knuckles, the red splattering the wall. But it wasn't enough.

Again.

But the voice wasn't Rosalie's, it was her own.

Cercel slammed her hand into the wall. The plaster broke, the blood sprayed. The skin around her knuckles peeled back to reveal her flesh. More blood. Then bone.

The red poured down her wrist. The blood instantly soaked her palm, dripping down her arm in a stream. It seeped into her sleeve, staining the gold a glimmering crimson.

Cercel exhaled, imagining the smoke of heroin coming from her breath. She ran her bloodied fingers through her hair, causing the red to fall down her straight locks.

Good, Cerce. The voice was familiar, its accent bright and bubbly. *Did that help?*

"What?" Cercel staggered back. "Lamia?"

Of course, Cerce. The calm voice stepped from behind her. *Are you blind?*

Honestly, a chaotic crack cooed. *This is insane even for you Cerce. Seriously, get a grip!*

The golden class stepped in front of her. Each detail, each feature, each minor freckle replicated to perfection. But something was... *off.* Their edges were blurred. The once sharp curve that was Ezekiel's jawline was more gentle. Lamia's neat curls hung in less predictable strands. Casimir's tight smirk curled too high on his lips. Something was terribly... *off.*

Killing your own kin. Casimir let out a stout cackle. *Really? Have you sunk that low? In the process to demolish a girl, you eliminate the most powerful squadron in Thine.* He touched her cheek, his ghostly fingers tracing her lips. *And the best part is, we were on your side!*

"No you weren't!" Cercel snapped. "You were never on my side. This is a game of jealousy. We all played it. You're just angry I *won.*"

Won? Lamia hummed a laugh. *Dear, if you won you wouldn't be in this room. Your hand wouldn't be bloody, and you wouldn't be alone.* Her icy fingers grazed across Cercel's throat. *Look at you; your only company is the shattered glass on the floor and the figures born from your shattered mind.*

Tell me, Cercel. Ezekiel took a strand of her hair, weaving it between his long, pale fingers. *What is victory to you?*

"What?" Cercel stammered. "I don't–"

Yes you do, Lamia licked her teeth. *What does victory look like? What do you imagine?*

The words sprang from her tongue like a rabbit. "Rosalie Ghan bleeding on the floor."

Hm, Casimir snorted, as if amused. *So easily, Cercel. And yet? Will that change anything? What will killing her do for you?*

"It will give me justice!" Cercel screeched, saliva spewing from her mouth with the rage.

Justice? Ezekiel asked. *For what? Running? Trying to bring you with her? Trying to save us? You're the one that tried to kill her, that actually killed us. If anyone deserves to die, Cercel, it's you.*

Cercel crumpled to the ground, covering her ears with her hands. "Stop it." She whimpered. "Please, leave me alone."

Do you really believe yourself right for this? Lamia touched her shoulder, the brush cold as ice.

Do you really think you can live beyond your vengeance? Casimir cooed. His sharp nails trailed along her spine.

You are nothing, Cercel. You are only your goal. Your only place in this world is as a villain. You have no point. Your life has no meaning. Only one goal.

Cercel opened her eyes, anger stinging with the tears rolling down her cheeks.

Well? Lamia brushed loose strands of hair from Cercel's eyes. *Be that villain.*

"I am going to kill Rosalie Ghan." Cercel growled. She chanted the words a million times before. They were with her when she fell asleep, when she woke up. They accompanied her when she ate, when she trained, every *second*. When the voices got too loud the phrase yelled over them. When she was bleeding on the ground, the words pushed her to her feet. It was her anthem, the only reason she was still alive. The only reason she had to *live*.

"I am going to kill Rosalie Ghan. I am going to kill Rosalie Ghan. I am going to kill Rosalie–"

Who's that? Cercel took a strangled gasp as the voice chirped behind her. It was so pure, so *familiar*. And yet the memory was foreign. She heard it before— yes— but time had chipped her remembrance.

Cercel turned, her eyes wide with disbelief. As soon as her gaze steadied, she recognized the figure. She recognized the straight hair, the way her black eyes glowed in the light. Her lips were small, the touch of the light glimmering off them. The paleness of her skin, the way her hair hung over her shoulders, and the gentle pull of her cheeks when she smiled, every inch of her radiated Cercel.

But it wasn't her.

"Siena?" Cercel choked, her voice shaky with disbelief. "Is that you?"

Of course, Siena smiled. *Been a while, hasn't it?*

"I–" Cercel stammered. "You– you died."

Did I? Siena gazed down at her arms. *I don't think I'm dead.*

"No," Cercel shook her head. "You were vaporized in the explosion. When– when I was five. Ghan took me. He made me a member of his Golden Class!"

Siena simply blinked. *Oh? And what's that?*

"Emperor Ghan's personal league of assassins. I was the least favorite. I was destined to be a failure, the fucking *runt*! But I won! Through hard work and pain, so much *pain*, I won. I was the leader. And when Ghan tried to take that away, I took over as Empress!"

Cercel didn't know why she said that. It wasn't exactly relevant to the conversation, nor did she think Siena cared. But as the words flooded from her tongue, Siena's gaze widened with disbelief. Not the vile kind of disgust, but of admiration, of *pride.*

Oh, Cercel, Siena croaked, wiping a tear from her eyes. *I knew it, I just knew it!*

"What?" Cercel murmured. "Know what?"

That you would be incredible. Siena smiled. *I told you once before, it doesn't matter what you do with your life, you will succeed in whatever you put your mind to. Because whatever you put your mind to, whatever task you want to achieve, you will break through bedrock to achieve it. Through dirt, through injury, through pain, you will achieve it.* Siena strode towards her, grasping her shoulders. *That's what sets you apart. It's not your cruelty, not your skills, not your ambitions. It's the fact that you will do everything possible to achieve your goals.*

Cercel gazed into Siena's black gaze. Her sister was twelve when she died, and remained young in front of her. But Siena brought a sense of security, a sense of parenthood. Sensibly, Cercel was older; yet Siena still felt like her older sister.

She barely noticed the tears pouring from her eyes. When they trickled down her neck, she didn't bother wiping them away. Instead, she pushed herself into Siena's chest.

But she phazed right through.

Cercel turned, but instead of the glassy, kind eyes of her sister, the gaze was darker. Siena's straight locks curled. And worst, her proud expression was replaced with demeaning amusement.

She's dead. Rosalie snorted. *Remember?*

Cercel simply stared at her. For a moment, her expression was blank. Then, it contorted. Her jaw shifted outward, her fingers curled into her palm, and her eyes squeezed into fierce glare.

"I *hate* you!" Cercel lunged at her. "Leave me the *fuck* alone!"

Rosalie dodged to the side, hands clasped behind her back. When Cercel made another swing, Rosalie simply weaved behind her.

Too slow, she commented. *Not enough power. Is that really all you have? Pathetic.*

Cercel lunged at her chest. This time, Rosalie didn't move. She stayed perfectly still, her arms folded and her grin spread wide.

Cercel should have seen it as a trap. But instead, she dove at her. Contrary to the satisfying flesh she expected, she phased right through.

She gasped for air, hands on her knees. She needed a clever response, she needed to pick herself up and try *again.*

But for the first time in a very long while, she couldn't. There was no witty comeback, no strength in her legs to swing another punch, no room in her mind for vengeance to consume.

She was simply *tired.*

Cercel rested her head on the floor, knees tucked in the fetal position. Her breath came in gasps, her lungs frantically sucking the air into her veins. But no matter how hard she tried, the blasted oxygen never reached her body.

Well, Rosalie demanded. *What are you waiting for? Get up, Cercel, get the fuck up!*

"I–" Cercel stammered. "I can't."

What do you mean you can't? Rosalie snapped. *Are you that pathetic? What happened to your drive? What happened to all the work you put in? What happened to the promises of death?*

"What if I don't want to?" Cercel retorted. "What if– what if I'm just tired."

Nonsense, Rosalie growled. *You don't get to be tired. You don't get to be weak. You gave up that right when you swore Rosalie would die. What? Did all that just wash down the drain?*

"Stop it," Cercel murmured, placing her hands over her ears.

You can't get rid of me, Cerce. I'm just as much a part of you as air is a part of your lungs. As acid is a part of your stomach. I am the wind beneath your wings, the push of your legs, the pull of your grasp. Without me, you would crumble.

Cercel took a breath. Her neck twisted and her eyes ignited into a fiery glare. She looked at Rosalie, gazing at her with nothing but pure *hate*. From her perfect coils to her mesmerizing eyes; she hated every inch of her.

"Fine," Cercel rasped. "I choose to crumble."

With those words, she pushed herself to her feet. It was as if her brain was on autopilot, running without command. She sprinted around the halls of the palace, frantically searching for *something*.

She didn't look back. She didn't want to see what was following her. Her only focus was the goal, the *escape*.

Then, she found it.

The infirmary was full of wounded soldiers and doctors tending to them. Cercel didn't pay any mind to the prying eyes that locked on her when she entered. Nor did she care about the several shouts of confusion when she made her way to the jar of pills.

She stuck her manicured fingers into the jar, tossing the smooth capsules in her palm. For a moment, she simply observed the way the tablets slid on her skin.

Then the voices got loud.

And she shoved the handful into her mouth.

Chapter Thirty One
Quilla

"What are you doing here?"

Quilla turned as the raspy voice choked behind her. Her eyes widened as she saw Nikolai heavily leaning against the railing. His face was hollow and white. Under his drooping eyes lingered bags that could carry all her knives. He looked awful, but at least he was standing.

Quilla raised her glass. She was sitting at the table, her tangled hair falling down her slouched shoulder.

"Care to join, Princely?" she asked, gesturing to the seat next to her.

Nikolai scoffed. "Drinking, really?"

Quilla looked offended. "I'm not drinking."

"Oh," Nikolai snorted. "Of course, my apologies."

He strode to the cabinets, only to stop short. "Where do you keep the alcohol?"

"Third cabinet to your left." Quilla said, "Oh, and they may be under a blanket. Florian thinks they're hiding them."

Nikolai gave a stout laugh. "How foolish."

He opened the cabinet, tore off the cloth and frowned. His eyes crinkled into a fine stare as his lips curled.

Quilla sighed. "Florian has weird taste–"

"No, it's not that." Nikolai said, grasping one of the bottles. "You hate Muscat wine."

Ah, of course. On the long walk to the Golden Palace, Nikolai sparked an interest in what sort of alcohol she liked. Quilla had then informed him she couldn't stand the cheap liquid. Its spicy sting was too much for her. Part of her wished she hadn't told Nikolai, because he spent the remainder of the walk teasing her about having the spice tolerance of a mouse.

"Yes, I hate Muscat," Quilla recoiled at the thought. "What about it?"

"Well, the only unsealed bottles are of it."

"Oh," Quilla took a sip. "I think Florian likes it."

Nikolai wrinkled his nose. "So what are you drinking?"

"I told you," Quilla waved the glass in the air. "I'm not drinking."

Nikolai rolled his eyes, grabbed a glass, and sat down with his spicy alcohol.

"Good luck," Quilla snorted into her 'not alcohol.'

"Thanks," Nikolai poured himself a glass. "I'm sure the taste will burn my tongue alive."

Just as he was about to touch the rim to his lips, Quilla snatched the wine from his grasp. He scowled and lunged for his drink. Quilla pushed it to the other end of the table, then gazed at Nikolai with the most innocence those black eyes could muster.

"Asshole," Nikolai growled. He reached for the bottle, even more eager to consume the narcotic.

"Nope." Quilla snatched the wine from his hand, dangling it over her head.

Nikolai snarled, his bandaged arms reaching for the glass. "What's your problem?" he made a jab at the alcohol, only to have Quilla tuck it behind her back. "Fuck off!"

Quilla simply cackled. She leaped from her stool, running around the kitchen with the alcohol dangling from her loose grip.

"Fine," Nikolai snatched her glass from the table. "You take the Muscat. I'll take whatever the hell you're drinking."

Quilla smirked. "Have fun."

She barely had time to say the retort. Nikolai chugged her drink so fast she was convinced he might choke. Then again, her assumption wasn't exactly wrong.

Just as the liquid sunk into his taste buds, he spat it out. The vinegar exploded from his nose and mouth, going nearly three yards before resting in bubbly droplets.

"That is *not* alcohol." Nikolai drawled, steadying himself on the table.

"I told you." Quilla laughed. "I'm trying to be better."

"*Better*?" Nikolai gazed at what was left of the liquid. "How does that taste better? What even is it? Cat piss?"

"No," Quilla hopped on the table, dangling her bare feet in the air. "Vinegar and lemon juice."

"Ew," Nikolai wrinkled his nose. "Why would you ever drink that?"

"I told you," Quilla said. "I'm trying to be better."

"*At*?" Nikolai urged.

"At being a person." Quilla tucked her knees to her chest. "I guess–" she took a breath. "I'm lucky to be alive, Nikolai. For the first time since I remember, I'm trying to *live*. I'm trying to enjoy this time I have. Because I know that at any time it could just..." Quilla extended her long fingers, mimicking an explosion. "Be over."

There was silence. For a moment, Quilla thought she said something wrong. But then, Nikolai released a breath.

"Woah," Nikolai sighed. "That's— *profound*."

Quilla released a small laugh. "I do try,"

For a moment, there was silence. Not an awkward one. It was a quiet that signaled familiarity, not lack of it.

"Quilla–" Nikolai breathed. "I never said I'm sorry."

Quilla huffed a laugh. "It's not me you should be apologizing to."

"Oh, right." Nikolai bit his lip. "I owe a very, very deep apology to everyone here. But too you–" he cleared his throat, as if the words were having trouble emerging from his throat. "Well, I'm sorry for trying to kill you."

"Oh," Quilla chuckled. "To be honest I forgot about that."

"You did?" Nikolai poked at his bandages. "I didn't."

"I see that." Quilla hopped from her perch and waltzed to him. Her long fingers gently pushed his hands away from each other.

Nikolai sighed, pressing his fingers to his temple. "You know, don't you?"

There wasn't any point in lying.

"I had my suspicions for a while. Alohi told me this morning."

"Oh," Nikolai dug his fingernails into the table. "I'm sorry,"

Quilla scoffed. "What are you sorry for? The only reason I care is because I'm worried about you."

Nikolai looked up, "The last time someone was worried about me, I betrayed them. I wouldn't advise going down that path."

"Alohi?" Quilla asked. "Well, she worried wrong. At least in my opinion."

Nikolai leaned against the table. "How so?"

"Well, she said it herself. She attacked the remedy instead of the pain."

"Hm," Nikolai gazed at his wrists. "Yeah, she did."

"Speaking of which," Quilla suddenly perked, as if her attitude did a one eighty. "I think I might've cracked it."

"Cracked what?" Nikolai asked.

"The key to stopping," Quilla beamed. "The key to a happy life. It's quite simple, really. Obvious, even. I believe the hard part is figuring out what it is."

Nikolai furrowed his brow. "What?"

"The trick is walking away." Quilla smiled. "Walking away from the source. For me, it was my attachment to the Empire, the attachment to my past. The belief that no matter what I did, it would always define me. Once I freed myself from that, once I let myself believe I wasn't simply my vengeance, I started to get... happier."

"Do you–" Nikolai stammered. "Do you think the same could happen to me?"

Quilla gave him a small smile. "Sure. I think if you find what is hurting you, and find the will to walk away, you can get better."

"The hard part is finding out what it is," Nikolai added, biting his lip. "What you think is your savior, might be your downfall."

Quilla nodded. "What saved you in the past, might kill you in the future."

There was silence, each not daring to speak. Nikolai placed two fingers on the bridge of his nose, closed his eyes, and bit his tongue. Quilla knew what he was thinking about. She knew the revelation that was to come. She knew it since she met him, Lilith figured the truth at the same time, and Alohi had known it since she entered the League.

"It's my father, isn't it?" he finally asked.

"From my perspective," Quilla nodded. "Yes."

"Do you think he's an ass?" Nikolai asked, his tone light with vulnerability.

Quilla scoffed. "Oh come on, Nikolai," she cackled. "When have you ever seen me and the Lone have a civil conversation? Yes, I think he's an ass!"

"Okay," Nikolai nodded. "Just wanted to make sure I wasn't imagining things."

Quilla's gaze turned sympathetic. "I get that," she whispered. "Thinking you're crazy, thinking you're the problem."

"Yeah," Nikolai breathed. "Do you think they have any remorse?"

"What? Our fathers?" Quilla cackled. "Come now, Nikolai. You're gonna make me relapse."

Nikolai gave a small snort. "Seriously, Quilla. What do you think was going through their heads?"

"When they abused us?" Quilla sighed. "The weird part is, I know why they did it. They wanted us to be great. The best there ever was. When we didn't meet that expectation, we needed to be punished."

Nikolai bit his lip, sinking into his stool. "That's fucked up."

"Sometimes you wonder if there was any little alarm in their brain that might've stopped them." Quilla growled, her voice beginning to raise. "Did they ever see the wrong when my arms were covered in scratches from their own blades? Did they ever regret the words of criticism— no, not criticism — *insults* that sprang from their mouth?"

"Or is it the fact that you are their child that is so regretful?" Nikolai finished. "I know the answer. I'm a failure in my father's eyes. His only regret was having me in the first place. But Ghan–" he took a breath. "Do you think he wishes he chose a different kid in your place?"

"I don't know," Quilla sighed. "Don't really care. Try not to think about it. You're welcome to ask if you like."

Nikolai shot up. "I beg your pardon?"

"Oh right," Quilla chuckled. "He's in our basement. I might need to feed him soon."

Nikolai's face seemed to go through every expression at once. His lips contorted into a motion of disgust, pity, anger, and utter confusion, until finally, it rested in smug amusement.

"Of course," he smiled. "Why am I not surprised?"

Quilla gave a small snort. She strode over to the cabinets, grabbed the vinegar and poured it into the glass. She then followed it by a generous amount of lemon.

Nikolai notably winced as the liquid curtled.

Quilla took a sip of her drink, finding petty joy in Nikolai's disgust. She waltzed to her stool and set her drink on the table.

"You know," she said. "You're not the only one who nearly died last night."

"Oh?" Nikolai asked. "What happened?"

"I was stupid." She murmured. "I made too many mistakes in a row, and the grief was too much. I felt like I was nothing, better off dead." Quilla took a shaky breath. "So I tried to jump off a cliff. Lilith found me and stopped me, only for the cliff to break beneath me. I clawed my way back to the beach, and well, broke a lot of trust."

"You tried to kill yourself." Nikolai swallowed. "I– I guess I don't really understand."

"It was a promise I gave myself when I was young," Quilla said. "For years, it was the only thing that kept me going. That one day, all this would end. I guess, life can get to a point where you either want to kill yourself or–"

"Take the easy path to happiness." Nikolai concluded. "That's why I cut."

Quilla looked at him. "You weren't trying to end your life, were you?"

Nikolai shook his head. "No. All I wanted was a break. But– well, I took too many. When you take a drug too much–"

"–you develop a tolerance."

"So you cut deeper."

"Drink more."

"Use more blood."

"Until your body is the one who needs a break." Quilla swallowed, afraid to say it.

"So you–" Nikolai stammered. "So you die."

"For me, addiction was never an issue." Quilla said. Nikolai raised an eyebrow. "No– wrong words– I mean I didn't mind it. I knew I was drinking myself to death, but I didn't care. I would drown my pain in the drink, and when I needed more, I'd drink more. Then, one day, I'd drink too much, and die." She shrugged. "Seemed like the best way to go."

"So–" Nikolai bit his lip. "What stopped you?"

A hint of a smile touched Quilla's lips. "I suppose it was the hope that I would have a reason to live besides vengeance. A future." The grin widened, indenting dimples in her cheeks. "A future with *her*."

Nikolai smiled. "I'm happy for you two. It's a stark contrast from when we first met."

Quilla laughed, remembering the hostile times between him, her, Lilith and eventually Alohi. Neither of them could bear more than fifteen minutes around each other without sparking a fight. "Memories."

Nikolai snorted. "Oh, how wonderful."

"Enough about me," Quilla placed her face in her palms, licking her teeth mischievously. "Let's talk about you and Alohi."

Nikolai's emotions did a one eighty. "Oh," he drew a sigh. "What do you want to know?"

Quilla heaved a sigh. "It's not so much what I want to know, but my opinion. And I want your stance."

"Well?" Nikolai raised his shoulders in question. "Go on."

Quilla took an exaggerated breath. On the exhale, words sprang off her tongue like a rushing flood. "It's no secret that you and Alohi are on... *questionable* terms. Between her hostile attitude towards your struggle and you trying to take her life, it's no wonder the relationship has suffered. However, I've watched you two for almost a year. When she was taken to Rock Highland, you went insane trying to get her back. She's told me things you did for her, things that could have gotten you in deep shit. Personally, that's a relationship that seems to be more profitable than not. So, like any good business operation, you should go to great lengths to make sure it stays afloat. Those lengths will be hard, given the fact that she screamed at you every time you cut and the amount of times you tried to kill her is equivalent to the amount of scars on your wrist. But I do think this relationship is worth fighting for."

Nikolai stared at her. A mix of shock, disbelief, and mild offence painted his features. He scoffed. "Thanks for sugar coating it."

Quilla grinned. "My pleasure."

He sighed. "You're right though, Quilla. That relationship... it's worth fighting for. I think we both fucked up—"

Quilla cleared her throat.

"Maybe—" Nikolai stammered. "Maybe a bit more on my end. But that doesn't mean I'm not going to try and make amends. My only worry is—" he turned to her, eyes pleading. "Quilla, be honest."

"Do you really have to ask?"

Nikolai drew a shaky sigh. "Does she hate me?"

For a moment, Quilla only furrowed her brow. Then, she giggled. Not a cackle, but a light, friendly chuckle. "No, Nikolai, she doesn't." Quilla hummed a laugh, remembering the conversation on the boat right before she strode into Florian's kelp filled base. "Don't get me wrong, she tried. The poor girl definitely wanted too. But in the end—" she turned to him, smiling. "I think all she could remember were the times when you were there for her."

Nikolai nodded. "How did you and Lilith do it? I mean way back when I remember you saying—"

"'Our relationship is purely professional.'" Quilla mocked, pushing her voice up a few octaves. "'She is valuable to me only as an archer.' 'Partner' as in 'crime.'"

Nikolai snorted. "The lip on lip action is purely platonic."

"Me and her? *Never.*" A rough grumble came from her throat as she struggled to withhold her laughter. "Everyone knows I've been sleeping with Coriolanus Dacnoff ever since I joined the League."

Nikolai burst out laughing. He placed his head on the table, his chest rising and falling with giggles. "Who tops?"

Quilla breathed, attempting to control her tyrannical cackles. "Who what?"

Nikolai gave her a look someone would give if they asked what bread was. Then, he let out a sound that vaguely resembled a laugh. "Forget it." He sighed. "But seriously, how did you and Lilith become... well, civil and able to–"

"Love each other?" Quilla finished. A hint of a smile touched her lips and her cheeks turned a rosy pink. "Well, I realized that when she was taken, I was never going to find anyone else who I loved— and who loved me— that much. I realized that if I let her die, then it would be a worse fate than the death of my own. When we both survived, we apologized. She kept my secrets from Ghan. I freed her. After that, I started opening up, and she was patient. She never pushed me, never dug too far. In turn, I told her everything. I cried with her, she cried with me. And now–" Quilla placed her cheek in her palm. "Well, I'm more comfortable with her than anyone else. It's like, for the first time, I don't have to earn someone's love. For the first time, it doesn't matter how much I do or how far I'm willing to go. All that matters is that I want her to be happy, and she wants the same for me."

Nikolai gazed at her with proud, happy eyes. "I'm happy for you, Quilla. I really am." He sighed and his face fell. "But– that just seems so far from me. It seems *terrifying*–"

"Dangerous?" Quilla asked.

"Yeah," Nikolai breathed. "That."

"For me it was too. There was never to be any vulnerability shown around Ghan or Gillen. If I cried, they'd yell louder. But I had to realize that wasn't normal. That isn't something someone does to a child, no matter the reason. For me, I started believing that the way I was mistreated was normal, and everyone would do that."

"But that's not true..." Nikolai dug his fingernails into the counter. "When my dad found out about my scars, he called me sick. He said as long as I didn't die, he didn't care."

"See that–" Quilla tilted her head. "Is not something a father should say."

"Alohi never did anything like that." He murmured. "Sometimes she would get frustrated or say something that hurt, but it was never intentional. She always– there was never any ulterior motive in the friendship. She just... wanted to help."

"Hm," Quilla drummed her fingers against the counter. "I guess that leaves the question; are you going to let her keep trying to help?" she gave a small smile. "And are you going to allow yourself to help her?"

Chapter Thirty Two
Alohi

Alohi hadn't realized she had fallen asleep.

So imagine her surprise when she woke up slumped in her chair next to Nikolai's unmade bed with no one asleep in it.

She got up so fast she tripped over the chair leg. Her bashed heel jolted to her grasp, as if that would help the throbbing pain, and left the chore of her balance to her left foot.

And her left foot failed spectacularly.

She toppled to the ground, slamming her chin into the molding floorboards. As soon as she hit the ground, she sprang back up, dashing to the door and bolting into the hall.

Lilith was standing just outside her room. By the look of her panicked face, Alohi guessed she had also gone to war with her bedroom to find her missing partner.

They locked eyes. "Lost yours too?" Lilith asked.

"Yeah," Alohi barely finished the word before leaping downstairs, Lilith on her heels.

Alohi halted around the fifth step. There, sitting at the table, were Quilla and Nikolai. A bottle of wine sat a few feet away from them. They're elbows sat on the counter, faces resting in their palms. A sly smile touched their lips, as if they were deep in conversation.

Lilith landed next to her. Her face shifted from panic to understanding, then the same small grin curved her features.

"There you are," Lilith said, striding to Quilla. "Will you ever stop being a morning bird?"

Quilla turned and flung herself around Lilith. "Sorry, did I worry you?"

Lilith snorted. "Not a smidge."

Quilla gave a small laugh in return. She then turned to Nikolai. "Look who decided to join us."

Lilith's smirk widened. "Would you look at that? Excited to join us in the wonderful land of smuggling and stealing?"

"'Excited' isn't the right word." Nikolai said.

"Would 'exhilarated' or 'sparked' suffice?" asked Quilla.

"Keep guessing," Nikolai urged. "Though I am glad to be back. The League was–"

"Hell?"

"A cage of suffering and regret?"

"The eternal incubator for abuse?"

Nikolai made a gawking sound that vaguely resembled a laugh. "Take all of those and combine them, then you'll have your answer."

"Sure," Quilla snorted. "And let's add incompetent as well. Grandez Lone, the motherfucker, led Cercel right to his little base."

"In my defense, I tried to point out the fallacies in his operation."

Quilla shrugged. "That probably would've helped, but I don't think he can hear constructive criticism."

Lilith picked up Quilla's cup from the table. "What's this?"

Nikolai and Quilla looked at each other, a glance of mischief glittering in their eyes.

"Not alcohol." They said simultaneously.

Lilith wrinkled her nose. "I don't believe you."

"Why don't you try it?" Nikolai urged.

"Right." Quilla said. "If you really think we're lying, why don't you take a sip yourself?"

"Fine," Lilith cautiously sniffed the liquid. "Ugh, that's *vile*!"

"Is it now?" Nikolai smirked.

Lilith pressed the cup to her mouth. As soon as the liquid entered her mouth, it came rushing back out. Quilla moved to pat her partner's back while Nikolai took cover behind a chair.

"That is *not* alcohol." Lilith choked, spitting the remnants into the cup.

"Told you," Quilla said, running her fingers down Lilith's braid.

"Don't be too hard on yourself," Nikolai said, putting his hands on his hips. "I made the same mistake."

"God, I think it's in my nose!" Lilith croaked. "Why would you drink that?"

"Well," Quilla rubbed the back of her neck. "It helps, I guess. I can pretend it's alcohol and not need to drink the real thing. No hangover, no sinking feeling in my stomach and I become less dependent on the liquid."

For a moment, Lilith's face remained neutral. Then, a smile touched her face. She flung herself around Quilla, pressing her face into her shoulder. "Thank you,"

"For what?" Quilla laughed, wrapping her arms around Lilith.

"For trying," Lilith murmured. "For wanting something better."

Quilla gave a soft smile, "You're welcome. Thank you for helping."

For a moment, Alohi just watched. Then, her eyes drifted to Nikolai. Their gaze met. The ice blue of his eyes was so unreadable. His expression was flat, as if he was simply observing. Then, the small quirk of his lip. It was small, barely noticeable.

But she noticed.

He smiled at her.

She smiled back.

Quilla laid a hand on Nikolai's shoulder. "I think you two have some catching up to do." She nudged him. "Go on."

Nikolai padded up the stairs, slowly inching towards her. Alohi gave him a warm glance; he returned it.

"Hey," she smiled.

"Hi," he returned.

They strode up to her room. Alohi's gaze wandered all over him. From his ice blue eyes to the way his feet lightly dragged against the stairs. She gazed at his lips, which had regained some of their color since she last saw him.

Her gaze wavered to his bandages. She watched the red slowly soaking through the white. Her face got hot. Her ears started to burn. And worse, her heart started to pound.

Because the worst part was, she had no idea how to help him.

She had been shooting in the dark.

And that turned out *awful*.

They strode into Alohi's room. Nikolai closed the door behind them, clicking the nob shut.

"Alohi–" Nikolai blurted at the same time Alohi spoke his name.

Nikolai gave a small smile. "You go first."

"I am so sorry, Nikolai." She stumbled. "I left you when you needed me most. I let my fear control me and I abandoned you. That was so, *so* wrong and I don't know what was going through my head but–" the words came out so fast, as if they'd been on the tip of her tongue for months. "It was wrong and I did it. There's no excuse and I don't know how I could ever make it up to you–"

"You don't have too." Nikolai interrupted. "I am more at fault here. I was the one who tried to destroy the pirate colonies. I was the one who tried to kill Quilla. Fuck, I tried to kill *you*. I was my father's dog. He had me on a tight leash. It's my fault–"

"But I drove you to that!" Alohi hollered. "I was the one who was a bitch. I was the one that drove you into his grasp. That was *my* fault!."

Nikolai gazed at her. He didn't open his mouth to retort. Instead, he just looked.

"I am so sorry," Alohi covered her face with her hands. "That's not how I should be approaching this. I am *so* sorry–"

Nikolai laid a rough hand on her back. "Politicians," he chuckled. "Do you ever stop talking?"

Alohi looked up. To her surprise, he was smiling. The typical gleam in his eye had returned. Her heart melted. She hadn't realized she missed his smile so much.

Alohi flung herself around him, pressing her face into his shoulder. He skeptically put his hands around her, entangling his fingers in her hair.

"I missed you, Nik." She mumbled.

Nikolai smiled."I missed you too, Lo."

For a moment, they stayed put, immersed in each other's presence. Alohi didn't want to let go. She didn't want to speak. In that moment, all previous grievances between them vanished. It was like they were thirteen again; too many cares, too little time. But at least they had each other.

"We do need to figure out how to get past this, though." Alohi pulled away, heaving a sigh.

"Yeah," Nikolai took a shaky breath. "We do,"

Alohi took his hand, placing his bandaged forearm in her lap. "Is this okay? Please tell me if it isn't."

"It's okay." Nikolai said. "Just– don't judge me, okay?"

Alohi nodded. "I won't."

She unwrapped the cloth, peeling away the bandage layer by layer. What she found sent tears to her eyes. Her friend's arms were tattered and torn. Scabs covered his arm, ripping through his flesh to his elbow. Over them, was a fresh, horizontal cut.

She looked at Nikolai, finding his eyes effortlessly gazing at his arm.

"It's not really disturbing to me." He explained. "It's just—well, I guess it's so normal for me."

Alohi simply nodded. She reached into her drawer and pulled out a fresh set of bandages. She took his arm, gently wrapping the cloth around his cuts.

"Can I ask you a question?" Nikolai asked.

Alohi looked up. "Of course."

"Are you–" he swallowed, as if the words couldn't come out. "Are you mad? And please don't lie to me, I want to know."

Alohi sighed, setting the bandages on the bed. "Yes, I'm mad. But not at you. I'm mad at the people who made you do this. I'm mad at the people who made life so unbearable that you had to cut."

"So–" Nikolai stammered. "You're mad at my dad."

"Well, yes," Alohi nodded. "But to be fair he's not a very likeable character. I'm mad at the League. I'm mad they put all that pressure on a teenage boy. I'm mad that they made us do their bidding. I'm mad at how incompetent they are." She took a shaky breath. "But to be honest, I'm mostly mad at myself— don't deny it, I know what I did— though I wasn't the original cause, I know I made things worse, and it's really hard to forgive myself for that. Especially when I did it to my *best friend.*"

"I don't blame you," Nikolai said. "You know that right?"

Alohi sighed. "Maybe now, but did you?"

Nikolai bit his lip. "Yes, but I was blind. I was so mad that I directed my rage at you. It was easier to believe that you were the cause rather than–"

"Your dad." Alohi finished. "I get that."

"You know, it's weird. Because even though I knew something was bad, and what he was doing isn't okay, I still loved him." Nikolai sighed. "Their approval is–"

"A drug?" Alohi finished. "Yeah, like a sense of security you've been looking for your entire life has finally been given to you."

Nikolai nodded. "I think I finally broke away when I realized they needed me. They were keeping me with the little praise I got, once I realized I could simply walk away, no one could stop me."

Alohi raised her eyebrows. "No one even tried?"

Nikolai snorted. "I didn't say that. They definitely *tried* to stop me, but they couldn't kill me. Once I realized that, I let my sleeves fall to my elbows and pressed my blades against my neck."

Alohi's mouth dropped. "You weren't actually–"

He shook his head. "No, showing the scars was simply insurance, in case they thought I was bluffing. They were fooled and I walked out of there scot free."

For a moment, Alohi simply looked at him. Then, she smirked. "God, I would pay good money to see Grandez Lone's face."

Nikolai ran his tongue over his teeth. "It was priceless. I'll be running that picture in my head for the rest of my life."

"I would do the same with my dad when I killed him." Alohi gave a harsh cackle. "Though, he didn't exactly have a face."

Suddenly, Nikolai became very quiet. He took a sharp breath. "I should never have told my dad about that. I am so sorry. He fed me sugar coated poison and I just *ate it*!"

"Hey, hey," Alohi laid a hand on his wrist. "I get it. Trust me, I get it. I'm not angry. If anything, I admire you for leaving."

Nikolai growled. "I should have left earlier."

"Me too." Said Alohi. "I should have left before I was elected to the council. Quilla should have left before she was nominated as Leader. That would have minimized the damage. But when push comes to shove, we were just kids. Kids facing enough pain and struggle to kill the average adult. The important thing is we *left*. We got away." She smiled. "That's better than nothing, right?"

"Yeah," Nikolai murmured. "It is."

"Just like getting something on the second try is better than not getting it at all." Alohi picked up the bandage, rewrapping his arms. "And we're going to get this, okay? I'm sorry I wasn't a support for you last time. But this time will be different."

"A do over." Nikolai whispered.

"Yeah," Alohi tied the bandage right below his elbow. "And now, we're going to do it right. I may make mistakes, but I'm going to learn from them. And no matter what, I'm going to be there for you."

Nikolai smiled, dimples forming on his cheeks. A tear rolled from his eye, trickling down his chin. "Come here."

Alohi wrapped her arms around him. They laid in her bed, Nikolai gently stroking her hair. Alohi pressed her face into his chest, smelling his scent. It was unplaceable, not anything she'd experienced apart from with him. It was his. Purely *his*.

"I'm sorry all that happened." Alohi murmured. "It's not fair."

"Well, it happened." Nikolai said. "There's no going back, all you can do is look at the future."

Alohi hugged him tighter. "I don't want the world to break me."

Nikolai sighed. "I think it already has. Us, Quilla, Lilith— hell, even Cercel— we're cracked glass. The only thing we can hope for is that we don't shatter."

"And–" Alohi stammered. "And if we do?"

Nikolai took a breath. "Then the rest of us try to pick up the pieces."

"Would you pick up mine?" Alohi asked.

"Yes," Nikolai said. "Would you?"

"Without hesitation." Alohi murmured. "But I think ultimately it has to be you who puts your pieces back together. Others can help, but it always has to be *you*."

"A full glass can't hold another's wine." Nikolai said.

Alohi chuckled. "Poetic."

"You're not the only one who's a politician."

Alohi sat up. "I missed this."

Nikolai joined her, flinging his feet over the bed. "The talks?"

"Yeah, the in-depth conversations about everything. Fuck, I even missed the arguements. Everything was just— *off* without you."

Nikolai laughed. "I missed you too, Alohi."

Alohi chuckled. "I guess those are the words I'm looking for."

"I'm really dehydrated," Nikolai stood up. "I'm gonna go get some water–"

"Wait–" Alohi grabbed his wrist. "Just a second, okay?"

She stood up, grasping his hands. For a moment, it felt like she was going to say something. But no words were passed, only their breath hung between the two of them.

Then, Nikolai lifted her chin. The last time he touched her face like this, it felt scary. Like a father's praise, it was addicting. But this was different. His grip was soft, his eyes were steady, and his lips weren't moving towards hers.

"Is this okay?" he asked.

"Yes," Alohi breathed.

He leaned in, his lips just inches from hers. They locked eye contact. His gaze was blue, pouring into her like a waterfall rushing into a lake. Her hands moved to his waist, just above his hip bones.

"Is this okay?" she asked, just before her hands landed on his skin.

"Yes," he said, hand gently brushing her jaw.

The warmth of his face touched hers. They were so close, closer than they had ever been. Then, he leaned in.

"Ahem," the notably fake clearing of a throat rang behind them. They sprang apart, hovering on opposite sides of the bed.

"Ah, to be hormonal teenagers." Florian's eyes drifted between them. They snorted. "Definitely don't miss that!"

Alohi rolled her eyes. "What do you want, Florian?"

The pirate shrugged. "So snappy. God, the teenage youth is so irritable." Alohi snarled. "Quilla wants you downstairs." A sleek smile grew on the pirate's features. "The kids got something up her sleeve, I can feel it!"

Florian turned with a triumphant fist in the air. Nikolai and Alohi followed behind them, giving each other skeptical looks.

Chapter Thirty Three
Quilla

"Sit down," Quilla commanded as Alohi, Nikolai and Florian trickled into the room.

"What is it, Quilla?" Nikolai asked.

"We're ending this." She announced. "If we let Cercel stay in power she will burn every last inch of Thine to the ground."

Alohi took a cautious breath. "And you plan to do that how?" she asked. "We know Cercel's mad. But she has an army. You can't argue with pure military strength. She has thousands. We have— well, us."

Quilla tilted her head. "You sure?"

"Me and Quilla have spent the last thirty minutes breaking into every gang leader's office." Lilith announced. Nikolai palmed his face while Florian looked heart wrenchingly left out. "Inside, we left a note telling them about a job with a *massive* prize. We told them to be at the town square by midnight tonight, bringing their entire gang."

Nikolai raised an eyebrow. "So you've gathered two gangs of bloodthirsty criminals in one place. They've been warring with each other since this city began and you think they'll just be at *peace*?"

"Not to mention the fact that you have no job and no prize." Alohi added. "May I remind you, we're broke. I'm failing to see the opportunities in this plan of yours."

"If you would let me finish–" Lilith growled. "I would have explained that there are four gangs, and we do in fact have a job and a prize. Both in one. The fall of the Empire."

Alohi snorted.

Quilla ignored her, continuing where her partner left off. "Since you two are obviously having some doubts, let me connect the dots for you. Why do you think most people are here in the first place? Do you think they just decided they wanted to become cold blooded killers? Do you think *I* wanted to become one?" Nikolai and Alohi gave a curt shake of their heads. "Every thief, every homeless child, every drug lord; they all have something in common. They're hurt. The Empire has taken a once full life and diminished it to nothing more than scattered ashes."

"What does this mean?" Alohi asked.

Quilla gave a sick smile. "It means the people are hungry. It means they have a rage inside them. A *fire*. When every ounce of life is stripped from you, when you've failed too many times to count, everything is too painful to feel. Everything except *rage*. The people of Hanslack need someone to blame. As did you, Alohi. And you, Nikolai. And Florian. And me, and Lilith." Quilla took a breath. "So we all turn on Ghan."

"That doesn't mean anything." Nikolai said. "We've established this. Everyone hates Ghan. But that doesn't change the fact that Cercel has the largest army in the world."

"Nikolai?" Quilla tilted her head. "Do you remember when I explained the organization of the Empire military to you. The organization it needs to work? They require neatness, but it's also the only thing they've ever fought against."

"And the people of Hanslack are disorganized..." Alohi finished, the revelation dawning on her.

Quilla nodded. "These criminals are all self taught. Each's fighting style is different from the rest. A combination of different tactics they've seen on the street."

"The Empire won't stand a chance." Lilith said. "The numbers of Hanslack are almost enough to match the number of Bronze soldiers. Plus the army of the League–"

"How are you going to get the League on our side?" Nikolai interrupted. "They're barely holding themselves together. They don't have the resources to help us, not to mention they're not very fond of us four."

"Correction," Quilla held up a long, pale finger. "The *councilors* aren't fond of you. The people on the other hand..."

"You're a symbol, Nikolai." Lilith explained. "Who was there to fight Cercel? Who is their White King? And Alohi? Who is their political prodigy? Who was always in control of the council room?"

Nikolai and Alohi looked at each other, a matching smile of ambition growing on their features.

Quilla grinned, a powerful glow radiating off her. "Grandez was never in control of the League. The council never had any power. It was always the people. Just like the people of Thine have more power than any Emperor. And you two–" she gestured to Alohi and Nikolai. "Are their symbols. You are the ones who tell them that freedom is possible. You're the ones who convince them of victory. And *you* are the ones that march with them every step of the way."

Alohi and Nikolai exchanged glances. "Fine," Nikolai said. "We'll take the League. But the problem remains, we are going up against the entire might of a criminal infested city. We are five people. You said it yourself, the numbers of all gangs could match the Empire's bronze battalion."

"They have a point, Quilla." Florian admitted. "Gillen and the other gang leaders are the most powerful men in this city. As talented as you are, you are just one person."

"One person," Quilla repeated. "One person who has openly defied the Empire and is still standing. Ghan's heir that turned her back on him. Everyone knows, Florian. It is no secret who I really am. But I'm still standing. I'm still here. That says something."

"Great." Nikolai growled. "We're going against the strongest forces of Hanslack and just expect to *walk* our way out of death."

Quilla licked her teeth. Power flooded her arms, seeping into her chest. The feeling infected her lungs, rose through her throat and embedded itself in her heart. She forgot what true power felt like. The feeling licked her skin like fire, the flames getting brighter by the second. She wanted the blood. She *missed* it.

"Trust me, if anyone opposes me, I will crush their beating heart with my fingers." She squeezed her nails into her palm, imagining the blood dripping down her arm. "Because none of the four gang leaders rule this city." She slammed her fist against the table, the echo thundering through the room. "We do."

Chapter Thirty Four
Cercel

Cercel awoke to a wave of vomit.

She scrambled out of bed and stumbled over herself, trying to get to the toilet.

In the end, she didn't succeed and lurched on the floor.

The bile rose from her throat as she heaved onto the carpet. She was running out of breath. Every time she gasped for air, another round of acid rose from her throat.

When all of the liquid had spewed from her mouth, Cercel coughed up a wad of phlegm. It was as if she was a cat, lurching over an owner attempting to dislodge a stubborn hairball.

"Hello, Empress."

Of fuck.

That voice did *not* come from her head.

Cercel stood, wiping the dripping vomit from her mouth. Her face burned with embarrassment as she saw the several generals standing beside her bed.

"Mor–" Cercel's voice came out jarringly cracked. She cleared her throat, making a second attempt. "Morning, generals."

It took much effort to hide her emerging scowl. These men had been Father's closest advisors. While they were supposed to be used for governing advice, Cercel was certain the bastard used them for emotional support. Most likely to complain about her.

The distaste must have been mutual, because though the general's lips remained civil and professional, their eyes held a steady, burning hate.

"Empress," the furthermost one spoke. He was a large man, a long beard hanging on his covered chin. Lamia and Ezekiel once wagered that he was killing himself with steroids. Cercel silently guessed he passed the time jerking off to Father's voice. The two always seemed unnaturally *close*. "Do you remember what happened last night?"

"Vaguely," Cercel croaked, another round of bile rising up her esophagus.

"Well," he spoke, rubbing the back of his neck. "To recap, you ran into the infirmary, clearly... well..."

"Incapacitated." A small man spoke. He was barely tall enough to reach Cercel's shoulder. His powerful stance reminded her of a screeching chihuahua. "The word you're looking for is incapacitated."

Cercel growled. "Whatever you are getting at, spit it the fuck out."

"For lack of better words, Empress–" The bearded man continued, urging the egotistical dog to continue.

"You are losing it." The chihuahua commented. "We feel that it would be better if someone *else* took over. At least until you get your shit together."

A hand landed on her shoulder. The touch was icy cold; the shivers rattled down her limbs, caressing her sides and consuming her mind.

Rosalie clucked her tongue, letting out a low hum of a cackle. *You know they're right, Cerce.* She licked her sharp fangs. *You've shattered. Who are you to lead a nation? Face it, you will always be in my shadow. Nothing but a failure. Second, Cerce. Always second place.*

Always second place. This time, the voice was deeper. It's cracked accent dripped with manipulative poison. Cercel kept her eyes on the ground, afraid to see the monster standing before her.

Second... Father rolled the word on his tongue like a ball of phlegm. *Third, forth... last? What do you think, Cercel?*

Cercel growled. "I think you need to fucking can it."

Now, Rosalie cooed, moving to stand beside Father. *Is that any way to talk to your elders?*

"I don't respect you!" Cercel spat. "Why should I ever talk to you in any manner other than *disgust*?"

Oh Cercel, Father hummed. *So egotistical, as always. There was a time I thought you would grow out of it but...* He waved a slim finger in her face. *I was wrong. You are, and forever will be, worthless.*

"Shut up!" Cercel screeched, covering her ears. "You're wrong, you're so *wrong*! I am Empress, Rosalie, not you. I imprisoned you, Father. I am in power. I have more power than either of you could've ever *dreamed*!"

And yet? Rosalie's glacial hands folded over her wrists, pulling them from her ears. *That supposed ethereal power is about to be stripped from you. Come now, Cerce, do you really think we're real? We're simply figures of your mind, here to torment and punish you.*

But your words are real. Father added. *Those generals? They hear everything you say. Yet they have no idea who you're talking to. Wake the fuck up Cercel. They're right. You're losing it.*

"Shut *up*!" Cercel flung forward, fist plummeting towards Rosalie's misty face. But instead of settling for the impact, Rosalie drifted into the air, fading from existence.

But her fist found something else to hit.

The bearded general recoiled in pain, clutching his red cheek. His friend rushed to his side, anger consuming his features.

"Look what you've–" Cercel assumed the chihuahua was trying to sound intimidating. However, as soon as the high spat of a cackle slipped off her tongue, he shut his mouth.

"Oh, look at you." Cercel grinned, running her bandaged hand through her hair. "You are so *stupid* to believe you have any right to talk to me! I suppose you have forgotten, blood nor favor binds me to your old Emperor. I am new. A new era. Father appointed you, yet I would slit your throat just as easily." Cercel turned to her bed. "Now, in case I have to remind you, I never invited you to my quarters in the first place. So if you may, get *out*."

"Cercel–" the man with the beard interjected. "We are simply worried for the fate of the nation."

"Well don't be," Cercel retorted. "It's my responsibility. It's also my choice who I bare it with." Her hand wavered to the nightstand. There, her fingers found the cold metal of a blade. She picked up the star, weaving it between her fingers. "And I choose to bear it *alone*."

For a second, the generals simply gazed at her. Their faces were blank, nothing but pure disbelief glittering in their gaze. Then they filtered out of her room. No one dared look her in the eye, no one even glanced.

They were afraid.

Cercel grinned. She liked it when people feared her.

Once the fearful, now the feared. Rosalie's crisp accent rang. *Once the tormented, now the tormentor. Feast on their terror, Cerce. Live off your vengeance. Savor it, crave more. This is who you are. Who you were always destined to be. Ever since you rose from that rubble, ever since Rosalie left you. Taste the blood on your hands, savor the feeling of a dying heart. You are your kills, Cerce. You are your revenge, and you are your pain.*

"I am feared," Cercel mumbled.

Yes! Rosalie chanted. *Let the fear crawl up your limbs. Let it sink into your heart. Let vengeance consume you!*

Cercel collapsed on the bed. She felt the fire of hate. It flickered, licking the sides of her skin. The flame thundered through her body, caressing the beating organ that was her heart. This feeling was her puppeteer. It controlled her actions with invisible strings of criticism. It was her captor.

And yet?

The rage was the only reason she lived.

Chapter Thirty Five
Lilith

The first stage of Quilla's plan was getting the four major gangs of Hanslack to gather in the town square. Of course, there were other smaller assemblies of criminals. But they were much too minor to care about.

The second step was for Alohi and Nikolai to filter in with the groups Quilla predicted would cause the most trouble. This was of course the Stripes and the Serpents. Quilla wanted to make sure Gillen didn't attempt anything. Her solution? Assign Nikolai to stand as close to him as possible.

"The fuck do you mean, *guard him*?" the swordsman growled when Quilla broke the news. "So I'm just babysitting?"

"Stop complaining," Quilla hissed. "You'll get a front row seat. Now shut up and listen. I'm not done."

The third level of the scheme was for Lilith to fire an arrow with a rose stuck to its point into the water fountain below. This part seemed a bit excessive. After all, they were giving away the precise location of their archer for only a symbol. But Quilla insisted.

"They need to know who it is by a trait they recognize. I'm not trying to surprise them, simply talk to them. However, the rose is something to fear. If this is going to work, they need to be equal parts threatened and civil." Quilla explained when Lilith expressed her clear distaste for the stage.

Nevertheless, Lilith had learned to trust her partner. Though her methods were... *unusual* to say the least, they worked. Lilth didn't trifle.

That was why she was stationed atop one of the many crooked buildings of Hanslack, overlooking the crowded square. One by one the gangs filtered in. First, the Hallucinogens. Though the name suggested they would constantly be high, the gang was surprisingly good at what they did. Getting others high.

Next were the Fouls, the Hallucinegen's main marketing target. Each one's gaze wandered around the square, searching for something that wasn't a drug induced image.

The Stripes followed them. Lilith immediately recognized Alohi's posture, mostly because it seemed to shrink amongst the other members. She stood alongside what Lilith assumed was a small boy. But he didn't look small, he looked powerful. *Dangerous.*

And finally, there were the Serpents. Once the weakest gang in the city, Gillen strode to the square with his head high. In the span of five years the Serpents had gone from watered down liquor to rich, aged wine and blades sharper than their seventeen year old murder prodigy.

Nikolai followed close behind the gang lord. His swords were strapped to his back and a dark hood concealed his face. Nonetheless, Lilith was sure it was him simply because of his posture. Much straighter, much more professional.

She let the gangs gather. Their eyes wandered around the square, realizing that the only job present was to watch the spectacle. She loaded her bow, nudging the rose stem deeper into the tip.

"Let them settle." Quilla had explained before the two parted. "I want you to shoot the silver lining. When they first get there, they'll be confused. In around ten seconds, that confusion will turn to bloodlust, and they'll be displaying each other's heads on pikes. The moment between that, you fire."

Lilith released her bowstring. The arrow flew through the air, rose clinging tightly to its tip. With a thud, the weapon planted itself in the water fountain below.

It took three seconds for everyone to realize what happened.

And by that time, Quilla had captured the crowd.

First, it was the click of heels echoing in the night. Then, the dark shifted to reveal a hooded figure. Her pace was long, confident, and drawing the eyes of every thug in the square. The crowd parted, watching as the woman strode to the fountain.

The click silenced as her coat wavered at her knees. She tipped her hood back, letting her long curls fall behind her back. She placed her hands on her hips, a sly grin touching her face.

"Hey," Quilla blew a stray lock from her face. "Did you miss me?"

For a moment, only the slight echo of Quilla's words hung in the air.

Then, shouts.

Anger, pain, confusion. But mostly– mostly death threats.

Lilith loaded her grappling arrow. She fired the weapon into a plank beside Quilla, looped her bow over the string, and leapt out of the window. She slid down the rope, landing next to her partner and tucking her bow behind her back.

The square silenced for Lilith's entrance. Just for a moment, there was stunned peace. When they recognized who she was, double the insults rained on them.

At first, Lilith couldn't pinpoint where the cackle rose from. Amongst the shouting, it was prominent. However, there were so many people in the square Lilith couldn't possibly identify the tongue that spat the chortle. But as the laugh grew louder and the crowd's screech halted, the air parted for Gillen's cackle to take the reins of sound.

"Oh, Quilla," Gillen stood a couple feet away from them. His grey hair continued to retreat up his scalp and wrinkles littered his face. He was old, sure. But underneath the appearance of an old man, there was a manipulative, power hungry monster. "You stupid little girl. You've cornered yourself in the center of hundreds of cruel criminals. You can't get out of this, little heir, no fucking chance."

For a moment, Quilla's eyes glistened. The slightest glimmer of vulnerability crossed her gaze, barely noticeable. Then, she smiled.

"Hm," Quilla hummed a chuckle. "That's the thing, Gillen, I'm not trying to get out of this. I'm done running. I'm done being on a leash in the city I own."

To this, Gillen responded with a cracked laugh. "You don't own this city, Quilla. You are a part of it. I took you in, I own *you*. This city, these thugs, they're the only reason you're still alive. You may be the queen of this chess board, but me– I'm the player."

"No," Quilla shook her head. "We're all pieces in chess. We're all the pawns, destined to die before making it halfway across the board. You and I, Gillen, we've never been the players."

"Oh?" the leader of the Hallucinogens chimed. She was an older woman, neon hair mixing with her greys. Jewels littered her long, extravagant coat, most likely bought with opiate money. "And in this analogy, who controls us?"

Quilla tilted her head. "Isn't it obvious?" the pitch of her voice raised to a level of simple question. "The Empire."

No one had a response.

"The Empire has been our puppeteers for years." Lilith spoke. "Think, how did you get here? Who put you in the city where thieves rot? We may have different versions, but when it's all boiled down, we share the same story." She took a breath. "We were wronged by the Empire, and the constant yearn for vengeance keeps us alive."

"So let me ask you this," Quilla stepped forward. "Do you want to let this city eat away at your bones, or do you want to take action? Would you like to sit here like ducks, waiting for Cercel to sink her teeth into your asses, or are you going to be on the offensive?"

"Who are you to talk?" Gillen growled. "We know who you are, Rosalie Ghan. Your face is plastered on this city's walls with the description of the Golden Heir. You aren't one of us, you're a fucking princess, Ghan's favorite. Don't pretend like we've ever played the same game."

Quilla let his words resonate. She seemed to roll the phrase on her tongue, running the words along her teeth. She breathed a sigh, Gillen's words coming out like smoke.

"Are we really that different?" Quilla cocked her head. "Ghan destroyed my home, my *family*. He may have called me his daughter, but when push comes to shove, I was nothing more than a weapon. But that weapon backfired. I defected, ran to this city, and became the most notorious failure the Empire has ever seen."

Gillen snorted. "Cocky, Quilla." He grinned. "You think your past defines you in any way other than weakness? Please, go ahead and demonstrate. Show us the most powerful *defect* in Thinian history."

Quilla smiled, her tongue tracing her fanged teeth with bloody, malicious intent. She gave the gentle wave of her palm, so discreet only Lilith could notice. Before anyone could stop her, Lilith pulled up her hood and slipped into the crowd, blending into the mass of thugs and thieves surrounding the criminal prodigy.

Quilla cackled, the sound low and cracked. "You were right about one thing, Gillen." She hummed, her voice low and dangerous. "This city is a game, but if you think you can play it better than me—" she drew her knives. "You are *sorely* mistaken."

For a moment, Quilla's words echoed through the square.

Then, Gillen clapped.

And a wave of criminals charged at her.

They came from all angles, blades drawn by their sides. Lilith rushed forwards, only to feel a hand on her shoulder.

She turned to gaze into Nikolai's ice blue eyes.

"She doesn't want you out there," he said, eyes alert. "This is her fight."

She jolted out of his grasp. "She's not the only one who owns this city," she growled. "Fuck her dramatics, this is my fight too."

With that, she charged into battle. She drew her arrows, and with a creative use of elbows, Lilith barged into the crowd. She found Quilla surrounded by several men, flinging her blades at an inhuman speed.

Behind her, a man raised his knife. Lilith acted on instinct, thrusting an arrow into his throat. The man gurgled, blood spewing from his gasping mouth. He crumpled to the ground, clawing at his dripping neck.

"Didn't I tell you not to follow me?" Quilla asked, not even trying to cover her grin.

"I've never been one for orders." Lilith laughed, backing up against her partner. "Never should've assumed anything different."

"Oh trust me," Quilla thrust her blade into the attacker's stomach. The blood flew from his wound, splattering her face in a crimson glitter. "I was counting on your defiance."

More thieves came at them, knives flying towards their throats. They moved in sink; while one attacked, the other one defended. While one made a move to the right, the other covered the left.

"Lilith!" Quilla called as a man with a dozen blades charged towards them.

"On it!" Lilith drew her bow, twirling it as Quilla taught her. The blades rested in its wood, sticking like an arrow does to a beating heart.

"Quilla, ammo!" Lilith screeched, placing her bow on her back for Quilla to pluck from.

She obliged. In fact, the criminal prodigy was quite pleased with the new opportunity. She smiled, grabbed the blades, and disappeared into the crowd.

As she ran, Lilith drew her arrows. A man charged at her; Lilith ran the arrow down his torso, spilling his organs in a bloody mess. A fraction of a second later, a thief slammed into her. She doubled forward, gasping for air. She held up an arrow, turning and impaling the man in the throat.

A third charged from behind. A fourth stumbled from the side. A fifth ran from the crowd. Lilith raised her foot, her boot landing in a chest. She flung her arrow into an incoming face. The bone held restraint, crunching as Lilith twisted her arrow deeper into the flesh. A crunch, a squirt of blood coating her skin, and a soft interior; she hit the brain.

Lilith gasped as a foot landed in the crook of her knee. Her leg twisted inward and a sharp pain shot through her thigh. She hit the concrete and raised her arrows in defense.

A man stood over her, blood drenching his wrinkled clothes. No, not just a man. Polar Zinglor.

Polar *fucking* Zinglor.

He raised a knife, vengeance burning in his black gaze.

Lilith brought her injured leg between his legs. Zinglor faltered, loosening his grip on his knife. With all her strength, Lilith flung herself forward. She pushed her arrow into his stomach, twisting around his ribs.

Zinglor doubled over, coughing as blood rose from his throat. Lilith slammed the arrow deeper, pushing its tip into his spine. Instead of the vengeful glare he once held, his gazed gleamed with despair.

He wanted her to pull the arrow out. He wanted to die quickly.

Fat *fucking* chance.

Lilith spat a wad of blood stained phlegm and slammed the arrow deeper. There was a loud crack; the spine had snapped.

The man hollered and doubled over.

But Lilith wasn't done.

She grabbed his chin, forcing him to lock eyes with her. His droopy gaze faltered, but he saw her.

"Look at me– *no*, look at *me*!" Lilith growled. "You may not remember me, but I remember *you*! I made a promise long, *long* ago that I would kill you! That my eyes would be the last thing you ever saw– *keep looking*– and that *I* would kill you. And it would be *painful*!"

Zinglor's eyes lingered on her. He opened his mouth to murmur something, but Lilith didn't try to decipher it. He was alive– that was all she knew– that was enough. The last thing she saw was her. Her *winning*!

She released him, watching as he fell to the floor, his own blood pooling around him. The red circled around her knees, drenching her pants. For a moment, it was only her and the corpse.

Then she was thrust back into reality. The battle resumed, blood painted the stairs like a crimson rug, and Quilla impaled people around her, guarding Lilith and Zinglor's body.

"Don't try to get up." Quilla stabbed a man charging at her. "You're hurt."

"I'm not–" Lilith started, then looked around. The battle had dwindled. The once endless crowd had become nothing more than a trickle of men.

Quilla threw a knife. The blade landed in a thieves chest and he crumpled to the ground. Quilla strode to Lilith offering her a hand.

"Don't put any weight on your leg." Quilla whispered, pulling her up. "I'm worried it's sprained."

Lilith took a shaky breath, scratching at the blood on her hands. "I didn't really know that was possible."

Instead of responding, Quilla clutched her hand. She weaved her bloodied fingers through Lilith's, and thrust their arms in the air.

"Well?" Quilla spat. "Who else?"

The men staggered back into the safety of the crowd. Fear lingered in the air. Lilith licked her bloodied lips. The terror the crowd's eyes was a stark contrast from when she first came to Hanslack. Back then, she was the one that was scared. Now, it was them who trembled in her presence.

"Here's a peak," Lilith said, clutching tightly to Quilla's hand. "We came here as nothing. Me? An orphaned slave girl with nothing but a yearn for a better life."

"And me?" Quilla continued. "Just another stray to die on these streets."

"Except we didn't!" Lilith screeched. "We survived. Through blood, spit, and grime, we became royalty in this city. We went from uncountable aspects to favorable contenders in this sick, blood filled game. And now–" Lilith spit on the ground. "We've won."

For a moment, there was only silence. Then, someone spoke.

"I don't care how powerful you are," Lilith turned to find a boy. His black hair hung loosely at his shoulders. He wore a coat that was clearly three sizes too big and a vengeful expression that– unfortunately– fit him perfectly.

"You killed my father," the boy continued, not a waver in his voice. "I would rather *die* than do what you want."

For a moment, Quilla's glare rested, prepared for another fight. Then, her eyes softened. She tilted her head, looking at the boy with a strange glimmer in her gaze. She let go of Lilith's hand, striding to the boy.

Their eyes met; his filled with anger, and Quilla's... filled with grief.

That's when Lilith understood.

She was looking in a mirror.

Quilla took off her coat, the fabric clinking with the blades inside. She dropped it to the ground, kicking it away. She grabbed a knife from her boot– the boy tensed– then she extended it, blade towards herself.

"Go on," Quilla tilted her head. "Kill me."

The boy snatched the blade, advancing on her.

"Come on," Quilla wasn't taunting, simply speaking. "I know you want to. This is what you've dreamed of, right? Sticking that blade in my throat? Ever since you were given control of the gang? You *want* to end me." Quilla raised her hands. "Go on, do it."

The boy let out a screech. He lunged at her, blade raised above his head.

Lilith tensed.

The boy held the knife over Quilla's throat. He sobbed, tears pouring down his face. Quilla, however, was calm. She gazed at the boy with understanding; they were a mirror reflection; cause and effect; past, present, and future.

Quilla lowered the boy's shaky hand from her throat. They gazed at each other– the previous rage absent.

"Olan, right?" Quilla's voice was so soft. "He killed my men, so I killed him, so you vowed to kill me. If you ended my life, then Lilith would kill you, and your men would kill her. It just goes on. One death after another. Another hurt bird caged by vengeance. And who wins?" Quilla stood, her voice echoing around the square. "The Empire. Always the *Empire*.

"I'm sorry about your dad," Quilla knelt next to the boy. "There's no excuse for what I did, there's no way I can make it right. But you–" she brushed the tears sliding down the boy's face. "You can be better than all of us. You can stop. Walk away. It takes strength, yes. Strength that I never had. But you are so, so strong–"

The boy flung himself into Quilla's arms. He buried his face in her chest, wrapping his arms around her torso. Quilla put her hand in his messy hair, stroking his head.

Everyone was silent. Too baffled to say anything. Too stunned to speak.

Until finally, Quilla stood. She laced her fingers with the boy, gazing at the crowd with fierce determination.

"I'm tired." Quilla growled. "I'm *tired* of being stuck in a game where no one wins. I'm *tired* of doing the Empire's dirty work. I'm *tired* of killing my kin just for a cycle. So I'm done. I'm not killing anyone else. The next person I raise my blades to will be the Empress."

For a moment, Lilith thought it would be that easy. She thought Quilla had won. Until she heard the rough, old cackle.

"Quilla," Gillen exclaimed. "You've never been a part of this game. You're fucking Rosalie Ghan! The Emperor's *daughter*. I think I speak for everyone when I say that I will not bow to any bastard who resides within Ghan's quarters."

Quilla tilted her head, looking at her former father with mild curiosity. "But I'm not Rosalie Ghan. I killed her when you found me holding that knife to my throat, so many years ago. I'm Quilla Thorne, the self made criminal prodigy, wrath and Hanslack and queen of con." She smiled, showing her bared, blood soaked teeth. Quilla could switch so seamlessly from kind to dangerous. She was an actor. These streets were her stage. "You don't have to like me. Fuck, I would wager quite a bit of money that very few of you do. But that doesn't change the fact that no matter how much you *despise* my existence; no matter how many times you've imagined dragging a blade through my stomach, you hate one person more." Quilla took a breath, a triumphant grin touching her bloodied lips. "Because I'm not the person who put you here. We all have one thing in common. The Empire dug this grave and buried us in it. The question is–" she licked her teeth, straightening her posture. "Are you going to keep turning in the mud, or are you going to climb *out*?"

For a moment, there was silence; the last syllable of Quilla's words ringing around the square.

Then, Olan's son got down on one knee, dipping his head in respect.

The stripes followed, lowering into a bow. Then it was the Hallucinogens, then the Fouls, and finally, one by one, the Serpent's lowered into a bow. Ily and Greg, anyone who Quilla had ever commanded. Then the ones she didn't like, the ones who were jealous of her power. Lilith recognized the people who laughed at her, calling her a defect. Now, they bowed in respect, heads dipped to the notorious criminal prodigy of Hanslack.

And last, there was Gillen, a hateful stare centered on the woman he used to call his daughter. Quilla tilted her head, eyes filled with a blank expression.

Gillen looked around, frantic. His eyes wandered around the square, desperate to find someone who wasn't complying. He was pleading for a victory.

Quilla pleaded to him once. It didn't work out for her.

Finally, his expression shifted into one of deep regret. Slowly, he lowered himself to the ground, dipping into a low bow.

Quilla looked around, disbelief shining on her face. Her eyes wandered around the square. Every single man, woman and child in this square saluted her. Every single person who tried to kill her, laughed at her, abused her, was kneeling.

She united the city of endless civil warfare.

Lilith limped beside her, grasping her hand. They held each other tightly, fingers intertwined. They locked eye contact, each gaze powerful and triumphant.

Then they thrust their fists in the air. They held each other's hands towards the sky, gazing at the stars of the night.

And one by one, the people of Hanslack rose. They interlocked hands, Hallucinogens with Fouls, Fouls with Stripes, Stripes with Serpents, and Serpents with Hallucinogens.

Then, with one united movement, they pumped their fists in the air.

Once a forever rival city.

United as one.

Chapter Thirty Six
Quilla

"Quilla–" Lilith raised an eyebrow as her partner ran her fingers down her knee. "Seriously, it's fine. It doesn't hurt."

"That's the thing," Quilla kept her eyes on the leg. "If it's the sprain I think it is, it wouldn't hurt. Did you hear a pop? Is your knee unstable, how–"

"Slow down," Lilith sighed, gazing at the ceiling. "Just– let me rest."

Quilla made a final, pleading glance at her knee, and sat beside Lilith on the bed.

They were back in the Link, a location that felt surreal. Surrounding them were the walls of Quilla's old bedroom. Everything was exactly how she left it. A neat, made bed. A desk scattered with papers and pens. And a window, cracked just slightly open.

Lilith laid down, resting her head on the pillow. "Do you miss it?"

"Miss what–" Quilla wrinkled her nose. "You're getting blood on my sheets."

Lilith gave the smallest quirk of her lips. "It's not mine."

Quilla stood, grabbed a cloth, and stuck it out the window, into the downpour of rain. With the damp rag, she took Lilith's hands and wiped the crimson stain.

Lilith let her, watching the blood wearily. "So, do you miss it?"

"Hanslack?" Quilla asked. "Or the Link?"

"Both."

Quilla sighed. "Some parts. I miss going on little missions with you, when everything was so– *far*. But I don't miss Gillen, or the rivalries– those were both chores."

"*Far?*" Lilith asked. "What do you mean?"

"Well," Quilla took a breath. "It was almost better when I thought Cercel was dead. It was so clear– I hated Ghan, I loved my siblings. But now, my family is–" her voice cracked. "Gone. Ghan rolled over like a puppy, and Cercel's the one I have to–" Quilla swallowed. "*Kill.*"

Lilith laid a hand on her shoulder. "If it makes it easier, I can do it."

Quilla raised an eyebrow. "Do what?"

"Kill Cercel." She said, "It won't be hard. You distract her and I put an arrow into her throat."

Quilla shook her head. "No. It has to be me. I need to give her that mercy. If she dies, at least she dies trying to do the thing she lived for. Killing me."

Lilith bit the inside of her cheek. "And then?"

Quilla raised an eyebrow. "What?"

"What happens after we kill her?" Lilith asked. "Will you take over? Will it be Nikolai? Or Grandez?"

Quilla shook her head. "I'd be fine with Nikolai, but if that bloodsucking hound of a father ever spits poison in his ear, I'm going to spit poison in his coffee."

"Hm," Lilith chuckled. "So we do have a plan. We appoint a ruler and if we don't like them, we assassinate."

"Seems like a pretty sound system of checks and balances." Quilla grinned. "In all seriousness, I don't trifle with politics. That's Alohi's job. If we win, I'm going to find a nice little band of immoral rich kids and shit on their parade."

Lilith laughed. "Sounds like a wonderful retirement."

"In the meantime," Quilla said. "It's almost morning. I need to make sure the gangs are ready for departure. I want to leave at ten."

"Where are we going?" Lilith asked. "The League isn't exactly *intact*."

Quilla tilted her head. "Yes it is. All the important parts are. The people, the soldiers. Let's be honest, all those wanna-be-tyrants are nothing more than nuisances."

"How do you know they aren't there?" Lilith asked. "You know, the executives."

Quilla huffed a laugh. "You really think they could stand to walk more than a mile to find their people?" she snorted. "And if they do happen to meet us there, Alohi and Nikolai will just prove they are the best of their kind– a matter which shouldn't be hard– and take over the League. If that doesn't work–" Quilla ran a delicate hand over Lilith's arrow. "We'll have to fall back on *other* methods."

Lilith grinned. "Is it wrong I'm hoping for the latter?"

"Oh I'm praying for the same thing."

There was a knock on the door. Quilla turned, opening it to reveal Florian standing before them. The pirate's hands were clasped at their waist, tangled locks falling at their chest.

"Kiwi," Florian started. "May I talk with you?"

Quilla furrowed her brow, worry creasing her expression. "Of course," she tilted her head. "Is everything okay?"

"Oh fine," Florian snorted. "I just thought I should tell you something."

Quilla snuck a glance at Lilith, who nodded. The archer picked herself up from the bed and strode from the room.

"Sit down," Quilla gestured to the bed. "What's up?"

Florian sat on the matress, leg bouncing restlessly on the floor. "Look, Quilla. I can't imagine any of that was easy for you. Honestly, I don't think any grown man could accomplish what you have in their entire life time– but you've done it in seventeen years. You escaped Ghan–" Quilla took a breath, a thunderous downpour of emotions raining in her mind. "Survived Hanslack– no not survived– *thrived*. You joined the League and made the organization, well– far less shitty." Quilla let out a choked chuckle. "And you united Hanslack. I guess I'm going on a tangent, but you should know, Kiwi–" Florian turned to her, sea green eyes glittering with tears. "I am so, *so* proud of you."

She didn't know why. She had no idea why the tears started coming. It was as if they were triggered, like a dam breaking. But once they formed in her eyes, there was no stopping them. They trickled down her cheek, curling around her chin and dripping lazily onto her blouse.

"Florian–" she choked. "Please, *please* tell me you mean that."

Florian's face softened, their own eyes welling with tears. "Of course I mean it, Quilla. Why wouldn't I?"

Quilla's head swam with possible motives. What was this? What were they using her for? It could be political leverage; a power trip over the criminals. But that wouldn't make sense– Florian had their own gang of pirates, and if they wanted the criminals of Hanslack, they could simply take them by force.

It could be to get an alliance— but that wouldn't make sense. Quilla wasn't close to anyone who would be of importance to the pirate. For all the alliances she made, Florian held stronger ones.

"Why are you playing with me?" Quilla snapped. "If you want something, you could just ask. You don't have to play with my emotions."

Florian looked taken aback. "That's not what I was doing."

"Oh?" Quilla wiped the previous tears from her face, contorting her expression into a scowl. "Then what the *fuck* were you doing?"

"Giving you a fucking compliment!" Florian threw up their hands. "Expressing my pride, my *admiration*! People can just do that, you know."

This time, it was Quilla's turn to stagger back. She gazed at him, eyes filled with confusion. She bit her lip, her glare slowly softening into a simple stare.

"Not in my experience." Quilla murmured. "They always want something."

"Oh," Florian laid a cautious hand on Quilla's. Their touch was gentle, soft. In all honesty, she wasn't sure what to do with it. "Okay, well let's put it like this. You have an army, I have an army. You are a skilled fighter, I'm a skilled fighter. I'm not one for emotional manipulation, Kiwi. Not my personal style. If I want something I'll write you a check or threaten you. But personally, I believe in honesty, especially when it comes to someone I admire and care about, *deeply*."

Quilla blinked. A tear spilled from her face, trickling over her chin. "I want to believe you, Florian, I really do."

"But it's hard." Florian said. "I get it, really I do. I can't imagine Ghan was kind. I don't believe Gillen was at all good. You have every reason not to trust me. But please Quilla, just take a leap of faith."

Faith. That's all they were asking for. What was so hard about that?

"One reason, Florian." Quilla said. "If you can show me one thing, give me one reason why you won't betray me, I'll trust you."

Florian smiled. With a heavily jeweled hand, they drew a necklace from their pocket. The thing looked as if a treasure chest threw up on it. Green, red, purple— about every color you could imagine— glimmered off the gold. In the center of the chain was a massive, obnoxious diamond.

Quilla wrinkled her nose. "And the rock puke matters... why?"

Florian waved the necklace in her face. "This is a very important jewel!"

"Ah, do pirates treasure all pieces of rock waste?"

"It's not rock waste." Florian snapped. "It symbolizes the entire might and history of the Pirates of Salenian! Leaders link their jewels to the chain. The large pendant is from our founder– Fezil Handle. Since then it's been passed down for centuries. If anyone else is found with the chain, they are now the leader, and the pirates must submit full loyalty to them. A leader must lay down their life before they allow the chain to fall into the wrong hands."

Quilla gazed at the jewel. The diamond wavered back and forth, light reflecting off its edges.

"My point is–" Florian continued. "I'm not even supposed to let you see this. If anyone found out about this encounter, I'd be tossed into the ocean for treason." Without hesitation, they tossed the chain into Quilla's hands. "Why don't you hold onto it for me?"

Quilla's eyes widened. "Florian I couldn't possibly–"

"Yes you could," the pirate tilted their head. "This way, if I betray you, you could kill me with only a few words. Consider it the insurance of our friendship."

"But–" Quilla stammered. "This is passed down for *generations*–"

"Yeah, I was never big on family traditions. Or heirlooms. When push comes to shove–" Florian grinned. "It really is just rock vomit."

Chapter Thirty Seven
Nikolai

If Nikolai had any hope for the League, it vanished as soon as he got Killen's letter.

"Why the fuck would they go back?" he exclaimed to Alohi, clutching the crumpled paper in his hand. "Camp Fifty is nothing more than a smoked out gopher hole! They'd have better luck simply waltzing into Brighan!"

Alohi shrugged. "The League gave them a home. Perhaps their loyalty prevents them from leaving."

Nikolai snorted. "I don't understand why anyone would ever have loyalty to my dad." He dug his nails into the taffrail. "He's a tyrannical political whore with nothing on his mind but power."

Alohi laid her hand on his. Quilla's massive fleet had set sail barely an hour ago, and Nikolai was already growing bored. While the massive parade of ships was impressive, after a while, the spectacle wore off. Nikolai was left gazing past the sea of stolen merchant boats and into the open ocean. The sea, though familiar, had grown exhausting. He found himself hoping that every passing cloud was the shores of Woodran.

"Your dad, though an asshole, is actually quite good at hiding his immorality." Alohi said. "And the people of the League are- for lack of better words- idiots. It's no wonder they follow Grandez's command like dogs."

Nikolai shook his head. "They're not idiots, they're followers. They know they won't survive on their own, so they go to the place where they have the most power." He growled. "My father's slimy clutches."

"Well," Alohi gave him a sly smile. "The bright side is, between you and me, it won't be hard to convince them Grandez is nothing more than a tyrannical, power hungry, less smart version of Ghan."

"And if you can't–" there was a thud behind them, followed by a second crash. "We'll be there to make the job more... *permanent.*"

Nikolai turned, head falling back in exasperation. "Aren't you two supposed to be at the front of the fleet?"

Quilla and Lilith had swung in from the surrounding ships. Stray ropes wavered over the ocean, gently blowing in the wind. Lilith stood on the deck, a smile gleaming on her face. Surprisingly, it was Quilla who crash landed. The criminal prodigy stood behind her partner, brushing off her tattered pants.

Alohi snorted. "Nice necklace, Quilla,"

The criminal prodigy growled, tucking the obnoxious chain into her blouse.

"Leading the fleet is boring." Lilith waved a hand. "Besides, all the gang leaders are up there, and those guys are *awful* to talk to."

"And they aren't exactly fond of us," Quilla added.

Lilith grinned. "Something about taking all their power. God, people can really hold a grudge these days."

Nikolai cracked a smile. "And you decided to come to this ship, why? It's not exactly eventful back here."

"There's always an event when you two are talking to each other," Quilla commented. "Besides, we have a plan to make."

"Oh?" Alohi raised an eyebrow. "I thought we already had our plan. You know, get Grandez in front of an audience and humiliate him? I thought that was unspoken."

Lilith wrinkled her nose. "You're way over simplifying it." She said, "Yes, that is the plan, but there needs to be a lot more thought put into it. How will we get in, how are we going to get Grandez in front of an audience? That stuff."

"Easy," Nikolai said. "We come in hooded, catch my father during an important council meeting, and then me and Alohi combat his tyrannical bloodthirst with citations of abuse and idiocy."

Quilla and Lilith looked at each other. Given the mischievous looks growing on their faces, Nikolai could tell he was about to be humiliated.

"Wrong," Quilla waved a finger. "First, it won't do us any good to convince a couple boring councilmembers. We need to convey the soldiers. The ones that really do the League's bidding. Second, if we march in there with veils covering our faces, that sends a message of fear, that we don't belong. But in reality, Nikolai, this is your home, your *power.*"

"So what?" Alohi snapped. "We just stride in there like we own the place? We'll be ambushed in seconds!"

Quilla grinned. "Exactly."

"As soon as we enter, we'll be swarmed. Of course, we fight them off, but we don't kill." Lilith said. "That solves two of our problems, a confident entrance and a crowd of the appropriate audience."

"So our plan is just to stride in with nothing but our wits?" Alohi snorted, clear skepticism wrinkling her features.

"Basically," Quilla smiled, laying a hand on Alohi's shoulder. "But don't worry, it's more fun than it sounds."

"I'm sure," Alohi growled.

They leaned against the taffrail, gazing into the ocean. The choppy waves slapped the boat with ferocity. The blue seemed to stretch forever, a never ending field of water. Once, this kind of thing comforted Nikolai– it was a place to hide.

But now– now he had nothing to hide from. The itch for vengeance had taken over. He wanted control, he wanted everyone to see what kind of man his father was. The everlasting calm of the open ocean did nothing more than infuriate him.

"Look!" Lilith exclaimed, pointing to the faded horizon. "Land!"

Sure enough, they were approaching the forested shores of Woodran. The smallest dots of trees traced the beaches. Waves crashed against the sand, creating white tints in the water. Nikolai dug his nails into the taffrail: no matter how boring the sea was, land always brought fear.

"Ugh," Quilla threw her head back. "I promised Gillen I'd be back as soon as we saw land."

Lilith drew a sigh. "Don't you think they can at least handle the task of docking?"

Quilla snorted. "Are you kidding? Gillen needs me to wipe his own ass."

Alohi laughed. "I can't imagine how he managed without you."

"Honestly," Nikolai picked at his cuticles, a grin peeling back his lips. "I'd be more worried about his genitals."

Lilith wrinkled her nose. "Disgusting, Nikolai."

"I really don't want to imagine it." Quilla drawled, repulsed. "Thanks, Nikolai."

"My pleasure."

"We should go, Quill," Lilith said. "Don't want to make them hate us more than they already do."

Quilla grinned. "But that's the best part!"

Lilith flashed a smile. With that, the two criminals stood on the taffrail and leapt to the ropes. For a moment, Nikolai was convinced they would plummet into the water. That was until he saw their silhouettes soaring above the waves, leaping onto the next ship.

Alohi chuckled, resting her face in her palm. Instead of her once tight bun, her hair was woven into several small braids. They hung over her shoulder, wind blowing the stray strands. The blue of the ocean reflected off her even bluer eyes. She looked so *different*.

"Do you miss it?" Alohi asked. "You know, the League?"

Nikolai placed his chin on his palm. "Of course not." He snorted. "It was awful."

"It was," Alohi amended. "But there must have been some good parts."

Nikolai shook his head. "Not after you left, not at all." He lowered his gaze. "I turned off, snapped. The only thing I could feel was anger, that was the only thing safe to feel. I was... *cutting* everyday." He chuckled. "Still hard to say."

"That sounds..." Alohi took a breath. "*Awful.*"

Nikolai shrugged. "Most of the time, I was high on my own blood. So honestly, I wasn't present much. The worst times were when I was with my dad or..."

"Or?" Alohi asked. "You don't have too–"

"No it's okay." Nikolai took a breath. "I hurt the people I love. That was the worst part. Killen tried to check in on me, and I laughed at him. I was more worried about preserving my secret than preserving a healthy relationship," he scoffed. "Probably the only healthy one I had left."

For a moment, the only sound between them was the ocean wind.

"You know he doesn't hold it against you, right?" Alohi asked.

"How do you know?" Nikolai rubbed his temples. "You weren't there."

"No," Alohi said. "But I know Killen. He's smart and he cares about you, Nikolai. He'll understand. Besides–" she gazed at the incoming land. "You'll have a chance to explain."

"Yeah," Nikolai smiled, a new ambition shining in his gaze. "I will."

"And–" Alohi grinned, her smile one of mischief. "You get to show everyone who your father really is."

Nikolai matched her expression. "That will be rewarding." He ran his hand through his hair. "And you? This is just as much your battle as it is mine. Aren't you excited to take the council that's always been yours."

For a moment, Alohi's eyes fixed solely on the ocean. Nikolai watched them change, her blue gaze shifting into one of dark, deep thoughts.

"No," she drawled. "No. I'm doing this only because I want to win. There's–" she swallowed, turning towards the deck. "There's nothing for me there."

~~~

"Here we are!" Quilla exclaimed as the four of them leaped off the ship. The criminals had joined them shortly before the fleet docked. The two seemed overly eager to be around them at all times, as if at any moment, a show could to start.
~~~

"So," Lilith started. The grin plastered on her face made Nikolai nervous. "You miss it? Home sweet home, Nikolai."

Nikolai groaned. "Not particularly, no."

The area around Camp Fifty wasn't exactly unscathed. The grass was trampled and crushed, the scars of the League's demise touching land. Near the water was a burnt patch. Through the haze of the heat, Nikolai made out turkey vultures picking apart the charred meat.

It took him a second to realize.

He grabbed Lilith's hand, his breath growing quick.

"What?" the archer snapped, "Is there a reason you pulled me back?"

"Lilith–" Nikolai gestured to the burnt patch. The blasted vultures picked at the bodies. "Don't let her–" he swallowed, turning away. "Don't let Quilla go over there."

Lilith tilted her head. Her eyes narrowed on the birds, wrinkling her nose at the bloody corpses. Then her eyes widened and her hand flew to her mouth.

"Oh–" tears brimmed the rim of her eyes. "Oh my god..."

"Go," the same droplets trickled down Nikolai's cheek. "Don't let her look. Don't let her realize."

Lilith blinked the tears from her eyes, wiped her cheeks, and ran to her partner. As if on cue, her entire demeanor changed. She grasped Quilla's hands, urgently discussing what Nikolai made out as 'the great comeuppance of Grandez Lone.'

Alohi chuckled, falling back to match Nikolai's side. "Nothing like gossip to ease the broken mind."

Nikolai scoffed. "Some would say the art of shit talking deepens previous wounds."

"Whoever said that obviously has no good gossip to discuss."

"Perhaps," Nikolai sighed. "Do you ever think the only reason to live is gossip?"

Alohi furrowed her brow, considering. She took one of her many, long braids and twisted it between her fingers. "No," she concluded. "It's a wonderful part of life, but not all it is. Life is running in the rain. It's crying into the arms of someone you trust. Life is diving into the cold ocean, or waking up to the patter of rain. Life is realizing that no matter how hard it is, there is always a way out." She smiled. "That's half of it. Gossip is the other half."

Nikolai snorted. "I suppose we'll have some good gossip after this incident."

Alohi shrugged. "The League always has gossip. When your people are so judgemental, there's always something to talk about."

"Well," Nikolai said. "There'll be plenty to talk about when we jump down that hole."

Before them was the grand, over dramatic entrance of Camp Fifty. Quilla and Lilith were standing at the entrance, their hair blowing with the light wind.

"I still don't understand why you two have to come." Nikolai growled. "You won't exactly be welcome."

Quilla snorted. "Neither will you, Princely."

"I'm their king. The child and heir of the League." Nikolai said. "I've fought beside most of the men who will be holding a blade to my throat. They'll listen to me, you–"

"If you do your job right, Nikolai–" Lilith waved a finger in his face. Nikolai snapped at it, baring his teeth. "We'll also be fighting beside the League soldiers. We need to be seen with their king– a notion of peace, of a common enemy."

"Right," Nikolai growled. "I still don't like this plan."

"Well then," Quilla grinned. "It's a good thing the plan is not your choice."

With those words, the two criminals leapt into the hole. Nikolai stuck out a desperate hand, screeching reluctant words to be swallowed by the fall.

"God dammit." He grumbled. "We should follow them."

Alohi looked at the fall and wrinkled her nose. "Let's wait. I want to see how they fare without us."

"They won't fare well."

Alohi snorted. "Of course, we know that. I'm just wondering how long they'll last before going assassin mode."

Nikolai tilted his head. "I give them five minutes tops."

"I'll wager ten on pure willpower."

Nikolai peered into the dark hole. Vines and rocks scattered the unfinished edges of the pit. It was well constructed, though it didn't look it. Camp Fifty's architecture was, in some way, ingenious.

Alohi knelt next to the drop. She tilted her head, listening into the pit. "There's no screaming." She commented. "Do you think something is wrong?"

"No." Nikolai shrugged. "I think our comrades are doing a remarkable, miracle induced job at following the plan."

Alohi snorted. "I didn't think they had it in them."

"Well," Nikolai dangled his foot over the cliff, bracing himself for the fall. "If we wait to follow them any longer, we may see the winner of our bet."

Chapter Thirty Eight
Cercel

"I'm failing to see the issue," Cercel groaned, placing her chin in her palm. "This matters, why?"

"It matters, Empress," General Huang retorted. "Because people are dying and standing at the palace doors, *begging* us to do something!"

Cercel tilted her head. "You'd be surprised at the effectiveness of a hose."

"You're missing the point!" General Forkel, who Cercel had grown accustomed to as the 'chihuahua.' "The people are starving! If they keep suffering, an uprising will start! We'll be overthrown and all our heads will be on pikes!"

Cercel bit her lip, contemplating. On the bright side, if her head was on a spike she wouldn't have to be around these imbeciles. On the not so bright side, she would be dead.

She chewed the inside of her cheek, considering the consequence.

"Okay," Cercel said. "Cool."

For a moment, the generals simply gaped at her. Huang's mouth was as wide as his biceps, and Forkel resembled an angered ferret ready to strike.

"Are you out of your mind?" Forkel snarled. "We will all *die!*"

The man seemed quite passionate about the topic, so to preserve her sanity, Cercel decided to play along.

"Right." Her gaze wandered to the ceiling. "Okay, we distribute more supplies from Woodran to Thine, the bulk of it going to Brighan. Problemo solved."

"Then the people of Woodran will starve." Huang retorted. "We're just shifting the problem farther away."

"Exactly!" Cercel grinned. "Farther away from us."

"No," Forkel clutched the bridge of his nose. "We are simply postponing the inevitable. There is going to be an uprising if we don't solve the agricultural shortage."

"Okay," Cercel said. "Grow more plants."

"That's not it!" Forkel snapped. "You're still not getting it. The farmers are not working. There are protesters. Strikes across all four countries. Criminals are rampaging!"

Cercel perked. "Criminals?"

"Yes, more and more–"

"I don't care about that!" Cercel screeched. "I care about *Hanslack*. What's happening in Hanslack?"

Huang and Forkel exchanged weary glances. "That city's an anomaly, the surge of crime as gone down–"

"Salenian!" Cercel interrupted. "Pirates, what are they doing?"

Huang dug his nails into the table. "Also a downsurge in crime. Our scouts haven't seen a single one. Why does this matter?"

"Rosalie..." Cercel stood brushing her hair behind her back. "Rosalie's coming. Rosalie and her little friends..."

Without thought, she started to laugh. Long, hard belts poured from her throat and rolled off her tongue. She doubled over, grasping the table as more chortles erupted from her chest.

A hand grasped her collar. She was slammed against the wall, still heaving the awful cackles. Huang's hand whipped across her face, leaving a hot, red implant.

"Pull it together!" Huang growled. "You are the Empress! Act like one!"

Cercel tilted her head, gazing at the man with a curious expression. Then, the laughs returned. They rose from her stomach, scraping her esophagus as they sprouted from her throat. Dewy saliva flew from her tongue, leaving droplets on the general's cheek.

For a moment, the man simply watched. His gaze widened, his mouth fell, and the anger melted into sappy defeat. Huang released Cercel, dropping her laughing mess to the ground. He wavered back, placing his rump on the table.

"We're all..." he breathed. "We're all fucked."

Forkel sat beside him, rubbing his temples. "We had our girl, god dammit! We had a capable person who would take over! But Rosalie left, and instead we're left with *this*!"

Cercel's cackle ceased. Her eyes ignited with fire, rage kindling each flame. She picked herself off the floor, not bothering to remove the hair hanging in front of her eyes.

Oh, Rosalie chuckled, filthy ambition shaping her tone. *A doubter, Cerce. The ones that don't fear you. Listen to that little voice, Cerce. You don't need them. You have me, you have your rage. That's all you need. They are extra weight. Cut them off.*

"Get the other generals." Cercel drawled. "Each and every one of them, I want them here."

Forkel stood. "Empress this is not–"

"*Go!*" Cercel snapped. "That is an order!"

Without another word, the two generals rushed off. The large doors slammed behind her, and Cercel was left alone.

She collapsed onto the floor. It wasn't a fast fall, not at all. It was a slow slump, as if she was simply laying down after a long night.

"Rosalie..." she murmured. "Rosalie's coming..."

She's still the best, Cerce. Rosalie chanted. *She's still better than you. You heard the generals. Rosalie will always be better. That's until you end this charade for good.*

"I am going to kill Rosalie Ghan." Cercel chanted, the words sending energy to her legs. "I am going to *kill* Rosalie Ghan!"

Yes, Rosalie growled. *She is going to come to you with all her little friends. You will torture her archer along with the rest of her allies, before leaving her to bleed on the concrete. But first–* she smiled. *You have to finish off the hindrance.*

Cercel matched her grin, reaching for her blades.

No, Rosalie ordered. *Not yet.*

Just then, the door swung open. Forkel and Huang stood in front of at least twenty generals. They seemed to want to shrink. Each had shoulders raised to their neck and fingernails dug into their palms.

Cercel's smile widened.

"Come!" Cercel waved a hand, gesturing to the large table. "Sit! We have much to discuss!"

Slowly, the men obliged. Cercel sat at the head, hands clasped together, chin resting on her knuckles. The generals watched her wearily, fear twinkling in their gazes.

Patience, Rosalie cooed. *It will feel much better if you're patient.*

"So," Cercel tilted her head, "A little birdy told me you have some complaints about the way I do things." She ran her tongue along her teeth, an ambitious glint shining in her gaze. "Spit it out. Don't be scared. I don't bite."

There was silence. The generals sent anxious glances around the room. Finally, Forkel opened his mouth.

"We believe, Empress," Forkel began. "That you may be mentally unstable. You may want to consider–" he swallowed. "Taking a break, and letting someone else take over."

Cercel tilted her head. "Someone *else*?"

"Someone more–" Huang continued.

"Like Rosalie!" a man spoke. "Someone more like her!"

At first, Cercel saw red. Her eyes stung with emerging tears and her heart ached with pure *anger*. It was always Rosalie. Always fucking *Rosalie*. It didn't matter that she was Empress, it didn't matter that she achieved all Rosalie failed to do. She was always *second*.

Calm yourself, Rosalie hissed. *You know what to do.*

Cercel obeyed, taking a breath. On the exhale she bounded onto the table. The generals flinched back, fear glimmering in their eyes.

"You, right?" Cercel knelt to the man who exclaimed her sister's name. "You're the one who believes my sister is better?"

The man swallowed. He was so small, only a few years older than Cercel. His black hair was slicked back and beads of sweat trickled down his neck. Cercel leaned closer, observing his terrified eyes.

"What's your name?" Cercel asked, smiling.

"Samuel," the man sniffed.

"Hm," for a moment, Cercel simply gazed into his terrified expression. She relished it, relished the fear. Honestly, it was better than the corpses she left in her wake.

No one saw her draw the blade, but about every head turned when she thrust her throwing star into Samuel's neck. As soon as the skin broke, blood poured from the wound, soaking her hand. The warm liquid trailed down Cercel's arm, staining her blouse a deep crimson.

Samuel made a choking sound. He made one last pleading, fearful glance before his eyes glazed over and his head sank.

Cercel grinned, standing on the table. "I told you I don't bite," she licked her blood stained teeth. "That would be very inefficient."

The generals looked on the verge of tears.

"Does anyone else have any complaints?" Cercel asked, running a red hand through her hair.

Nothing but the smell of death lingered in the room.

"No?" Cercel's lips quirked into a grin. "Well then, I suppose we don't have anything else to talk about."

The generals stayed unmoving.

"Well?" Cercel snapped. "I believe that was hint enough for you to leave."

Like a flicked switch, the generals scrambled from their seats and hurried for the door. Cercel turned, gazing at her blade. Little dots of crimson slid off the gold, landing at her feet.

You aren't done, Rosalie's cold hand grasped her shoulder. *I know you want more, Cerce.*

"On second thought," Cercel flung a blade into Huang's face. The general crumpled to the ground, blood pooling around the other's feat. "Why don't you stay awhile." she drew her blades, holding them like cards along her knuckles. "It'll be fun."

Chapter Thirty Nine
Alohi

Alohi and Nikolai plummeted into the hole. At first, they attempted to cling to each other. That plan failed miserably, and they ended up flying down the shaft solo.

She didn't expect the landing and the soft net felt more like concrete. She fell on her stomach, the air promptly leaving her lungs. She flew upwards, collided with Nikolai, and toppled into the net.

"Little late?" the crisp accent drawled. "Don't you think?"

Nikolai sat up, dusting off his clothes. "Or right on time."

Quilla and Lilith were backed against the wall, a plethora of guards pointing swords at their throats. It seemed to take both of them quite a bit of effort not to kill their attackers on site. Instead, Quilla raised her hand and flipped them off. Her silent offence was slapped down by Lilith, who shot her partner a sharp glare.

"Well?" Lilith growled. "Go on, do what you're good at. Argue!"

Nikolai cleared his throat. "Take us to Grandez Lone."

Quilla threw her head back, sliding to the floor. She let out a sound Alohi assumed was a noise of exasperation.

"That was *not* the plan." Lilith snapped.

"Fuck the plan," Nikolai retorted. "I want to see my father."

Quilla rested her chin on her knees, groaning like a toddler. "I hate family reunions, why would you initiate one on *purpose*?"

This time, it was Alohi's turn to speak. "We cannot simply take the League's men without pointing out their fallacies."

Lilith raised an eyebrow. "Can't we?"

Nikolai cleared his throat, asking a final time. "Take us to Grandez Lone."

The guards gazed wearily at each other. A few glances later and they weren't closer to a decision. Their eyes seemed to fleet from Quilla and Lilith to Nikolai and Alohi, then back to their peers.

"Don't listen to them," Quilla murmured. "They're mentally deranged."

"We are not!" Alohi shot back.

"I'm done messing around!" Nikolai growled. "I don't care what my father told you, I want to see him! I am the White King and his son! You will do as I say!"

For a moment, the guards continued with their fleeting, scared glances. Lilith joined her partner on the floor, barely acknowledging the sword pointed at her throat. Quilla rested her head on Lilith's shoulder, letting out a bored breath.

Suddenly, a steady clap broke the silence. The two criminal's sprang up, a new panic glittering in their gazes. They knew that clap, and they knew the stride that came with it. Slowly, the crisp click of Grandez Lone's shoes echoed around the very halls surrounding them.

"No need for dramatics, my boy," Grandez grinned. "Father dearest is right *here*."

Nikolai stiffened; Alohi reached for his hand.

"Well?" the Lone tilted his head. "Haven't you brought me a fine harvest? It took a sword to your throat to get it done; funny enough, your own blade, but Black Cyanide is here and alive." He licked his viscous, white teeth. "Now, answer me this, are you on their side, or the League's?"

Nikolai raised his chin. "Both."

Grandez put his hands on his hips. "This should be interesting." His smile widened. "Well men, let's give the boy the audience he so obviously desires."

Suddenly, League soldiers swung down from the massive hole above them. They came from ropes, one after another, blades pointed at Nikolai and Alohi. More emerged from the bright caverns, surrounding them with weapons aimed.

Alohi took heavy breaths, gazing at the army before her. It must've been the whole of the League gathered before them. But it wasn't a kind audience, if Grandez Lone gave the order, they would be dead within seconds.

For a moment, Nikolai's face remained captured by hostility. Then, without warning, it broke. Not into tears, but into something much more maniacal. Laughter.

It wasn't funny. He wasn't laughing at a joke. The chortles were much drier, much more *terrifying*. The cackles could be categorized into nothing more than insanity.

Alohi understood.

He wasn't insane. He wasn't laughing because he had lost it. He was laughing because he simply had *enough*.

And so had she.

She was done with the pressure. Done with the constant criticism. Done with the control, with the abuse. She was tired of being great only to be treated as *pathetic*.

So she joined him.

Together, the rough cackles ripped from their throat in high, off-tune echoes. The noise radiated around the room, heard by every soldier, every politician, and every child in the hall.

Eventually, Alohi stood up, gathering herself. Nikolai followed, wiping the tears that rolled down his cheeks.

"This is hysterical!" Alohi cackled. "All of you! All of you fucking idiots! You are so, so *stupid*!"

"This place is *pathetic*!" Nikolai joined. "You have no morals, even though you pretend this place was built on them. You are a bunch of dogs, leashed to a man with no fucking idea what he's doing!"

Quilla sunk to the floor. "We're so fucked."

"And for what?" Alohi snarled. "A home that belongs to you anyway? A life of dying for a hopeless cause? Why the *hell* are you here?"

"They are here, Miss Windlem," Grandez shot back. "Because they want to otherthrow the Empire. We are their best bet."

"*Best bet*?" Nikolai cackled. "Father, you cannot even run two feet. Your political skills are equivalent to a monkey, you have no grasp of war strategy and are basically as tyrannical as Empress Ghan, though less good at it."

"Tell me, Grandez," Alohi smiled. "When was the last time you actually *won* a battle? The League's troops are fine— skilled, even. But you?" she chuckled. "The council hasn't made a good decision in *years*. You have no conception of war, no grasp of strategy. The only thing putting you in power is money and greed. So let's face it, you have no idea what you're doing!"

The Lone tilted his head. "Oh, and you do?" he cackled. "Let me remind you, Nikolai, I was the one that trained you. I taught you everything you know! You can't beat your teacher."

Nikolai shook his head. "You were never my teacher. I was taught by the waves I sailed. I learned from the crew I called family. I learned my swordsman skills from Killen. Quilla taught me to be ruthless, Lilith taught me the bounds of my cruelty, and Alohi showed me the balance. The only thing I learned from you was to be scared." He bared his teeth. "And that hasn't done me much good."

Grandez matched his son's furious expression. He advanced on him, low heels ticking against the concrete. They came face to face, Nikolai's chin at his father's eyes. It was just then Alohi realized how much taller he was compared to Grandez. Normally, Nikolai seemed shorter– shrunken.

The Lone scowled, wrinkling his nose. "You're making excuses for your failure."

"Not failure," Nikolai shook his head, his voice soft. "Defiance. You're angry because I've learned things, Father. How to keep going when my body screams to stop. How to remain triumphant when the world wants me to die— when my own father pushes for my death-" Grandez's face twisted into one of horror. "How to predict when you strike. How to resist against the knife to my throat. You taught me how to be scared, Father, nothing more." He tilted his head. "And even at that, *you* failed."

The Lone frantically looked around, gazing at the horrified eyes of his colleagues. "You're lying, that's not-"

"You're really trying to deny it?" Nikolai scoffed.

The League gazed at Nikolai, then his father. Their eyes flashed with concern, then doubt.

"I did no such thing!" Grandez cried, throwing up his hands. "You are accusing me of abuse! Are you that desperate for attention, Nikolai?"

"No," Nikolai murmured. "I am not crying wolf over a dog. I am not lying for pity. I am telling the pure, unfiltered truth. You hit, scratched, threatened and screamed at me." He straightened his posture, turning to the League. "Do you really want to follow someone who hurts their own blood?"

Grandez scoffed. "You have no proof of such allegations!"

Nikolai opened his mouth, but it wasn't his voice that rang about the walls.

"No," Killen spoke. "But he has a witness."

"Multiple," Tnil's crisp cut joined.

The two stepped from the crowd, locking eyes with Nikolai, then his father. Killen wore a long rope, the end of the cloth flowing at his heels. His long, strawberry hair was pulled into a tight braid which fell down his back. Though his dress was professional, his face betrayed his poised display. Bags hung under his eyes and tear stains left a salty residue on his cheeks.

"When Nikolai left," Tnil began, a slight tremor shaking her voice. "I became Mister Lone's lab rat. At first, when he came to me with the opportunity, I was overjoyed. Then, I began to realize the reality of the spotlight. I never got to sleep; Mister Lone kept me training until I was perfect. Sometimes, I would be in that training center from dusk to dawn without a wink of sleep. When I didn't do well, I was met with a flurry of criticisms and demoralization. But when I finally met his enormous expectations, the validation felt so damn *good–*"

"Like a drug," Nikolai breathed.

Tnil nodded. "Like a drug."

"I can concur," Killen said. "I've trained Nikolai for years. He would always come to practice with bruises he couldn't explain. I knew what was going on, though the matter was quite hard to discuss. Eventually, the fact that Mister Lone beat him weaved its way into our conversations. But Nikolai never looked at it as a sorrow. He looked at it as a simple fact. Something that simply happened."

This resonated with the crowd, Killen's words shifting around the walls. Each member of the League glanced between Grandez and Nikolai, a mix of shock and anger resonating on their features.

"I don't announce this for pity." Nikolai said, breaking the silence. "I don't yearn for your sympathy. All I want is the truth. Not for my sake, but yours. If you follow my father, I want you to know exactly what kind of man he is." He took a breath. "A man who uses his son as a pawn.

"I was never to be in control of the Empire," Nikolai continued. "There was never going to be a balance of power. It was all going to be him. He controlled every councilmember's movement like a puppeteer. There was no democracy, no oligarchy. The League is the same as the Empire in every way but one. We have a different tyrant."

"But it doesn't have to be like that." Alohi interrupted. "You don't have to follow Grandez Lone's pull like a rope. We won't replicate Empress Ghan's tyranny. We aren't perfect, but we know what our processors did wrong. Unlike every other organization, we aren't fighting for ourselves. We are fighting for the future of our nation."

For a moment, there was silence.

Then, the familiar, earsplitting cackle of Grandez Lone.

"You really think they're going to follow *you*?" he spat. "You really think the League will pledge loyalty to a bunch of teenagers who abandoned them?"

Nikolai shook his head. "I never abandoned them." His voice was so soft, like a leaf landing in a puddle. "You did, remember? You were the one who hid in the bunker leaving your citizens to die. You were the one who held a knife to my throat when I voiced my reluctance." Nikolai took a breath. "It was never me who abandoned my people. I was the one who took on the Empress. I was the one who undid their ropes and steered the ship away from Camp fifty. What you call *abandonment* is my choice to no longer be your lapdog."

Grandez scoffed. "That's not true." It was as if he was murmuring it to himself rather than the League. "None of that is true! All this boy wants is power. He's out of his mind. *Insane!*"

Nikolai cocked his head, a slight smile growing on his lips. "And who's fault is that?"

Grandez opened his mouth to respond, but there were no words on his tongue. He shut his jaw, sinking into the shadows.

"Well?" Nikolai asked, projecting his voice throughout the room. "I won't force you to come with me. I've said all I need to say. The choice is yours."

First, it was Killen who got down on a knee, his long braid running down his shoulder.

Then, Tnil.

And the members behind them. Soldiers, farmers, bakers, and politicians knelt before Alohi and Nikolai. One by one, like a wave, the entire League bowed their heads in respect.

Until it was just Grandez Lone and the council members.

"Well?" Alohi asked. "Make up your mind."

Dacnoff, Spin and Bolian lowered to their knees, their expensive cloaks pooling at their feet.

Last was Grandez Lone and Unighast. The counselor sent an apologetic glance at the Lone, and sank to his knees.

Grandez shot Nikolai a glare. They locked eyes, neither relenting. Alohi knew what he was planning. The Lone was trying one more, desperate time to manipulate Nikolai. And he was failing spectacularly.

Quilla, perhaps growing bored, approached with silent, steady feet. She drew a blade, and shoved the hilt into the small of Lone's back.

Grandez's eyes rolled back in his head as he toppled to the ground. His unconscious body rolled onto Unighast before resting on the concrete.

Alohi shot her a glare.

Quilla shrugged. "I didn't kill him."

The two criminals strode to Nikolai and Alohi, resting their eyes on the sea of bowed heads.

"Well, Nikolai," Lilith smirked, resting her hand on his shoulder. "Nice job."

Nikolai didn't respond. Instead, he knelt next to Killen, extending a hand.

His master looked up, lacing his fingers through Nikolai's. With him, the entire League rose to their feet. They gazed at Nikolai, awaiting an order.

Killen smiled, resting his hand on Nikolai's shoulder. "Well played, kid."

Chapter Forty
Quilla

"Shut *up!*" Quilla screeched, her hands crumpling into fists.

What the hell was the point of gathering three armies at your command if none of them would fucking listen?

Her, Lilith, Nikolai, Alohi and Florian stood on a rather large rock. Below them were three armies. The Thugs of Hanslack, the League of Red Doves and the Pirate colonies of Salenian stood before them, each intertwined in some nervous but incredibly loud conversation.

"Florian," Quilla drawled. The pirate perked. "Get down there and knock out anyone who dares say anything."

Florian gave a quick, excited nod before leaping into the crowd and disappearing.

"You know they're gonna take that literally, right?" Alohi asked.

Quilla wrinkled her nose. "How else would they take it?"

Alohi gazed at the crowd, then shrugged.

Quilla opened her mouth to speak, only to be interrupted by the constant hum of chatter. Her lips twisted into a scowl and her eyes tightened into a glare.

"*Quiet!*" she hollered. This time, the armies sunk into an obedient silence, gazing at her with expectant eyes.

"You better shut the fuck up," Quilla drawled. "If I hear one more conversation, my friend Florian will come down on you with the hilt of a knife and you'll have quite a severe concussion. The choice is yours, shut up voluntarily or be *silenced*."

The crowd fell to a hush.

"Wonderful," Quilla clasped her hands together, a wide grin spreading on her face. "I have a lot to explain, so cram it and listen. Our strategy will be one of skirmish and trickery, but before we can begin that, we need to sail to Thine. As long as we stay off of the Empire's main ship routes, we shouldn't be caught. However, on the rare occasion that we are, we sink any ship that's in our way. I don't much care who is still alive on the vessel, only that they cannot get back to shore before us. Is that understood?"

The sea of soldiers nodded below her. Each of their eyes gazed at her with silent obedience.

Quilla grinned. A little fear made them into proper soldiers.

"The arrival is a bit more tricky. We don't want to march right into Brighan; our soldiers will be exhausted from the walk and won't have enough energy for the fight. Instead, once we dock we will wait for a train to come by. A small squadron of assassins from Hanslack will ambush it and bring the engine to a halt. If there are any prisoners inside, we set them free. But any soldiers? Kill them. I want no loose ends.

"Once we have our train, we load our supplies and soldiers onto the engine and ride. We will journey past the last mountain range, just before the Golden Palace. Pirates and League– you wait there. Hanslack, we're the first to march. Our attack will come in skirmish; a steady stream of strike and retreat. I want to draw the bronze battalions out and lead them to the base of the mountain. Rivious Olan will lead the Stripe to the front of the palace, baiting the north patrol. Felicia Tornstead will take the Hallucinogens to the south, Garmond Felick will lead the Fouls to the west, while me and Miss Cole round up the back with the Serpents."

Quilla took a breath, checking that the army was still listening. Sure enough, a thousand glittering, vengeful eyes stared back at her. *Perfect.*

"As soon as you capture the attention of the battalion, you run. Understood? I need you to keep the Empire soldiers with you. Don't let them wander or retreat back to the Golden Palace. They need to be constantly aware that you are still a threat. I don't care much how you do it or what route you take, but I want four squadrons of Bronze soldiers at the base of that mountain.

"Pirates, League– this is where you come in. As soon as the first battalion comes to the clearing, you attack. I want you ready to pounce, no delay. However, you are to spare as many lives as possible. If this doesn't go our way, I want an entire army as our hostage."

Quilla took a shaky breath. This was a part of the plan she wasn't looking foreward too.

"After that is done, I will lead a small squadron into the Golden Palace to assassinate the Empress. That will consist of me, Miss Cole, Miss Windlem, and Mister Lone. I won't bore you with the details, given it doesn't concern you. All there is to know is that if we do not come out of the palace in an hour, blow the fucker up."

Unlike the last few words, this conclusion drew a reaction. While the crowd seemed to shoot her skeptical looks and cautious protests, most of the objections came from the man walking onto the rock.

"I don't believe that is the best course of action." He said, the words dripping from his mouth like syrup. The man couldn't have been older than her: his long, brown hair fell down his unnaturally yellow shoulders. While he looked poised, the blue bags below his red eyes and the yellow glow of his skin told Quilla otherwise. This man was an addict, through and through. "Quite reckless, in my opinion."

Nikolai and Alohi let out an agitated growl.

Quilla took one glance at them, then her eyes fled back to the man. "Sorry," she wrinkled her nose as the distinct smell of cocaine drifted into her nostrils. "Who are you?"

"Tanor Unighast," he puffed. "The representative from Woodran."

"Oh, okay," Lilith drawled. "Congratulations, you're fired."

If Unighast heard the phrase, he didn't show it. Instead, he took a long, strung out exhale. Smoke drifted from his mouth, curling into the air and evaporating with the wind. "Why would you blow up a perfectly fine structure? You have no need for explosives– or to kill the Empress for that matter. To me, it sounds like you're just itching to go up against Cercel Ghan."

Quilla wanted to backhand him, but she didn't take the bait. "Fine, I'll explain." she snapped. "We need to kill Empress Ghan because she is our largest loose end. This is not a petty chase but a strategic move. If the Empress escapes, she'll spark a rebellion. No reign lasts forever, but I want this newfound government to at least outlive me."

"So why–" Quilla threw her head back at the salty rasp crawled up the rock. "Do we need to blow up the palace?"

Lilith scowled, turning to Grandez Lone. "Why are you here?"

The Lone tilted his head. "To point out your fallacies, of course."

Nikolai snorted. "I would trust a duckling over your strategic incompetence."

"Nikolai, Alohi," Quilla clutched the bridge of her nose. "Can you please babysit this round? I really *don't* have the energy."

The two politicians shot her a nasty glare, but didn't contest.

Quilla turned to the army, raising her voice to the necessary octave. "I will clarify the logistics with the necessary people later. For now, let's ready the ship for departure." She let out a breath. "Dismissed."

The army scattered, each section bolting to a ship and preparing the vessel for the journey. For a moment, Quilla simply watched them. Then, as the voices raised behind her, she slowly turned to face the imbeciles.

"I don't see why you have to go into the place, then." Unighast argued. "We simply blow up the palace. Your sister dies in the explosion and no one else gets hurt."

"That woman is not my sister," Quilla snapped.

"And why would we destroy years of architecture and historical value for a fight that can be won with a squad of assassins. " Alohi retorted. "It's one woman against four trained fighters. What's the harm?"

"The harm is that you are drastically underestimating the Empress." The Lone argued. "She is not just a woman, she is the greatest fighter in the country."

"She is *not* the most powerful fighter in the country." Lilith scoffed. "She is no greater than any of us. The Empress is simply a girl with a shattered conscience and way too much power. It's an easy fight."

"An *easy* fight?" Unighast turned to Quilla. "Was it an easy fight when you wanted to free your archer? Was it such a breeze when you were tasked to kill the Golden Class and Ghan? How *easy* was it when you attempted to save the League from your sister's grasp. Remind me, who are those vultures feasting off of?"

Quilla's breath caught. Her eyes wandered to the patch of grass where birds picked at burnt, charred flesh. She had seen it before; she wanted to pretend she hadn't. She wanted to convince herself that the vulture's meal was simply a deer. But in her heart, she knew those bodies were the only remnants of family she had left.

"It's different now." Quilla murmured. "I was still looking at the Empress like the girl I knew all those years ago. But now I see my sister is long dead. Right now, my goal is to avenge her death."

For a moment, Lone and Unighast stared at her. Then, their faces fell in defeat.

"I can tell you won't be swayed." The Lone drawled. "But be warned: I don't care how powerful you *think* you are, never underestimate the power of a broken mind."

Chapter Forty One
Nikolai

"This is a bad idea," Nikolai commented as he leaned against the taffrail. "I can feel it. This is a bad idea."

Alohi gave him a look. "Then why are you grinning ear to ear?"

"Because for once–" Nikolai licked his teeth, ambitious power blooming on his cheeks. "It's *my* bad idea."

Alohi snorted. They were standing on the leading ship in the first fleet. Quilla arranged for the army to disperse in five parts, each sailing in different routes. That way, if Empire scouts found one fleet, they still wouldn't know the strength of the entire army. For some reason, Quilla wanted them all on the same ship. Perhaps it was strategy, or perhaps it was the fact that she preferred to have them out of fondness. Nikolai secretly hoped it was the latter.

"Keep in mind," Alohi grinned. "It wasn't your plan, it was Quilla's."

"Right," Nikolai returned her gleam. "And I wholeheartedly agree."

Alohi hummed a chuckle. "I see, and are you sure this isn't just because it's pissing off your father?"

Nikolai shrugged. "Perhaps that's part of it." He gazed into the ocean, an excited glow thrumming throughout him. "But more so, I think it's a good plan. I believe Quilla knows what she's doing and there's no reason to waste a perfectly good structure."

"Sure," Alohi's tone darkened. "But, Nik–"

Nikolai turned to her. "Hm?"

"What if one of us doesn't come back?"

Surprisingly, this thought hadn't occurred to him. He always figured the four of them were indestructible. They survived so many battles together; he himself had survived so many times. Over the years, he'd come to think of himself as unkillable.

"I hadn't thought of that," he murmured. "I suppose I never considered it."

Now that the thought entered his mind, it was hard to get it out. What if it was Lilith? Cercel could throw a star into her forehead– she'd be distracted with her aim. Quilla would be a more likely target. If for some reason she held back, Cercel wouldn't hesitate to strike her in the chest; to drag her star down to her intestines. The criminal prodigy's guts would paint the concrete red, and she'd be dead within seconds.

And then there was Alohi. Nikolai couldn't help but imagine all the ways Cercel could kill his friend. A blade to her heart, a brick to her head, the Empress could propel her foot into Alohi's throat and do some damage. There were too many ways– too many options of death. Nikolai's mind only dared to wander to the less horrific ideas. He didn't want to imagine the vivid image of Alohi's organs.

"That won't happen." Nikolai snapped. "I don't care how it goes, we're all making it out of this alive."

"And if we don't–"

"We don't think about that," Nikolai answered. "I don't want to think about that." He turned to her, his eyes glossy. "Please, Lo, don't make me think about *that*."

Alohi gave him a small smile. "Then we won't think about it. But for now–" she moved closer to him. "I want to enjoy this as much as possible."

Nikolai wrapped his arm around her as Alohi leaned into his side. They watched the ocean, the gentle bump of the turquoise water as they sailed over the waves. The sun was dipping into the horizon, its bright glow turning to a deeper orange. Somehow, the day before battle was always beautiful, as if the world was giving them one last gift before the end.

"Nik?" Alohi asked, leaning her head into his chest.

"Yeah?" he murmured.

"If this is the last time we ever have this–" she swallowed. "Have *each other*, can we at least make it worth it?"

Nikolai turned to her, a gentle smile touching his lips. "Of course? How so?"

Alohi grasped his shoulders, nudging him to face her. Her long braids hung over her shoulder in long, neat strands. The blue glow of her eyes reflected the gleam of the ocean, and her dark skin radiated in the setting sun. The world had swallowed her– molding the light of the sun and the lap of the waves into her features.

Alohi reached up, stroking his jaw. Nikolai cupped her face; her features pouring into him like a waterfall. His fingers wavered to her chin, gently lifting her to face him.

Their eyes locked. Blue against blue, gazing into each other like it would kill them to break contact. Nikolai leaned down, his lips brushing Alohi's. He stayed still, afraid to go further.

"Go on," Alohi whispered.

His hand wavered to her neck, his fingers weaving themselves through her braids. Alohi's hand drifted to his waist as she stroked his side. Her grasp wavered to his back, feeling the clothes with gentle curiosity.

Then, their eyes made their way back to each other. The seawater gaze radiated between them: it seemed to halt time, movement, and anything meaningful.

Nikolai leaned in.

"Ahem," they sprang apart to find Quilla leaning against the taffrail. "Having fun?"

Alohi shot her a glare. "You enjoy this, don't you."

"Thoroughly," Nikolai turned to see Lilith. "It's about fucking time. You two have been pretending like nothings between you for months now. It's been fucking *aggravating*! You better believe we're gonna witness when you too finally snap and dive into each other's pants."

"Ew," Nikolai leaned against the taffrail, clutching the bridge of his nose. "You two have no decency."

"And you–" Lilith strode to him and tapped his nose. "Have no sense of humor."

"It's just the fact that our taste in jokes isn't miserably broken that upsets you." Alohi retorted.

"Hm," Quilla bit the inside of her lip, considering this. "Killen wants you guys in the cabin. He wants to show us something– or whatever."

Alohi glanced at Nikolai and shrugged. "What for?"

"I haven't the slightest clue," Quilla grinned. "But he said we'd like it."

~~~

When the four of them wandered into the cabin, they were met with the largest display of artillery that Nikolai had ever seen. Arrows, swords and knives lined the walls in neat, organized sets. Killen was leaning against the doorframe, gleaming with a smile that both scared and excited Nikolai.

"Welcome to my pride and joy," Killen said, plucking one of the arrows off of their shelf. "The result of several months of blackmail and connections."

Quilla took one of the blades from the walls, tossing it in the air.

Before the trinket hit her fingers, Killen snatched it from her. "Careful, Dear." He grinned, brushing off the blade. "This isn't an ordinary dagger."

Killen strode to the targets on the opposite side of the room. He handed the blade to Quilla, gesturing for her to throw it.

"I've never been good at the little swords." He commented. "Besides, you better get used to handling these."

Quilla launched the blade into the target. The knife struck the center ring, a blue powder dusting the area around it.

Quilla narrowed her gaze. "What's that–"

Before she could finish her sentence, Killen clapped. The target exploded, blue fire reaching out to touch the walls. When the flames cleared and the smoke lifted, the targets were completely unscathed. The walls looked as if they hadn't been touched and the blade was still neatly stuck in the target.
~~~

"Not inside the ship, please." Nikolai drawled, pressing his fingers against his temple.

"Oh relax," Killen snorted. "Everything in here is completely blast proof. You couldn't destroy these walls if you tried."

"Woah," Lilith marveled. "What strings did you have to pull to get this?"

Killen shrugged. "Called in a couple favors. My associates were more than happy to accommodate."

Nikolai barely heard him. He was too busy scouting out the blades on the wall. They were dark black, gold stripes caressing the sides. He grasped the hilt, lifting the blade with care.

"What does this do?" he asked.

"It's poisonous." Killen said. "Venom comes from the tip. Whenever you stab someone, it will sink into their skin."

Nikolai ran his finger over the sharp edge of the sword. "I don't want to kill every time I strike. Sometimes I stab to demobilize."

"Yes, I know. Your sick idea of mercy." Killen shrugged. "But don't worry, the poison doesn't kill, only paralyzes. And besides, it'll wear off in a few hours."

"What does this do?" Alohi asked, holding up her needle.

"Same thing as the sword." Killen said. "Stab and it paralyzes. It allows much less precision than your usual tactic."

Alohi grinned, staring at the needle with malicious ambition.

"And mine?" Lilith strode to her arrows, running her finger along the smooth surface.

"Same thing as your partner." Killen said. "Shoot and it spreads explosive powder. Basically like the knife but better."

Quilla glared at him, running a protective hand over her daggers.

"Cool," Lilith drew an arrow and fired it at the target. The weapon struck the inside ring, powder spraying the outer circles.

Lilith clapped. Nothing happened.

She clapped a second time. Still, silence.

She turned to Killen. "It's broken."

"No," Killen scowled. "It's not broken. You're just doing it wrong."

"Oh?" Lilith raised an eyebrow.

"I have a sensor." Killen held up his palm, inside was the silver metal button. "See? When I clap–" he swung his hands together and the target exploded. "It goes *kaboom*."

"Okay," Quilla said. "Where's ours?"

Killen wrinkled his nose. "Greedy much? You don't get one until the battle, Dear."

"You don't trust us?" Lilith snapped.

"Are you kidding?" Killen retorted. "We are on a vessel currently in the middle of the ocean and the only thing keeping us above the waves is this floor. Believe it or not, I'm quite fond of the deck."

Quilla rolled her eyes. "I'm not going to blow up the boat, I'm an esteemed general."

"Maybe." Killen admitted. "But you're also a seventeen year old girl who has an unhealthy obsession with things that go *boom*."

Quilla and Lilith glared at him, but didn't contest.

"Anyway, you three should go." Killen waved to the door. "I'm far too tired to babysit."

"We are not *children*." Lilith shrieked.

"Pish posh," Killen waved his hand. "You're child enough. Go, shoo, get out of here. I don't care where you go, just stay here."

The two criminals sent him a scowl as they sulked towards the door. Nikolai and Alohi followed them, each sending longing gazes towards their poisonous weapons.

"Nikolai," Killen called. "You stay."

Nikolai held back, leaning against the door while the rest of his crew trailed out the door.

"Could you please close it?" Killen asked. Nikolai pulled the handle and the door clicked shut.

"What's up?" Nikolai asked.

"Nothing much," Killen shrugged. "Just wanted to check in."

Nikolai offered him a smile. "Thank you, that means a lot."

"Of course, kid," Killen matched his grin. "You don't have too, but if there is anything you–"

"I'm sorry." Nikolai blurted. The words came out so fast it took time to completely comprehend what he said. "I'm sorry I snapped at you. I'm so, so sorry I acted that way at Camp Fifty. You didn't deserve how I treated you–"

Before he could finish, Killen flung himself around him. His hug was warm, soft, and comforting. A comfort he had never felt. But it was pleasant; the kind of pleasant that brought tears to your eyes.

"Shut up, Nikolai," Killen mumbled, pushing his face into Nikolai's shoulder. "You owe me nothing, much less an apology."

Nikolai tried to retort, but found he didn't have the words. Instead, he pushed his face into Killen's shoulder, relishing the scent of his master's perfume.

When they finally pulled apart, Nikolai was surprised to see tears staining Killen's cheek. He had never seen his master cry before. The fact that it was happening now was surreal. Strange– but comfortable. This whole conversation was new, but somehow, Nikolai found it resurrecting. Like someone had doused him in cold water.

"Why aren't you mad?" another thing Nikolai noticed is that he wasn't in control of his own words. "I don't understand! I did something stupid–"

"I'm not mad because I understand." Surprisingly, Killen's words were soft; a whisper, almost. "Because it wasn't stupid. The cutting was survival, Nikolai. That drug was the only way you could survive. The stupid thing about survival is that once you don't need the habit, it becomes a hindrance."

For a moment, Nikolai stayed silent. Then, he slumped against the wall, lowering himself to the ground. Killen matched his movement, sinking next to Nikolai.

"How long have you known?" Nikolai asked, not daring to look at him. "About my... cutting?"

Killen shrugged. "I always had my suspicions. I've seen a lot, Nikolai, and I know when someone is at risk for something like that. You were definitely at risk. So when I noticed the sleeves and the change of personality, I knew there was *something*."

"I'm not the only one?" Nikolai asked.

Killen shook his head. "No. There's a reason why people hurt themselves. It produces a hormone; the same one morphine stimulates. Said hormone numbs pain– and not just the physical kind."

Nikolai buried his head in his hands. "It almost killed me, Killen."

"Yeah," Killen released a breath. "It can do that."

There was silence for a moment. Nikolai kept his head in his hands, afraid to look up. It was like he couldn't move; for if he raised his face from his palms, the entire world might collapse.

"Killen?" Nikolai murmured.

"Hm?"

"I want it gone." It was with those words Nikolai found the strength to move. "How do I make the urges go away?"

Killen put a hand on his shoulder. "Honestly, you've already taken the first step. You've gotten away from the cause; from your dad. Now, the urges will naturally subside. It will take time and patience, but they'll fade."

Nikolai took a shaky breath. "Promise?"

Killen gave a gentle smile. "Promise."

Their eyes rested in one another. Killen kept a gentle gleam on his face, while Nikolai's smile crumpled. He didn't try to withhold the tears. They were coming anyway.

He flung himself into Killen's arms, pressing his tearstained face to his velvet robes. Killen laid a hand on his head– he didn't need to say anything, all words were already spoken. Right now, Nikolai simply needed someone to hold him.

Chapter Forty Two
Cercel

"The people are starving–"

"They're rioting, Empress–"

"The trade routes are being ambushed–"

"Our trains are breaking down–"

"Oil production in Courna is striking–"

The messengers swarmed Cercel, coming at her with problem after problem. Everytime she dared to emerge from the halls, she was instantly surrounded by people.

She wanted to say something. She needed to come up with some sort of solution for this. But she couldn't. The reports kept coming faster than her brain could think.

Before, her advisers handled this. But their bodies were rotting on the floor of the meeting room. After killing them, she bolted the door shut and forbid anyone from entering the room. Now, the only time she had to think about what she had done was when the scent of decomposing corpses drifted into her nose.

Rosalie didn't let her forget the fact she was fucked.

You've killed your advisers. She cooed. *You slaughtered your siblings, and Father left you. Now–* She let out a strangled, sarcastic gasp, which was quickly overcome with sadistic giggles. *You actually have to do your fucking job.*

"The trade routes, Empress–"

"The starvation, Empress–"

"They're ambushing–"

"Armies spotted on the sea–"

"We need–"

"Shut up!" *What are you going to do Cerce? Kill them like you killed everyone else. Or are you finally going to do something useful and stop being such a pathetic mess.* "Shut up, Rosalie!"

Rosalie, Rosalie, Rosalie. Kill Rosalie. You can end this. All you have to do is end one, tiny girl.

Suddenly, and without warning, Cercel felt the overwhelming urge to kill herself.

Her legs moved without her telling them. She broke into a run, sprinting down the hall. The messengers followed her, their steps beating in her ears like a pounding heart.

She raced around the corner, her shoes skidding on the glazed concrete. For a moment, the army of problems vanished around the turn. Before thinking, she shut herself in a supply closet.

Congratulations, Cerce, Rosalie's ice cold fingers wrapped around her heaving shoulders. Her fingers dug into Cercel's skin, the pain almost refreshing. *You've hidden from your issues, again.*

"Stop it," Cercel placed her hands over her ears, tucking her head between her knees. "Shut up, shut up, shut up."

You know, Rosalie murmured. *Father was right about you, Cerce. You should've died in that explosion. You're a failure– disgusting. The only thing you've ever done right is thwart. Kill, destroy, revenge. That is all you're good at.*

Cercel drew her throwing star. She raised the blade above her head and plunged it into her thigh. The pain was supposed to make Rosalie leave, but instead, her hallucination only wavered.

Rosalie's grip on her shoulder tightened. Blood dripped from Cercel's wound, the red droplets curling down her thigh and drenching her pants.

Maybe you should stick to what you're good at. Rosalie cooed. *Destruction. Revenge. Death.*

With trembling hands, Cercel raised the star to her throat. Tears trickled down her face, looping around her chin and drenching her robes. She pressed a blade to her neck; a warm rush told her she had broken the skin and blood was trickling from her throat.

No! Rosalie screeched. *Not before you kill Rosalie Ghan. Not before your only purpose in this world is complete. Death is a mercy, Cerce. You don't deserve it.*

Cercel let out a strangled sob. The star slipped from her hand as her head slammed into her knees. She kept screaming, the belts sending more droplets down her skin. Her hair was drenched with a mix of blood and tears, the substance sticking to her face. Cercel dug her fingers into her scalp, the flesh giving way and crimson running down her head.

"Stupid hair." Cercel scowled. She yanked the strands off her face, gazing at the greasy locks. She needed to cut *something*. She needed to dement herself *somehow*.

She raised the blade to her scalp. With messy, shaky hands, she cut the unbrushed hair from her head. The leftover locks drifted from her scalp and landed on her legs. Cercel kept cutting, the hair flying in messy, blood drenched tangles.

When she was finished, half of her hair hung at her back while the other half was cut to her ear. Stray locks ran down her shoulders, still soaked with red. Cercel let the long hair fall over her eyes; her gaze resting on the blood entangled within the strands.

Without warning, Rosalie started laughing. The sound wasn't sadistic, it wasn't cruel. Instead, it was simply *there*. Nothing was funny, nothing was sad. The laugh was just a laugh.

And Cercel joined.

She pressed her forehead against her knees, cut strands of hair sticking to her sweaty forehead. She cackled while tears leaked from her eyes. She cackled while the wound in her leg poured blood. And she cackled while her hallucination became stronger. She laughed while her broken mind consumed her; fake residue of her own sister taking over the sanity that was once pure and innocent.

Chapter Forty Three
Lilith

"Did they make it?" Quilla asked as she hopped from the ship onto the sand. Lilith trailed at her heel, taking mental note of where the ship was parked.

"Yes," Felicia Tornshed matched her stride. "I got word from my men in the Hallucinogens that the third fleet docked an hour ago. The rest sent me the confirmation letter within that hour."

"So we were the last to dock," Quilla jutted out her jaw. "Good. Do they all know to get on the train at sunset?"

Tornshed nodded. "Yes, that was mentioned."

"Then we're set." Quilla's eyes flitted to the sun. It was just above the mountains– minutes away from sinking into the jagged peaks. "Where is the hijacking team? I want them ready."

Tornshed gave a swift jerk of her head and ran to find the team. Quilla had chosen four people from the Hallucinogens which Lilith had a tremendous amount of respect for. Each were skilled, experienced killers with the moral compass of a blade. The only people they cared for were each other, and all had a unique craving for chaos.

"They're going to kill everyone in that train." Lilith had commented.

Quilla shrugged. "I'm counting on it."

"You do realize we'll be ruling the Empire soldiers if we win," Lilith retorted. "We can't kill all of them."

"I'm not planning on killing all of them." Quilla said. "But a few deaths is nothing to fret over. Later, they may be allies, but right now, they're enemies. Besides, what's a few soldiers over a thousand? The men in the train are a sacrifice. A necessary calculation."

Lilith always noticed a separate gleam in Quilla's eyes when blood spilled. But this was different. While her partner was smart, Lilith had never looked at her as a strategist. That was because Quilla Thorne wasn't. This woman was trained by Emperor Ghan to command wartime. While her partner kept it under control, Lilith couldn't help but notice the appearance of Rosalie Ghan.

"You understand why I'm doing this, right?" Quilla tapped her shoulder. "These are calculations. I don't like it, but in order to win this, lives have to be sacrificed."

"Quilla, I don't care about their lives." Lilith bowed her head. "No– I don't think about them. It's easier that way. What I'm worried about is the fact that I am seeing more and more of your past self."

"We're one person." Quilla said. "I'm simply using Rosalie's knowledge."

"Of course." Lilith retorted. "I just hope that when the time comes, you won't adopt her morals."

The sun had retreated behind the mountains by the time the train came. The hijacking team was sent ahead to stop the train before it reached the ship. The machine was already screeching to a stop when it met them. Quilla and Lilith strode to the doors, weapons drawn in case it wasn't their men who emerged from the train's cabin.

But as the door to the car slid open, Lilith peered to find bloodied corpses littering the train floor. The hijacking crew stepped out, their tattered cloaks soaked with blood.

"General Thorne." Alrik Fruin stepped from the car, landing next to Quilla. "I hope you're satisfied."

Quilla peered inside the car. A steady stream of blood dripped from the doorway and seeped into the gravel.

"Could have done away with the bodies?" Quilla asked, wrinkling her nose.

Fruin smiled a heavy grin. "We're hired to kill, not clean, Darling."

If Quilla registered the insult, she didn't show it. Her voice sharpened, like a dagger digging into Fruin's heart. "You're not hired at all, *Alrik*. In fact, you chose to be here, under my command. You have a choice here, you can clean your mess or I can leave you here with no food or drinking water. Thine is a desert and that ship is guarded with military personnel five times stronger than you. If you don't like taking my orders, fine. I hope you like starvation or an arrow to the neck better."

Fruin scowled. For a moment, he leveled Quilla's glare. Then, he turned away and fled back into the train.

"They're not people," Quilla murmured. She wasn't speaking to Lilith, nor to herself. She was talking to the air. "They're numbers. A strategic advantage. I'm– *we're* above ethics when it comes to war."

"Quilla what–" Lilith lay a hand on her shoulder. She flinched away. "I know why you're doing it. I've killed before, Quill. You don't have to explain yourself to me."

Quilla swallowed, her glare hardening on the ocean. "It's not you I'm trying to convince."

Before Lilith could respond, Quilla brushed past her. She came to face her army, who were hauling supplies off the ship.

"Bring only what you need. Only the lightest foods are necessary." She commanded. "I want you on that train in the next ten minutes. We ride through the night. As soon as the sun peaks from the mountains, we send our battalions into Brighan."

<p style="text-align:center">~~~</p>

The train raced through the dark, the moon shining on the mountains. The soldiers had been told to sleep, but they all knew that wasn't possible.

Instead, they lay face up on the floor, eyes resting on the ceiling. In the past, the low click of the train had lolled Lilith to sleep. Now, the constant hum of the wheels only heightened her anxiety.

She leaned against the car door, gazing at the dark landscape. The rocky wasteland didn't look as barren in the moonlight. Instead, it gave a mystical, silver gleam. As if the light of the moon was pooling into the valley.

Lilith took a final look at the moonlit landscape, and hauled herself to her feet. She padded through the cabin, careful not to disturb the soldiers pretending to sleep.

She found Quilla just outside the car. She sat with her knees tucked to her chest, fondling one of Killen's explosive blades.

"Careful," Quilla jumped at the sound of her voice. Lilith laid a steady hand on her shoulder. "Wouldn't want to get that powder on you."

Quilla gave a gentle smile, the initial fear in her eyes resting into a calm. "Aren't you supposed to be asleep?"

Lilith sat down next to her. "I should ask you the same thing."

"I think we both know sleep isn't a possibility tonight."

Quilla rested her head on Lilith's shoulder, moving her body closer to hers. They watched as the train clicked by; the dark, moonlit landscape slowly fading as the train raced into the distance.

For a moment, Lilith hoped her partner had fallen asleep. The steady rhythm of her breath and the gentle rise and fall of her chest hinted at the fact. But she knew better. They both knew better. This night was not one for rest.

"I'm going to have to kill her, Lili." Quilla's voice was so soft it could've been mistaken as the wind.

"Cercel?" Lilith whispered, her tone matching her Quilla's. "Yeah, I know."

"There's no second chances this time. I can't fuck up. If I can't do this, Lili–"

"Hey, hey," Lilith cupped her face. "Let's not think about that. It's okay–"

"No it's not!" Quilla screeched. "*Every single time* I've tried to kill Cercel, I failed. What's different now? That she killed my siblings? That she's lost it? It's still those same eyes, Lilith. That same face, that same gaze that laughed with me as a kid. I can try to separate my sister from that woman, but no matter how much she's done, the tips of her hair are still the same roots I once brushed."

For a moment, Lilith just sat there. She wanted to pull Quilla into a hug; to let her cry. She wanted to tell her that it would be okay, that in the end, everything was going to work out.

But she couldn't. Because that was a lie.

"I'll do it." She whispered. Her words were so low they barely made it over the wind. "I'll kill her."

Quilla's eyes widened. "What? *No!* I can't ask that of you–"

"It won't be hard." Lilith said. "You distract her and I'll put an arrow in her heart."

For a moment, Quilla looked as if she had a rejection. But she kept rolling the invisible words on her tongue, desperately searching for a response she didn't have.

Lilith tilted her head. "Quill, it's okay that you don't want her to die."

Quilla's eyes rested on the mountains. She placed a hand over her mouth, lowering her head into her knees. At first, Lilith thought she was crying, but when she looked closer, there was no rise and fall of her shoulders.

She laid a hand on her partner's back. "It's okay to cry."

Quilla lifted her head, tucking her knees to her chest. She refused to meet Lilith's eyes; refused to even look at her.

"No, it's not." Quilla drew a shaky breath. "I can be as weak as I want after this is over. But for now, I can't cry. I can't curl up in a ball and hide from the world, as much as I want to."

"Crying isn't weak," Lilith said, her voice gentle. "It's a show of emotion."

"Emotion is pathetic–"

"Emotion is what makes us human."

Quilla rested her chin on her knees. "I hate being human. We aren't strong enough."

Lilith draped her in a hug, resting her head on Quilla's shoulder. "You're strong enough. As far as I've seen, you're the strongest person I know"

Quilla pressed her face into her legs. "Don't lie to me."

"I'm not." Lilith murmured. "I'm being honest. I'd never lie to you, Quill. Never."

Quilla lifted her head. Lilith joined, gazing into her partner's black gaze. Tear stains trickled down her face as more droplets formed in her red eyes. "Promise?"

Lilith gave her a small smile. She brushed her finger over Quilla's cheek, catching a tear falling down her face. "Promise."

For a moment, their gazes rested on each other. Then, a shine entered Quilla's eyes as her lips contorted into a sob. Tears poured from her puffy eyes, tricking around her chin and soaking her shirt.

Lilith pulled her into her blouse, cradling her partner's curls. The train continued to click through the night, the landscape flying by with the wind. She rested her chin on Quilla's head, pressing her lips into her hair and watched as the world passed by.

Chapter Forty Four
Quilla

Ironic how the world worked, wasn't it?

Just five years prior, Quilla was defending the Golden Palace. Now, she crouched before the massive gates, strategizing about how she would draw the entire bronze army out.

"Would you shut it?" Lilith hissed at the troops behind them. Quilla sent a silent thanks. The chatter made it increasingly hard to focus. "I don't care what you're talking about! Unless you want to get shot I suggest you *zip it!*"

The squadron quickly came to a quiet.

Quilla had divided the armies of Hanslack into four groups which now circled the Golden Palace. She instructed they wait until they see patrol on the gates, and then strike. She had already heard three massive explosions, meaning everyone else had already made their move.

Now it was their turn.

"Lilith," Quilla tugged at her sleeve. "Look!"

A large bronze squadron walked along the palace. Each looked deep in conversation– like school children after a long day. Quilla was not deceived. They may have looked innocent, but they were loyal to the very woman who murdered her siblings.

Lilith loaded her bow, one of Killen's explosive arrows resting in the drawstring.

"Say when." She said, eyes resting on her targets.

"When." Quilla commanded. Lilith let the arrow fly. The weapon soared through the air and landed in the brick. As soon as the arrow hit, the patrol leaned over the edge and gazed at the mysterious object.

Quilla turned to her squadron. "As soon as it blows, we charge."

The men got into position, weapons drawn at their sides. The Empire squadron gazed around the forest, anxious to find who fired the stray arrow. They were alert– expecting a potential fight.

Perfect.

"Now." Quilla said.

Lilith squeezed her fist, pressing on the button that rested on her palm. The wall exploded, fire dancing along the charred bricks. The patrol scrambled back, clutching to the stable structure as the debris fell.

Quilla wanted them alive. She wanted a *messenger*.

Her squadron lept from the bushes, weapons drawn at their sides. The dust of the explosion provided a perfect disguise for enemy troops. The shuffling and crunching of leaves told her that the Empire soldiers had surrounded them. She could deal with a threat. She couldn't deal with a threat she couldn't see.

"Get behind me!" Quilla snapped. Her troops filed into a crowd behind her, blades outstretched and ready to strike. She reached into her coat, drawing her daggers.

"Surrender!" the Empire voice called. "Drop your weapons and put your hands in the air. We have you surrounded."

Quilla kept her blades in her palm.

"We have the upper hand." The Empire accent repeated. "Lay down your arms and your fate will be merciful. You made a feeble attack without preparation of arms. You're lucky. The Empire forgives its imbecile perpetrators."

"A shame," Quilla hummed, her accent cutting like fresh meat. "Stupidity can be transformed into such a powerful weapon."

As her tone echoed the last word, the knives exploded from her grasp. They flew at the dust, wails and grunts following the blades departure. Quilla didn't aim to kill– she simply couldn't. She aimed to get a reaction.

It worked.

The soldiers emerged from the dust. Their blades at their hilts, ready to plunge into a waiting chest. But they were material, visible targets. That's all she needed.

"All fire power to the back!" Quilla hollered. "Now!"

Like a bomb, her squadron exploded. Knives, swords and arrows flew towards the rear of the crowd, clearing their escape route. Quilla and Lilith guarded the sides, plunging a blade into the heart of anyone who dared attack.

Sweat beaded on Quilla's forehead as she plunged her blade into a soldier's shoulder. The man screeched and fell to the ground, clutching his crimson wound. She turned to see her men had created a clear entrance to the forest.

"Go!" Quilla shouted. "Run!"

On que, her squadron bolted. They took to the trees like squirrels, hoping over bushes and stomping on debris. This was their terrain: though not trees, the men and women of Hanslack had leapt from buildings and weaved around crowds. The Empire was used to a clear battlefield. This was messy; *chaos*.

Chaos was her home.

Quilla and Lilith leapt over bushes, tumbled under branches and weaved around trees. A warm, loose substance trailed down her neck; she couldn't tell if it was blood or sweat.

The squadron raced ahead of them, tracing the path back to the base of the mountain. It was as if they were deer galloping to the nearest watering hole. No soldier took the same route as another. They leapt over their own obstacles, but followed the same trail.

Quilla was so immersed in the sprint that she didn't notice no one was following her. She gazed behind her, saw the empty forest, and her heart stopped.

The Empire never left a chase. Their motto was to never let even the smallest enemy get away unpunished. There was no shortcut they could take; Quilla chose the most direct route and the enemy had no idea where they were running.

Like an arrow, a flash of memory hit her.

"Get behind a tree! Now!" Quilla hollered. Her squadron rushed behind the trunks, invisible to the perspective of their perpetrators. Quilla rolled behind a tree just seconds before an arrow punctured the air where she once stood.

More followed suit. Hundreds of weapons flew from the trees. Their heads slammed into the bark of the trees as more flew into the dirt. Quilla hugged the rough bark, watching as the weapons soared past her.

Slowly, the arrows died down. Instead of the thuds in the bark, battle cries echoed throughout the forest. The Empire squadron exploded from the trees, bows strung to their back, swords held at their waist.

"Disperse!" Quilla ordered, sprinting into the woods. Her men exploded through the trees, each finding their own path to the larger battlefield.

She raced through the grub, the sound of bowstrings and orders close behind her. The air parted, and an arrow flew towards her. Quilla propelled herself into the air and watched as the weapon soared under her stomach.

Her back foot landed on a fallen tree. With the planted boot, she flung forward. The Empire's cries sounded close behind her: orders and swords clashing against the forest.

Quilla snuck a glance at her chasers. They were far, but running to catch up. She grinned, this would be—

She slammed into something that felt disturbingly like flesh. She crumpled to the ground, dazed. She met the eyes of one of the Stripe's archers.

Quilla flung her blade at the same time that the archer shot his arrow. It hit the opposite's closest perpetrator in the chest. There was a disfigured grunt, and the enemy fell.

As if on cue, both broke into a run. Instead of separating, they ran side by side, weapons drawn to guard the other's weak spots.

"Thank you, General," the Stripe panted.

"Don't mention it," Quilla heaved as she leapt over a bush. "The murder came on both parts."

They sprang through the woods, their shoes skidding against the dry tuft. Quilla sprang over the plants, pushing stray branches out of her way. She ran so fast she forgot about her destination. The sweat dripping down her throat and the adrenaline pumping through her veins made everything else vanish. For a moment, she forgot she was even at war.

She pushed through a branch, flew over a thorned bush, and stumbled right into a bloodbath.

Chapter Forty Five
Alohi

Alohi ducked as a blade flew over her head. The sword caught on her bun, pulling her braided locks. She yelped and flung her needles into the enemy's armpit. He collapsed to the ground, gasping and flailing. Alohi patted her hair.

The next one came at her from behind. She ducked, flinging her needles into the man's pelvis. His legs went limp, crumbling under him as he collapsed to the ground.

She wasn't aiming to kill. She aimed to immobilize. There was no point in bloodshed. It was better that the fate of these men was decided with a clear head.

Suddenly, something grabbed her shoulder. Before Alohi could react, she was pushed to the ground. A foot landed on her chest and a blade touched her throat. Her breath grew short as the boot pressed harder into her ribs. The air slowly slipped from her lungs, refusing to return with her desperate, heaving breaths.

Alohi clawed at the leg, her futile attempts growing weaker as more oxygen fled from her body. A cold rush doused her like a plunge in a glacial river. Her heart thudded with panic, beating under her crushed chest. She let out a gasp, and the boot moved to her throat.

The soldier was grinning ear to ear. His silver armor gleamed in the rising sun; a bright reflection that was unsettlingly blinding. Blood dripped from his lip and seeped between his smile. He was beaten up, sure. But that wouldn't stop him from savoring her death.

Her vision blurred, the panic rose, and the cold grasp turned frigid. Alohi closed her eyes; she didn't want to see the blade plunge into her throat.

But there was no piercing pain, no blood rushing down her neck. Instead, there was the soft snap of a bowstring.

Alohi's eyes sprang open as the soldier toppled off of her. She sat up, clutching her throat and gasping for air. As her vision cleared and her gaze landed on a red arrow lodged in the silver's armor.

Lilith charged, an arrow resting in her fingers. The soldier dislodged her weapon from his armor and tossed it to the side. The archer attacked first–aiming her weapon towards the soldier's thigh. He retaliated by swinging his swords towards Lilith's crouched figure. The blade narrowly missed her, nicking the hair of her braid. In one movement, Lilith leapt onto the sword and drew her bow. Within seconds, she had an arrow planted in the drawstring, ready to shoot.

The soldier withdrew his blade, but not before Lilith jumped. Time slowed as the archer flipped over him, bow aimed at his head. The silver didn't have time to turn before the arrow flew into the back of his neck.

Alohi sat dumbfounded as the head of the weapon ripped through her attacker's throat. Blood poured from the wound; first a trickle, then a steady stream. His eyes rolled back in his head and his knees buckled. His crumpled figure collapsed on the ground, blood pooling under his face.

"Get up, Alohi," Lilith snapped. Alohi hadn't realized she had been sitting there, watching the blood pool. She scrambled to her feet, tightening her grip on her needles.

"Silvers are always annoying." Lilith conceded, firing an arrow into the crowd. "They aren't incredibly hard to kill— if you know how. They're incredibly organized; used to one style of fight— on your left."

Alohi swung her needles into the hip of a soldier. The man collapsed, clutching his paralyzed leg.

"The silvers have no idea how to fight someone without their style." Lilith continued. Alohi couldn't comprehend how she could talk so casually in the middle of a bloodbath. "They're fit for the best. But when they're met with an opponent who knows street style, they're basically fucked– duck."

Alohi lowered to a crouch as Lilith's arrow flew over her. The weapon struck a soldier's arm and he crumpled to the ground.

Of course, Lilith wasn't trying to kill. She was doing the same as Alohi. Stall, immobilize, paralyze.

But an arrow was quite inefficient for that type of fight.

"I'll cover for you." Lilith ordered. "Go into the crowd and paralyze as many people as possible."

Alohi nodded and bolted. She sprang from Lilith's side and ran into the crowd. It was a mess of limbs and blades. One second, an elbow propelled into her gut; another a sword swung over her head. Alohi stuck her needles anywhere they fit. Bodies collapsed around her, yelping from the pain and shock of paralyzation. Throughout all of it, she snuck by unnoticed. If anyone tried to resist, an arrow flew into their throat.

She snuck around the bloodbath, crouching at the height of people's waists. Like a hunting tiger, she struck her prey. The hip, the shoulder, the knee. One way or another, her victims collapsed into the dirt.

A sword flew over her head. She ducked, identified who held the weapon, and flung her needles into his knee. She narrowly avoided a second attack and flung her needle into her perpetrator's armpit. .

Dust flew, kicked up by the raging battle. To her, it was just a mess of limbs and weapons. She struck the people that aimed at her– not paying any mind to which side they were on. Empire, League, Hanslack, Pirate Colonies; Alohi didn't discriminate. The paralyzation would wear off in due time. In the end, what was a few hours of immobility?

Alohi snuck behind a soldier, flinging her weapons into the muscle of his thigh. There was a yelp, and a thud. She didn't pay any mind. He'd be fine.

A hand struck her shoulder. The touch was so light it might have been a tap, but the severity didn't matter. Alohi flung her needle at the man's knee, but was stopped by a firm grip.

Someone yanked her above the commotion, struggling and screaming. She was so busy trying to unhand herself that she didn't realize her captor until she spoke.

"Oh do shut up, Alohi," Quilla rolled her eyes, holding her wrist like a dirty diaper. "If I wanted you dead you would be so already."

Alohi stopped struggling and faced her. Quilla and Nikolai looked strikingly bored, an emotion extremely out of place in the battle. Quilla's unruly curls sprouted in every direction and Nikolai was covered in a mixture of dust and blood.

Alohi nervously glanced at Quilla. "Did I try to–"

"No," Quilla said. "You tried to paralyze *him*. Trust me, Alohi, I know the urge, but now really isn't the time."

Nikolai growled, elbowing her.

Suddenly, heavy footsteps rushed towards them. They ducked in unison, dropping to the dusty ground. Quilla's blade sailed overhead— Alohi didn't notice it leave her palm. The dagger struck the soldier and blood poured over his armor.

"It's thinning." Nikolai said. "It's almost time for Tnil to lead the attack on the silvers, and–"

"And our siege of the Palace." Quilla finished. She wouldn't meet his eye. "I know. Alohi, where's Lilith?"

Alohi pointed to her right. In the center of the chaos was the archer. Lilith's arrows fired in every direction at every second. When the soldiers got too close, she would use her weapons as blades and push them into her attacker's forehead. Occasionally, arrows would fly towards her and she would twirl her bow to block them.

"Holy shit," Alohi conceded. "She's amazing."

"I know," Quilla grinned. "She's been amazing for years. Keep up, Alohi."

Alohi glanced skeptically at Nikolai. When she returned her gaze to Quilla, she found the criminal prodigy was already sprinting into the battle. Without a word, they followed her.

They ran through the dust; Nikolai making a creative use of elbows to get through the battle. When they reached Lilith, she was joined by her partner. They fought back to back— a technique that seemed old as time.

Lilith fired an arrow past Quilla's shoulder while Quilla stabbed Lilith's opponent. They moved in symphony, a song so loud it hypnotized everyone within a distance.

"Move, assholes!" Lilith screeched. Another detail of their song was that it was incredibly rude. "We aren't going to do this by ourselves!"

Alohi and Nikolai snapped out of their trance. They drew their weapons, moving to fight beside Quilla and Lilith. Alohi barely had time to use her needles, because as soon as she was about to strike, Lilith pushed her hand to her side.

"Look," she said, pointing. There, on a high rock, was a man waving a white flag. As if in unison, the entire army dropped their weapons. The atmosphere turned from one of battle to sorrow in the blink of an eye. Suddenly, soldiers were counting their dead instead of making more.

Quilla watched the flag with an unreadable stare, as if calculating if the thing was real. She didn't let go of her knives— if anything, she held on tighter.

"Quill," Lilith tapped her shoulder. "We need to negotiate the terms."

Quilla nodded. She tucked her blades into her coat, ran her hands through her hair, and straightened her posture.

"Killen!" she screeched. "Florian!"

The two materialized at her side. Each was covered in blood, the crimson liquid splattered on their face. Killen was the most unruly Alohi ever saw him. His straight, tailored hair stuck out in bloody strands and blood crept between his grinning lips.

"Your trusted advisors are here, Kiwi," Florian smiled. A deep crimson lingered between their teeth. "Glad to be of service."

Quilla ignored them. She strode to the rock, her crew close at her heel. Just before the last stretch, she nodded at Alohi. On cue, she dispersed from the group.

Instead of meeting them at the bottom of the stone, Alohi was to take a different route. She scaled the rock, brushing plants and debris out of the way. The nature in Thine was quite annoying; dry, spiky and uneasy to move.

Alohi snuck around a brush and crouched behind a boulder. Behind the large rock, she heard Quilla's crisp cut accent.

"Generals who hide while their armies fight are a peculiar type of coward." She cooed. "I find that fear is a luxury fighters and their commander's don't have. Yet you seem afraid to get your hands dirty."

There was a shuffle of clothing. Alohi assumed someone shrugged. "A safe perch for commanders means the head of the flock is out of harm's way. I can't say the same for your army of rag-tag delinquents. Any sort of organization seems a far feat."

Quilla's stark cut of a cackle echoed around the boulders. "Possibly, yet you are the one who bears the white flag. Our methods seem victorious compared to your socially constructed 'organization.'"

"I find the true meaning of the battle is in the negotiation." The silver general hummed. His Thinian accent was sharp, the words coming out blended together, yet slowing at any vowel. The tongue was bizarrely posh —as if the accent was a language itself. "Battle proves the threat— compromise decides the fate."

"I suppose you have a point." Alohi snuck from behind the boulder. Her padded soles crept along the dry dirt, needles clutched between her fingers. The silver's armor gleamed in the sun, not a splotch of blood splattering the new material.

Alohi went for the two guards first. She struck the first behind the neck. Before he could gasp, she flung her needles into the second's hip. Their legs broke beneath them. This time, a scream escaped their lips. The general whirled around.

She didn't waste any time. Her needles struck his collarbone, knee, ankles and hip. The general didn't have time to draw his sword; he was gasping on the ground before Alohi broke a sweat.

She kicked him off the rock. His limp body landed on the hard dirt with a thud, dust sprouting around his incapacitated form. Alohi jumped after him, landing next to Quilla.

"You're right about one thing, General," Quilla gestured to Killen and Florian, who lifted the coward to her height. "Negotiations do decide a nation's fate. That is why I plan to achieve the upper hand in *every* compromise I participate in." She grabbed the general's chin, forcing him to look at her. "That way, *'compromise'* is only a grain of salt in my plan."

The general spat on her face. "You fucking whore."

Quilla wiped the saliva off her cheek. For a moment, she gazed at the sticky substance on her fingers; then smudged it in the general's eyes.

"Let me level with you." Quilla grinned. "I am no leader, and certainly not a politician. I am a fighter, through and through. I know the human body— how to make and break it. So let me assure you, if you or any of your men lay a finger on someone who has pledged their allegiance to me, I will have you and your family strung by your genitals to these very trees." Quilla lifted his chin, a hungry look blazing in her gaze as she looked at the general's terrified expression. "I don't make rules, General. I don't handle compromise or political quarrels. My only job is the punishment if they don't go as planned."

Chapter Forty Six
Nikolai

Battle nerves came before the fight and left shortly after.

At least for Nikolai they did.

Quilla and Lilith seemed more alert than ever. As quickly as the battle ended, Quilla gathered her trusted advisors and leaders to organize the next motion of their attack.

"Tnil." Quilla ordered. "Take one hundred soldiers. I don't care which. It's your choice. Go into the Golden Palace and finish off all the remaining soldiers. I want them injured— not dead. We want to limit our casualties."

"About how many are still in the palace?" Tnil asked. "If you were to guess."

"The casualty and captor number add up to around eighty percent of the Empire's total military." Lilith explained. "It's just the stragglers. Stragglers play a massive role in the rise and fall of nations."

Tnil nodded. "And–" she cocked her head to the side. "I believe titles are in order. General, perhaps?"

Quilla and Nikolai glanced at each other. "We assumed you already gave yourself the title."

Tnil had been in charge of the League, along with Killen. Quilla had given her the role assuming she would straighten the organization to her liking. That included being unnecessarily harsh and naming herself their esteemed commander. Quilla and Nikolai had discussed it, and agreed that her prickly personality would be a perfect fit for the role.

"Honestly," Tnil shrugged. "I've been introducing myself as General Limpana since the boat ride."

"Well," Lilith said. "Good to make it official."

"Choose men who you know and trust." Nikolai added. "Make sure you are aware of what each of them can do and where they may need assistance. We can give you guesses, but in reality, you are going into an assassination blind."

Tnil pierced her lips. "I prefer visually impaired."

"The only realistic preference is your choice of troops." Quilla said. "Which you may want to choose."

Tnil shot her a glare, which quickly turned into an over exaggerated smile, and fled the tent.

After she left, the only sound was the wind rustling against the fabric. Nikolai, Quilla, Lilith and Alohi sat cross legged on the floor, not daring to meet each other's gaze. They were waiting for someone to speak. Someone to tell them it was time. They all knew what came next, but an order felt... *right*.

"I'm forcing anyone to come with me," Quilla said. "It's your choice. If anyone— throughout any point in this— wants to back out, I won't hold a grudge."

Lilith spoke first. "I'm going with you. No matter what we are doing this *together*."

"Come on, Thorne," Nikolai shot her a grin. "You think you can get rid of me that easily?"

"We've stuck together this far," Alohi added. "Seems wrong to split up now."

Quilla's lips parted in a half hearted smile. They quickly returned to a fine line. "I just want you to know what you're getting into. Cercel is the most powerful person we've fought— and she's completely off the rails. What's worse is that I don't know if I have the strength to–"

"Then we'll do it for you," Lilith finished. "She's one woman. We're four trained fighters. If you can't kill her, one of us will."

"Thank you," this time, Quilla gave her a real smile. "Thank you for not letting me do this alone."

Nikolai patted her on the shoulder. "We're not going anywhere. You're stuck with us whether you like it or not."

"In this case," Quilla said. "You are very welcome to stay by my side."

"What do you need us to do?" Lilith asked. "What's your plan?"

Quilla nodded. "There's a courtyard in the center of the palace. The Empress already knows we're coming— there's no way a messenger didn't get back to her. We'll enter there, a scout will let her know we're there. Lilith," the archer perked. "There are several trees overlooking the area. I want you to set up your perch there. Alohi, Nikolai, you are the safety. If everything goes to plan, you two won't have to bloody your weapons. Nevertheless, I want you to hide behind the pillars. They're large enough that they should conceal you; but if Cercel seems to be going towards you, do your best to hide."

The three nodded. "What's our plan for killing her?" Alohi asked.

"I'm the only one who will be in her range of sight." Quilla said. "Cercel will come after me, thinking I've come alone. I'll engage her enough for Lilith to get a clean shot, and she will pierce Cercel's throat."

Nikolai tilted his head. The plan caught him off guard. For the dramatic, long awaited death of Cercel Ghan, the scheme seemed rather... plain.

"That's it?" he asked.

"Yes," Quilla said. "I want this to be done as quickly as possible. In and out, never look back."

"That's... good–" Nikolai took a sharp breath. "I guess I just expected–"

"Me to kill her?" Quilla's gaze drifted to her feet. "Everyone expects that. The expectation is what I'm counting on. Cercel's stayed in the palace because she knows I'm coming for her. But the truth is, I don't know if I'll be able to put a blade in her heart."

"So I'm the insurance." Lilith finished. "Quilla's only the decoy. As soon as Cercel is in range, I'll kill her."

Alohi nodded. "And you're sure you can."

Lilith scoffed. "The bitch strung me up like poultry and covered my arms in scars. I think my rage is more than enough to manage."

None of them responded. None of them could find the words. There was no phrase to be spoken, no conversation to be exchanged. The only appropriate noise were the sharp breaths echoing around the tent.

After what felt like minutes, Quilla stood. She dusted off her pants and gazed at the blazing sun.

"Come on," she said, her eyes resting on the landscape. "Let's go kill ourselves an Empress."

~~~

As expected, Tnil made short work of her title.

She had gathered a hundred soldiers— most from the League, but a few from other organizations, and informed them of their job. Nikolai had expected some pushback; after all, none of them knew what they would find behind the Golden Palace walls. But the entire squadron seemed to hum with ecstatic energy. He supposed after years of suffering under the Empire, it was euphoric to have the upper hand.

Tnil took their buzzing bliss and transformed it into hungry, powerful bloodlust. In the matter of minutes, the exhausted soldiers who could barely lift their own feet were converted into angry lions anxious to attack a herd of cattle.

"I don't care if you're tired!" Tnil stood at the center of her troops, hands placed on her hips. "Guess what? We all fucking are. We've been tired for *years*. We are exhausted from grieving loved ones, fighting for our food, and trying so damn hard to win a hopeless war. But now we've *won*! Do you know what that means?" Tnil drew her sword, a malicious smile carving across her lips. "It's time to clean up the stragglers."

The army drew their weapons, raising them in the air with triumphant screeches. Tnil's grin widened as her squadron rallied around her, waiting for her command.

"I really didn't expect her to–" Nikolai whispered to Quilla. "Well, I don't know what I was expecting, but certainly not this."

"She's quite..." Quilla pressed her fingers to her lips. "Extravagant, isn't she?"
~~~

Nikolai snorted. "You should have seen her when she was younger."

"I get the feeling we would get along."

Nikolai shrugged, weighing the possibility. "If you were on the same side, you would be the best of friends. If you weren't, I think you might loathe each other."

Tnil's army surged forth. By the look of the soldier's giddy feet, it seemed they were trying not to break into a sprint. Quilla, Lilith, Nikolai and Alohi brought up the back. They would follow the army until they got to the Golden Palace. Then, they would split. The battalion to kill the stragglers, the four of them to kill the Empress.

The squadron marched through the trees, leaves crunching under their feet. As they grew closer to the Golden Palace, the plant life grew greener and thicker. Nikolai found himself wacking green vines out of the way and jumping over pools of water.

"Brighan's an oasis." Quilla explained. "It's how it became the center of all power. Other oppressors can have as much military personnel as they like, but fire power is next to nothing if you don't have water. Brighan will *always* have water."

They continued to march through the forest. Sticks and brambles tugged at their ankles while mud and dirt crusted around their shoes. Around them, Tnil's squadron still buzzed with anticipation. While Nikolai was relieved at their joy, he couldn't help but feel terribly out of place.

For the army, this was the happiest time of their life— a long awaited victory.

But for the four of them, this was a solemn occasion.

Quilla kept her eyes trained on the ground. Nikolai gazed ahead, Alohi tugged at her clothing, and Lilith dug her fingertips into an arrow.

There was no ripple of emotion when Nikolai cleared a branch and revealed the Palace. There was no yelp of excitement, no flinch of fear. They all just stared at the building, silent understanding rippling between them.

It's time.

"Last chance." Quilla breathed. "If you want–"

"We don't," Nikolai interrupted. "Or... at least I'm staying."

"So am I," Alohi agreed.

"No matter what happens," Lilith reached for Quilla's hand. "We are all staying with you."

Quilla dipped her head in thank you. She offered them a smile. "Can we have one last moment? Before we go?"

Without hesitation, they embraced each other. Lilith put an arm around Quilla, and the other around Alohi. Nikolai towered over them, placing his hand on Quilla's shoulder and chin on Alohi's hair. They wrapped their arms around each other, pressing their faces into each other's clothes.

"This won't be the last time," Alohi murmured. "We're going to run this country together."

Quilla snorted. "*You two* will run this country together. After this, it's retirement."

Nikolai gave her a look. "You can't go into retirement at seventeen."

"Oh?" Quilla tilted her head, grinning. "Who's gonna stop me?"

Nikolai had a response, but decided not to use it. This moment was too precious to be burdened with quarrels.

"I look forward to our future spats." Nikolai said.

Quilla dipped her chin. "As do I."

"This is not the last time," Lilith breathed. "You all have to promise to come back alive."

They gazed at each other, unsure of what to do. Of course, they would all promise, but none of them knew a ritual worth the occasion.

"Promise," Quilla withdrew a blade. "One mark into your palm, just enough that it'll scar. That's our promise."

Quilla did the cut first. She dug the blade into her skin, blood leaking out in wake of the dagger. When she was done, she withdrew the knife, let the blood fall into the dirt, and passed the blade to Lilith.

The two criminals did the ritual with so much ease it looked like it didn't hurt. But when he was passed the blade, he realized the act was much harder than they made it look. He had to grit his teeth so he wouldn't yelp as he slid the blade across his palm.

Alohi made the mark, and from the look on her face, it must have been just as painful as his. When it was done, she handed the blade back to Quilla and gazed at her wound.

"Good," Alohi said. "That's the promise. If any of you die, you break it."

They nodded in unison. Once again, a state of wordless bliss had come over their group. It wasn't awkward— no one was trying to force needless conversation. Instead, it was a comfortable, calm silence.

"It's time," Quilla murmured, her voice barely coming over the breeze. "Let's go."

The two criminals stepped out of the forest. They didn't try to conceal themselves, they simply walked to the Golden Palace in full light. Like two soldiers coming home from war.

Alohi stepped to follow them, but Nikolai grabbed her hand. "Wait," Nikolai said. "Just– just one second."

Alohi stopped, gazing at him with bright, blue eyes. Nikolai pulled her into his chest, wrapping his arms around her. He rested his chin on her head, watching the Golden Palace glimmer in the sunlight.

"Nik?" Alohi murmured. "I know you promised already. But I really, *really* need you to survive."

"I know," Nikolai said, pressing his lips into her hair. "But all I can promise is that I'll try my best not to die."

Alohi tightened her grip on his waist. Nikolai cupped his palm over her head. For a moment, there was silence. Nothing but the wind flowing through the trees.

"Promise me you'll take me to the snow." Alohi said. "After this, we'll go to Courna together, just you and me, and play in the snow."

Nikolai gave her a sympathetic look. "Lo–"

"Promise me, Nikolai," Alohi pushed him away, grasping his shoulders. Her blue eyes bore into his; a silent, vibrant weapon. *Promise me* we'll see the snow."

"Okay," Nikolai leaned in, pressing his lips to Alohi's forehead. "We'll see the snow, Alohi. I promise."

Chapter Forty Seven
Quilla

"*Cercel!*" Quilla screeched. Her hands tightened around her knives as the silence thickened.

The courtyard was like any place in Thine; eerily quiet with a low wind to keep it company. Trees hung over the concrete like chandeliers, their golden leaves drifting to the ground with a slight breeze. A long time ago, she and Cercel had played there. Now, they were meeting for one final game.

Except the Empress was missing. Her cackle was silent, and her footsteps echoed around another part of the building. Demolition teams were stationed outside of the palace at this very moment. The clock was ticking. If Cercel didn't show herself soon, the entire palace would be blown into the sky.

Quilla tried again. "Cercel!" she screamed, her voice echoing around the pillars. "I'm here! This is what you want, isn't it? Fucking fight me!"

For a moment, the silence remained. Then, there was a rustle in the trees. Quilla bolted to Lilith's hiding place without thinking.

There was an ear splitting scream followed by the crack of branches. Her archer toppled out of the tree, bow and arrows nowhere to be found. Lilith landed on her feet, but her knee bent inward, and a horrifying snap confirmed Quilla's fear.

As soon as she hit the floor, Lilith screamed in pain. Her knee flung to her grasp, the limb swelling rapidly. Loud, painful cries rang from her mouth as she clutched the sprain.

Quilla rushed to her side, kneeling beside her partner. Lilith's eyes were shut, tears sinking down her cheeks. Her teeth pressed together hard enough to snap her jaw. She was in so much pain, but as soon as Quilla touched her cheek, Lilith's eyes flung open.

"You need to *go*!" Lilith drawled. "Cercel is *here*. I'll be fine."

Quilla bounced back as Lilith pushed her off. "Lili, are you sure–"

"*Go!*" Lilith screeched, fire burning bright in her gaze.

Quilla stood, surveying the grounds for the Empress. There was no evidence of her; once again, the wind was her only companion.

That was until she heard the blood curdling cackle.

The noise echoed around the courtyard, bouncing off of the pillars and springing around the building. It was distorted, as if a new woman had taken over Cercel's laugh. But Quilla recognized it. *No one else* had that fierce a tongue.

"Alohi!" Quilla called. "Get Lilith out of here!"

The politician leaped from the pillar and sprang into view. She raced across the courtyard, hauled Lilith to her feet, and limped away. It took all of Quilla's strength not to race after them, but there was a job to be done. Lilith would be fine. The question is, would she?

"Where is she?" Nikolai asked. Quilla didn't realize he was back to back with her until he spoke. His swords were drawn at his sides and his ice blue eyes glowed with anticipation.

"What are you doing?" Quilla snapped. "I told you to *hide*!"

"The plans gone to shit." Nikolai retorted. "I'm not letting you face her alone. If we win, we win together. If we lose... well..."

"Together," Quilla repeated. "We die together."

They were interrupted by the stout cackle. Cercel's hard rasp filled the courtyard, her voice so rough if might have scratched the concrete. Quilla flinched, tightening her grip on her blades.

"Look who it is," she drawled. "The Golden Heir and the White King. Back to back, side by side. How *wholesome*."

The words bounced around the courtyard, their syllables lingering before absorbing into the floor.

"You wanted a fight, Cercel." Quilla yelled. "Now you've got one. Do us the courtesy of showing up, won't you?"

"Hmm..." Cercel hummed. "Family gatherings are usually only *family*. I find the boy is a bit out of place, don't you think, Rosey?" the Empress sounded like a child, toying with the words as she spoke them. "Then again, he will be easy pickings. I suppose an extra toy never did any harm."

"This isn't a game, Cercel!" Quilla snapped. "People's lives are at stake! A *nation* is at stake!"

Cercel's low hum of a rasp split the air. "Oh, Rosey Rosey, always the moralist." She let out a stark chortle. "Funny, how things turned out. But I always find life is funner with a risk. They're like pawns... you know, people?" she clicked her tongue, the snap vibrating throughout the walls. "So easy to just... tip over."

Quilla and Nikolai bristled, bracing themselves for an attack.

"But..." Cercel's rasp scraped the atmosphere. "I suppose I have been waiting for a while. I guess I should be thankful— thank you, for finally showing up, Rosalie."

Quilla whipped around as the click of heels rang out. Long robes drifted at Cercel's feet, swaying gently in the wind. The black cloth ran up her sides, tying at the waist. Gold stripes caress the robe's side— eerily similar to their old uniform.

The Empress— for lack of better words— looked manic. Her hands were wrapped in bloody bandages and her face was blood-crusted. Her hair was messily cut, as if someone had taken garden tools to it. Strands running down her back were mixed with the jagged mess cut at her head. A crimson shine splattered in her hair, the oily feel matching the sparkle in her black eyes.

"Rosalie," Cercel hummed. "It's been too long."

Quilla dug her nails into the hilt of her knife.

The Empress tilted her head. "You aren't usually this quiet. You were so... *chatty* growing up. What happened?"

She spoke like it was an actual question. Her voice scraped low, but the octave rose with emphasis. Cercel was either trying to dilate her accent or extinguish it.

"I don't want to draw this out." Quilla said. "We both know niether of us came here for conversation."

Cercel scoffed. "So serious, fine." She waved to Nikolai, as if swatting a mosquito away. "Pretty boy goes. Just you and me, Rosalie. We don't want to *complicate* things."

"Fine," Quilla retorted. Nikolai grabbed her arm.

"What are you doing?" he hissed. "You know you can't take her alone!"

"There's something different about her," Quilla said. "I'll be fine."

"It's Cercel, something's always *different*."

"But something's really *off*." Quilla responded. "I don't know what it is, but she's lost it. In this state, my skills best hers."

Nikolai shot her a glare, but stepped back. "You know that's not what I'm worried about."

Nevertheless, the swordsman retreated to the pillars, swords resting by his sides. He was ready. He may have moved off the battleground, but he was still in this fight.

"Well isn't this nice." Cercel strode towards her. "Sister, *sister*. I really did miss you, sister. Can you believe it?"

Quilla squared her shoulders, silently calculating her first action.

"*Boring*!" Cercel cackled. "Right to the point, I suppose."

The Empress's robes slipped off her shoulder, sliding down her arm and revealing a training uniform. The jumpsuit was stuck to Cercel's muscular figure, only the pads on her shoulder accentuated her body. The same gold stripes ran down her figure, glittering where the sun touched them.

"It's so sad," Cercel cooed. "This was the same uniform we used to wear together. You know, with our *family*."

Quilla's fist crumpled around her dagger. "You *killed* our family!" she screeched. "Dammit! *fight*!"

This time, Cercel's smile fell, molding into a scowl. She drew two stars and hurled them at Quilla. She was faster; Quilla flew to the side, throwing two of her own blades.

Cercel ascended into the air, twirling around the attack. She drew more weapons from her belt and charged at Quilla.

Quilla expected her attack. Cercel came at her left, foot swinging into her side. Quilla's fist pummeled into the Empress's stomach, only to be blocked by Cercel's wrist.

They flew apart, regrouping. The two circled each other like vultures, scouting each other's weak spots and avoiding the other's strong attacks. Cercel had a slight limp in her left leg. A deep crimson soaked through the gold stripe of her pants. The Empress was injured. A weak spot.

This time, it was Quilla who made the first move. With her blade extended, she lunged at Cercel's thigh. Cercel swung her fist into Quilla's face, but the blow was poorly aimed. The Empress's hand grazed her cheek, and Quilla dug her blade into Cercel's wound.

Cercel toppled back as fresh crimson covered her uniform. Quilla pounced on her fallen figure, raising her knife above her head.

"Well?" Cercel spat, blood leaking from her lips. "Go on, do it. *Kill me*! That's what you came here to do, right?"

Quilla tightened her grip on the blade. Tears sprang to her eyes and the adrenaline of the fight was replaced with a heavy grief.

When she looked at Cercel— the Empress who killed countless people— she didn't see a murderer. She saw glowing black eyes, straight hair that was effortlessly maintained, and a smile she used to adore. Those same, bloody locks that stuck out from her head were the same strands she once brushed.

No matter what Cercel did, no matter how much she lost it, Quilla would always be her sister.

Cercel let out a cracked cackle. Blood flew from her lips, splattering Quilla's face. The Empress swung her knee into Quilla's chest. In the same motion, she hit the knife out of her hands. Quilla staggered back, reaching for another blade. The weapon was virtually useless— what good was a dagger if you couldn't wrench it into a heart?

"Oh-ho!" Cercel cried, deranged laughs interrupting her speech. "Oh, *Rosalie*. No matter what I do— you still can't put a blade in my chest."

Quilla took a shaky breath, the air suddenly very cold. She couldn't respond. She had no retort on her tongue. No matter what, she could *never* kill Cercel.

Cercel's blades came spinning at her. Quilla leaped in the air, twirling as they whistled around her. As soon as she landed, Cercel charged, stars in hand.

Quilla didn't use her blades. Instead, she simply dodged Cercel's attack. This wasn't her style of fight. She preferred to be on offense. Defense was a liability— defense was her weakness.

"You're not even trying!" Cercel cackled. "Oh, come now, Rosalie. I thought this would at least be a bit fun!"

Quilla didn't have the energy to respond. Cercel's blades flew faster and faster. As soon as a star whistled by her ear, Cercel's fist came at her chest. She dodged every blow, her form getting sloppier with each movement.

There was a piercing pain in her stomach. Quilla glanced down to see crimson blood soaking through her blouse. Before she could react, Cercel swung her foot into her chest.

Quilla fell to the floor, rolling across the concrete and curling up in a ball. Cercel's footsteps clicked behind her, the distinct smell of blood drifted into her nose as the Empress knelt beside her.

"You're rusty, Rosey," she cooed. "I've dreamed of this day, when I kneel over your broken body and slit your throat. But— it's come so *easy*." There was a ruffle of fabric, Quilla assumed she shrugged. "Oh well- I suppose not everything can be as beautiful as a dream."

The cold touch of a blade pressed against her throat. Quilla tried to turn around, but Cercel's boot landed on her chest. Quilla closed her eyes. She didn't want to watch as Cercel slit her throat.

"Get away from her!" Nikolai's voice rang over the courtyard. Cercel stepped off of Quilla and faced him.

"Nikolai!" Quilla warned, scrambling to her feet. "Don't-"

But it was too late. Cercel had a new target. Her stars came fast. At first, Nikolai was able to dodge them. His swords flew to block the blades, but he was getting tired.

Cercel charged at him. Nikolai tried a blow at her chest, but the Empress jumped onto his sword, flipped to his opposite side, and landed two paces away.

This time, Nikolai didn't have time to turn around. His swords weren't ready to block, and he wasn't in the position to dodge. He only had time to turn before Cercel flung a throwing star into his throat.

Chapter Forty Eight
Quilla

"*No!*" Alohi screeched.

Quilla turned to see the politician, she was standing near the pillars, Lilith leaning against her. Her bright blue eyes shined with tears and her mouth opened in a scream of terror as she watched Cercel twist the blade into Nikolai's neck.

Before the Empress could make another move, Quilla fired a blade at her head. Cercel withdrew her star and dodged Quilla's attack. More knives rushed at her, anger in each throw. Quilla wasn't blind anymore. Her morals had dissipated. Now, all she had was rage.

"How dare *you*!" Quilla growled. "This was between you and me, Cercel!"

Cercel's low cackle echoed around the walls. She was striding next to the pillars, stars resting in her bandaged palms. "Rules are simply guidelines, Rosey. Ones that I don't like to follow."

Quilla fired another blade. "You *slaughtered* my family!"

"*I'm* your family!" Cercel screamed. Her voice was pained with sorrow. Sorrow Quilla had no time for. "I'm your *sister*!"

Quilla tightened her fist. "Not anymore."

She charged at Cercel. This time, she had the offensive. Cercel fired futile, rushed attacks, but Quilla's blades were precise. She went for the Empress's hip, and Cercel barely blocked her. A half second later, Quilla lunged at her stomach. The blade scraped the flesh before Cercel twirled away.

Quilla wasn't hesitating anymore. Everytime Cercel dodged, her attacks became quicker. Next, she lunged at Cercel's face. Her fist made contact, and a sickening crack crumpled the Empress's nose. She clutched the bloodied flesh, tears filling her fiery eyes.

The Empress made a move at her stomach, only for Quilla to kick her chest. Cercel toppled backward, but not before flinging a star in Quilla's direction. It was poorly aimed, not a kill shot. But through luck or skill, the blade found itself in Quilla's shoulder.

She toppled backward, clutching her wound. Quilla drew the blade from her shoulder, and another wave of blood fled from her body. The warm liquid trickled down her arm, flooding her white blouse.

"So this is how it ends?" Cercel stood over her. Blood trailed down her face, and her eyes were no longer vibrant. Instead, the fiery glow was replaced with a dull, saddened gaze. "A blade to your heart, in your friend's, and a one in my own."

Quilla lunged forward, only to be kicked back. She tried to reach for her blades but Cercel stepped on her hands.

"*Argh*!" she screeched, squirming under Cercel's grasp. The Empress leaned down, holding Quilla's wrists with her hands. She gazed at her with curiosity— but there was a mix of sadness. Almost *regret*.

"A shame it has to end like this." Rasped the Empress. "I would rather slaughter all your friends and torture you for a while. But honestly, that seems like a far feat. We're both going to die, Rosalie. It's just a matter of who goes first."

Quilla tried to yell. She tried to scream. But she was paralyzed with fear. This was it, all other options were gone. As Cercel drew her throwing star, Quilla realized it would be the weapon that killed her.

Unless she let go.

Let go of her sisterhood, let go of her past. Forget the fond memories she shared with Cercel, the woman about to send a blade into her heart. They weren't the same person. The child she loved and the woman she became were separate. There was no salvaging their relationship— no returning to what they once were.

Cercel had gone too far.

It was Quilla's job to make sure she stopped there.

Cercel raised the star above her head, an insane smile gleaming on her face. Her straight hair dangled in front of her eyes as she laughed hard, terrifying belts.

"Goodbye, Rosalie!" Cercel cackled. "Farewell, sis—"

Her face crumpled. The star she was holding slipped from her grasp. The crazy glitter in her eyes was replaced with a shining gloss. A tear rolled down her cheek. For a moment, Cercel looked sane.

Quilla wasn't fooled.

She kept her gaze steady, breathing rhythmic and fist tight as she pressed the blade further into Cercel's chest.

Cercel let out a gasp.

Quilla twisted the knife.

Blood leaked down Quilla's fingers, trickling over her wrist and soaking her blouse. In a smooth, gentle movement, Quilla moved Cercel onto the concrete.

She pulled the knife from Cercel's rib cage and stood. When she looked down at Cercel's bloodied, broken figure, she didn't see the woman that tried to kill her.

She saw the child that cried in her arms. The kid who had lost everything. The daughter deprived of affection. A person who so desperately wanted to be *loved*.

The story of Cercel Ghan was a true tragedy.

Both of their tales were. They were children of a broken dynasty, survivors of an unsurvivable event. Those kinds of people— those kinds of children— have tragedy written in their blood.

The only difference between them was who followed the story of their past, and who defied it.

"Rosalie..." Cercel choked. Blood started to come up her throat. Everytime she opened her mouth, a pool of crimson liquid dripped down her cheek. "Rosalie please... stay."

Quilla tilted her head. Cercel may have looked weak, but those were still the same hands who cut open Lilith's arms, who burned the Golden Class alive, and who thrust a throwing star into Nikolai's throat.

She turned, heading towards her friend's fallen figure.

"*No!*" Cercel hollered, her screech choked with blood. "No, Rosalie, please! *Stay!*" the stumble of sobs entered her tone. "*Rosalie!*"

Quilla stopped. She turned her head just enough to see Cercel's body on the floor. Blood crusted around Quilla's face, her long curls drenched in the red liquid. Her tattered cloak wavered at her knees, the edges covered in Cercel's crimson.

Quilla ran a bloodied hand through her hair. "Try again."

For a moment, Cercel lay silent. Her bloodied, broken form held still. For a split second, Quilla thought she had died. Then, she started begging.

"*Quilla!*" Cercel screeched. "Please, Quilla. Stay. Just while I die. *Stay!*"

Quilla didn't look back. Cercel's screams echoed in the distance as she strode away, heels clicking, knives clattering in her coat. She no longer wanted to see the Empress.

Cercel was no longer her family.

Quilla strode across the concrete, ignoring her former sister's pleading screams to be with the people who *really* loved her.

Chapter Forty Nine
Alohi

"Nikolai!" Alohi grasped his shoulders. "No! No! *No!* You're going to survive this. Everything is going to be okay!

Nikolai extended a shaky hand. His fingers were drenched in the same blood that slowly seeped through his shirt. The crimson pooled around him, flooding from his wound and turning his skin an awful, pasty white.

"Lo," he touched his trembling fingers to her face. "It's okay–"

"No, *shut up*!" Alohi sobbed. Tears poured from her eyes, coming like a storm. No matter how hard she willed the droplets back, the sting in her eyes persisted. "Don't talk, Nikolai. You're going to be *okay*!"

"Alohi–" Lilith put a hand on her shoulder. She jumped around to find tears trickling down the archer's face. "We can't save him–"

"No! Shut up!" Alohi screeched. She grasped Nikolai's shoulders, burying her head in his chest. The warmth of his body was retreating. His life was–

No, she wouldn't finish that thought. She couldn't. He *promised* he wouldn't die. He couldn't break a promise. Not now. Anytime but *now*!

"Alohi," Nikolai's shaky, pale hands picked up her face. "Alohi, I need you to listen to me."

Though her entire body was trembling, Alohi nodded. She found the strength to look into her friend's ice blue eyes; though every part of him seemed to be drifting, Nikolai's gaze held the same vibrant sparkle.

"You're going to rule." He choked. "I don't care what my dad says— I don't care what my dad *does*. He doesn't get a snippet of power, understand? This is your country now–"

"Nikolai, no!" Alohi screamed, tears soaking her blouse. "*You're* going to rule–"

"No," his voice was so steady, but blood was creeping along the edge of his lips. "I'm going to die. This country has been in shambles—" he was interrupted by a sputter of coughs, crimson mixing with his saliva. "—for years. You make sure that it doesn't stay that way. Take all the corrupt people in this world and silence them. You have control. Do good with it."

Alohi let out a strangled sob. "*Nikolai*!"

"Promise me Alohi."

"You promised *me*!" she screeched. "You promised to take me to the snow! You *promised*, Nikolai!"

"Alohi," Nikolai choked, tears glossing over his eyes. "Please."

Alohi wanted to form a response. She wanted to promise that she'd create a Utopia, that this country would outlive all four of them. That she wouldn't let Grandez Lone get his hands on their nation.

But she couldn't, because every time she opened her mouth sobs erupted out. Tears continued to flow like a river, and her jaw could do nothing but tremble.

"I promise, Nikolai." Quilla knelt beside him. He reached for her hand, and Quilla took it. "Tyranny will be a distant memory. I cannot promise Utopia, because it doesn't exist. But I can promise that we will spend our entire lives striving for that goal."

With these words, Nikolai let his head rest on the concrete. The three of them stood over him, gazing at his conscious figure for a final time.

"Thank you, Lilith." He choked. "Your power is in your reason. Keep your level head, keep your rage, keep your balance. There's glory in the good in bad, and I am honored to have known someone with the perfect balance."

"I'll miss you Nikolai." Lilith sobbed, tears running down her neck. "I don't think I'll ever meet someone like you again."

Nikolai offered her a smile. It was small, as much as his draining face could manage, but it was genuine. The greatest gift a dying man could give.

"Quilla," Nikolai squeezed her hand. "Before I met you, the concept of a sibling was far off. But now, I am proud to call you a sister."

Quilla clasped a hand over her mouth as tears raced from her eyes. "I'll miss our talks, Nikolai."

"I'll miss your unsolicited advice."

"And I'll miss your stupendous ideas."

Nikolai gave her a smile. "Love you, Quilla."

Quilla choked a sob. "Love you right back, Nikolai."

Slowly, Nikolai turned to Alohi.

His face was so pale. His lips were turning a blue-purple. Around him, his own blood spread like a lake. The red soaked through her pants. It was so cold it felt like rainwater.

But it was *still* Nikolai.

For a few more seconds, he was still with her.

"Lo," he rasped. Alohi choked a sob.

"I'm never going to stop loving you, Nikolai." Alohi gasped, holding both of his glacial hands. "*Never.*"

"I love you, Alohi." Nikolai sobbed, a tear trickling down his chin. "I've always loved you. I hope that you find peace without me, but know I will always be holding your hand."

Alohi cried a sob. She pressed her soaked face into Nikolai's shirt. "You're just going to sleep." She chanted. "You're *just* going to sleep."

Nikolai lifted her head. His face was almost completely white and his entire body shook. Still, his eyes were the same. The light hadn't gone out. Not yet.

"Don't think of it as falling asleep." He murmured. "Think of it as waking up from a wonderful dream."

Chapter Fifty
Nikolai

Nikolai rested his head on the concrete. The pain, which had been so unbearable earlier, numbed to euphoria. Above him were three tear stained faces. The faces of his family.

He gazed at each of them a final time. One last clear glance. Then, his vision blurred. Their faces molded into unrecognizable bursts of color, and the sun suddenly got a lot brighter.

The light grew, opening a tunnel for him. It was so bright, so *beautiful*. A million different colors, some he didn't know could be formed. It was a path the human mind couldn't wrap its mind around. And yet he was standing in front of it.

A man came striding down the colors. His League uniform was pure white and his skin glowed in a way Nikolai never thought possible. The last time Nikolai saw him, the man was simply trying to survive. Now, he strode down the path with a calm, restorative youth.

Rex extended his hand; a shining beacon. An invitation.

"You ready, Commander?" Rex asked.

Nikolai gave a smile.

The last thing he heard was Alohi's blood curdling scream.

And he took his first mate's hand.

Chapter Fifty One
Lilith

Quilla didn't let anyone touch the bodies.

Somehow, she found the strength to race to the army and tell them not to explode the palace. Once everyone was inside the building, she forbade anyone from going into the courtyard.

Well, not everyone.

Florian, Killen and Tnil arrived shortly after Quilla called for them. No one had to break the news. Nikolai's body was lying in the sun, his blood shining like a pool of silver.

As soon as he saw him, Killen screamed.

He rushed to Nikolai's side, cradling his fallen figure in his arms. Alohi had rested her tearstained face on Nikolai's chest. The two made eye contact, and flung themselves into each other's arms, sobbing over the boy they had loved more than anything.

Florian rushed to Quilla's side, pulling her into their chest. They rested their chin on Quilla's curls, tears trickling down their cheek. The pirate didn't let go of her, they kept her close to their chest, as if they were expecting her to be dead.

"You did good, kid." Florian murmured. "You did so well."

Quilla squeezed her friend, pushing her face deeper into their chest as she sobbed.

Tnil moved to Lilith's side. She barely noticed as the swordswoman rolled up her pant leg and started working on her knee. The limb had gone plump and purple, and if Lilith hadn't known better, she would've guesses the kneecap was in shards.

No matter how many times Tnil wrapped her leg in bandage, Lilith knew it would never be the same. No matter how many bottles Quilla drank, it wouldn't erase that she killed her own sister. And no matter how many tears Alohi cried, Nikolai wasn't coming back.

Band-aids didn't do shit against stab wounds.

And the three of them were covered in blood.

~~~

The next month was awful.

The first event that took place was Nikolai's funeral. The three of them made none of the arrangements— barely any effort to honor his memory. The three agreed they wouldn't cry. Crying showed weakness, and they couldn't afford to show their new citizen's any of that.

To their credit, they managed not to shed a tear.

Alohi stood over Nikolai's casket with dry, empty eyes. She said her goodbyes formally, as if addressing a distant relative. There was no emotion in her eyes, no trace of anger or grief on her face. On one hand, there was power in her blank expression. On the other, Quilla and Lilith both knew it killed her.

Cercel didn't get a funeral.

Quilla took her ashes into the woods. Lilith offered to come with her, but she refused. Hence, only Quilla knew where her sister was buried, and only Quilla visited Cercel at least once a day. Lilith didn't know where she was, and she didn't ask. Some secrets were not meant for sharing.

The first days of their new Republic were dedicated to the loss of the past. The next were for the opportunity of the future.

A future that was theirs to shape.

Grandez Lone was hard to convince. Of course, the asshole wanted to take all the power for himself. But the three of them stood their ground, showed their evidence, and persisted until the Lone was given nothing but a small hut on the outskirts of Courna. Quilla's courtesy.
~~~

And once Alohi sat on the throne, there was a country to shape.

They started by identifying the problems. Rising famine, protests and riots, extinguished trade routes, a crumbling military and an entire world dependent on one ruler.

Once they had listed around ten inconceivable issues, they decided it was time for a less overwhelming subject.

Appointing officials.

Alohi made it quite clear she wanted to establish a democracy eventually, but the world was in shatters, and voting was nowhere on anyone's mind.

Florian was in charge of the riots. Killen took control of the hunger. Tnil started to establish trade routes. Quilla was in charge of the military and arms. Lilith moved to abolish slavery and the unjust rule of law. And Alohi shot to establish the four nations as four different balances of power.

And so they got to work.

It was nothing short of grueling. They would wake up before the sun rose and get to work on tasks they had no idea where to begin with. Lilith wrote endless letters to malicious slavers, who wrote back requesting she go fuck herself. In turn, Lilith sent Quilla's newly crafted battalions to force their hand.

But no matter how much work there was to do, every night, just for an hour, the three of them slumped against the wall with a bottle and fantasize about the opportunities of their dynasty.

"I want the punishment for sexual assault to be to cut off your own dick and eat it." Lilith hiccuped.

"And the one for child abuse should be to walk the streets naked and have children whip you." Quilla snatched the bottle from her and took a swig.

"Racial discrimination and unfair legal justice should be a fair vice for lawsuits." Alohi grabbed the wine. "And the courts should gravitate towards the victims."

They sat talking like children who thought they ruled the world. A pipe dream for most. But for them it was real. They *did* rule the world. And as soon as they figured out how to run this country, their word *would* be law.

The downside of rulership was the fact that they had rulership. No matter how clueless they were, they had control over this country. But why? When everything was boiled down, they were just deeply hurt, confused kids with no fucking idea what they were doing.

And in the deepest depths of the night, it showed.

Quilla found Lilith curled up in a corner, trying to dislocate her sprained leg. The medics told her it couldn't be healed. She would have to live with a cane for the rest of her life and she figured if the damned limb didn't work, it might as well be amputated. Quilla sat with her that night, no words could comfort her, no phrase would make her pain go away. All she could do was let Lilith cry into her shoulder and promise that she wouldn't leave.

At first, Quilla's panic attacks came nightly. No matter how hard she tried, sleep wasn't an option. Lilith and Alohi took turns staying with her, not because they were worried for her safety, but because they knew it was an unbearable fate to go through the panic-filled nights alone. After Cercel's death, her nights consisted of constant flashbacks and overwhelming guilt. Quilla would put her hands over her ears, muttering names and constant apologies. The only thing Lilith could do was hug her. The truth is, the only thing that would ever help her pain was the reassurance that she was still loved.

To her credit, Quilla never once tried to kill herself.

"It's bad now," she told them. "Awful. But I know it'll get better. If this was simply reality, I think I would have every right to die. But I know it'll get better. And that better is worth it."

Alohi, by far, had it the worst.

Nikolai gouged a hole so deep in her chest, Lilith doubted it would ever heal. It was weeks before she smiled again. She always had her head in work; facing her thoughts was too painful, she preferred to distract herself.

Late at night, her sobs filled their shared room. It was always Nikolai's name she muttered. Sometimes she would tell him she missed him; how much she loved him, and sometimes she would curse him. Curse him for leaving, curse him for letting her do this alone.

Quilla had caught her multiple times with a noose. Sometimes she was tying the rope, sometimes it hung from the ceiling, and sometimes her neck was through it. The criminal prodigy treated her with kindness, gently coaxing her away from the thoughts. Alohi would yell at her, tell her awful things she knew hurt. But Quilla never raised her voice and never took the insults personally. She knew the pain Alohi was feeling, and every single time she got the politician away from the noose and into her arms.

But even though she wasn't dead, Alohi still *hurt*.

So when she started taking ketamine, not even Lilith tried to stop her. By Alohi's request, they left her alone with the drug. Her hallucinations would paralyze her, but she didn't care. Though most of her mumbles were incomprehensible, sometimes Quilla and Lilith would catch Nikolai's name. Alohi would ask him questions, tell him secrets she didn't even tell the two criminals, or simply be with him. Lilith supposed it helped with the grief.

The spoils of royalty did nothing to ease their woes. Originally, they were each given their own room. Massive beds rested on marbled floors. Gold and black walls supported the ceiling in high, decorated pillars. At first, they tried to occupy the beds, but they felt like a trap. A spoil they didn't deserve.

On the first night they all rushed into Alohi's room, pulled the blankets off the bed and curled up on the floor. Each night they would stay up late, telling stupid stories they made up on the spot. It was the only thing that remotely resembled the life of children.

And so was their routine. Everyday, they would set to work on making their country a bit more progressive. Slowly, famine vanished, the military was reassembled, slavery was abolished, and the four countries turned into just that. Four countries.

Eventually, the new Thine got it together just enough to have an election. Quilla nearly suffocated laughing when she saw Grandez Lone's name on the ballot list. The criminal prodigy seemed unusually jolly that day. Both Lilith and Alohi found it particularly bizarre, until Quilla cracked and revealed she had the entire military deliver pamphlets to the doors of all citizens with a detailed list of the Lone's crimes.

When election day came, it wasn't a competition.

President Windlem's cabinet won by a landslide.

Chapter Fifty Two
Theodore

The door swung open to the dungeon. Ghan picked up his head to find a woman striding past the many cells. Her long, tailored cloak was out of place in the dark, messy corridor. Every inch of her was put together, from her heeled boots to her black blouse. The only thing that was remotely messy were the unruly curls hanging over her shoulders.

Ghan sat up, brushed back his hair, and folded his legs below him. This should be a fun conversation.

"General Thorne," One of the guards said. "We weren't expecting you."

"You weren't supposed to." The crisp, Renelian accent responded. "I came on my own accord."

"What can we do for you?" the guard asked.

The woman tilted her head. "Leave."

The guard opened his mouth to respond, but shut up when the woman gave him a look. He strode past her and closed the door of the dungeon behind him.

"Rosalie," Ghan smiled. "It's been too long."

Rosalie tilted her head. "Has it?"

"There are whispers, you know." Ghan continued. "I've heard you took control of the Empire with an army of delinquents. Single handedly led the battle to demolish the Empress's army and put a blade in Cercel's heart." He chuckled. "Such a shame. You two were always so close."

"Cercel was off the rails." Rosalie retorted. "I don't regret her death, but I miss her dearly."

"Ah," Ghan shook his head. "I never quite understood that about you. Your..." he paused, rolling the words on his tongue. "*Attachment* to people. Useless, in my opinion, but it never quite left you."

"That's the thing about attachment," Rosalie said. "It doesn't ever leave you. There's always a voice in your head that clings to your past. Your choice lies in if you listen to it."

"Wise words," Ghan smiled. "Then again, you were always wise. Always the smartest, daughter dear." He stood. The shackles tugged at his ankles, but the heavy metal didn't stop him from approaching the bars. "I could help you. We both know President Windlem has no fucking idea how to run this country. But you do. I can help you, Rosalie. Together, we'll have full control of the world. Just like it was supposed to be."

Rosalie stepped towards the bars. For a moment, her expression was emotionless. But then her lips quirked upward, and a dangerous spark glittered in her eyes as she ran her gaze down Ghan's body.

"Tempting." Rosalie ran a tongue along her teeth. "But I'm afraid I have to refuse. President Windlem is a competent politician and a fair leader. Without her help, I'm afraid I'd be lost in this world of politics."

Just for a moment, Ghan showed his frustration. His face twisted into a sneer and he banged his fist against the bars. The clang rang through the air, echoing off the walls. "Don't you see?" he took a breath, returning to his defaulted calm. "I know all the ropes. I know how to snatch all the power, and I know how to rule a country! You could have all the blood you so desperately crave and every single citizen in the *world* would bow to you. We could rule together, Rosalie. Side by side. Father and daughter. A *family* again."

Rosalie only tilted her head, her curls shifting down her shoulder. Ghan could read his kid's emotions, especially Rosalie's. Their facial expressions told the stories of their past and the hopes of their future. But he couldn't predict when she showed nothing.

"Unfortunately for you," Rosalie grinned. "I already have a family. I found them through trial, anger and *tons* of mistakes. They've stuck with me through my failures, shortcomings and faults. I rule this country with *them*." She hummed a cackle. "Unfortunately, my love for you has *permanently* shut off."

Ghan scoffed, matching her hum of laughter. "You can never get rid of me. I live in your head, prospering in your dreams and poking where I please. You can pretend I don't matter all you want, Rosalie, but you know you'll always care for me."

"Maybe," Rosalie tilted her head. "Maybe there's a part of me that will never stop loving you. Maybe there's a part of me that will always be easy to manipulate. But those parts are small." Rosalie took a step closer, her face inches away from his. "Do you know what the vast majority of me feels towards you?"

Rosalie's mint breath was cold on his cheek. Her eyes poured into his, an emotionless power radiating off her like her rose scent. Ghan had to fight the urge to step back. He hadn't felt that urge in years.

"What?" he spat. "What do you feel towards me?"

Rosalie blew a stand of hair from her black eyes. "Nothing."

Ghan had a counter for every emotion. He could manipulate love, grief, guilt, anger; everything. He could spin feelings into a web of deception and power. But what could he make of human emotions if there were no emotions dealt?

"I've figured out your game, you know," Rosalie clasped her hands behind her back. Her heels clicked against the floor as she strode along the bars of his cell. "You are quite brilliant, Theodore. I hope you take solace in the fact that your tactic worked well. But now–" Rosalie stopped, humming a small laugh. "Well, you take emotions and spin them. Take whatever someone wants most, give it all, and take it away. You make them think they can have it all, and you rip it from them. You create a vulnerable shell, beckoning to your every phrase. Because emotionally, you hold all their strings." Rosalie met his eyes. "Am I in the ballpark?"

Ghan staggered back, horror slithering up his legs in cold, icy movements.

"But what happens when you have no control?" Rosalie asked. "What happens when all emotions are blank? I think–" she cracked a grin. "You turn into a simple, frail old man."

"Oh come now, Rosalie." Ghan growled. "No one is free of emotions. No matter how hard you try, they sneak into your mind like venomous snakes. You stabbed a blade into your own sister's heart. You led your archer into battle and now her leg is permanently damaged. President Windlem is a bloody mess and has to manage a country on her own. And let's not forget that Lone boy." Ghan cracked a smile. "How do you feel about that, Rosalie?"

"How do you feel that your Empire didn't outlive you?" Rosalie retorted. "How does it feel to watch your nation crumble at the hands of your daughter?"

Ghan's gaze tightened into a glare. That was all he had to give. No quick, snappy reply, and no way to manipulate his way out of this hole.

"Of course it hurts." Rosalie continued. "Of course the guilt rips me apart at night. But those feelings are deep, deep inside me. They can be defied with logic. The logical part of me knows that I did what was necessary." She paused, reaching inside of her coat and drawing a golden blade. "Besides, there are ways to combat the hurt."

This time, Ghan had something to say. "Oh come now, Rosalie." He cackled, the sound drifting from his breath and echoing around the room. "We both know you can't kill me. You were barely able to kill your sister— not to mention your *father*. To do that–" he cocked his head. "You'd betray everything you've built yourself to be. A politician doesn't kill for a cause such as vengeance."

For a moment, Rosalie let his words echo around the corridor. Then, a grin cracked her lips; the smile was sadistic— a blatant show of power. Ghan recognized the split of her lips; it was his own.

"Who ever said I was a politician?" Rosalie cackled. "Sure, I may play lawmaker, but if I'm being honest–" she flipped the blade. "I prefer to deal with President Windlem's... *dirty work*."

"Dirty work requires the absence of a conscience." Ghan retorted. "Something you fail to possess, Rosalie."

Rosalie took a step towards the bars. "Unfortunately, I have to disagree with you." There was a click, and the door to Ghan's cell slid open. "The only necessity for bloodshed is a yearn for justice and an urge to finish what's started."

Ghan snorted as Rosalie stepped into his cell. They were face to face, Rosalie's blades by her side and Ghan's ankles shackled to the floor.

"Call it what you like, daughter dear." He breathed. "But we both know justice is a synonym for vengeance. That's one thing you and Cercel have in common. You are always controlled by your anger. It's the only thing that keeps you alive— being hopelessly *awful* is in your blood." Ghan tilted his head. "What separates you from the people you claim to hate so much? If you are bound by your vengeance, what makes you better than me?"

Rosalie let out a stout laugh. "I'm not here to be better, Theodore." She raised her knife, the blade glimmering in the dungeon's firelight. "I'm here to get even."

Chapter Fifty Three
Alohi

The inauguration party was a dull necessity.

Originally, Alohi guessed it was a simple meeting with batshit crazy politicians and power hungry, wannabe monarchs. That's what most political parties were— ploys for power.

But when the event was debriefed to her, she found that it could be whatever she desired. The event's only purpose was to showcase Thine's newfound leadership. It didn't have any structure unless Alohi dictated the fact.

So with Lilith's advice, Alohi created her celebration in a way that honored the people. It was less a party, and more a formal greeting.

She requested to stroll the streets of Brighan alone. Though there was initially backlash, Alohi shut it down. She had word of law. Whatever she said went.

So on the first day of her presidency, on the first day of her *democracy*, Alohi strode along the streets in trousers and a cream blouse. Her hair was pulled into a messy, loose bun and her muddy, worn boots crunched against the rocky pavement.

The company of citizens was... well, a relief. Alohi found that it wasn't political questions they asked, but simple, humane greetings. There were no demands, no angry disputes. For once, it seemed the people surrounding her were truly people.

At first, they were hesitant. The citizens of Brighan huddled on the side of the street, murmuring frantically as she strode through the city. They whispered to their partners and friends, debating whether to approach Alohi or retreat back into their houses.

Eventually, a boy tugged at her pants.

"Hello," his big, round eyes poured into hers with innocent curiosity. "Do you want to play ball with me?"

Alohi gave him a grin. "Of course," she leaned down, meeting him at his eye level. "But I must warn you, I am quite horrible."

The boy tilted his head. "That's okay." He grinned, displaying his missing front teeth. "Me and my friends can teach you! We're really good!"

Before Alohi could respond, the boy tugged at her hand. He pulled her to his group of friends, each grinning as wide as he was. They were kicking a ball in a circle, trying to get the thing to roll past their friends.

When they saw Alohi, their smiles widened. Without any words, they let her into the circle. As expected, she sucked at the game. The children kicked the ball past her with minimal effort– but Alohi tried her best. Soon, she was diving on the ground, catching the ball with her hands and being swiftly told she was breaking the rules. The children started to laugh as she continued to mess up. Soon, they were all covered in mud and laughing to the point of tears.

Alohi hadn't noticed the citizens gathering around them until one offered to help her up. Alohi dusted off her trousers and met the woman's eye. She was tall, her blonde hair tied back in a baker's bonnet. She offered Alohi a smile, but it was noticeably more fearful than the children's.

The woman fell into a bow. "Don't feel bad, your Highness. I fear they make up rules as they play."

Alohi extended a hand to her, returning a toothy grin. "Call me Alohi. Your Highness scares me too much."

The woman hesitated, and with Alohi's reassuring smile, took her hand and stumbled to her feet.

"What's your name?" Alohi asked. "If you feel comfortable telling me, of course."

The woman matched her smile— this time, the grin remained free of fear. "Lisa. I'm a baker. Would you like some bread?"

Alohi's hands shot up. "I couldn't—"

"No, please," Lisa insisted. "I feed all of the people who play with my son. It's a taxing affair."

Alohi released a small chuckle. The children were laughing over their ball, unaffected by Alohi's sudden absence.

She took Lisa's hand and put some change into her palm. It was the least she could do. She was here to earn these peoples trust; not as a ruler, but as a friend.

For the next few hours, she ate bread, danced to local music, and mingled around the locals. Slowly, they grew more accustomed to her. She was led around Brighan, shown the local shops and treasures of the city. The citizen's stuffed her with food until her stomach was bulging out of her blouse. She danced until her feet ached, and when it felt like her toes would fall off, she ignored the pain and continued.

When the sun had long set behind the mountains, Lilith came to get her. The archer was dressed in a soft blue dress, her neat braid hanging over her shoulder. As she limped through the crowd, a smile formed on her lips. She moved through the people like she was one of them, leaning on her walking stick as she listened to the music.

When Lilith had done away with the crutch, she had been offered the most beautifully crafted canes. She refused all of them, and instead sent Alohi and Quilla into the forest to find the best piece of driftwood. They had made it a game— whoever found Lilith the best piece of wood got to choose the whiskey they drank that evening. In the end, Alohi had found Lilith's walking stick, and Quilla was quite salty about her loss. Even more so after Alohi chose Muscat.

"It's beautiful, isn't it?" Alohi said, moving to Lilith's side. "All of this?"

"Yeah," Lilith breathed. "Breathtaking."

"You know, you forget." Alohi said. "When you're in the midst of struggle, simply trying to survive. All you think about is how you'll avoid that beating, win the battle, or have your next meal. Sometimes, your horizons become so thin you forget the point. But this—" Alohi gestured to the people. "This is why we survive. This is the part of life that's worth it. This is *living*."

"I think we all forgot." Lilith said. "When we were so wrapped up in killing Cercel, or running this country. But look–" a crowd of children ran through the crowd, carrying handfuls of sweets. They didn't even have food a month ago. "This is why we're doing it. It may feel hard, but slowly, we're making a difference."

Alohi looked at her, then back to the dancing crowd. "We're never going to be the same, are we?"

Lilith shook her head, staring at her leg. "No."

Alohi gazed at her, tears pricking her eyes. "Are we broken?"

"No." Lilith said. "We're scarred. We've changed. But we aren't broken. I'm not who I was when I rescued you from Rock Highland. You're not the person who came out of that place. Some parts of the old me I wish I kept, but that doesn't mean I can't like the person I've become."

Alohi tucked her knees to chest. "He would've loved this."

"He would have loved all of this." Lilith crossed her good leg over her bad one. "The opportunity of a new country would delight him. But I think what you've done with it, Alohi–" she placed a hand on the president's shoulder. "Would make him so, *so* proud."

A tear dropped down Alohi's cheek. As she watched the people dance— her people— she realized that he would be proud. Even though Nikolai wasn't with her, she could feel his happiness shine through the firelight.

You've done something good, Lo. He said. *Enjoy it.*

<p style="text-align:center">~~~</p>

Unfortunately, Alohi had to give a speech.

Lilith had led her to the stage— a grand thing surrounded by velvet curtains and decorated pillars. She didn't like it. It felt too royal; too *godlike*.

But nevertheless, when she walked behind the platform, she was met with her entire cabinet, along with some people she didn't exactly appreciate.

"Where's our third part?" Alohi asked. "She'd handle *him* perfectly."

At first, she wasn't sure that Lilith heard her. The archer had rested her glare firmly on Grandez Lone. The bastard was in conversation with Florian, who looked quite scared.

"I don't know." Lilith said, breaking her eyes away from the Lone. "Quilla said something about finishing the unfinished. She said she'd be back in time for the ceremony."

Before Alohi could respond, she was called to the front of the crowd. Florian practically sprinted away from Grandez's side, joining her, Lilith, Killen and Tnil before the stage.

"Where the fuck is Quilla?" Killen snapped. "In situations like *this* she's quite useful."

As if on cue, the door flung open. Quilla toppled through the crowd, her neat general's uniform hanging loosely on one shoulder. She stumbled forward, landing next to Alohi and wiping a bead of sweat from her forehead.

"Inconspicuous," Lilith drawled.

Quilla smirked. "Quite."

"Good," Alohi said. She knew she had to address the politicians gathered before her. She didn't have a speech prepared, but she had to say *something*. "Now that everyone's here–"

"I have your speech, Miss Windlem." Grandez Lone waved a piece of paper above his head. He handed it to Alohi, who glared back at him in disbelief. "I wrote this the day I founded the League. I wanted Nikolai to read it, but—" his voice choked. Quilla's eye roll was palpable. "My son is dead. So I would like you to honor his memory."

"Alohi," Quilla whispered. "Just say the word and I'd be delighted to–"

"No," Alohi said. She read over the script, her mind instantly pointing out the fallacies of Grandez Lone's shape of government.

... the Lone family lineage...

... a birthright to the heir...

... appointed officials chosen by the current ruler...

Alohi scoffed. An oligarchy.

How childish.

"Killen," Alohi held out her palm. "A light, please."

Killen placed a match in her hand. Alohi flicked the switch, and a small flame sprouted from the top. She watched it dance in front of her face. Through the orange, she was delighted to see the Lone's horrified expression.

She touched the paper to the fire. It caught easily, Grandez's jagged handwriting disappearing as the speech turned to ash in her hand. As the fire crept towards her hand, Alohi dropped the paper. The thing turned to ash before it hit the ground, and all that remained of the Lone family was a pile of dust at the bottom of her feet.

When she got on stage, she laced hands with Quilla and Lilith. Without a script, Alohi told the citizens of Thine exactly how their government would be. She admitted that she didn't have all the answers, and she knew it wouldn't be easy. But she promised the people of Thine she would do *everything* in her power to create as close to a Utopia as possible.

In Nikolai's name.

<center>~~~</center>

The ball took place in the Golden Palace.

Alohi didn't even know the structure had a ballroom until it was shown to her. As soon as she saw it, she proclaimed that during the inauguration the dance would be open to anyone who wanted to come. There would be music, food and open arms to anyone who wanted to celebrate their survival.

The towns-people seemed to enjoy it.

Alohi, Quilla and Lilith hovered on the outskirts of the dance, the music thundering in their ears. They kept moving, trying to avoid reporters or politicians who wanted to ask them questions. They could be criticized and manipulated tomorrow, today was for them.

Right now, they were perched at one of the many snack tables. They sat on the ground, leaning on each other. Once in a while, Quilla would reach to the table and grab a handful of cookies. She would then pass the treats down to Alohi and Lilith, who ate them without blinking.

"It might be fun?" Quilla finally said, looking at Lilith. "You know, to dance?"

Lilith gave a small chuckle. "You know I can't."

"Well, conventionally you can't." Quilla stood, offering her a hand. Lilith took it, hauling herself to her feet. "But what if you were to put your arm around my shoulder, and I'll support you by the waist— good, does that feel comfortable?" Lilith nodded, smiling at her. "Okay, then I can sort of be your crutch."

Lilith put her hands on Quilla's cheek, kissing her. "Well, you've figured it out! What are you waiting for?"

Quilla laughed, brushing a strand of hair from her partner's face. Lilith put her free hand on Quilla's hip, and Quilla supported her partner by the waist. Together, they waltzed through the room, stepping with the beats of the music.

Eventually, their dance slowed. The music's melody came to a rhythmic hum, and Lilith put her head in Quilla's chest. Their movements were gentle, simply moving for the sake of being with each other. They cradled each other, pressing their bodies closer. They held the other like they were afraid to let go— like they were grateful their partner still breathed.

Alohi couldn't help but feel a pang of jealousy. She could've had that. She *did* have that. But unlike them, she couldn't hold her love like she might lose him. Because she *had* lost him. Nikolai might show up in her ketamine highs, but he was still gone.

The music sped up. Quilla and Lilith's dance matched the melody. They intertwined their movements with the other's, just like they had done when they were in battle. They could predict where the other would move, where their partner might need catching. When Quilla fell forward, Lilith caught her by the chest, and when Lilith dipped backwards, Quilla fell with her, catching her back before she hit the ground.

Eventually, the music slowed to a halt. Quilla picked Lilith up and carried her back to their perch by the snack table. Both of them were grinning ear to ear, sweat beading on their cheeks. Quilla placed Lilith next to Alohi and plopped between them, resting her head on Lilith's shoulder.

Alohi tucked her knees to her chest. "You guys are very good."

"Really?" Lilith raised an eyebrow. "Never did anything like it before."

"You can predict my movements." Quilla shrugged. "I can predict yours. All we had to do was intertwine our positions to the music. Simple, really."

Lilith scoffed. "Are you this good at everything?"

"Yes," Quilla smirked. "I am."

Lilith tapped her nose. "The thing about dancing is you only get to do it once. After that, you're too exhausted to think."

Quilla let her head fall against the wall. "The loud music is starting to sound like screams."

Alohi stood, grabbing a handful of cookies from the snack table and stuffing them in her pocket. "Let's get out of here." She said, "Grab as much food as you want. Let's go hide in the halls."

Quilla stood, helping Lilith up. They stuffed their pockets with so many chips and cookies that the cloth nearly burst. Alohi couldn't help but laugh at the fact they looked like drug smugglers.

The three of them weaved between the dancers, each too intertwined with the music to realize the three most powerful people in the country were walking beside them. As soon as they left the ballroom, they burst into a sprint.

Like children, they galloped throughout the Golden Palace. Alohi led them, Quilla taking the courtesy to stay behind with her partner. Eventually, the criminal prodigy got fed up with losing the race and made Lilith get on her back.

Alohi couldn't keep her lead for long. Quilla's athleticism strongly outmatched her own. Soon, Alohi was gasping for air, nearly doubling over. It also didn't help that midway through the chase Lilith's walking stick came spiraling at her head.

Alohi fell against the ground. She heaved for air as cackles encased her, making her blue eyes glow. Quilla leaned down, Lilith holding onto her shoulders, and pressed her nose.

"Had enough, Windlem?" Quilla smirked. "Come on now, dump out the goods."

Alohi took a breath, containing her chortles. She then turned her pockets inside out, emptying the treats into her palm.

Quilla set Lilith down on the floor. Each of them displayed their findings. Alohi had snatched a display of cookies and biscuits from the table. Quilla stuck to the chocolates, her fingers a deep brown from the melting candy. Lilith on the other hand, had gone with a different approach.

"Of all options, why would you choose *those*?" Quilla asked when the archer pulled a handful of licorice from her pocket. "It's disgusting!"

Lilith popped a black swirl into her mouth. "You just have the taste buds of a fish."

"You have the taste buds of an elderly man!"

Lilith smirked. "Better than a fish."

"Fine," Quilla shoved her sweets away. "Have fun with your old people candies. Alohi and I will stick with our chocolates."

"Actually," Alohi reached to grab Lilith's licorice. "I quite like it."

Quilla looked appalled. "You two have both broken a lot of my trust."

"Oh Quill," Lilith waved a piece of licorice in front of her face. "You know, if you get used to it, your fishy food tolerance might strengthen."

Quilla flinched back. "I'm perfectly content with my weakened palate, thank you."

Lilith grinned; Quilla returned a horrified expression. The archer pounced. She pinned Quilla to the floor, pushing the candy against her lips.

Quilla cackled, pushing Lilith off of her. As the laugh broke her lips, Lilith was able to force the candy into her mouth.

The thing came out as soon as it entered. Quilla spat the black licorice onto the floor, stomping on it with her heel. Lilith lay beside her partner, joyful chortles mixing with her playful giggles.

"Oh come on!" Lilith said. "You didn't even give it a try!"

"I tried it." Quilla retorted, pulling the archer into her chest. "You forced it down my throat."

"And you spit it out before you could get a sense of its taste!"

Quilla scowled, but pulled Lilith closer. Just for a moment, they stopped talking, simply enjoying each other's company. Lilith nuzzled her face in Quilla's chest, and Quilla rested her head on her partner's hair.

"Hello," they sprang apart as the sharp, Thinian accent scraped the air. "This came for you."

Alohi scrambled to her feet, brushing the cookie crumbs from her clothes. "Thank you, what is it?"

The messenger shook his head. "It's not for you, President." He gazed down at Quilla, who met his gaze with a curious look. "It's for you, General Thorne."

Quilla took the letter, gently unfolding the envelope. It wasn't sealed with a well known stamp, instead, a simple flower rested in the clear glue. Quilla peeled back the paper, careful not to hurt the seal, Alohi and Lilith watching over her shoulder.

"This flower is Renelian." Quilla said, pointing to the plant. "It's a rare rose; one that can only be grown from a certain type of soil. It's thought to be extinct. The only way they could have it is if–"

"They saved it." Lilith finished. "From a doomed country."

With trembling hands, Quilla pulled the letter from the envelope. She opened the paper with tender fingers, gazing upon the messy, jagged handwriting.

Quilla put a hand over her mouth, tears pouring down her face as she read the writing. Alohi and Lilith clutched her arm, tears pricking at their own eyes.

"They're pulling my leg," Quilla murmured, her entire body shaking. "This isn't real. This is some cruel joke."

"No," Alohi whispered. "This– this is genuine."

Hello, General Thorne,
Thank you for taking the time to read this. I understand that

you are very busy, but I think I have some news that may hold meaning to you. I'm no writer, so I'll simply spit it out. I, along with my husband, survived the Lunan Renel explosion with only luck. We left our five year old daughter, Rosalie, with her grandparents to go see our distant relatives in Thine. When we heard the news of the country's demise, we assumed our daughter went with it. But when you stepped on that stage with President Windlem and Miss Cole, your appearance was so unmistakably Renelian. I did some digging, and well, I think you may be our daughter. I know that Rosalie was, or still is, a swimmer. She learned things very quickly, and loved to show off. Her curly hair was incredibly hard to brush and she never cared for anything that was too spicy. If these traits align with your personality, please consider looking into this. I know you may go by a different name, but if there is any chance that we are related, I beg you to consider meeting with me and my husband. Of course, this is completely up to you, but I would love to meet my daughter as whatever woman she has grown into today.

    Best,

Riven Slitheen.

Epilogue
Quilla

"What if they hate me?" Quilla put her hands over her head, staring at the ground as they walked. "What if they think I'm too cruel— or I've changed too much. Or what if they find out—"

"Hey," Lilith put a hand on her shoulder. "Hey. Look at me– Quill, look at me." Lilith tilted her head up, boring her green eyes into Quilla's gaze. "They aren't going to hate you. Yes, you did things to survive; but you had too. Your past isn't your fault, how you recover from it is. And honestly, Quilla, you're the most resilient person I know. They're going to love you."

"Besides," Alohi shrugged. "If they don't, I'm the fucking president. They have to at least pretend to be okay with us."

Lilith shot her a glare. "Not helpful, Alohi."

"I want them to genuinely like me." Quilla said. "Not because they're scared of me, and not because I'm their daughter. I want them to *like* loving me." She turned to Lilith. "How many people do that?"

Lilith gave her a bored look. She took her cane and bonked her partner on the head. "Look in front of you, imbecile."

Alohi swung her arm over Quilla's shoulder. "We both genuinely care about you, even if it took some getting used to."

Lilith raised her walking stick, eyeing Alohi. "Oh come on, you loved her from the moment she dragged you out of that cell."

Alohi eyed the cane wearily. "We all admire you, Quilla." She said, "But I didn't trust you until *way* later."

Lilith sighed, resting her cane in the dirt. "Acceptable response. Well done, Windlem."

"Seriously," Quilla folded her arms. "I don't want them to be scared. Even you two can admit you were afraid of me. These people— I don't want to frighten them."

Lilith reached for her hand. "You won't, Quilla."

"But I have to tell them about what I did eventually–"

"And that day is not today," Lilith finished. "Besides, they'll understand. I'm sure they did things they aren't proud of. If they really love you as parents should, they won't give a shit."

Quilla drew a shaky breath. "Promise?"

Lilith brushed a strand of hair from her partner's face. "Promise."

"Hey guys?" Alohi squinted at her map. "I, uh— I think that's it."

In front of them was a small cabin. They'd been wandering through the woods for so long Quilla was actually starting to think she'd been sent on a wild goose chase. But when she saw the cabin, it felt so— *homelike*. She had to stop herself from running to the door like a lost child and jumping into the arms of whoever inhabited the place.

Lilith squeezed her hand. "You ready?"

Quilla released a breath. "Yeah, I think so."

Together, they strode towards the house. Smoke drifted from the chimney, and as they approached the door, the distinct smell of bread drifted into their noses. A growing pit swallowed Quilla's stomach as she stood before the concrete steps. Her shaking consumed her body, and her teeth were chattering so loud Lilith must have heard her.

"Hey," her partner's bright green eyes bore into hers. "Right here with you, okay?"

Quilla took a breath. "Okay."

Her fist hovered over the door as she contemplated the knock. She couldn't do it too hard, or they might think she was an intruder. But if she knocked too soft, they might not hear and then she'd have to knock again—

"Quilla," Alohi put a hand on her shoulder. "It's a door. You've encountered them many times before. Now is no different."

Quilla offered the politician a grateful grin, and tapped the door. The handle turned as soon as she withdrew her fist. The three stepped back as two men stepped onto the porch.

They were old, probably in their fifties. White streaks mixed with their long, brown curls. Wrinkles tattered their pale skin, and their dark eyes sank with years of grief and loneliness. But nevertheless, when they saw her their faces lit up. Quilla recognized the sharpness of their features, she had seen them in the mirror.

Quilla's hand flew to her mouth as tears flooded her eyes. "Oh– oh my god."

"Hi." The one to the right breathed. His accent was so crisp– a tongue Quilla hadn't heard in a *long* time. "I'm Riven and this is Richard. It's nice to meet you, Quilla—"

They didn't have time to finish before Quilla flung herself into their arms. She pressed her tearstained face into their chest, inhaling their scent for the first time in twelve years. To her surprise, she remembered it. She remembered a time where all her troubles evaporated in her parent's grasp. She *remembered* their arms.

"It's good to see you," Quilla choked. "Dads."

Her parents held her close, as if she might be ripped away again.

"Come on," they choked, tears pouring down her dad's cheeks. "Any friend of our daughter is family to us."

Alohi and Lilith flung themselves into Richard and Riven. They pressed themselves into one another, savoring the comfort of their friend's touch.

Quilla knew that everytime she hugged these people, she'd hug a bit tighter. If her life taught her one thing, it was never to expect that someone would live another day. But these people, as long as they would live, loved her. They were the ones who would pick her up when she fell, the ones who would be there for the highs and lows. The ones who truly mattered.

She had been in many families before.
But those had used her.
This group of people wouldn't dare.
And they were the ones she wanted to spend the rest of her life with.

The End

Authors Note

Hi. I've never written an authors note, so here goes my solid effort. If you're reading my attempt at a heartfelt message, congratulations! Chances are you've finished the trilogy.

It means a lot that people read my writing. At first, it started as a simple way to understand my emotions through another person's perspective. Little fourteen year old me who wrote at 5:30 AM because she didn't want anyone to know would go into a coma if she saw how far we've come.

When I was writing the early drafts of A Life of Morals and Murder, it was just a way to let out emotions I didn't think I was supposed to have. Writing helped me overcome a lot, so when I finished my first manuscript, I wanted to help teens who were also in my position.

Teen mental health, in countless pieces of media, is poorly represented or romanticized. My goal with this trilogy was to represent this reality without villainizing the victims, defending abusers, or watering down the trauma that teens experience. With this representation, I wanted to give my readers a clear idea of how to heal from mental health challenges. For example, the way Nikolai stopped his self-harm was by escaping his abusive household, and the way Quilla halted her suicidal ideation was by realizing she didn't owe anything to the past.

While I research teens mental health extensively, I am not a professional. If you are experiencing a mental health concern, please reach out to a trusted person. You can also text or call 741-741 or 988.

They occasionally respond.

Anyway, if you've stuck with this story until the end, I can't thank you enough. I hope the messages I conveyed helped you overcome or understand mental health issues and I hope you grew to love these characters as much as I do.

Acknowledgements

There are so many people I want to thank for the publication of this book and this trilogy in general.

First, Wallace Baine and Lookout Santa Cruz. Your article about me brought my book a bunch of publicity and popularity. Book Shop Santa Cruz and those who support it, you've been an invaluable ally and extremely understanding when complications come up with my business.

Of course, I have to thank IngramSpark. While most of said *complications* come from you guys, you get my book out there for people to buy. Publishing as a teenager wouldn't be possible without you guys. While your customer service... has room to improve, you are a great self publishing company and the only one who isn't a complete scam.

Onto personal relationships— thank you so much Camilla for proofreading the last two books. You are an amazing woman and profoundly smart. I'm lucky to have you as a friend and ally.

Thank you Mrs Pendell, my English teacher, for teaching me how to reach out to people for knowledge and advertising. I hope to come to your classroom every time I accomplish something in this industry.

Fiona— I'm so glad you enjoyed this book. You pick up on a lot of the little pieces of symbolism and details that most people miss, and I love talking to you about the hidden gems of literature.

Daniel— you have always been an amazing mentor to me, and even though you're not a writer to my knowledge, your compliments and confidence in my career mean the world to me. I hope that I can continue to coach with you and learn about the game we both love.

Amy— oh my god how can I even sum up your help in this trilogy? You're my friend, my mentor, and at times, I teach you. We come to each other with every question, no matter how vile or weird. I hope we're friends for a long, long time and I can come to you with my crazy— probably god awful ideas that you somehow spin into a piece of literature.

Sadie— You're literally the person who keeps me smiling. You help me take rests when I need and hype me up when I'm feeling down. Maybe you have to wrestle me down to get me to sleep, but I'm grateful for your effort. I love our talks— about my writing or yours. I hope I can be a useful asset to you, and I assure you, I will continue to make use of your amazing smarts.

And of course, to everyone who has ever read a word of anything I have written. It's actually amazing to me that people read my writing and *enjoy* it. So to anyone who's followed this story till the end— I can't thank you enough. I hope you'll continue to enjoy my work in future novels.

And trust me, there will be future novels.